SO-AIU-615

MOONSTRUCK

A CROSSBREED NOVEL

USA TODAY BESTSELLING AUTHOR

DANNIKA DARK

All Rights Reserved
Copyright © 2019 Dannika Dark
First Edition: 2019

First Print Edition
ISBN-13: 978-1-0965-8450-6
ISBN-10: 1-0965-8450-6

Formatting: Streetlight Graphics

No part of this book may be reproduced, distributed, or transmitted in any form
or by any means, or stored in a database retrieval system, without the prior
written permission of the author. You must not circulate this book in any format.
Thank you for respecting the rights of the author.

This is a work of fiction. Any resemblance of characters to actual persons, living
or dead, is purely coincidental.

Edited by Victory Editing and Red Adept.
Cover design by Dannika Dark. All stock purchased.

www.dannikadark.net
Fan page located on Facebook

Also By Dannika Dark:

THE MAGERI SERIES
Sterling
Twist
Impulse
Gravity
Shine
The Gift (Novella)

MAGERI WORLD
Risk

NOVELLAS
Closer

THE SEVEN SERIES
Seven Years
Six Months
Five Weeks
Four Days
Three Hours
Two Minutes
One Second
Winter Moon (Novella)

SEVEN WORLD
Charming

THE CROSSBREED SERIES
Keystone
Ravenheart
Deathtrap
Gaslight
Blackout
Nevermore
Moonstruck

The most sublime act is to set another before you.

– *William Blake*

Chapter 1

O F ALL THE PAWNSHOPS IN Cognito, Pawn of the Dead sold some of the rarest antiquities I'd ever seen. After hours of relic hunting, this was our fourth and final destination for the day. Our unannounced inspections always inspired shopkeepers to find creative ways to conceal their contraband, but they all knew the drill. While our confiscating illegal paraphernalia cut into their profits, it certainly didn't deter them. Weapons like guns, axes, machetes, knives, and so forth were permissible—they could even sell cannons for all we cared. What made an item banned from public sale was infusion with magic meant to subdue or kill Breed. Impalement stakes included, even though they were found in nature. It wasn't illegal to own a stunner or carry one, but the higher authority outlawed those items from sale in public stores. They not only felt it sent the wrong message, but humans could easily get their hands on the weapons.

It had been a few weeks since I'd moved out of my father's house and back in with Keystone. Viktor had wasted no time taking on new assignments. Christian and I had spent a week tracking down a Vamp who was leaving corpses in the human district after draining them dry. Blood addiction was a nasty thing, and this guy had been so out of control that it didn't take long to apprehend him.

In the act.

I hefted a vase and studied the inscription on the bottom.

"Lookie what I found!" Gem bounded toward me, her arms clutching a book tightly to her chest, her eyes lit with excitement.

With each step, her wavy hair bounced, the pale lavender locks just as vibrant as her violet eyes. Watching her run in stacked shoes was amusing, but she managed to do it with grace and flair.

I glanced down at her discovery. "What's so exciting about a book?"

Claude barked out a laugh from the next aisle over.

Ignoring him, Gem set the book on a shelf and gingerly lifted the cover to let me peek inside. "Fifteenth-century Portugal, written by a Relic scholar. Just *look* at the calligraphy."

Her bright pink fingernails hovered above the page but didn't touch.

"What's the significance?" I asked, setting my vase on a higher shelf.

"It proves that Breed existed in Portugal! Immortals like to trace back their ancestry just like humans, but it's a little easier for us to go further back. Shifters insist that no Breed dwelled in Portugal until they claimed territory in the eighteenth century. This book not only proves unequivocally that they're wrong, but there's also mention of a Mage architect. Who knows how many others were there? That's why I love pawnshops. We're literally discovering history."

Gem acted as if someone had rolled her up in unicorn sparkles and tossed her in a pink cloud of joy. She always got excited when discovering uncommon objects, but historical books were her catnip.

I scratched my eyebrow with my pinky. "What's the point of learning history? All you have are these books written in secret or a few illegal paintings and photographs, but you're not allowed to make them public. The higher authority doesn't want us to know about our past. We're not allowed to document or record details about our lives. No pictures, no names, nada."

Unaffected by my cynicism, she lifted her chin. "Maybe someday that'll change. If we ever go public and reveal ourselves to humans, names won't matter anymore. But in the meantime, we have to save everything. Our history is just as important as theirs, if not more. Before the higher authority was around, there were simply elders who would try to maintain order. Most of them banned us from writing books, and they worked hard to destroy them. So the very fact that some survived is a miracle. Most wound up in personal collections, but think of how many were tossed as scrap after the owner died!"

A tall man appeared at the far end of the aisle with a mask on his face. I recognized Claude's white T-shirt and V-shaped torso. While the paint was faded, the mask's expression was exaggerated and demonic.

Gem rocked on her heels, oblivious to Claude's antics as she closed the book and lifted it off the shelf. "It's even written in a rare dialect spoken by Relics. They had a language that was code so that only they could read it."

"Why would they write it all down if they pass it in their DNA?"

"Not all Relics have children, so some of them used to document all their knowledge in books that would become their legacy."

Claude inched closer behind her.

I regarded him impassively before looking at Gem's new treasure. "What do you do with all the books you find?"

"I translate them. Not everyone understands these languages, so I copy all the text in English to new books and preserve the originals in the archive."

"Maybe they belong in a library."

She gazed up in wonderment. "A Breed library? Imagine, piles of books as tall as the ceiling and rows that go on forever. Alas, my dreams are dashed by politically enforced laws that prohibit the exhibition of Breed literature." Gem spun on her heel like a cartoon character and shrieked at Claude.

The book hit the floor with a *thwack*.

Claude's long arms reached for her, his fingers curled like claws.

"Jiminy Christmas! Look what you made me do, you big scamp." She bent down and cradled the book in her arms before springing back to her feet. "And just so you know, that Polynesian mask is inhabited by an ancient spirit. Anyone you look at through its eyes is cursed."

Gem strode away, her pleated skirt swishing from side to side. She was so petite that from behind, she looked like a teenager.

Claude removed the painted mask and shook out his curls of golden hair. "I love her vernacular." He gave me a sheepish grin and set the mask on the shelf. "Do you think it's really cursed?"

I looked up at Claude, who was a good ten inches taller than me. "Everything in here is probably cursed. You didn't look at *me*, did you? I've got enough hexes going on. I don't need another."

Claude's winsome smile could thaw an iceberg. "No, but I wonder what Cosmo would do if I put it on and had a little chat with him about the stunners he keeps selling."

Cosmo was the surfer-looking guy with dreads who ran the shop.

"April Fools' Day was weeks ago. He'll never fall for it."

Claude raised the sleeve on his shirt and scratched his arm. Wearing clothes that covered his muscular shoulders must have been hard for him. If Claude wasn't in a tank top, you could usually find him shirtless. All that rope climbing in the gym paid off, and he liked displaying the fruits of his labor. But while on Keystone assignments, Claude dressed as if he was trying to avoid Viktor's judgmental gaze.

He noticed my empty hands. "Didn't you find anything?"

I reached in my back pocket and pulled out a long blade. "What do you make of this?"

He studied the gold handle and dull edges. "It looks like a letter opener."

"I figured as much. Does it feel strange to you?"

His brow furrowed. "How do you mean?"

"I pricked my arm with it, and it's not a stunner. But it feels weird."

Claude chuckled. "Is that how you test them? You stab yourself?"

"This one hurt like a bitch. Dull blade and all." I took back the object and admired the white stone in the handle. "You didn't notice anything weird while touching it?"

"Perhaps there's residual energy only a Mage can detect."

I twirled it between my fingers and passed by him. "I think I should keep it. Better safe than sorry."

Claude swaggered up beside me. "Careful or you'll turn into one of those hoarders they show on TV. We'll have to use a wrecking ball to get inside your room after an avalanche of useless shit buries you alive."

"I'm not a hoarder."

He clasped his hands behind his back and fell into an easy stride. "First it's letter openers. Next it's three hundred egg cartons."

I poked his side with the dull blade. "Perish the thought."

The pawnshop had a lot of tall shelves on the left side of the building. Cosmo spent most of his time at a glass display counter that ran along the right side of the shop and the back wall. Security guards watched for shoplifters, but most of the expensive stuff was beneath the glass or mounted on the wall.

Viktor sealed up a cardboard box on the counter, the tape dispenser loud enough to make heads turn.

Cosmo watched with a look of derision, his arms folded and the lines on his forehead deep. "What happens to all the shit you confiscate? Oh, wait, it gets sold."

"It is sold to responsible people," Viktor informed him.

Cosmo snorted. "Yeah, who turn around and sell it for a higher price on the black market."

"You know the laws. If you choose to make personal transactions out of your home, that is not my concern. But when you store them under this roof or sell more than one or two, that is where I come in."

I offered the letter opener to Viktor. "I've got another one for the pile."

"I just finished taping the box," he said. "Add it to Gem's."

"Wait a second," Cosmo sang, reeling in closer to have a look. "That's not an illegal weapon. You can't just take whatever you feel like from my store. This isn't a charity."

"It looks suspicious."

He swept his arm to the headsman's axe on the wall. "Lady, everything I sell looks suspicious. If you want to collect stunners in the name of the law, fine. But you can't just steal my bread and butter because it suits your fancy."

Viktor always paid a fair price for anything of historical interest, so I didn't want to raise a ruckus.

"Fine. How much?"

Cosmo tapped his fingers against his puka shell necklace, which matched his shipwrecked wardrobe. By his gaunt face, you'd think he'd spent the past five years on a deserted island instead of behind a counter. "Two hundred smackeroos."

I marveled at the play of colors within the milky-white stone on the letter opener. The handle fit nicely in my palm. Too bad it wasn't a weapon. "It's not real gold," I pointed out. "This looks more like brass."

"You're getting a deal. That stone is an opal, and I could charge a lot more in a human store for it."

I gave him a sardonic smile. "So what you're telling me is that it has no value in a Breed shop. I'll give you fifty dollars."

"Lookie, you people take more than enough from me. If you run me out of business, what'll you do with all your free time?" Cosmo was probably a master haggler, so no matter what, he was going to walk away ahead of what he paid for it. "I'll go as low as one seventy. Take it or leave it."

I almost turned away, but then I considered what a cool gift this would make for Gem. Hooper's death had been rough on her, and maybe we hadn't done a good job of making her feel appreciated. Gem loved surprises, and I knew how she felt about gemstones. This one was probably loaded with all that chakra energy she was always going on about.

I took out my wallet and counted the bills before setting them on the counter. Meanwhile, Viktor and Claude collected two boxes and hauled them out to the van.

"So what's the history behind it?" I asked.

Cosmo put the money in his cash drawer. "Beats me. That's why it's not in the glass counter. People like a good story tied to their shit. Enforcers confiscated it in some sting operation on a

Mage who was buying and destroying artifacts and historical goods. He's dead now. That's all I know."

"Why would anyone destroy history?"

"To hide secrets. That box your pixie friend made off with includes a few books from that bust. She's lucky she got anything. The Mageri got dibs on everything pertaining to Mage history; the rest of it they hauled here. Most of the shit was unsellable. The spines were rotting and paper decayed. The only thing salvageable was leftover junk from his personal collection. Sometimes people keep old stuff from their past for sentimental reasons even though it's damaged. Can you believe they also gave me his toothbrush and shaving kit?" Cosmo rolled his eyes. "Do I look like I have time to go through a dead man's toiletries?"

Cosmo turned away, still rambling about all the extra work he did. I didn't have anything against the guy aside from the fact he was an asshole.

We all had our faults.

Once we made it home, Gem dashed off to her secret room to sort through her newfound treasures. Viktor disappeared with his box of weapons while everyone else gravitated to the courtyard. The weather simply demanded it. After weeks of gloomy skies and abundant rain, the grass had overgrown, making it perfect to lie on. While Kira had done a magnificent job pruning the native bushes and vines, Viktor scheduled for the lawn service people to stop by on their riding mowers.

Instead of joining everyone out in the sun, I relaxed on the veranda, sipping my tea and watching Hunter leap around the courtyard like a frog. Bees hovered near a holly tree as if they had found their oasis.

Blue strolled along one of the pathways, the breeze ruffling her long brown hair. Unlike mine, her hair was as straight as a board. She was barefoot, her cargo pants rolled up to the knee. After passing Wyatt and Shepherd, who were chatting on a bench, she stopped by her favorite winged statue of a grief-stricken man. I had to admit there was nothing angelic about the statues around Keystone. They were either battling or suffering. Niko snoozed on a patch of grass, his fingers laced across his chest and his eyes closed. How regretful that he couldn't see how vibrant the sky looked against the stone exterior of the mansion, like a sapphire jewel in a crafted setting.

Christian stepped outside with dark sunglasses shading his sensitive eyes. He sat down between the arches of the short wall in front of me. "Where's Claude?"

I crossed my legs and looked into the courtyard behind him. "I think he passed out in the grass somewhere. Hunter wore him out. They were playing tag for about an hour."

"That's hardly fair. A wee lad against a Chitah."

"Wyatt made him wear a blindfold, so he kept smacking into things."

"'Tis a shame I missed that spectacle." Christian's gaze swept down to my bare legs, and he licked his lips. "Will you be wearing those shorts all summer? They don't cover much, lass."

I stretched my long leg in his direction so he could get a better view. "I'm a bad girl."

His fangs descended slightly. "Indeed, you are."

Christian wasn't wearing his usual grim attire of a trench coat over a Henley. He looked so out of character in a black tank top and jeans.

"I didn't know you liked jeans."

A crooked smile wound up his face. "It's laundry day."

"You should buy a pair of those tight bicycle shorts."

"Over my rotting corpse."

I uncrossed my legs and widened them just a little bit. When I did, I couldn't strip my eyes away from Christian's growing erection, visible as it pressed against his jeans. "What a shame. It's nice wearing shorts in this weather. I couldn't dress like this on the streets. They would have drawn too much unwanted attention."

Christian got up and strolled over to the chair beside me. After he sat down, he reached across and put his hand on my leg, his fingers tucking between my thighs. "I can see why."

Awareness burned in his eyes, and I felt feverish from his touch. Christian and I were navigating our way through a new relationship, and we didn't want to create unnecessary rules or pressure. We hadn't opted for a shared bedroom. Some nights he stayed with me, and other nights I stayed with him. We didn't always have sex; it wasn't about that. I was discovering a new kind of intimacy with a man that had to do with trust, conversation, and patience. Sometimes we both wanted privacy and slept alone, and that was fine. Nobody got jealous or sparked an argument. Our arrangement was unconventional, and it worked. It built up the sexual tension between us to a crescendo, and I had no complaints.

He retracted his arm and sat back. "What's on your mind, lass? You've been quiet all morning."

I wasn't sure how to broach the topic as it had been stirring in my thoughts for a while now.

After another sip of cold tea, I set the glass on the flat armrest of the Adirondack. "Tell me what you think before I mention this to Shepherd or Viktor." I shifted in my seat to face him, my eyes scooping up the deliciousness of his biceps and tight-fitted shirt. "Shepherd's busy with work, and Kira can't keep an eye on Hunter with all her responsibilities. Viktor didn't hire her to be a nanny, and I think he's beginning to see that. None of us have time to give this kid schooling. I'm assuming Breed kids have to be educated like everyone else."

Christian tipped his head to the side. "It depends on your definition of *educated*. Most Relics I've met don't waste time teaching their children about history or economics. Their innate knowledge keeps them focused on their future career. With Shifters, it depends. Some of them have family businesses. The packmates teach the wee ones what they need to know."

"But Hunter's special. He needs a well-rounded education. We don't know if he'll grow up to do anything with his Relic knowledge. He's also a Sensor. Not only that, he lives with a bunch of killers. I know Shepherd doesn't want him neglected because we're all busy. What do you think of a live-in nanny?"

Christian drummed his fingers on the armrest. "Viktor has trust issues, so I don't see that happening. He only took in Kira because of the friendship he had with her father."

I leaned on the armrest. "He's gonna have to trust someone. If that kid doesn't get some structure in his life, he'll be a nightmare to deal with. Like a mad dog. Face it—nobody who lives with us is going to come out of it well-adjusted. Not unless they have a good mentor."

"And where do you think Viktor will be able to find a nanny who won't spill our secrets?"

"What about Switch?"

Christian dipped his chin so I could see his black eyes over the top of his shades. "Are you fecking with me? You want that numpty to move in here… with us? Well, that's just grand."

"I thought you settled your differences. He's not a bad guy."

"You didn't think I'd be vexed over a man living in the next room who has his eyes on my lover?"

I gave him an impish grin. "I love it when you call me that."

He turned his head away. "I'll not have it."

"Are you really jealous over someone I'm not interested in? Switch romanticized over the old me, but he doesn't want anything to do with the new and improved Raven Black. The one who can kill a man with her thighs."

I stood up and scooted onto his lap. When I nuzzled against his neck and felt him harden beneath me, I knew he wasn't as mad as he pretended to be. "Think about it," I said, nipping his neck with the tips of my fangs.

Christian hissed and wrapped his arms around me. "You're not playing fair."

If only we didn't have an audience, I thought, glancing at the courtyard.

I nestled against him and ran my fingers through his beard. "I've given it a lot of serious thought. Switch is the perfect solution. This is what he does for a living, and whatever Viktor paid him would be better than what he earns from the packs. He's not happy about his situation, and we're not happy about ours. I owe him for putting his life on the line to protect my father. He would never break my trust, and he'll protect Hunter with his life. I told you about what got him in trouble with the packs in the first place."

"Aye. He might have admirable qualities, but that doesn't mean I want your ex living here."

"He's not my ex. We never dated. We've never even kissed. Switch is good-looking, but I always liked those clean-cut guys."

"So that's your type? The all-American quarterback?"

I pinched Christian's scruffy beard. "You're my type. And I know you trust me."

"It's him I don't trust."

I stood up and raked my fingers through my hair. "I don't know how to change that. Would you trust a different man, or is it just him?"

Christian gave me a mirthless smile. "Do you not know how persistent Shifters and Chitahs are by nature? They're not only territorial, but they love a long courtship. Rejection among their kind is incentive to improve themselves and become worthy of a woman's affections. What if Viktor sends me to some godforsaken country for another month? Your friend's tail will start wagging, and you'll see what I'm going on about."

I sat down on the low wall and sighed. "It was just an idea."

"So we find someone else."

"He's the only one with the right qualifications. I didn't want this to be an impulsive decision. I gave myself weeks to mull it over and decide if Switch was the best fit. Isn't it better to have workers with a personal connection to someone in this house? That's the only reason Kira's here. Besides, Switch is practically family." I stood up and squared my shoulders. "I get that you're jealous, but you need to think about what you're saying. If you really trust me, then it wouldn't matter if ten horny men who wanted me as their wife moved into this house. If you and I have an argument, I'm not the type who'll run into the arms of another man. If you go on a long trip, I won't become so desperately lonely that I'll sleep around. That's not who I am. And if that's who you think I am, then you don't really know me at all."

He crossed his legs and stared in my direction. "Perhaps Lenore has experience."

"Sleeping with men? That I don't doubt."

"I think you know the point I'm making."

I did, but Switch and I had a platonic relationship, whereas Lenore and Christian's was mired in years of manipulation and blood sharing. And none of it by force. No, Christian had delighted in drinking her ancient blood, so I had reason to be jealous of someone like her in the house. It had nothing to do with my trust for Christian and everything to do with the control she had over him. Switch had zero control or influence over me, and that should count for something.

I stared at my elongated reflection in his glasses. "This isn't about us. It's about what's best for that little boy running around on the lawn. If we don't give him a fair shot in life, you might be the lucky Vamp who has to scrub away ten or twenty years of his life when he betrays us out of spite. I want you to sit here for a while and consider that."

"Why did you not just go around me and ask Viktor?"

I strode up to Christian's chair and planted my hands on the armrests. "Because if I pitch this idea to him, it would be nice to have your support. He's known you a little bit longer. Maybe it's not my place to get involved in what Shepherd wants to do with his kid, but I see an opportunity to help two people. Switch might not even agree to it, but maybe we should entertain the idea before tossing it out the window."

Over the top of his sunglasses, I could see the aim of his gaze was straight inside my blouse. Good thing I'd skipped the bra this morning and wore a wide collar.

I kissed him on the lips. "What are you willing to do to please me?"

He lifted his chin. "Another man living here would please you?"

"Your support turns me on." I playfully nipped his bottom lip, and he growled low and sexily. "Think about it."

While heading back inside, I could feel Christian's hot gaze all over my legs and ass. Reluctance was his middle name. It was his nature not to trust anyone, least of all someone he perceived as competition. But Switch had shown loyalty to my father and to me. Anyone who would put his life on the line for my father was family in my book, and I couldn't turn my back on the opportunity to repay him. Why hire a stranger when we could invite someone whom I trusted with my life? It might give Keystone peace of mind that Switch would never betray us.

The real question was: Would they go for it?

Chapter 2

AFTER JOGGING UPSTAIRS TO GRAB something from my room, I ventured down to the first floor along the east wing. When I reached the first alcove on the left, I noticed the lantern that usually hung on the wall was gone. Gem used it to light her way when she went into her private study, so when it wasn't on the wall, I knew she was working.

When I pushed on the stone wall, the door pivoted and created a gap on the right side. I slipped through the entrance and entered a dim room with lofty ceilings and bookshelves for walls. A lantern and several candles lit up the large wooden desk in the middle where Gem was sitting, studiously working on translating a book. Lanterns affixed to the dividers between bookshelves added extra light to the windowless room.

I walked barefoot across the cold floor until I reached the green area rug beneath the table. "Why do you work in such a dark room? You could have chosen one of the larger rooms upstairs with oversized windows."

Gem set down her pen and gently turned the page of an old book. "Ultraviolet light is bad for paper. Some of the light bulbs are also harmful, but I can't keep track of all the new technology. It's better to store books in a cool, dry place with no ambient light." She sat back in her chair, her eyelids still sparkling with the glitter she'd put on earlier that morning. The false eyelashes only enhanced her round eyes. "I store some of the older books in acid-free boxes. The temperature in here stays cool and dry most of the year, so it's an ideal storage room." She pointed to what looked like a clock on a shelf. "That's my thermo-hygrometer. I'm the guardian of history. If you have any photographs or notes you want to preserve, let me know and I'll give you some tips."

"I hadn't thought about it."

Her brows arched. "You should. You're an immortal. You'll last longer than your keepsakes if you don't know how to store them. Wyatt can also scan them, but like I said, technology is always changing. They might not have USB ports in the year three thousand."

"You work too much."

She gave me an elfin smile. "Tell me about it. I've been so buried in work these past weeks that I haven't even gone swimming once since the last snow. Such is the life of a bibliophile."

"I didn't mean to barge in, but I've got something for you."

She hopped out of her chair and clasped her hands together. "Oh, I love surprises!"

Gem still had on her platform sneakers but had changed into a pair of pink shorts and a long-sleeved white shirt.

"I know how you like stones, and I thought you might like this." I retrieved the letter opener from my back pocket and presented it to her.

Gem's eyes widened like saucers. "It's gorgeous!" She snatched it from my hand before the words were spoken. "The opal is divine! How much did you pay for this?"

"Apparently less than it's worth in a human store. I got it for a steal."

"I'll say." She turned it in her hand. "I love white opal. Black is the most prized, but I've never been a huge fan. Someday I'd like to get my hands on a harlequin opal. Stones are magic. They can store and emit all kinds of energy. Did you know that many ancient cultures used them for healing?" She brushed her fingers over the gem. "The energy feels so strong. This is a good one."

"I thought you'd like it," I said with a nod.

"The colors are brilliant, but what an odd choice for a letter opener." She raised the dull blade and studied it. "The handles are usually narrower than this or flat."

I looked at the cross guard. "I thought the same thing, but what else could it be? The tip and edges are too dull to be a weapon."

"Thank you so much for this. I can use it to open my boxes and supplies." She set it on the table. "What's the occasion?"

"It just looked like you. Plus you helped me paint my armoire."

"Black is so dreary. I just wish you would have let me paint it blue instead of red, but I guess it goes with your décor."

I tensed when I saw her coming in for a hug. Gem wrapped her arms around me, pinning my arms to my side. "You're so thoughtful."

I lightly patted her back and stepped away. Physical affection sometimes made me uncomfortable. My father loved me, but he wasn't a demonstrative guy. The only people I'd ever felt comfortable hugging were him and some of his buddies, whom I considered family. And now Christian. But I didn't go around hugging him for no reason. He'd probably wonder what I was smoking if I did.

Gem whirled around and sat back down. "When Viktor found out the contents of the books I bought today, he wanted me to translate *all* of them. So I've put my other projects to the side for now, and I suppose I'll be living in this room until the next century."

I glanced at her ballpoint pen. "You don't type it out on the computer?"

"I tried that once, and it was an epic fail. I didn't save the file. I thought I did, but then it restarted and got this blinking cursor. Two weeks of work... wasted. You can't trust computers. People can steal that data, and the higher authority doesn't like the idea of digital archives floating around. Paper you can trust. So I translate all the books to English and store them on *that* shelf," she said, pointing to my right.

I snorted. "Sounds daunting."

She wiggled her fingers. "My hand cramps up sometimes. At least I can't get carpal tunnel syndrome. The perks of being a Mage," she said with a roll of her eyes. "If I'd done this kind of work when I was a Relic, I probably would have dropped dead." After a brief lull in the conversation, Gem tucked her chin in her palm. "Why hasn't your father come over? Viktor invited him to dinner."

"Crush isn't a dinner kind of guy. Viktor's a little formal, and my dad doesn't like feeling out of his element. Besides, I think he's just keeping his distance from my job. Two different worlds. He's pretty good about giving me my space, even if it's to a fault."

"I simply adore him. I still can't believe he's been a trusted human all these years and you never knew. And yet… here you are, living in the Breed world."

I twirled my hair around my finger. "Yep. Here I am."

When Gem's phone vibrated, she swiped her finger across the screen and read the message. "Viktor's asking if you're with me. Are you?"

I shrugged.

She typed in a message and waited. "He wants you and Christian to meet him in the front study. *Pronto*."

"Duty calls." I pivoted on my heel.

"Thanks again, Raven. I love the gift."

I waved my hand as I left the room. I was indebted to the team. They'd come to my aid when that loan shark and his lion pride decided to kill my father and me after making off with our money.

Keystone truly cared, and that thought nestled in my heart.

When I reached the study, Christian had beaten me there.

"I have a quick task for you two," Viktor said as he shut the door. "I am logging today's inventory of weapons and noticed that we have too many in-house. Shepherd takes what we need, but I cannot store them all here. When we have too many in our possession, I transport them to an arms dealer. He distributes what he can to Enforcers or Regulators."

I hooked my thumbs in the belt loops of my jean shorts. "Why not just take the boxes directly to him each time we do a run?"

"And risk exposing his identity? Nyet. Everything we confiscate must be logged and reported. I cannot travel to his place each and every time. We would set ourselves up for an ambush." Viktor scratched his forehead and looked toward a lantern on the table. "Claude and Blue are usually the ones to go, but I think it's time to test how you and Christian can handle an assignment such as this. Transporting valuable goods is something we do on many levels."

"You're asking us to deliver a few boxes?" I folded my arms. "Aren't Christian and I the killers on staff? Seems like we should be given the dangerous assignments."

Viktor wagged his finger at us. "No assignment is too small. Everything we do comes with risk. Many would kill to get their hands on these weapons and sell them on the black market. If that happens, every innocent life lost is blood on our hands. Christian, I want you to load the boxes into the van. Do not discuss your mission during your drive. Keep the conversation to a minimum. Talk about wine and travel."

I chortled and looked at Christian. "Like our memorable trip to Washington?"

Christian winked at me but didn't comment on the infamous spoon fiasco that left one man dead and a house torched. He turned the onyx ring on his finger. "At what hour is he expecting us?"

Viktor tossed Christian the keys. "He does not know you're coming. It is never good to have a routine with jobs such as these. When you are near his home, send me a message and I will alert him that you are en route. Is this a problem?"

"No sweat," I said, nonplussed as to why Viktor would hand us such a straightforward assignment.

"Says the adrenaline junkie," Christian quipped.

"Maybe you should just stay home. Go bite a few holes in the water hose with your fangs and make a sprinkler for Hunter to play in. I got this."

"With your atrocious driving, I'd be surprised if you made it there in one piece. Or would you rather I drive so you can strap yourself to the roof while we hit the freeway?"

Viktor ambled to the door and gripped the knob. Before opening it, he glanced over his shoulder at us. "Some days I cannot tell if it's hate or love between you two."

Christian flashed him a wicked smile. "That's what makes it interesting. I can't tell either."

I watched Christian adjust the passenger seat after he climbed inside the van. "Everything loaded?"

"Aye. All five boxes. That's a shiteload of weapons."

Once we hit the main road, I accelerated past the speed limit until we entered the edge of the city. "Why is Viktor giving us such a boring assignment? Aren't we supposed to be the hired assassins on the team?"

"You seem vexed that you can't always be putting a knife in someone."

"He's made it clear that Wyatt and Gem are intelligence and Claude and Blue are the trackers. Shepherd and Niko are not only healers but also backup. That means you and I are the killers who do all the dangerous shit. And yet here we are, driving a delivery van."

"Has it ever occurred to you that this *is* the dangerous job?"

"Come on. Viktor's gotta be getting some juicy offers after what we did for the higher authority during the blackout. He's holding out on us. We've had one big case since, and that one was too easy to solve. The Vamp was practically sucking on people in front of 7-Eleven. This is child's play."

"I once knew a lad who washed windows for a living. Great view, fresh air, privacy—a man couldn't ask for an easier task. Until the harness breaks and you plummet thirty stories to your death. Never underestimate the perils of a simple job."

"Brushing a shark's teeth is inherently dangerous. Washing windows has enough security measures in place that the chances of falling are slim."

"Are you afflicted in some way?" Christian rested his arm on the door. "They don't have men who brush sharks' teeth. If so, I'd be the first in line to watch that."

We hit a bump, and Christian reflexively threw his arm in front of me.

"You should wear a seat belt," he grumbled, retracting his arm.

"I thought you were just trying to feel me up."

"Speaking of that, it didn't occur to you to put on a brassiere? You can't just walk around the city, flashing your knockers to every man with a set of eyes."

"You mean a bra? I hate to break the news, but you're living in the twenty-first century. It's a woman's prerogative to dress how she wants."

When I abruptly hit the brakes, his arm flew out again. I barked out a laugh at his chivalrous gesture. *Not bad... for a Vamp.*

"*Jaysus wept.* Will you keep your foot on the gas? I don't feel like plucking a box full of knives out of my back."

"Are you a red or a white wine kind of guy?" I turned a corner and smiled at him so he understood why the sudden change in topic. "You're pretty quick on the reflexes, Poe."

"I get my practice around you."

When I reached a stoplight, I decided to buckle up. My truck didn't have a shoulder belt, so I'd gotten used to disregarding the safety rules of the road.

Christian tilted the visor and adjusted his sunglasses. "How's your da?"

"You should come with me on my visits. I don't know why you're so scared of him."

"Don't be daft. I'm a Vampire near three times his age. The man hardly puts a fright into me."

I chortled. "You sure about that?"

He glanced out the window. "I've not had the time, and you know it."

"What does Viktor have you doing that's so secretive?"

"I have special skills."

I flicked a glance down at his crotch. "I'll say."

"Keep on with that, lass, and I'll have you pull the van over so I can flatten you in the back."

"Why can't you tell me what you're working on?" I pressed, steering him away from the sex talk.

Christian stretched out his arms. "Afraid not. We both have given Viktor our loyalty. Your magical fanny isn't enough to tempt me out of a job."

I recognized the confidential nature of our relationship with Viktor, but where was Christian disappearing to for days at a time? He wasn't just my lover—he was my partner. I wanted to be included in his work, but Viktor always had a plan for everything. Solo assignments were a necessity, so I just had to accept it.

I tapped my fingers on the steering wheel. "Does this light seem extremely long, or is it just me?"

He twisted in his seat and scanned the sidewalk. Car horns impatiently honked, and a few vehicles up ahead were entering the intersection despite the cross traffic moving through. The lights weren't blinking red as they often did when there was an issue.

"I don't like the looks of this," Christian said under his breath.

"I know what you mean." I studied the side mirror, the traffic backed up behind us.

Christian leaned toward me and pointed up ahead. "What's that shitebag doing?"

"Who?"

"The one standing with his hand on the light pole. If he wanted to cross, he could have done it already. But he's just standing there. Can you feel anything?"

"I'm not sure." I rolled down my window and leaned my head out. The hair on my arm tickled, but it was hard to tell if it was from the wind or a current of energy. "There are too many people around us—too much energy bouncing around from all the road rage."

"Jump the curb," he commanded. "Do it."

I hit the gas, turned the wheel, and sent a metal trash can flying into the street. The wide sidewalk made it easy to maneuver around the newspaper stand and pedestrians. I slowed before reaching the corner. The cars turning right were at a standstill, unwilling to turn since traffic was no better in that direction either. We had a gap in front of us with a clear view of the buildings ahead.

"Floor it," he said.

"What about all that?" I gestured to the café up ahead. Empty chairs surrounded small round tables just outside the door.

He rolled down his window. "Hurry up!"

Sensing something was about to go down, I switched from "good citizen" mode to "crazy mercenary behind the wheel of a death machine" and ripped through the café. Tables went flying, and one chair caught beneath the van and dragged until the undercarriage spit it out. Cars were honking, but I didn't give a damn.

Pedestrians scattered like mice in a field, diving inside banks and jewelry stores. I spotted a break in traffic at the intersection ahead and held down the horn. Two wrecked cars had freed up the street heading east, so I jerked the wheel right and sailed onto the street.

When I checked my side mirror, I noticed a flashy red car tailing us. Christian must have heard or seen something to make him panic.

"What now?"

The wind from the open window blew back his hair. "Keep driving."

"I can't outrun a Corvette," I informed him.

"Cut through the park!"

"Shit. We're gonna get arrested." The van flew over the sidewalk with a bang and landed on the grass. "Just so you know, the local news just loves car chases. They even have police helicopters with that infrared technology."

All the weapons in the back were rattling around as we sped through the park. I glanced at Christian, who was on his phone.

"Wyatt, I need you to ring your contact with the police. The emergency department. Tell him to ignore any calls involving a red car and a black van on a citywide chase. … One more word and I'll drain you. Just do it."

I nearly struck a man reading a newspaper on a park bench before jerking the wheel to the right. We went careening toward a pond, ducks flapping out of the way in a frenzied panic. I quickly turned before we ended up submerged in water.

Christian glanced in the back of the van. The boxes were making a racket, but nothing had spilled open. "Take a right," he said tersely, referring to the road up ahead.

"No."

"Shut your gob and do as I say."

"That goes right to the Bricks. Do you want to add a new level of fuckery to this situation?"

"Well, you can't go left. The coppers are down that way."

I couldn't go straight either. That was nothing but a long row of buildings.

Or could I?

"Let's have some fun," I said in a singsong voice.

I scanned the street left and right before plowing straight ahead and snapping the wooden gate of an indoor parking garage. The tires squealed on the smooth surface as I sped up a ramp and turned left, following the arrows painted on the ground.

Level one.

Level two.

Level three.

The Corvette stayed on our ass as we ascended the garage.

Christian wiped his pants as if there were something on them, a sure sign he was irritated. "You're gonna trap us at the top with no escape."

"I work best under pressure."

The car engine behind us throttled, and I weaved, afraid he might try to jump ahead and block me.

I leaned into a turn. "Any other cars back there?"

Christian gripped the door. "Just the one."

When I reached level eight, we sailed onto the roof.

"What's your plan, Miss Black?"

I parked the van at the far side and left the keys swinging in the ignition. "In case you haven't noticed, I have special talents when it comes to baiting men."

"Aye, that you do."

Christian and I hopped out at the same time to face the car speeding up behind us. The sticker on the windshield was a Breed mark, one I often saw on the doors and windows of Breed establishments. Rarely had I seen them on someone's car, but the driver's ego didn't surprise me.

I sauntered up, Christian by my side.

Two men slowly got out and gave each other a furtive glance. The husky passenger had on long red shorts, and the driver looked as yuppie as they come in his polo shirt and loafers. All he needed to complete the ensemble was a pink sweater tied over his shoulders.

He ran a hand over his gelled hair and tossed his sunglasses into the car.

Christian and I knew better than to underestimate anyone, but this guy didn't strike me as a hardcore thug.

"What's in the van?" the yuppie asked.

Christian tucked his sunglasses in the collar of his tank top. "Your mother with her legs spread wide."

Red Shorts turned his baseball hat backward and put his hands on his hips. "Something's in the back," he said to his friend. "I'm tellin' you."

I smothered a laugh. "You don't even know what you're chasing after?"

Red Shorts turned to his friend and said something under his breath.

"He thinks we have something worth a lot of money," Christian relayed to me quietly. "He's just got a funny feeling about it."

"I call bullshit. Our van isn't marked."

The yuppie gave his friend a look and jerked his head toward their car. Red Shorts walked back to the window and reached inside. When he stood up again, there was impalement wood in one hand and a knife—one I could only presume was a stunner— in the other. He held them both out to his friend as if he were offering him a choice between candy bars. Yuppie contemplated for a moment before choosing the blade.

These guys actually thought we played by the rules.

I checked to make sure my shoelaces were tied. "This is your last warning to get lost."

"Afraid to fight a real man?" the yuppie said, taunting me. "I can feel your energy leaking all over the place, Mage."

Annoyed, I leveled down and sharpened my light.

He laughed haughtily. "Show me some of those girlie moves."

I shot a look at Christian. "Let's have some fun."

Instead of going after the yuppie asshole with the stunner, I flashed toward Red Shorts. His arm swung down, and the impalement stake narrowly missed me. I clutched his trachea and threw him off-balance. When we hit the ground with a thud, the air knocked out of his lungs. I scrambled to my feet before he had a chance to recover. The buildings next to us were lower, offering us plenty of privacy.

Christian attempted to fight the other man, but the yuppie was a Mage and flashing all over the place. I heard his blade hit the concrete.

"Get over here, you blundering eejit!"

"Get on his car!" I shouted.

Certain that Red Shorts wasn't a Mage, I stepped closer to blast him with energy. His arm swung toward me, and pain lanced through my leg when the stake grazed my calf.

I picked the wrong day to wear shorts.

I released enough volts to singe the hair off his chest. After he quit convulsing and foaming at the mouth, he lay still—conscious but not lucid.

Incensed by the cut on my leg, I ripped off his red shorts and underwear and flung them over the edge of the building. Then I marched over to their flashy red car. While Christian taunted the Mage by denting the roof, I searched the ground for the stunner, but it was nowhere in sight.

So I pulled the keys out of the ignition.

"You win! Get off my car," the man pleaded. "I just bought it."

"Did you now? It's a real dandy." Christian put his hands on his hips and flashed him a wicked grin. "How did an insipid little man with no socks and bad hair manage to get his hands on a classic beauty such as this?"

"My Creator bought it for me."

"Ah. Daddy's little boy."

I tossed the keys in the air and caught them with my hand. "Why did you follow us?"

Panicked, he looked at me and held up his hands. "My friend.

It was all his fault. He had this harebrained idea that you were hiding something valuable inside. I thought it would be an easy robbery. I didn't know you were Breed."

"Taking advantage of helpless humans?" Christian asked. "Tsk-tsk." He hopped from the roof to the hood of the car, leaving a solid dent.

The man cringed. "Come on, man. I didn't plan to hurt anyone. I just wanted to see what was in the back."

"Is your friend psychic?" I tossed Christian the keys.

Something shifted in his expression, and like a bullet, he flashed toward the front of our van. I chased after him and grabbed his shirt. It ripped at the collar, and a struggle ensued as he tried to climb into the driver's seat. Before he could do something stupid, I reached beneath the steering column and pulled the keys from the ignition.

Afraid the man would drive away with the van, I flung the keys as hard as I could over the edge of the building. Instead of fighting me, he got inside.

"Christian, he's climbing into the back!"

I couldn't get a firm grip to pull him out, and he slipped through my fingers. I went after him. The last thing I needed was this idiot getting into a box full of weapons.

I tackled him, and we fell over the boxes. As we scuffled, I kept waiting for the rear doors to burst open, but they never did.

The yuppie crawled away and knocked me off with his legs, but he lost his shoe when I grabbed his foot. My fangs punched out, but the only target within reach was his ass, and that was a road I wasn't about to go down.

Frustrated, I punched through the box beneath me. The tape pried away from the cardboard, leaving an opening between the flaps. I slipped my hand inside and felt around for something— anything—before the Mage could escape through the rear doors. When my fingers touched what felt like a blade, I pulled it out and impaled him in the butt cheek.

A groan rattled his lungs, and his body went limp.

Out of breath, I took a minute to savor the victory.

Christian slowly clapped from the front seat. "Now *that* was the finishing touch."

I sat up and realized I'd stabbed the man with a crucifix infused with magic.

"Great," I muttered. After scooting onto a bench, I glared at Christian in the driver's seat. "You're a real fanghole, you know that? Why didn't you help?"

He arched his eyebrow. "Since when do you need rescuing? Besides, you were handling things quite well. I enjoy a good performance, especially when I get to admire your arse in those shorts."

"I just assumed you were going to open the rear doors."

"You'll never win a fight if you're expecting someone to save you."

I stumbled over the boxes and shoved at him. "Get out."

"Are we going to quarrel over whether or not I should have rescued the damsel in distress?"

I followed him out the door and then stared down at my bleeding leg. "No, but we're a team. If I tell you he's getting in the back, you're supposed to head him off at the pass."

"I couldn't break the doors. You tossed the keys over the side, remember? How the feck would we transport all those bloody weapons with the rear doors swinging wide open?"

I leaned against the van and caught my breath. "Point taken. What do you think we should do with these guys?"

Christian had a wicked sense of humor, and something was spinning like a carnival ride in that twisted head of his. "You leave that to me."

With my hand held out, I captured the rays of the sun on my fingertips and pulled in healing light. It entered my body like hot water, and the long gash on my calf mended together, leaving behind only a smear of blood.

Christian hurriedly snaked his arm about my waist and whirled me around. His lips pressed a kiss to my neck. "I get hard watching you in action."

I nipped his earlobe. The feeling was mutual. Despite his lack of chivalry, I liked that he let me fight my own battles. Most men wouldn't. Christian had spent years working as a bodyguard, so it couldn't have been as easy as he made it seem to stand on the sidelines. It proved he respected me as an equal.

I leaned back and ran my fingers across his nape. "Do what you want with these guys, but hurry. We've gotta go."

"Go where, Precious? Your keys are on the roof of another building. We're stranded. Perhaps we should make the most of it."

As much as the idea of having sex on a bed of weapons titillated me, I slipped out of his grasp and peered over the ledge. The building next door was shorter, but they weren't apartments. There was no way we'd be able to infiltrate business offices without them calling the police. They probably had security cameras inside and employee badges.

I strode back to the van and worked a kink out of my shoulder. "I've got an idea."

He stared at me carefully. "You're *not* thinking about it."

I gave him a cocksure grin and tapped the toe of my shoe against the asphalt. "Doing is better than thinking."

Before he could retort, I balled up my energy and flashed toward the low ledge. As I hurtled over the wall, I kicked off the edge to launch myself farther. Ten feet of thin air separated me from the adjacent building, and for the first time, I knew what Blue must feel when she soared across the sky.

Free.

Powerful.

Alive.

Chapter 3

C HRISTIAN AND I DIDN'T TARRY with delivering the weapons. After stripping the clothes off the yuppie, Christian drank him almost dry so he could remove the crucifix without a fight. By the time I returned with the keys, Christian had placed the Mage spread-eagle on the hood of his car. He'd also destroyed their phones and crushed their keys to make sure they had a memorable walk home.

Aside from the unexpected ambush, it was a simple operation. Shortly before arriving at our destination, Christian called Viktor to alert the arms dealer. Despite our success, Christian and I decided that Viktor didn't need to know the finer points of our mission. We'd completed the task, and that was all that mattered. Besides, we enjoyed the diversion.

Perhaps more than the mission itself.

I snuck into Shepherd's medical room on the first floor and used wet paper towels to wash the blood off my leg.

How in the world did that guy know we were transporting something valuable? By the way those men were acting, the ambush hadn't appeared to be planned. Their Corvette could barely fit two men, let alone five boxes of weapons. But the timing of the traffic lights screwing up was also kind of strange. I wadded up the paper towel and tossed it into the trash.

"A quick trip, huh?"

I whirled around.

Shepherd leaned against the doorjamb and stared at the bloody paper towels in the wastebasket.

"I started my period," I said flatly.

We both knew that I would never have a monthly cycle again, but it didn't stop me from enjoying the joke.

"I've never had trouble dropping off weapons. You two go out, and it's a bloodbath."

"Nothing we couldn't handle."

"Whatever you say, honey." Despite his steely expression, Shepherd's eyes danced with amusement.

He scratched his neck, his eyes on the paper towels. "You might want to dispose of your bodily fluids in the other trash can. The one with the lid and plastic bag."

I lifted the small wastebasket and then stepped on the pedal to the larger can, dumping the contents inside. "Are there psychics in the Breed world?"

He shrugged. "Haven't you heard of Mentalists?"

I leaned against the counter. "Yeah. But the guy who singled out our van wasn't a Mage. I'm not sure what his Breed was," I said, thinking about the guy in the red shorts. He couldn't have been a Shifter, so that narrowed it down to a Relic or Sensor.

"Anything goes in our world." Shepherd dipped his chin. "You weren't talking about the weapons while in the van, were you?"

"No, Viktor told us not to. Besides, neither of these guys were Vamps. I don't know. It just doesn't make any sense."

He sighed heavily. "Shit happens. Just make sure you've got a big mop to clean it up."

I nudged him aside as I exited the room. "That's a visual I didn't need."

"On that note, dinner's ready," he announced, following behind me.

Up ahead, Hunter went flying toward the dining room. All I saw were his little flailing arms and wild black hair.

I slowed down to let Shepherd catch up. "Is he still sleeping in his room?"

"As far as I know, he isn't sneaking out."

"That's good. Have you taken him shopping?"

"Nah. I think he's afraid of leaving Keystone too many times.

Like maybe one day I won't bring him back. I'm not gonna push it." Shepherd heaved a sigh. "I don't know if he'll ever recover from Patrick's brainwashing."

Despite having grown up in a wealthy home, Hunter had been denied love and given too many restrictions. Someone must have shown him physical affection as a baby, perhaps a nanny who cared for him in the early years. Viktor said that children completely deprived of interaction and touch often became emotionally unstable. Hunter was smart and occasionally affectionate, but he was also quiet. The poor kid had grown up without a name—without an identity. Living with Keystone was a whole new world for him, and everyone did their best to give him attention when he was around.

We strolled down the dark hall that led to the dining room. The last remaining hours of sunlight were trickling in through the window behind Viktor's chair. As always, Kira had lit the candles on the iron chandelier and sconces on the wall. The candles on the table brought out the golden hues in the aged wood.

Viktor had already filled everyone's glasses with red wine, with the exception of Gem's. It looked like she and Hunter were sipping on apple juice. I passed Niko, then Blue, and finally Christian as I took my seat to Viktor's left. I shook out my napkin and set it in my lap, curious to see what was on tonight's menu.

"May I?" Gem asked, eyeballing the large silver bowl in front of her.

Viktor gulped his wine and nodded.

Her eyes widened as she lifted the silver dome. Steam clouded in front of her face for a moment before her excitement deflated. "That's a lot of white rice."

Wyatt tapped the dome between us with his fork. "How much you wanna bet we got more in here?"

I lifted the lid, revealing what looked like a quinoa salad. "How much did we bet again?"

He took off his loose beanie and hooked it over the ear of his chair. "Doesn't count."

Kira appeared from the kitchen with a long platter in her hands.

She always had on a plain dress, and tonight was no different. Her sleeves were rolled up, and the blue apron tied around her waist had stains. Gem and Shepherd parted like the Red Sea as she set the platter in front of them.

Gem drew in a deep breath. "That smells divine!"

We devoured the dish with our eyes because there was a lot of artistry in her presentation. Lemon slices were neatly arranged across herbed chicken. We weren't exactly sure how Kira did it, but she tenderized her chicken and infused the flavors in the meat so skillfully that it was fit for royalty.

"Dibs on the drumsticks," Wyatt called out as Shepherd reached for a thigh and a breast.

Kira returned with two baskets of yeast rolls, and Viktor gave her an appreciative nod before she left the room. She never interrupted us during dinner. After an hour, she would serve dessert or a cheese platter. Kira ate her own meals separate from the team, which felt a little sad but necessary since we discussed sensitive cases at the table.

While we passed the plates around, Viktor refilled his glass. The only time he drank wine that generously was when something was troubling him.

"Are there any small bowls?" Niko asked.

Gem blinked and shot to her feet. "Oh, I'll get one."

Niko rarely asked for special accommodations because of his blindness. He told us that in the early days, before there were forks or spoons, he would use either chopsticks or his hands. Niko had no trouble with silverware and eating most foods, but spoons were easier, and a bowl allowed him to eat rice faster.

Gem returned and set the bowl in front of his plate. "It's in front of you."

"Thank you."

Blue split her roll and buttered the inside. "Are you going to share what's on your mind, Viktor?"

He cut into his chicken. "I have accepted an important group assignment. If any of you are still working on individual jobs, please bring them to a stopping point tonight. With the exception of Gem—continue the translations I've given you. Wyatt, I will need to pull you aside for assistance."

Wyatt gave him a two-finger salute. "Aye, aye, captain."

Christian drank his wine and set it by his empty plate. "What's the job?"

Viktor finished his bite and wiped his beard with a napkin. "I cannot tell you anything until we get there."

I jerked my head back. "Get where?"

"I do not mean to imply that any of you will spill our secrets, but there are too many risks, so I cannot give you information at this time. A Vampire might charm you and accidentally discover the details of our assignment. If he commits memory theft and scrubs you afterward, how would I know that our mission is compromised? A gifted Sensor might read your emotions and know you're hiding something big. Nyet. I have given this much thought. Christian knows a small piece of the plan but not everything, including the destination. Wyatt, I will need you to secure travel arrangements. I do not want you sharing this with anyone."

"Can't we all collaborate?" he asked.

"Better the right hand does not know about the left."

"What the left is doing." Gem corrected him, her eyes never leaving her plate as she gobbled up her quinoa salad.

"Spasibo." Viktor lifted his fork and knife. "Once we arrive at the first location, I will explain everything."

Niko's spoon clinked against his plate as he set it down. "When do we leave?"

"When I say."

"What shall we pack?"

"Only what will fit in a small bag. I do not want you to weigh yourself down with nonsense you do not need."

That narrowed it down to comfortable shoes and a hoodie.

"Pack tonight," he continued. "Keep your phones turned on. I am waiting for my contact to give me the signal, and I do not want to be searching for you. Nobody leaves the house unless I say."

Holding a pensive look, Shepherd cracked his knuckles. "How long is this trip?"

Viktor pushed food around on his plate with his fork but said nothing.

Claude gulped down his water and cleared his throat. "Viktor, I have a business to run. Can I at least have an estimated time of return so my employees don't panic? Two weeks? Two years?"

Viktor chuckled and scooped up his rice. "Days or weeks. No more than that unless we run into trouble. Tell them you are going on vacation."

Shepherd removed a box of cigarettes from beneath his sleeve and wedged a brown filter between his lips. Instead of using a match, he craned forward and lit his smoke on a candle. "Is this something you need me for? I've got... responsibilities."

"We all have responsibilities," Viktor reminded him. "We have spoken about this. You cannot turn away from your obligations due to your... responsibilities."

Neither of them said Hunter's name aloud, but that was who they were talking about. The little boy ignored the adults while he tore his chicken into a million pieces on his plate.

Viktor picked a grain of rice off his silver mustache. "Kira is here."

Shepherd blew out a cloud of smoke. "Kira is busy doing all kinds of shit, and you've got Gem and Wyatt working on stuff. That doesn't give me any peace of mind."

Sensing a well-timed opportunity, I folded my arms on the edge of the table. "Gentlemen, I have a proposition."

Wyatt steepled his fingers and studied me closely. "This should be juicy."

I looked between Shepherd and Viktor. *Better now than never.* "I think everyone here would agree that Hunter needs a tutor. None of us have the time or skills to educate him, not unless you want to give him classes on how to break legs and hack into the FBI. Trips like these are exactly why we need a nanny. Someone whose sole job is to look after him."

Viktor sighed, and when he spoke, his hands were animated. "I have reservations. There are too many secrets within these walls. Too many artifacts, books, weapons, Wyatt's computers, paperwork, and our conversations. I cannot look over my shoulder in my own home, worried that someone might be listening."

"Do you worry about Kira?"

"She is family to me."

"Switch is like family to me."

Gem's eyes widened. "You mean the long-haired Shifter we met at your father's house? He's kind of dreamy."

Christian shifted in his seat.

I lifted my wine and swallowed a mouthful before setting the glass back down. "This is what Switch does for a living. He's not only a nanny but also a teacher. He educates kids of all ages, and besides, he's a wolf. That's better protection than if you hired a Relic. Maybe he'll act as Hunter's watchdog. Look, I trust him with my life. He comes from a good pack."

Viktor struggled with his words before switching to Russian.

Gem bit her bottom lip for a second as she mentally translated. "He says that Switch belongs to a pack. We need someone as a… live-in."

"Spasibo. Why is it simple words I struggle with?"

Gem's necklace tapped against the edge of the table when she leaned over her plate. "Nothing is simple when it comes to language."

Gem often conversed entirely in Russian with Viktor. Just not when others were in the room.

I sat back and redirected the conversation. "That's not a problem. Switch comes from a good pack, but he doesn't belong to one. He's independent. He hasn't chosen a permanent family to live with yet."

Viktor's grey eyes narrowed with that look he sometimes got when we were withholding information. "And why is that? If he is so talented, Packmasters would be fighting over him."

I tried not to make the next sentence sound as dramatic as it really was. "There's something you should know, and I hope you'll keep an open mind. We're a second-chance group here, and I think it's only fair the same should apply to anyone who works for you."

Shepherd flicked his cigarette ash into the candle tray. "Spill it."

"One of the kids he was watching was being abused by an uncle or something. Instead of reporting it to the Packmaster, Switch took matters into his own hands and killed the man. That's why he's not in a pack. People trust him with their kids, but the Packmasters won't take a chance on packmates who might break the chain of command."

Everyone stole a glance at Hunter, who was blowing bubbles in his drink through a straw. He giggled when he noticed us watching. After a few more bites of his food, he crawled underneath the table.

"Is that all there is to the story?" Shepherd pressed, his dark eyes searching mine.

"You can verify it with any of the Packmasters in his territory."

"That's it? The packs don't want him because he killed a lowlife who had it coming?"

"That is the pack way," Viktor interjected. "The alpha has absolute power, and when Switch killed the perpetrator, he took that honor away from the Packmaster."

Shepherd stared at the tendril of smoke rising from his cigarette. "Do you trust him?"

I shared a glance with everyone at the table. "He's loyal. I don't know if he'll even want the job, but his prospects aren't exactly looking up. He's living in a shitty apartment, and I think this would be a good way for him to build up his income. We could be the substitute pack that he's been looking for, and you can trust him with Hunter. I grew up around Switch, and he's always been good with kids. Patient, kind, attentive—it's like he was born to do this job."

Viktor quietly listened, his eyes fixed on his plate. Even if Shepherd was all in, it was still up to the boss.

"We're not exactly a pack," I pointed out. "He'll respect your rules, but if—God forbid—someone ever hurt the boy, do you really want the kind of person who would sit on their ass and do nothing?"

Shepherd stubbed out his cigarette. "If anyone *ever* lays a finger on my son, I want them six feet under."

"Then Switch is your man. He's not a killer; he's a protector."

Viktor stared at his plate. "I do not know."

All hope seemed lost.

And then Christian spoke. "Perhaps you can bring him on for a trial period. See if he's as good a teacher as Raven suggests. We don't exactly know if he's teaching arithmetic or how to bake bread, so this will give you a chance to look into the matter. I don't see any other options if you're waiting for someone to come along who'll be loyal to Keystone. The man doesn't know us, but he knows Raven. And if Raven trusts him, well, that's a good enough place to start."

I stared at Christian, his unexpected support leaving me speechless.

"Very well," Viktor agreed. "We have an important job ahead, and it would give me comfort knowing that the boy is under someone's constant watch. If the packs still employ your friend, they must trust him immensely. But first his wolf must meet the boy, and I will need to supervise this. There is not much time."

I scooted my chair back. "Do you want me to call him?"

"Nyet. Give me his number. It would be best if I present him with the opportunity directly. We'll invite him over so I can decide if I have a good feeling about the arrangement, but we must do all this immediately."

My heart did a quickstep at the idea of Switch living in our home. This would be an opportunity for him to make good money and earn respect from the packs, but more importantly, I selfishly wanted a friend around. Someone not linked with Keystone secrets.

Christian coolly sipped his wine and then gave me a long look. Though no one else caught my excitement, Christian could no doubt hear my racing heart and quickened breath. I wondered if the tables were turned, how I would feel about him inviting a beautiful woman who was attracted to him to live with us. I decided I wouldn't care. If they had no relationship history, I'd trust him. But I wouldn't trust her, so I understood Christian's reservations.

"I'll give you his number after dinner," I said to Viktor. "If he accepts, Christian's idea about a trial period is a good one. That'll give us a smaller window to scrub his memories if we decide it's not working out."

"He'll have to prove himself in more ways than one," Viktor tacked on as a condition. "Shepherd, do you have any issues?"

"Nope. But I want to talk with him before I decide."

"Perhaps I should have a private talk with him as well," Christian muttered before finishing his wine.

Maybe this wasn't such a good idea.

Chapter 4

IMMEDIATELY AFTER DINNER, WE SKIPPED the usual wine and conversation and went to our rooms to pack. Well, everyone except for Wyatt and Gem, who stayed behind to have extra helpings of apple torte. I grabbed a camouflage backpack and considered Viktor's instructions to pack light. Without knowing where we were going, I packed a grey hoodie, a T-shirt, underwear, sweatpants, socks, gloves, and daggers. Just in case we had to look presentable, I threw in my toothbrush, hairbrush, and a little makeup. Uncertain if we were heading north, I draped my leather jacket over the bag.

I took inventory and glanced around my dimly lit bedroom. "What else?"

Clothes I could live without. I certainly wasn't a stranger to wearing the same thing for weeks at a time. As long as I had weapons, that was all that mattered.

"Pack light," I muttered. "What's light?"

Did that imply a short trip, or did it mean we were going to be carrying our bags for long distances? With Viktor, you never knew.

I ventured toward Wyatt's World on the second floor. His desk lamp was on but the TV off. "I'm out of change. Can you open your machine and give me some of those packaged peanuts?"

He wiped up torte crumbs from his plate with his finger and licked it. "What do I get in return?"

"To live another day?"

"I'll take the jerky," Shepherd said from behind me. "Hurry it up, Spooky. I've got shit to do."

I noticed the holster on his belt. "Great minds think alike."

"Always pack for survival, not comfort."

Shepherd's dark hair was so short that he didn't have to do anything with it after a shower. It looked glossy, and his face was freshly shaved.

Wyatt stood up and straightened his threadbare orange shirt, which had somehow survived since the 1970s. "Seeing how this is a special assignment, I'll make an exception." He jingled the keys as he opened the front panel. "Switch working as a nanny at Keystone, huh? That's a twist I didn't see coming."

I caught the peanuts he threw my way. "I like easy solutions. Hunter needs a good teacher, and Switch needs a better-paying job."

Wyatt tossed a couple of bags of beef jerky to Shepherd, one of them sailing off in a different direction.

Shepherd ambled over and dipped down to pick it up. "You don't trust anyone, so that's saying something."

I glanced down at my peanuts. "You got that right."

Wyatt shut the front panel to his vending machine and locked it. "I'm offended. Who's the one who gives you pertinent information at the drop of a hat when you're *supposedly*"—he used his fingers to make air quotes—"on a routine errand?"

I gave him a frosty glare for bringing up Christian's call earlier regarding the red Corvette.

"Your lethal stare doesn't frighten me, buttercup." He sat in his chair and spun around. "If you don't mind, I'm doing super top secret James Bond shit around here. Privacy please."

"Thanks for the snacks."

When he looked over his shoulder at me and flashed his green eyes, a smile line carved into his cheek. "I'll collect interest later."

I went back upstairs and tucked the snacks in my bag. Curious what Christian was up to, I snuck over to his room and peered inside. Only one candle was burning, and I noticed a small bag by the bed. Smaller than mine.

When I turned around, I must have jumped a foot in the air as Christian was standing not an inch away.

I smacked him on the chest. "Holy crap! You nearly gave me a heart attack."

"Now that I'd like to see. The first Mage to ever die of a coronary."

"Do you know CPR?"

He cocked his head to the side. "If you ever see a Vampire administering chest compressions to revive a corpse, be sure to take a picture. Aside from crushing a person's ribs in the process, Vampires are famous for stopping hearts, not making them start again."

I leaned into his warm body. "You started mine."

A crooked grin touched his lips, and he wrapped his arms around me. "Aye, lass. I did. Before me, it was just a cold dead thing taking up space in your chest."

I kissed his neck. "Is that a purse or a travel bag?"

"Vampires know how to pack light."

Christian definitely wouldn't need all the "just in case" clothing items since he was impervious to cold and heat. He didn't even need weapons since his hands and fangs were weapons enough.

"I hope you at least brought a change of underwear."

He stepped back and stared daggers at the door. "Your wolf is here."

"Switch?"

Christian folded his arms. "Could you turn down the excitement a notch?"

I gazed up at him earnestly. "Thanks for having my back earlier."

His eyes lowered to my ruby necklace. "Don't make me regret it."

I could have hashed out all the reasons why he didn't have to worry about Switch, but I didn't need to. Christian's support had given me all the affirmation I needed.

With lightning speed, I flashed down the long hall. The wide staircase curved to the first floor, the stone steps porous and easy to tread over. I jogged to the dining room and spotted Switch through an archway that divided the two rooms.

I strode into the gathering room and steadied my heavy

breathing. No sense in showing that I'd raced all the way down to greet him like an excited puppy. "What are you doing here?" I asked.

Switch turned to face me. His long brown hair hung past his shoulders, but I guessed he'd wanted to neaten it up for his meeting with Viktor because it was tied at the nape.

Switch's wolfish eyes met mine. His dark brows slanted down, no smile greeting me this time. "Raven." He inclined his head, speaking to me as if we hadn't grown up together.

"You have an impeccable record," Viktor said, ignoring my presence. "Before summoning you here, I called the Packmasters in your territory. They speak highly of your work with children."

The wood in the fireplace snapped as the glow intensified in the otherwise dark room. Both men stood before the massive hearth, Viktor with his hands clasped behind his back. I lingered by the entryway and quietly listened.

"Then you heard the full story," Switch said flatly. "You know why I haven't joined a pack."

Viktor gazed up at the high ceiling. "Not every man can hold his head high when his good name is dragged through the mud. You could have fled to another state, but you continued working here. That is admirable."

Switch hooked his thumbs in his jean pockets. "I love my job, and I'm not the kind of man who runs off with his tail between his legs. I regret how I handled things, but I'm not ashamed of what I did. In the end, that kid is living a better life because of me. Who's to say if the Packmaster would have believed me? Kids don't confide in just anyone. He hadn't even told his parents."

Viktor glanced at his watch. "I am satisfied with that answer. As I said before, this is only a trial period."

"When can I get back to you?"

"We have an emergency and no time to wait for an answer."

"If it works out?" he asked.

"Good money. I will ask you to live under my roof and follow my rules. You will eat with Kira and not ask questions about our work. We need not only a teacher for the child but also someone to watch over and protect him when we are away. More specifically, when his father is away. You cannot interfere with his father's discipline or rules."

"Understood."

"You will find that Shepherd is more than lenient with the boy, perhaps too much. You can help provide the structure and education Hunter needs. Your responsibilities also include confidentiality. We will not discuss sensitive matters in your presence, but there will be times you hear us talking about work. I expect you not to pry into our business, discuss it with anyone on the outside, or betray my trust."

"That's not a problem. And what if this doesn't work out?"

Viktor turned around and paced. "Then we will scrub your memories of this place and release you. As you can see, it is very important that you make this decision while in your trial period. The more time that passes, the more we have to erase. You must consider this offer carefully and whether or not you can commit long-term. This job will exist until the boy is grown."

"And then? I'll have no place here and you'll scrub my memories?"

"Nyet. I have decided that is an unjust decision. You will not be leaving by choice but by circumstance. The less you meddle in our business affairs, the easier it will be on my conscience to let you go. No spying, no eavesdropping, no going through our papers. If you betray us, I will be forced to take action."

Switch stroked his circle beard. "What about the thing you mentioned earlier about dating?"

Viktor pursed his lips and fidgeted with the buttons on his cardigan. "You are a male with certain needs. This I understand. But as long as you live here, mating is not an option. She cannot live here, and if you leave, that will be by choice. I will be forced to scrub your memories, and that may include memories of your chosen one."

Switch walked to the leather sofa on my right and took a seat. He held his hands in a prayerlike gesture, his gaze pensive.

"You are a wolf." Viktor gripped the back of a chair facing

Switch. "That means you have hundreds upon hundreds of years to settle down. All we are asking of you is thirteen years of service. Is that not a reasonable number?"

I hadn't given that any consideration and felt a sudden pang of guilt that Switch had to sacrifice his love life. How much did settling down and having children of his own mean to him?

"This job will not only give you stability but also good money. Substantial money," Viktor stressed. "That will put you in a stronger position for entering a reputable pack. I believe a good alpha will overlook your past. Your service with us will outshine all that nonsense, and I can provide a glowing recommendation. Because I am also a wolf, that will mean more. In a few years, you will have much to offer a pack."

Switch rubbed the hair on his arms. "That's a nice offer. Too nice. Why would you single me out above anyone else?" Then he turned and looked at me, disappointment playing on his features once he figured out that I'd had something to do with it.

Viktor motioned to me. "Raven offered your name, but I am very particular about who I trust within my organization. She feels you are loyal, and we have seen you show that loyalty to her family. That is a noble quality. Every Packmaster I spoke with said the same thing. They were not willing to let you join their pack, but they trusted you with their children."

I could tell that Viktor's answer pleased Switch more than the thought of a pity offer.

Switch brushed a stray tendril of hair away from his face. "Just one kid?"

"Hunter is a special boy who requires special attention. It is not just an education or nanny we seek but someone who can help him overcome his challenges."

"I'm in."

"Not until I say you're in," Shepherd barked from the dining area as he strode into the room. He walked right up to Switch and squared his shoulders. "Give me your hand."

Switch looked up at him with trepidation but did as he was asked.

Shepherd seized his wrist and gripped it tight. "Have you ever hurt a child?"

Switch's face turned red, and his eyes blackened. "No."

"Will you protect my son with your life? Without hesitation?"

"Yes."

"Are you just here for the money?"

Switch met his eyes. "Fuck you."

Shepherd let go and nodded at Viktor. "I approve."

Viktor gave him a curt look. "Hunter is in the kitchen with Kira. Go fetch him."

Shepherd pivoted and did as instructed.

Viktor folded his arms over the back of the chair and smiled. "Shepherd is a Sensor. Forgive his boorish behavior. Your wolf must meet the boy, but not when you are in control. I must see how your animal behaves without your influence. I'll supervise you for fifteen minutes. That should be long enough."

Switch sat back and gripped the armrest. "You wanna do this now?"

"If we have an agreement, your duties begin immediately. I would advise you not to make any drastic decisions like breaking a lease or spending money. I will know more about your abilities when we return from our trip. But you may hurry home to retrieve clothes and additional items you require. No pets allowed."

Switch snorted. "What kind of idiot do you take me for?"

Viktor turned his palms up. "The newer generations these days are not like the old. They do not see the insult behind owning an animal. They call it love, and they dress their animals like people. But they have not experienced slavery firsthand to recognize that animals are meant to be free."

I mentally laughed at the idea of wild poodles.

"I have integrity. You got nothing to worry about, old man. My former pack taught me well." Switch stood up and stripped out of his T-shirt, his muscles flexing. "In here or outside?"

Viktor glanced at the windows over his shoulder and then back. "In here is acceptable. The courtyard is much too dark."

I stepped inside the room. "Is this a good idea? It might scare the kid."

"We have no choice," Viktor said. "If there is trouble and Switch changes to a wolf, I need assurance that his animal will not turn on the child." His eyes darted over to Switch. "And do not do anything foolish. I may look like a polite old man, but my wolf is anything but civilized."

The idea of their wolves tearing each other apart made my stomach do a flip. "Maybe there's some other way—"

Switch winked at me. "Don't worry, Raven. I do this all the time." In a fluid movement, Switch morphed into a wolf. He lumbered forward and raised his snout, his nostrils widening as he took in the scent of his new surroundings. Unlike Viktor, who was a grey wolf, Switch was an earthy brown. The chestnut color was darkest on his ears and neck, his coat silken and incredibly soft to the touch from what I remembered.

He caught my scent, and his tail wagged. But the moment he spied Viktor, a low growl settled in his throat. His toenails clicked against the floor as he weaved around furniture to approach Viktor.

When he bared his teeth, I rounded the chair.

"Stay out of this, Raven," Viktor commanded, his tone calm and collected as he slowly turned to face the wolf.

When the two were close enough to kill each other, Viktor stared down at him. He spoke softly in Russian and extended his hand.

I flinched, thinking Switch might bite off his fingers. Instead, his wolf sniffed Viktor's palm and then licked it. Switch could have still been in control, but I had doubts that he would lick another man's fingers.

Viktor spoke in a soothing but dominant voice, and after a moment he knelt down and ran his fingers over the wolf's ear.

"I guess he likes you," I said in utter relief.

"One must establish who is the stronger wolf. I am not an alpha, but I am his superior. He will not touch me."

Shepherd brushed past me. "I'm having second thoughts."

Viktor stood up and wiped his wet palm against his trousers.

"I will not let the wolf harm the boy, if that is your concern. I'm quite skilled at reading the body language of wolves. If he behaves aggressively, I will throw him out on his haunches."

Shepherd ran his hands over his buzz cut and swung his gaze to one of the archways where Hunter was peering through. "Come on, little man. There's someone you need to meet."

Hunter tiptoed into the room in his blue pajama bottoms and white shirt. He didn't have his Sensor gloves on since it was bedtime.

Switch's wolf gave Shepherd a cursory glance. Unable to see Hunter, who was standing behind a chair, he lifted his nose and drew in a scent. A different kind of growl settled on his tongue.

Hunter clung to Shepherd.

"I'm not letting anything hurt you," Shepherd promised him. "We'll go together."

Viktor shook his head. "Nyet. The boy must come in alone."

Shepherd clenched his jaw. "That's not part of the deal."

"I am here to control the situation. You do not know the language of wolves, so you must trust me."

"He'll tear him apart."

"Let's not be dramatic. Come, little one. There is someone you must meet. This is your new teacher."

My heart pounded against my rib cage as Hunter circled around the chair, his blue eyes wide and fearful.

When Switch saw him, he whimpered and his ears went flat.

Hunter shuffled up to Viktor and cowered behind him.

The wolf barked and lowered his tail.

"You must not be afraid," Viktor encouraged him. He reached around and cradled the boy's head with one hand. "Animals talk to us using their body. You see how his ears are flat and tail is down? He is submitting. With cats, it's not the same."

Hunter didn't seem to have a clue what Viktor meant.

Viktor furrowed his brow. "That is a friendly hello."

A high-pitched whine sounded, and Switch yelped excitedly.

When Shepherd moved toward them, Switch swung his head and bared his fangs.

Viktor extended his arm, warning the both of us to remain still.

My breath caught when Hunter gathered enough courage to approach the animal.

The wolf crouched and lowered his head. Then he turned it to the side to peer up at the boy. I wasn't sure that I'd ever seen a wolf smile until that moment.

"Do not be afraid." Viktor knelt beside the two and stroked Switch's ear. "You must show him how brave you are, and he will respect you."

I wasn't sure if the little kid grasped concepts like respect and submission, but then I considered how Patrick had raised him. He probably knew a lot more about those topics than most kids his age.

Switch's wolf rolled onto his side, exposing his belly.

When Hunter squatted in front of him and touched his paw, the wolf barked playfully. You could see the joy in his face, and he licked Hunter's hand and then his neck, making the boy giggle uncontrollably. Switch wiggled to a new position as the two got to know each other.

Hunter ran his fingers over the wolf's ears and long muzzle, dangerously close to sharp fangs that could rip him apart in seconds.

Meanwhile, Shepherd was sweating bullets. "All right, that's enough."

When he moved toward them, Switch launched to his feet and shielded the boy with his body. He bared his fangs at Shepherd, and his tail shot up high.

"Get back!" Viktor shouted.

Hunter shot up and dashed over to Shepherd. He gripped his arm and desperately pulled him toward the wolf. I realized he wanted the two to get along and was acting as a mediator so his new friend would have a trusting relationship with his father.

Smart kid.

The wolf kept snarling, and when Hunter neared it, I realized he had his father's bravery and perhaps his mother's wisdom. He let the wolf sniff his palm that still carried Shepherd's scent. Then he leaned over and touched the wolf's ear. I wondered if he was using Sensor magic to convey his emotions. Kids his age weren't supposed to know the hard stuff, but Patrick had started him young. Hunter didn't talk out loud. When he did speak, it was to whisper in Shepherd's ear. In many ways, Hunter was like the wolf; they didn't need words to communicate.

After another moment, he held Shepherd's hand. I couldn't see Shepherd's face but imagined he was as dumbstruck as I was. Christian and Claude were in the dining room, watching through the archways.

"Hold out your hand with the palm up," Viktor instructed him. "Slowly."

"I like my fingers. Why don't you let someone else go first?"

"Gem, Wyatt, and Kira will get their turn before we leave. Everyone else will have to wait, except you. I cannot risk an accident with the boy's father."

Shepherd grumbled a curse word before holding out his scarred hand.

I inched forward, ready to tackle Switch's wolf if he so much as took a nibble. I didn't know his wolf well enough to predict what might set him off, but I sure as hell didn't want Shepherd taking his head off with the gun strapped to his side.

Hunter stood between the two, but his eyes were on his father.

The wolf sniffed Shepherd's palm. After a beat, he licked it and sat down.

I blew out a breath and looked at Viktor. "Why was meeting *your* wolf a death match?"

Viktor smirked and gripped his cardigan. "I am not easy to love."

"You're fine," Christian remarked. "It's your wolf who's a fecking lunatic."

Switch went back to tail wagging and cleaning Hunter's face with his tongue.

After circling the furniture and leaving the room, I heard Viktor say, "Bring Gem and Wyatt down. Time for a little fun."

Chapter 5

A KNOCK AT MY BEDROOM DOOR woke me. I blinked, staring at the inky blackness outside my window. My internal clock told me it was two in the morning, and if this wasn't important, I was going to put Christian's spleen on a spike. I groggily stepped out of bed, not bothering to light a candle or put on a pair of pants. As if the ice-cold floor against my feet wasn't enough to wake me, there was more pounding on the door. Why the hell was he waking me up at this hour?

I yanked the door open. "Since when do you knock?"

Switch raised his arm and rested it against the doorjamb. "Since my mother taught me manners."

A heady scent wafted from his body, and I wrinkled my nose. "You smell like you've been digging a grave."

"Maybe my own." His long hair covered half his face. "Can I come in?"

I turned away and trod over the white rug in front of the fireplace. The door clicked shut behind me, but Switch stayed where he was.

"Can you really see in the dark like Vampires?" he asked. "It's like a tomb in here."

I could make out a grainy image of everything, but I located a box of matches as a courtesy. "I don't have to worry about stubbing my toe in the middle of the night," I quipped, lighting a lantern affixed to the wall by the desk. "Have a seat."

He swaggered to the bed and sat down.

"Not there, smart-ass. Take the chair."

The bed creaked when he stood up. "You need a new interior decorator."

I sat on the bed, facing the desk. "I like my room. I've got a nice painting, a warm bedspread, fake flowers—"

"And no chairs."

I gestured to the desk chair. "That's all I need."

He straddled it and folded his arms over the top. "Not very cozy for guests."

"This is my private chamber, not a bar. Since you'll be living here now, don't get too comfortable. I like you, Switch, but if you ever walk in without knocking, I'll cut off your wolf's tail."

He smiled. "No worries. My affection for you has limits."

"Since when?"

"Since you started cuddling up with a Vamp. Speaking of which, why isn't he in here? Don't you share a room with your mate?"

"We're not mated. Not officially. I don't even think there *is* an official ceremony for our kind. Bonding doesn't really apply, and most Vampires don't mate for life since we live a little longer than Shifters and Chitahs."

"So I've heard." He rubbed his chin against his arm while staring at my bed. "If you've declared your intentions to each other, that's as good as mating. Which brings me back to my question. Where is he?"

"We have flexible sleeping arrangements."

His eyebrow arched. "How convenient for him."

"And me. Christian doesn't sleep. What's he going to do, lie here and stare at the ceiling all night, lulled into boredom by the sound of my breathing?"

"I pity a man who can't appreciate the simple things."

I pulled the cover over my legs since his gaze was drifting south. "You don't know what it's like to be a Vampire. I'm only half, but on sleepless nights, time moves like molasses. It's hard to sit still, and your mind wanders. Those are the nights we enjoy spending time together. And sometimes we sleep together."

"Sometimes?"

"Sex and sleep are two different things. Did you come all the way up here to pry into my sex life?"

His long hair curtained his face when he rested his chin on his hands. "After my wolf met your other housemates, I went home to pack. Viktor said you're taking off at any moment. I wasn't sure when I'd see you again, so I thought I'd come up and visit for a minute."

"If it's to thank me, don't bother. I just threw the idea at Viktor, but you earned it."

"Actually, it wasn't my choice to come in the first place."

I jerked my head back. "What do you mean?"

"Crush had a hand in my decision. After Viktor and I spoke on the phone, I called Crush to tell him about the offer. He already knows about you and Keystone, so Viktor didn't have a problem with my calling him for advice."

"My father made you come?"

"It's a good offer, but I had my reservations. For one, it's not a pack. All I've ever known is pack life, and I don't know if this is helping me toward that goal or taking me away from it. Your old man gave me some good advice."

"And what was that?"

"That I should stay here and keep an eye on you."

I chuckled and fell on my side, my head hitting the pillow. "Please tell me that's not why you accepted the position. Your job isn't to be my guard dog."

He leaned back. "No, it's not. My priority is watching over Hunter. But it doesn't hurt to be close by, just in case you need me. Well, not me personally, but my help. Your dad says that you bottle things up and need someone to listen. He doesn't think your boyfriend will give you sound advice, so I'll be here if you need to talk. No strings attached."

I rubbed my eyes sleepily. "Thanks. It's nice having a friend around." I yawned noisily and nestled into the covers. "How did it go with Gem and Wyatt meeting your wolf?"

His dark eyes sparkled. "From what they tell me, Gem was

nervous, but my wolf has never harmed a woman. In fact, he's quite gentle with them. Your friend with the hat wasn't so lucky."

"Wyatt?"

"I bit him in the ass. Not sure what he did to provoke it, but he shouldn't have fled. Running incites the beast in me." Switch sat up straight and grinned. "Don't worry. He'll live."

Between Shepherd and Niko, I wondered which man would have the honor of putting his hands on Wyatt's ass to heal him.

"What are you laughing at?" Switch asked.

"Nothing. I just have a tickle in my throat."

He rose from his chair. "Anyhow, I just wanted to say that I'm here for you. I'm not keeping a torch lit in hopes that you'll change your mind, so you don't have to worry about things getting weird between us." Switch lingered by my bed and gave me an ambiguous look. "He's a lucky man. I just hope he knows how lucky."

"I make sure to tell him every chance I get."

Switch smiled ruefully and strode toward the door.

"Switch?"

"Yeah?"

The words caught in my throat. I wanted to tell him that someday he'd find a life mate, but those were the wrong words. Switch cared for me, but we barely knew each other. I didn't want to give him the wrong idea. Despite our fumbled attempts at rekindling our childhood friendship, we had forged a bond that I felt certain would last.

So instead I settled for the right words. "Congrats on the job. It's a long commitment, but it'll be worth it in the end."

"I hope so." He glanced at me over his shoulder before closing the door. "In fact, I know so."

Shepherd woke up early, his nerves in a jangle. He always got restless before a big job, but this time was different. His anxiety was compounded by the fact he had to leave his son behind. He'd spent five years without his son, and now he couldn't imagine a day without him. Hunter was turning six this year, so every moment with him mattered. Before long he would be grown and off to live his own life. Shepherd had mentally prepared himself for jobs that were dangerous or took him away from home, but he was quickly discovering that his coping skills were nonexistent.

His bags were packed, but his heart wasn't ready to go.

Not yet.

Shepherd sat still on the edge of Hunter's bed, not wanting to rouse the sleeping boy. His kid could snooze through the apocalypse, and it was adorable as hell.

Each day he spent with Hunter managed to lessen the guilt of Maggie's loss. That cavernous vacancy in Shepherd's heart had slowly begun to fill with a new kind of love he'd never known. Hunter was an extension of Maggie. Shepherd saw her in Hunter's smile, and it forced him to think of her in an abstract way. Instead of remembering the last moments of her life, he thought about what her opinions might be on Hunter's room or his education. It made Shepherd a better man... and a better father.

This little guy had never left Shepherd's thoughts in the past five years. He used to imagine what his child might have looked like, what his first word might have been, what kind of ice cream he might have liked. He'd spent many nights wondering what their child would have grown up to be, and each time, Shepherd had to close those thoughts with regret for a life that never was.

And yet by some miracle, Hunter lived. He was here, sleeping under the same roof.

Alive.

The fates had truly blessed him. Hunter's will to live was innate from the moment he was ripped from his mother's womb, and Shepherd owed him a good life. He owed him his full protection, and that meant casting his pride aside to do what was best for him. Switch wouldn't have been his first option, but there were too many positives to turn his back on the offer. Hunter needed more than a teacher; he needed a protector. A wolf was a good companion—a loyal one. And during his brief questioning, Shepherd sensed that Switch was a noble and trustworthy man. Maggie would have wanted to give Hunter the finest education. So far the only thing Hunter had learned at Keystone was how to tie his shoes and how to clean a mansion.

Shepherd peeled back the comforter when he noticed Hunter was a little sweaty. Maggie had known that the child within her would be a crossbreed and live the life span of a Sensor, but would he also be vulnerable to human viruses? Relics had to worry about contagious diseases, but Sensors didn't. How much of Shepherd's DNA would play a role in Hunter's well-being? Only time would tell what his strengths and vulnerabilities were.

Shepherd felt Hunter's forehead. No fever, just a little warmth from the abundance of blankets. He ran his thumb over the scar that marked his little boy's face. It started near his left eye and curved down his cheek. That scar made Shepherd want to hit something. His son's first moments should have been in Maggie's arms, not hanging upside down in the grip of some maniac.

Shepherd glanced over his shoulder at the large windows. Hunter didn't get direct sunlight in the morning, but it was bright and cheery, and sunshine flooded the courtyard. A robin landed at the base of the window, peering in before flying away.

This was the hardest damn thing Shepherd had ever done, but time was up. Viktor had sent a text message instructing everyone to be downstairs in twenty minutes. Instead of eating breakfast, Shepherd had spent every last minute in Hunter's room. He didn't consider himself a doting dad, but it was somehow easier for him to let down his guard when the boy was asleep.

A light knock sounded at the door. Shepherd stood up, his shoulders tensing until Switch ambled into the room.

"He awake yet?" Switch asked quietly. "I like to get them used to an early schedule. It helps create structure. That way he'll always know when it's time to eat, time to learn, and time to play."

"Right now it's time to sleep."

Switch stroked his short beard with the palm of his hand and looked around the room. "Nice setup. The rest of the house looks like something out of the Dark Ages."

Shepherd chuckled. "Viktor likes it that way. Don't expect to have electricity in whichever room you pick out."

Switch leaned against the dresser by the door and gazed ahead. "I should find one with a window. Do they open? My wolf likes to go out at night."

"Not all."

An awkward silence fell between them. Shepherd folded his arms and glanced back at Hunter to see if the talking had woken him up. But he was in the same position on his side, his teddy bear snuggled under his arm.

"Is that his favorite toy?"

Shepherd masked a smile. "Yeah."

"I'll make sure he has it at bedtime. Is there anything else I should know?"

Shepherd sighed, not ready to have this conversation with someone he barely knew. But he had no choice. It was only a matter of time before Switch found out, and besides, what kind of teacher would he be if he didn't know the most important fact about his pupil? "Hunter's a crossbreed."

Switch's dark eyebrows popped up. "Which Breeds?"

"Relic and Sensor."

Switch tipped his head to the side as if unsurprised. "I've heard of that happening. Not very common, but it's a shame about them losing their gifts."

Shepherd took a few steps forward. "Yeah, but there's something you need to know. He's got both gifts, and that's not something we're advertising."

"Are you shittin' me? *Both?*"

"Make sure he wears his Sensor gloves, and don't take him out of the mansion while we're away. The courtyard is fine, but no public places. I still have to train him, but he knows not to touch things with his bare hands. There won't be much for him to pick up on since most of us will be gone, but I want him to get used to wearing them."

Switch dipped his chin. "Just so you know, I respect parental guidelines. You're his old man, so whatever you say goes. All I need to know are the boundaries."

"Leave bath time to Kira. If he has to use the bathroom, he knows he can use mine."

Switch glanced down at Shepherd's gun holster. "You got any weapons in your room?"

"I locked them up. He knows not to mess with those things, but I installed a lock on the armoire just the same."

"Got it. Anything else?"

"Lock all the doors and windows at night. He used to wander, but since I gave him this room, he only wanders to my room if he gets scared. But I won't be here."

"How about I take one of the rooms in the hall for now? If this trial period works out, I'll move to a different spot when you come back. I don't want to confuse him. Just so you know, I understand how important boundaries are. I'll be his teacher and his watchdog, but you're the alpha and omega in his life. I'll make sure to reinforce that."

Shepherd nodded, surprised by Switch's candor. "I appreciate that."

"No worries."

"And one more thing—don't stare at his scar."

"Why the fuck would I?"

"Because people are assholes and do it anyway. He doesn't talk, and I'm not pushing it. He's been through a lot."

"Understood. Who puts him to bed at night?"

"Me."

Switch drummed his fingers on the dresser. "He needs a substitute. Kids cling to rituals, but I can't be the stand-in. If he wakes up in the night, I can walk him back in here and read him a story. But tucking him in is a dad thing to do, and I don't want him forming that kind of bond with me."

After a second, Shepherd decided Switch was right. "Kira used to do it before. She doesn't speak English, but she'll understand if you lead her in here with him."

"What language does she speak?"

"Some archaic shit that nobody knows but Viktor."

Switch nodded, his eyes darting over to the bed. "Good morning, sleepyhead."

Shepherd turned and smiled at Hunter, who was sitting up and rubbing his eyes. "Hey there, little man. I got something to tell you." He sat down on the bed as the door closed behind him. "I'm going away for a little while."

When he touched Hunter's hand, he felt excitement, and it confused him.

Hunter jumped out of bed and scampered to the dresser where he kept his clothes.

"No, little man. You have to stay here."

Hunter turned. His sharp blue eyes filled with worry. He adamantly shook his head.

"I need someone to stay here and look after Gem and Wyatt. They need your protection. Switch will also be here—the wolf you met last night. He's gonna be your teacher for a while. If you like him, maybe longer."

Hunter dashed into his arms, and Shepherd felt a pang of guilt. He rumpled the boy's disheveled hair. "It won't be for long. Sometimes I gotta go away for work. But I'll come back." He put his hands around the boy's cheeks so he'd feel his sincerity. "I'll always come back. I promise."

Emotion flooded into the boy through Shepherd's hands and calmed him. Sometimes it was the most honest way that the two could communicate.

"I want you to be a good boy and do as you're told. I've got to follow the rules too, and sometimes it's hard. But we can do it together."

Teary-eyed, Hunter nodded and backed away. He dug in his drawer until he found his black Zorro mask and put it on.

Crestfallen, Shepherd watched as Hunter reverted to the child who'd lived with Patrick, the one who hid from the world behind a mask when he felt unsafe and alone.

Shepherd rubbed his clean-shaven jaw and briefly entertained the idea of staying. "Tell you what. When I get back, we'll go buy you some new shoes. Just the two of us on a special trip, and I'll let you pick out anything you want. Maybe after that we'll get some ice cream. Or cupcakes."

Hunter's eyes lit up. Kids were too easy to distract with bribes. But in this case, Shepherd had every intention of following through on his promises. He had a lot of lost time to make up for.

"And after that we can ride on that mechanical horse you like. Remember?"

Hunter beamed and then galloped to his play table. Wyatt had given him a couple of his toy cars from his work desk, and Hunter rolled them from one end of the table to the other.

Shepherd didn't want to make this into a big production and wind him up again, so he stood behind him and bent over, letting his hands rest firmly on Hunter's shoulders.

I love you.

Give me a kiss.

Those were words that Shepherd couldn't bring himself to say. He'd never said them to anyone but Maggie, and he didn't feel like he'd earned the right to with Hunter.

So instead he said the only thing that would make sense with the emotions leaking from his fingertips. "I'm gonna miss you, little man. Be good."

Chapter 6

"WHERE DO YOU THINK WE'RE going?" I asked Christian.

He put his arm around me just as the van hit a bump. "To a land of enchantment."

"Definitely not your bedroom then," Blue said, her delivery deadpan. She sat across from us, flanked by Niko and Shepherd.

Christian nudged her boot with his foot. "I'll have you know that there are plenty of enchanting activities that occur in my chamber."

She studied her unpolished nails. "None of which include cleaning, I'm sure."

Shepherd barked out a laugh. "She's got you there, buddy."

Rushing to Christian's defense wasn't something I did often, but I suddenly felt the urge to stick up for him. "I can vouch for the cleanliness of his room. Except for the spiders, there's hardly anything in there."

Niko snorted and looked away. "Apologies."

Shepherd checked something inside his coat, a smile widening his thin lips. "I envisioned a coffin with candy jars everywhere."

Christian shot him a baleful look. "You're a real comedian. Anyone ever tell you that?"

Claude slowed down and looked at Viktor. "Which way?"

"Left," Viktor said from the passenger seat.

None of us had any inkling of where we were going or what our mission would be. Sensing Viktor didn't want us talking business while in a moving van, we kept the conversation as light as our luggage.

The brakes squealed as we came to a stop.

"I need to check those," Shepherd muttered.

Blue pulled her loose hair out from the oversized hood of her blue cloak. Both Shepherd and I had on our black leather coats, while Claude was in his brown suede. Even Christian had worn a trench coat, and his pockets must have been stuffed with candy as he unwrapped another butterscotch and popped it into his mouth.

I looked at Blue's knee-high boots. "Are those comfortable?"

She crossed her legs and patted one. "They're waterproof. I've got a regular walking pair in my bag."

"Are they hot?"

She tipped her head and gave me a "no shit, they're hot" look. Blue's brown skin was flushed and dewy. The sun was heating up the van like an oven, but she looked hotter than the rest of us. While blessed with a womanly body, her features floated between feminine and masculine. Long lashes framed her sapphire-blue eyes, but her thick eyebrows and bone structure gave her the face of a warrior.

I glanced down at my black sneakers. "I was hoping we weren't going to Canada again. If we are, I'm screwed."

"You can never tell with Viktor. What did you pack, amigo?"

Niko raised his head. "Sandals."

I chuckled. "Sometimes I can't tell when you're serious or joking."

Blue's smile was as relaxed as her attitude. "We'll soon find out, and I'm afraid someone here will be ill-prepared."

"Or maybe we're all screwed, and Viktor is taking us to a palace," I suggested.

Viktor turned in his seat. "We're not going to a palace."

Blue uncrossed her legs. "Thank the fates."

Shepherd thumped Christian on the knee with his hand. "Guess that means you should toss your ball gown out the back."

I could already tell by the banter that this was going to be a lively trip.

Viktor leaned around to look at us. "Your comfort is not my concern. This will teach you a valuable lesson on how to pack lightly for any situation I might throw at you. If you choose poorly, that says less about me than it does about you." He turned to face the front. "Are you missionaries or tourists?"

We all held back a laugh, certain that Viktor had meant to say *mercenaries* and not *missionaries*. That would have been a whole different kind of trip.

"Down here?" Claude asked.

"Slowly," Viktor instructed him. "Keep the lights off."

Darkness enveloped the van as we descended a ramp. By the squeal of the tires as we made slow turns, it sounded like a parking garage.

"Make room," Viktor said.

Room? I thought. *Room for what?*

"Weapons," I whispered to Christian.

He retracted his arm, and I scooted directly behind the passenger seat. "I don't think that's what we're doing."

"What makes you say that?"

Viktor got out of the van while Claude kept the engine running. Christian cocked his head to the side, and I stayed quiet so he could listen.

"*Jaysus wept,*" he whispered.

"What's going on?"

"Come on," Blue pressed. "Tell us."

"You're about to find out," he said grimly.

The rear doors opened, and three figures climbed inside. My heart ratcheted in my chest when I couldn't see their faces. It was too dark, and they were all wearing hooded jackets and looking down.

Moments after they sat on the benches and the rear doors closed, Viktor got back inside.

"No talking," he instructed us. "Not one word until we reach our destination. Do you understand me? Not a single whisper out of any of you."

"Gotcha," Blue replied, her posture tense as she stared at our passengers.

Two of the figures sat on Christian's left, and the third took up the empty spot next to Shepherd. In the dark cab, dimly lit by the instrument panel in the front, I noticed the anxious looks on everyone's faces. I wondered what Niko could see and what Shepherd felt. They probably had a better sense of what was going on.

As the van ascended the ramp, daylight flooded the interior from the front windows. I leaned forward and got a better look at our passengers. The person next to Christian wore a dark denim jacket with a grey hood. His hands were soft but definitely male. The only other distinguishable feature I could make out was his brown skin and how it matched the person next to him. Not anything like the pale individual sitting beside Shepherd, whom I guessed to be a woman by her slim frame and small feet. She wore a thin ring on her slender finger, her face completely covered by her hood.

What had Christian heard them talking about?

Claude briefly glanced back when we stopped at a light. His nostrils flared, and his golden eyes burned bright.

Viktor reached over and turned on the radio. After skipping over a few channels, he settled on the peppiest song he came across—"Faith" by George Michael.

Blue and I exchanged a look as he cranked up the volume to an uncomfortable level.

The woman sitting beside Shepherd pulled her hood even farther down as she bent over and giggled. The person sitting across from her kicked their foot against hers, and the laughter cut off. Seconds later, she sneezed. When she pulled a tissue from her jacket pocket and blew her nose, I shot Christian a startled look. It sounded like she had a cold. Breed don't get colds, not unless they're Relics. Were these people defects?

The only Breed I could definitively rule out was Mage. When I tested my theory by flaring, Niko's gaze snapped up. He shook his head, showing his disapproval. Shepherd must have felt something, because he eyeballed Niko, trying to figure out what had him alarmed. Niko frowned when he didn't read any guilt or regret in my light. Viktor had said no talking, but he hadn't said anything about flaring. Because we did it in human establishments to avoid conflict, any Mage would have flared back.

But they didn't. Not one of them reacted. Even if they'd chosen not to flare back, someone would have recoiled or sat to attention at the amount of energy I'd put out.

I brushed my hands down my jeans to wipe off the residual energy.

Shepherd reached in his coat pocket and pulled out a smoke. When he struck a match and lit up his cigarette, the woman sneezed again.

We all glowered at Shepherd as the van filled with smoke.

He didn't need to verbalize a curse; it was written all over his face as he stamped out the cigarette beneath the thick tread of his boot.

The woman next to him fanned the air and then pulled her hood tighter over her face.

The next hour was uneventful, nothing but Viktor's bizarre music selections to fill the silence. I kept my light concealed after that one flare, deciding it was prudent not to draw unwanted attention.

Eventually the van came to a full stop, and the eighties pop music did as well.

Viktor twisted in his seat. "I want everyone to follow behind me. Avoid eye contact, no talking, and conceal your light. Christian, did you bring any sunglasses?"

Christian reached inside his coat and pulled out his dark shades.

"Good. Claude, put yours on as well."

When Christian put on his glasses, I laughed. He still looked like a Vampire to me.

After we piled out of the van, I took a quick look around. A loud whistle sounded, like the kind a referee uses. With our luggage in hand, we followed Viktor, our guests centered between us. Were these higher authority officials? Arms dealers? The woman who had been sitting by Shepherd was petite like Gem, but she could have been a dangerous felon for all I knew.

An automated announcement came on about warning signals

at pedestrian crossings. The clanging grew louder as we walked along a concrete platform, and the whistle was near constant as a train went by the platform at a sluggish pace. The brakes squealed until eventually the train came to a stop.

Blue pretended to be messaging on her phone while Viktor looked at his watch. I didn't bother to read the company name on the side of the train—it might have been Breed for all I knew. Viktor had told us to keep our eyes low, and that was what I did.

I slung my backpack over one shoulder and followed our group toward the rear. People rose from the outside benches as the doors opened and passengers spilled out. It wasn't a big station, so there wasn't a huge crowd to deal with. Not like the subway. That place was a madhouse.

When we reached the last car, a gentleman in a blue shirt and cap greeted us. "Tickets?"

Viktor handed him a stack.

"Very good, Mr. Watson. This is our luxury car, which I'm sure will meet all your needs. Our latest model is roomier than the average passenger train. There's comfortable seating and a bedroom with two beds. In addition to a private restroom, you'll have our service staff on call. There's a private door that separates you from the next car, and it only unlocks from your side. Feel free to roam about the train and join us in the dining car if you need to stretch your legs. Do you have any questions?"

"No," Viktor said tersely, his American accent forced. "Thank you."

"My pleasure. Step inside and proceed through the open door to your right. Have a good trip."

Everyone boarded, one at a time. When I got on, I spied people through a window on the connecting door to my left. Our door was half-open, but there was no window that would allow someone to spy on us.

I moved inside an open space that led to a passageway on the left. The first room was a bathroom, spacious with a toilet, standing shower, and sink. I walked farther down and stopped at the next door on the right. My jaw dropped when I poked my head in to take a look. It was nothing like the pictures I'd seen of passenger trains. Pastoral paintings hung on the mahogany walls, and a small wooden desk to the left added a dash of sophistication. Above it was a mirror, allowing anyone sitting on the leather stool to gaze at their reflection. Someone had switched on the green desk lamp, which gave the room a warm ambiance. No one would have to worry about a cold floor because a beautiful red rug with intricate gold designs covered it. There were two single beds—one against the left wall and the other straight ahead in the corner. Drapes covered the windows, and a ceiling fan above allowed the air to circulate.

Christian came up behind me. "Now this is what I call traveling in style. I claim the left one."

"Nice try, Vamp. You don't sleep."

He waggled his eyebrows. "Who said anything about sleep?"

We strolled to the open area of the car, and I gaped at the design and layout. This place was like a miniature palace. Red carpet blanketed the floor, and a thrill moved through me when I caught sight of the corner bar on my immediate right. Since we were in a moving train, they had locked the alcohol inside wire cabinets to keep the bottles from tipping over.

Claude set his stuff down in a breakfast nook near the bar.

The three figures lingered at the rear of the train, looking out the window.

Viktor approached us. "Relax until the train leaves the station. Then we'll have drinks."

That was code talk. Viktor wanted us to keep our mouths shut.

Just past the breakfast nook were booth seats with tables where passengers could play games and look out the window. I could only imagine how beautiful it looked at night when the light from the fixtures mounted between the windows would soak into the mahogany wood. The seats were a plush red fabric with brown tufted leather backings and dividers with wood tops to set your drinks on. Both sides of the train had wide seats facing center in addition to some facing front. You could easily fit two or three people in them. A sofa ran along the left side of the train in front of a large panoramic window, and the back of the car had corner couches that looked comfy as hell. Between the variety in seating and décor, this car was designed for socializing.

I dropped my bag on one of the tables and collapsed onto the seat.

Viktor handed Christian a note. After reading it, Christian disappeared down the hall, and I heard a door shut.

Shepherd inspected every nook and cranny with the meticulousness of a police detective. He looked behind the curtains and jiggled the lamps to make sure they were attached. After removing her cloak, Blue unzipped her tall boots and crawled onto the sofa across from me. We both watched Niko walk the car and memorize everything about it.

"Anyone thirsty?" Claude asked from the bar. "There's a fridge under here stocked with cold drinks."

"Me!" an unfamiliar voice called out.

All of us turned to look when our passengers drew back their hoods and revealed themselves.

I blinked in surprise. They were just teenagers. The two Latinos were a boy and a girl. Despite the height difference, they looked like twins. Same dark brown eyes, same broad mouth—though hers had pink lipstick—and even the same ears that stuck out a little. The only real difference was that he had a very short buzz cut and her hair was past the shoulders and parted on the side. By the looks of his pudgy face, I suspected the boy was overdue for another growth spurt. The other girl had milky-white skin and thick, beautiful hair. The golden-blond tendrils barely reached her shoulders and somehow made her heart-shaped face seem even smaller. She must have been our sneezer.

The train began moving, and the station slid out of view.

Shepherd tapped one of the sconces that ran along the panel above the windows. "How do you turn these on?"

"Did you try the switch?" the boy asked facetiously.

Blue smirked at Shepherd as he grumbled and stalked toward the bar.

The blonde unzipped her black jacket and tossed it onto a

chair. She fluffed her wavy hair, which held a natural frizz. Her clothes were slightly too big for her, but that might have been the style. Her finger looped around the thin gold chain on her neck while she explored the room. I couldn't help but notice the dismal look in her eyes, one I was all too familiar with. Our surroundings should have warranted some enthusiasm and curiosity from a kid her age, but she looked upon everything as if it didn't matter.

She sneezed, kicking her foot out comically when she bent over.

Viktor removed his coat and draped it across his bag. "We'll wait for Christian."

Claude walked up with an armload of bottled drinks. The boy grabbed an orange soda, and the girl took a grape. They both sat together in an oversized seat to Blue's left.

Claude drifted toward the blonde and bowed his head. "I won't harm you, female."

I didn't need his keen nose to see that she was afraid of him. She refused to look up and kept staring at his brown shoes.

Claude examined his inventory and offered her a bottle. "I bet you like root beer."

"I just want water," she replied softly, her accent surprisingly Southern. It was so heavy that I had no trouble imagining she'd grown up in the backwoods of Tennessee.

"Are you sure? Whatever you want is yours."

The pixie-like girl took one of the bottles and escaped to my table and sat across from me. She set her drink on the table and took out a tissue to blow her nose. "I have a stupid cold. Usually it's allergies, but I'm pretty sure this one's a cold because my throat kinda hurts." After she blew her nose, she wadded up the tissue and left it on the table. "I have a sensitive nose."

I tapped my finger on the table, eager to ask all kinds of questions. Like who the hell were these kids, and why were we transporting what I could only assume were Relics?

Christian finally returned, his sunglasses still shielding his eyes.

"You can take those off now," Claude said, offering him a bottle of water.

"Unless you want to close the drapes, I'll be leaving them on."

He strode up to Viktor and lowered his voice. "I checked every car. It's all clear. No Vampires."

Viktor nodded. "My contact assured me that no tickets were sold to Breed for this trip, but you can never be too sure. A Mage or Chitah we can deal with, but not a Vampire with prying ears. This train was not soundproofed."

Blue peeled off her socks and rubbed her foot. "Are you going to tell us what's going on?"

Viktor pivoted and held the posture of a general. "Our assignment is to protect these children with our lives and transport them to a new location."

Blue looked at the boy to her left. "¿Cómo se llama?"

The boy screwed the top back on his drink. "I don't speak Spanish. Do you speak Indian?"

She frowned. "No."

"There you go."

Blue stood up. "I don't speak Indian because I'm not from India. And technically speaking, that would be Hindi or another language. I'm Native American, so make sure to get your geography right before opening your mouth. It's respectful to speak to new friends in their mother tongue, and I wanted you to feel welcomed."

The girl poked him in the stomach, and he winced. "We're originally from Mexico," she explained, "but they brought us here when we were babies. We're as American as you."

"I doubt that. Even *they* aren't as American as me," she said, gesturing to the rest of us.

"Well, you know what I mean."

Blue didn't take shit from anyone, including smart-mouthed teenagers.

Viktor accepted a bottle of water from Claude and guzzled it before setting it down. "This is a high-risk job, and that is why every step of our trip has been carefully orchestrated. These three young people are Potentials. Do you all understand the meaning?"

A bottle slipped from Claude's arm and struck the floor, and he looked dumbfounded. "Are you serious? I've only heard of their existence among ancients, but that was from the drunkards at the bar who reminisce too much."

The girl across from me sipped her water and then wiped her wet hands across her beige shirt, an anime cat printed on the front.

Viktor groomed his beard with one hand. "For most, Potentials are a myth. They are an arcane Breed in which few believe. Potentials who have chosen to live as Breed do so quietly, and we have taken care to keep their existence a secret."

"So what makes them special?" I asked.

"They are humans who have the potential to become any Breed they so desire. Once they choose, they will stay that way for as long as they live. If they do not choose, they will live and die as a human. For years, secret organizations have sought to locate these children and protect them. Some doctors are able to identify them in hospitals, but we do not have insiders at every location. They are easier to find in orphanages, and some are discovered later in life. Children and young adults are prime targets. It is unlikely that nefarious men would find any interest in a married man with a family."

Blue put her hands on her hips, and the boy's eyes skated down to her tomahawk. "Why would our kind be interested in someone who can choose their fate?"

"Because the choice can be taken away." Viktor looked between the kids. "Apologies for any crude language, but you must have heard all this before." He sat down on the sofa where Blue had previously been sitting, the scenery blurring behind him. "For centuries, there have been those who've hunted Potentials. Some were killed, but others coveted them. Humans are so much easier to manipulate and control than someone born as a Chitah or a Shifter. Those who are born Breed have innate qualities of strength and defiance. Humans are malleable. A Vampire can make their own progeny, so they have little interest in Potentials. But not every Mage is a Creator."

Claude frowned. "But most other Breeds can mate and have their own children."

"They do not want these children to raise; they want them for other purposes. Mates, perhaps even slaves."

Spotted patterns rippled across Claude's arms and neck, and a growl settled in his throat as he dipped his chin. Blue nudged him, probably so he wouldn't scare the kids.

"There are those who believe Potentials become the purest Breed," Viktor continued. "Because they have human blood, it is a clean slate. No mixture of different Shifter animals in their lineage, no inherited defects. But it does not matter what they believe. It only matters that we protect the children."

"Stop calling me a child," the boy snapped. "I'm sixteen."

Ignoring him, we all took a moment to digest the new information. Christian didn't appear surprised to learn about Potentials, and neither did Shepherd.

"How do they choose?" I asked.

Viktor loosened the collar of his turtleneck. "A Potential becomes Breed with the first person they have intercourse with, even if they have been with humans."

The boy's face turned beet red.

"Cool necklace," the blonde said, eyeing my ruby with interest.

I tucked it beneath my sweatshirt. "Thanks. So what are your names?"

"I'm Carol. It's an old-fashioned name, but the people at the orphanage named me, so that's what I got stuck with. Carol. Probably someone's great aunt."

"I think it's a lovely name," Blue said.

Carol shrugged. "It means champion, but I don't feel like one. I just do what everyone tells me so I don't become somebody's love slave."

The hair on my arms stood up when Claude snarled and backed up.

Carol slinked down in her seat, her eyes fearful.

"He won't harm you," Viktor assured them. "Claude is very protective, and if he does not go into the bedroom and calm himself, you will see just how protective he can be."

Taking the hint, Claude separated himself from the group. I wondered if anyone brought tranquilizers.

"I'm Eve," the other girl chimed in. "And this is my brother, Adam."

"Whoever gave us our names is an idiot," Adam said. "She's my twin, and that's just gross."

"Hey, don't call me gross!" She shoved him, but he didn't shove her back. Adam took it and rolled his eyes. Despite their bickering, I sensed a bond between them. They had each other, whereas Carol had no one.

"How old are you?" Blue asked Carol.

"Fourteen. I'll be fifteen next month. Does anyone have any gum?"

No one moved, but then Christian reached in his pocket and handed her a pack.

"Thanks." She peeled off the top. "I prefer bubble gum, but whatever."

Blue sat to Viktor's right and rested her arms on the divider as she looked at Adam. "Why did they bring you all the way up here from Mexico?"

"Our mom died after we were born. They never told us how or why. Someone down there must have seen our marks and reported us. I guess they didn't have any secret hiding places, so they moved us up to Jersey, then Nashville, then here. They don't like to keep us in one place for too long."

"Why not?"

"I guess they think we'll get bored and run. But they don't have workers looking after us. They barely have anyone guarding the building. We could have run away if we wanted."

"But you didn't."

"No way," Eve replied, drawing her legs up and wrapping her arms around them. "I don't want to go out there. Not if bad people are looking for us."

I scooted toward the aisle to snag Viktor's attention. "What happens when they turn eighteen? They can't live in hiding forever, can they?"

"They release them," he said matter-of-factly. "We have intelligence working in pediatrics and orphanages in hopes of identifying Potentials. Orphans are vulnerable because they are passed around to foster homes. There is more chance that they will be discovered."

"How would anyone know what they are?"

"Because of this." Adam pulled his shirtsleeve up and revealed what looked like a small tattoo on his bicep. "We're all born with the same mark. Not in the same spot though."

I shot out of my seat to look at it, just as everyone else did. The mark looked like a spade in a deck of cards, the edges well defined. It resembled a tattoo more than it did a birthmark.

Eve gaped at me. "Your eyes are so cool! Adam, look. That one is so blue, like one of those sled dogs. Are you some kind of mutant?"

Christian sputtered out a laugh. "Aye, lass. They call her the Shadow."

Eve tried to dissect his remark, but Christian had perfect deadpan delivery. "What does that mean?"

"It means she'll eat your soul."

I shook my head. "Ignore him. I was born with these eyes, so it's nothing special. I'm just an ordinary Mage."

"Really? Can you show me?"

I jerked my head back. "You've never seen a Mage?"

"We've never seen anyone," Adam complained. "All the workers were Relics, and they can't do anything special."

Shepherd's jaw set. "Yeah. Nothing special about knowledge."

Adam shifted in his seat. "You know what I mean. They can't do anything cool, like shoot lightning from their fingers or climb walls."

Viktor stood up. "This is your first time seeing Breed?" He clapped his hands together. "Fascinating! Shepherd, you must come tickle them."

Adam scooted against Eve. "I don't want anyone tickling me. Especially your crazy ninja standing by the wall. Does he talk?"

"Maybe we can do this later," Blue said quietly to Viktor.

"They're probably overwhelmed with everything happening. Let's not freak them out with a ticklefest of sensory emotions followed by your crazy wolf making an appearance."

I looked out the window at the city moving by. "So where are we headed?"

Viktor glanced at his watch. "Top secret for now. In the meantime, we have drinks. Shall we?"

I hooked my arm in his. "We shall."

Chapter 7

A FTER A FEW HARD DRINKS, I had a nice buzz going. The kids hopped around from seat to seat, and when they got bored, they retreated to the bedroom to avoid the adults. Because we couldn't take any chances on them sneaking out and exploring the rest of the train, we decided to take turns guarding the door.

Shepherd took the first shift and stood in the connecting space between the cars. He was probably relieved to get away from the kids and light up a smoke. Adam wanted to know how he got all the scars on his body. Eve asked if his tattoos were permanent and if he used liquid fire. Then they wanted to hear all about how liquid fire worked and where it came from, which he didn't have all the answers to.

Snuggled on the corner sofa in the back, I admired the view. As the tracks created a never-ending trail behind us, I thought about the time I had left with my father slipping away. I also didn't like the distance between us growing with each mile, and it gave me a sliver of understanding of what Shepherd must have been going through with Hunter. If something happened, I wouldn't be there to help.

Christian sat down next to me and sighed. "Leave it to Viktor to pick a sunny day for a train ride. And you call these curtains? They're as thin as an Irish mother's patience."

I stared at his sunglasses. "We should ask the conductor if he has any tinfoil so we can darken the windows. Or maybe you can sit on the toilet for the rest of the trip."

"You have a tongue that could clip a hedge."

I put my hand on his thigh and gave it a firm squeeze. "But you like my tongue."

He moved my hand away and crossed his legs. "Best not be doing that in here."

The drinks were making me a little tingly, so I stretched my legs across the sectional that ran alongside the rear window. Blue was zonked out on the sofa beneath the panoramic window, her long hair hanging to the floor. I looked around to see if anyone was paying attention to us, but they weren't. Claude and Niko were chatting at a table by the bar, and I wasn't sure where Viktor had gone.

"I never knew people like them existed," I said, my thoughts steering back to the kids. "Born human, but they can become any Breed they want to?"

"Only if they find someone to fornicate with. Some go their entire lives without ever knowing what they are."

"Where do you think we're going?"

"Maine?"

"No, we're heading south."

"And how do you know that? The sun's too high up."

I folded my hands across my stomach. "Think real hard."

"Sometimes I forget you're a Mage." He put his arm around me. "When I look at you, all I see is a gorgeous Vampire."

I kissed him softly.

Tenderly.

"But I'm also a Mage. You can't just love half of me."

"Would you like me to prove my unflinching love for you?" He waved a finger at my shoes. "Take off your trainers, and I'll rub those dry hooves."

"Why don't you take off your coat? You look like a spy aboard the Orient Express. Viktor doesn't want us to draw attention to ourselves. Remember?"

"No one's back here."

"You're scaring the kids."

"Wouldn't be the first time that happened." He leaned forward and shook off his coat, revealing a soft V-neck beneath. When he sat back, I got what I wanted—to curl up against him and feel his heat. I held his bicep and rested my head against his shoulder. Christian tucked his hand between my legs. I liked sharing moments that weren't sexual, where I could breathe him in and enjoy his company.

"Don't get too comfortable," he said. "Lay off the alcohol, you hear?"

"Why? Viktor had a glass."

"Viktor wouldn't assemble a team if this wasn't a dangerous job."

"You said no one on the train is Breed."

"We can't be too careful. Those young ones need us at our best. There's no telling what we might encounter."

Viktor emerged from the narrow hall that led to the main door. He set a paper bag on Claude and Niko's table and then made his way to the back.

I curled up my legs to give him room to sit by the rear window.

Viktor sat down and unrolled another paper bag. "Hot dogs. They serve meals on plates, but I did not want their staff coming in here. You like?"

"I'm not hungry, but thanks."

He took one out and folded away the wax paper. "The children asked for snacks, but cookies are not what growing children need. I asked them to bake french fries instead and leave them with Shepherd. Dinner will be much later, so you won't have another chance to eat for a while."

The smell tempted me, but not enough. I hadn't yet gotten acclimated to the motion of the train, plus I'd had a few drinks.

I let go of Christian's arm and sat upright. "Why didn't we fly?"

Viktor dusted crumbs off his short beard. "Our destination has no landing strip. A train is safer and closer to the ground. Men can hide on a plane, and then where would we go? It is not uncommon for Vampires to travel for free by charming the employees." He took another big bite of his hot dog. "And what happens if I were to shift on a plane? Or Claude flips his switch around humans?

People would take pictures and put it on social media. If there is a battle and the pilot loses control… Nyet, I cannot risk such things."

"Private jet?"

"These children are in my care. What happens if the plane goes down and we perish in flames?"

"What happens if the train crashes?"

"Train is close to ground. You can jump, break bones, but nobody dies unless it goes off a mountain." He finished off the hot dog and wiped his fingers on a paper napkin. "It's too much money to rent a private jet that is large enough to accommodate everyone, and that would only be half the journey. An old friend owed me a favor, so he gave us this luxury car free. No questions asked. This is how collecting favors can work to your benefit."

"Why are we moving them?"

He peered into the bag as if contemplating eating another hot dog but rolled the bag up instead. "There is a facility that is much safer for these children, and it has been such a success that they've built a few others like it. Cities are not a safe place for Potentials." He gestured to the window. "They look outside and are tempted by the world around them. There is a high risk of runaways in the city, but there have been no reports of problems in the newer facilities. They are larger and safer, but the operation to transport the children has been slow going."

"Ah. So what you're saying is that we're going into the woods." I suddenly regretted my shoe choice. I'd been thinking about comfort and speed more than practicality for any situation.

Viktor picked at his teeth before wiping his mouth again. "Children are less likely to run away if they know they will be lost in the wilderness with wild animals. Once they are old enough, they are free to make their own decisions. Become Breed, stay human, or go into hiding with fake identification. There will always be a risk of discovery if they visit a doctor or hospital and someone sees their mark. Less so as they age. I have heard stories that some cut it off their body."

I shuddered at the thought.

Christian stood up. "I'll be walking the train now." With his sunglasses still in place, he strode out of the room to do another security check.

"Can they really be anything they want?" I asked. "What if the person they have sex with is a crossbreed like me?"

Viktor rested his arm over the back of the seat, his leg crossed. "It is my understanding that there are no limitations, but crossbreeds are so rare that I do not believe anyone has tried such a thing. The Relics who look after them have specific knowledge about Potentials. Only they know all their secrets." Viktor scratched his nose and gazed out the window behind me. "Let us say there is an alpha in search of a mate, but he does not want a dominant woman. He seeks a woman he can control, who will do his every bidding. Perhaps one he perceives as a pureblood. You see, among Shifters, purebloods only exist in the royal line. They have no mixture of other animals in their... genetics? Gem would know the word."

"I know what you mean. So how does it work? The first person a Potential has sex with determines what they are?"

"Not entirely. It is only with the first Breed that they sleep with. Even if they have intercourse with humans, they can still become Breed. It involves DNA and chemicals in their reproductive system. It cannot happen by kissing or..." Flustered, he fiddled with the paper sack next to him.

Yeah, Viktor didn't really want to get into the nitty-gritty of what I wanted to know. Like could a Potential become Breed through oral or anal sex. It was a fair question.

"Very few know about Potentials," he continued. "Most of the young ones have never heard of them, but the elders cling to folklore as truth. So I ask that you not discuss these details with anyone outside of Keystone. Not even your father. It is not our place to convince the world of their existence. Do you think they would be accepted with open arms? Throughout history, men have destroyed what they fear or do not understand. We have sought to eradicate other Breeds, and some successfully. Thank the fates that the higher authority has not adopted this way of thinking."

"What happens to the kids who have parents and don't wind up in orphanages?"

"We cannot protect them. Some manage to live ordinary lives. Others are not so lucky. Often you hear stories in the news about runaways or kidnappings. If the wrong person finds them, that is their fate."

I pulled my messy hair back and tied it with an elastic band I'd kept around my wrist. "What about those who choose to become Breed? Aren't they afraid people will see their mark and not realize they've already turned?"

"Some tattoo or burn away their mark to keep the secret. Others are less concerned about hiding even though the higher authority condemns talking about it. I once heard of a woman telling her story to an unbelieving audience. People wrote her off as insane or eccentric."

I reclined my head. "So what comes after this?"

Viktor patted my knee. "Sleep, Raven. Our stop will be in approximately fourteen hours."

"And then what?"

He stood up with his bag. "A less comfortable ride."

Gem shook her sore wrist and sat back in her chair. She had been transcribing the books that Viktor had assigned to her for weeks on end. Only one would be of interest to him as it contained the names of immortals in the seventeen hundreds who'd been accused of high crimes but had escaped. Time often erased a person's sins, but documentation such as this could help carry out justice in the modern world.

Viktor had asked her to focus on the books she'd recently acquired at the pawnshop, but after going through them, she didn't see the rush. They were historically interesting but didn't contain anything juicy like her other project.

Gem rested her cheek against her palm and stared at her bookshelf. Because she'd been the first in the house, Viktor had given her the choice of any room in which to do her work. So she'd wandered from room to room like a nomad, going through all the books that were already shelved or in boxes. Some of them went to charity, others to the pawnshop, and the rest became part of her private collection. But as Keystone grew, Gem decided she needed privacy to do her work. A place that was dark, secure, and hidden.

When Viktor showed her the secret passageway to this room, she fell in love with it. He promised to keep it a secret so she could work without any interruptions. Someone had loved this place and built it with the same idea in mind—to store precious books. The tomes must have belonged to his extended family that he never talked about. It had taken her time to go through each book, and most of them were boxed and relocated to a private study upstairs. After she finished, she filled the shelves with her own private collection, some of which she'd found in the house. Not long after that, she stumbled upon an old one with a red leather cover. Had it been there all along, or had she just forgotten about it? The old leather binding showed signs of wear but no significant damage. The pages were thick, and the writing was like nothing she'd ever seen before. So the red book had become her pet project. She cross-referenced many languages in search of a common thread between the symbols—anything to give her a head start on the etymology. But instead this book had become the bane of her existence.

Her eyes darted down to the box with her latest purchases, and she noticed a few had slipped beneath the heavy papers she'd used for packing.

"Alas, a girl's work is never done."

Gem hopped out of her seat and retrieved three small books from the box. If she didn't shelve them now, they might end up in the wrong pile. After she tucked the books under her arm, she positioned the ladder by the left-hand shelf. Gem was proud of her organizational system and never had any trouble locating a book. As she ascended the ladder, one of the books slipped from her grasp and hit the floor.

Gem cringed. There was nothing worse than dropping a book. Nothing!

She heaved a sigh. "Nothing to see here, ladies and gentlemen. It's just me, destroying history, one page at a time."

Her sneakers hit the floor as she hopped down from the ladder and set the other two books on the desk. Their fallen brother was facedown, his spine bent and covers splayed open. Just seeing the pages beneath, all folded and bent, was like watching the death of a butterfly. She gingerly lifted the book and turned it over to assess the damage. To some, books were portals through which to escape. But to Gem they were her children.

"That's not so bad," she said, straightening a crease on one of the pages. With an old book, you could never tell how it would withstand the impact of a fall. Sometimes the paper tore away from the spine, and other times the hinges would break open.

Before she closed it, the writing inside caught her attention. She studied the handwritten symbols and recognized them to be Akkadian, an extinct Semitic language of ancient Mesopotamia. But what interested her was that above some of the writing, someone had scribbled symbols of an unfamiliar language.

She cocked her head to the side. Gem had so much knowledge in her head that sometimes it was like trying to sort through a massive Rolodex. Focusing her attention back on the main text, she pulled out a volume of her Assyrian dictionary.

Her phone buzzed on the table. "Jiminy Christmas! Can't a girl work in peace?"

She read Wyatt's message.

"Dinner's ready? Who can eat when I'm on the brink of a great discovery?" She blew out the candles and walked jauntily out the door.

Too bad her skates were upstairs. Gem adored the freedom and whimsy that roller-skating gave her. Because she hadn't experienced a real childhood, she indulged in everything a child would. Why on earth did adults give up such cheerful activities? Bicycling wasn't her thing, and she'd never grasped Rollerblades, but the old-fashioned skates with wheels on four corners made her feel like the wind.

She flashed down the hall and around the corner until she reached the dining room. The only person at the table was Wyatt.

Gem steered right and sat across from him in Raven's chair.

"That's not where you sit." He folded his arms and pretended he cared.

"No one's here, Spooky. Pick any chair you like."

"I like mine."

"I bet your heinie is just too sore to move."

His mouth turned down. "You try sitting with a wolf bite in the ass."

She giggled. "Why didn't you let Niko heal it?"

The heels of his boots knocked against the floor as irritation flashed in his eyes. "By the time I woke up, everyone had split. Nobody ever thinks of Wyatt. It's all about me, me, me. It's just gotta heal on its own."

"Any news from Viktor?"

He touched the light dusting of whiskers on his face. They weren't coarse like Shepherd's but looked soft and grew in patches. "Not yet. I was busy setting up travel arrangements for their next stop."

"Where?"

"Can't tell you."

She poked out her tongue. Wyatt loved secrets, but he was horrible at keeping them. He loved to taunt people with his insider's knowledge until he finally revealed enough details that a person could figure out the secret.

Gem rested her elbows on the table. "I wish *we* could go on travel adventures."

He stifled a laugh. "No you don't, buttercup. Remember what happened on their last getaway? They had to jump out of an airplane into the freezing ocean. After the plane exploded, they hiked in wet clothes through the snow. Raven almost got her eyes scratched out by those Shifters who cornered her in the woods. And poor Blue was busy fighting off some horny mountain hermit." He sighed wistfully. "I wish I had been there to see it all. Maybe I should make them wear body cams."

"I thought you said you didn't want to go on those trips."

"I don't wanna live it—I just wanna see it."

What Gem really yearned for was a vacation, without all the

crazy assassins. She just didn't want to go alone, and the group never took holidays together. There was always work on someone's plate, and Viktor didn't like them all gone at once.

Wyatt kept his loose grey beanie on instead of taking it off as he often did at the table. His hair didn't play by the rules, but it was adorable in a boyish kind of way. Maybe that was why he always covered it up. Men were silly when it came to their perception of masculinity and attractiveness.

He glanced at the entryway when footfalls quickly approached. "Hey, little monkey. You ready for some chow?"

Hunter pulled out his chair at the end of the table and sat down.

"It's just us, kiddo," Wyatt said. "So you're gonna have to do all the talking."

Gem gave him a reproachful look. "That's not nice."

"The kid needs to talk eventually."

"Does he? There are other ways to communicate in this world. Sometimes your mouth is the least effective."

Switch swaggered into the room and took a seat in one of the booths along the wall. Gem had been so preoccupied with work that she hadn't taken the chance to get to know him. He was about the same height as Niko and Christian, but to her, anyone taller than five-ten made her feel like a garden gnome.

"Why don't you sit with us?" she asked, inviting him over with a wave of her arm.

"I'm not even supposed to be in here. Viktor wants me eating at different hours because of the confidentiality."

"Viktor's not here. He just doesn't want you overhearing any work stuff, but I am *so* done talking about work today. Don't make me yell over my shoulder!" she said loudly.

Switch rose to his feet and walked over. He didn't just walk, he had a swing in his shoulders and a heavy gait, like a man with an extra dose of confidence. He pulled out a chair on Hunter's left and took a seat.

Gem hopped over to Christian's chair to move a little closer. "We should roast marshmallows in the fireplace later. Have you ever done that?"

He tucked a chunk of long hair behind his ear. "Kids do that."

She put her foot on the chair, her knee bent. "I didn't know sugar was just for kids. I'll make sure to inform Kira of your special dietary restrictions."

His lips twitched.

"Your wolf is an asshole," Wyatt blurted out.

Switch turned his head and glared.

Wyatt flinched and looked down at the tattoos on his hands.

"How long have you known Raven?" Gem asked, genuinely fascinated that Raven had grown up around Shifters without ever realizing it.

"Since we were kids. We didn't really hang out because of the age gap, but her dad and mine were friends, so we saw each other at all the get-togethers."

Wyatt propped his elbows on the table. "And you two never…?" He used his fingers to simulate sex.

Gem rolled her eyes at the vulgarity.

"No," Switch said firmly. "She was a *child*."

"Only by a few years," Wyatt countered.

"Maybe that's how they do it in your neck of the woods, but not mine."

Kira appeared from the kitchen entryway, her red hair tied back in a blue kerchief. Gem thought her fiery hair was exquisite. The ombré effect was like nothing she'd ever seen before in natural hair.

Without a word, Kira set down a platter of hamburgers in the center of the table.

"Bravo!" Wyatt applauded. "You're my culinary hero. Anyone ever tell you that?"

Gem was certain she caught a smile on Kira's lips before she hustled out of the room and returned with bowls of sliced avocados, tomatoes, onions, arugula, and cheese. She had mastered the art of American cuisine but hadn't figured out when it was appropriate to put condiments on the table.

Wyatt's eyes lit up when she returned with a cloth-lined bowl filled with homemade french fries. He grabbed the tongs and filled his plate.

"You better eat some meat with that," Gem remarked. "You'll turn into a potato."

Switch stood up and fixed Hunter's plate. Instead of asking him what he wanted, he'd simply point to an item and wait for Hunter to shake or nod his head.

What a thoughtful thing to do.

After assembling Hunter's meal, Switch sat down with his own plate. His large hands covered the entire bun, and Gem couldn't stop staring as he ravenously chewed into his burger. People fascinated her. Everyone had their own unique styles, idiosyncrasies, and manner of speaking. With little to go on, she found it easy to read people. When Raven had come to Keystone, Gem sensed right away that she had a good heart. But Switch wasn't easy to read.

"What happens if he never talks?" Wyatt salted his fries. "Doesn't that make it hard to teach him anything?"

"Speaking isn't a sign of intelligence," Switch answered. "When and if he decides to use his voice is up to him. If he doesn't want to, I'll teach him and everyone here sign language. Sometimes it's easier for children to communicate using sign. He's not a toddler anymore, but his social skills are delayed." Switch smiled at Hunter. "That's not a bad thing. It means you're a very special boy."

Gem didn't know much about kids, so she often forgot how they absorbed everything like a sponge. Even if they pretended they weren't listening, they were. Sometimes she and the others had a habit of talking about Hunter in his presence as if he weren't there.

Kira reappeared and took note of everyone's plates before setting down a bottle of wine and apple juice.

After she made a silent exit, Gem fixed her plate and filled her glass.

"Can you pour me one?" Switch asked.

When Gem grabbed the wine, he shook his head.

"Don't you drink?"

"Not when I'm on the job. I'll have what you're having."

Gem poured him apple juice and then filled Hunter's glass with the same.

"Maybe you can teach that one some English," Wyatt said, jerking his thumb at the kitchen.

Switch finished his burger and wiped his mouth, mustache, and beard with his napkin. "If a grown woman doesn't want to talk to you, maybe you should take that as a hint."

Wyatt pulled the patty out of his bun and ate it all by itself. "Wanna play darts later?"

"Sure."

The symbiotic relationship between men perplexed her. Just when you thought they wanted to kill each other, they'd go out for a beer. Christian had once explained that men didn't dwell on the little things, and that quality was how primitive man survived in a time when large numbers mattered more than shoving a jackass into a tar pit.

Which meant women were the only ones who had evolved, and men were still living in the Stone Age.

"Gem, you in?" Wyatt asked before cramming a handful of fries into his mouth.

"Tempting, but I'll take a rain check on male bonding. While you two get chummy, I'm going to take a dip in the pool."

Switch gulped down half his drink. "You swim at night? Isn't it cold?"

"Heated pool." Wyatt shoved a few fries inside his now meatless burger and held it to his lips. "Gem is our resident mermaid."

Switch's eyes widened.

It made Gem giggle. Couldn't be helped. Naivety was so adorable. She made a tiny little ball of light in her hand and quickly crushed it. "I'm a Mage."

Wyatt scooted back his chair. "Whoa, Nelly. What did Viktor tell you about no lightning balls in the house?" He stood up and limped around his chair to push it in. "I've got one last thing to finish up before I kick your ass at darts."

Switch claimed another burger when he saw that Wyatt was leaving. "Keep dreaming. I'm a badass at any bar game."

With his plate in hand, Wyatt stopped behind his chair and

glared at the back of Switch's head. "Hopefully my limp doesn't affect my aim."

Switch piled tomatoes on his burger. "If you have any intention of pinning the tail on the donkey with those darts, just remember who the wolf is."

Chapter 8

WHEN NIGHTTIME ROLLED AROUND, WE had the most magnificent view of the sunset from the back of the train. Bronzed light poured through the windows, and the treetops shimmered before turning into black silhouettes against the painted sky. The landscape had changed from buildings and telephone poles to trees and low mountains. Viktor switched off the overhead lights since the accent lamps between the windows and by the tables were sufficient. Blue closed most of the curtains shortly after dusk once there was nothing to see but our own reflections. While there were heaters, the night air had a cooling effect on the car.

Christian relieved Shepherd of guard duty, and after a shower, Shepherd put on his boots again as if ready to start his day. I watched him take inventory of his bag before heading to the back of the train and nodding off.

I stared out the window to my left but saw only my reflection in the glass. Many hours had passed. The alcohol had long worn off, and without the landscape to admire, I was bored out of my mind. If only we had a deck of cards.

Niko sat across the table from me and steered his gaze in the same direction.

"It's pitch-black out there," I said.

"Not from my view."

"What do you see?"

"Blurred energy from animals. Some are on the hunt based on

the intensity of their light, and others are resting. Sometimes the trees give off energy left over from the sun. It's quite a view."

I looked at the narrow bag of peanuts in front of me. I'd eaten a few but had no appetite to finish the rest.

Niko was wearing all black, as usual. He swept back his ebony hair and used small hair bands to secure it in a thin braid.

"Why do you grow your hair long?" I asked. "Wouldn't short hair be easier to manage?"

"In part, I did so to disguise myself from Cyrus. I cannot wear contacts or change my features, but I can use my hair to obscure my face. After a while I just grew accustomed to it." A smile softened his features, and his pale blue eyes sparkled with amusement. "I never have to worry about a bad haircut."

"Claude wouldn't let that happen."

Niko scanned the room. "Where did he go?"

"You really took a long nap, didn't you?"

"I hope you did the same. It sounds like we'll be moving to a new location after midnight."

I closed the curtain next to me. "Claude went to stretch his legs. Or so he said. You know how women flock to him. He's probably fighting them off in the dining car." I sat back and rubbed my neck. "Blue jumped off the train."

Niko leaned back with a startled look. "Are you telling a joke?"

I rolled up the bag of peanuts. "Nope. Her bird was itching to come out, and she didn't want to shift on the train. Don't worry, she asked for Viktor's permission. I think she's back though. I heard her a few minutes ago talking to Christian outside the door. Maybe she went to find Claude."

"Hopefully with her clothes on."

We both laughed.

Niko rested his arms on the table. "I hope Viktor's animal doesn't get the sudden urge to run."

"At least we'll have privacy." I took my hair out of a ponytail and combed my fingers through the messy strands. Brushing it seemed like an exercise in futility. My hair had a mind of its own, and usually it suffered from multiple personality disorder.

The kids emerged from the bedroom and stampeded into the car. Adam darted over to the bar and disappeared from sight.

"No alcohol," I said loudly.

He popped back up, holding two bottles of soda. "Chill out, lady. You sound like a prison guard."

Eve caught the bottle he tossed her way. All three kids had on their jackets. I felt fine, but Niko might have been leaking off a little heat. He sometimes did that on the sly as a courtesy. Niko had the heart of a warrior and the soul of a saint.

The twins moseyed to the back of the train where Shepherd was sleeping. Adam leaned over and cupped his hands on the glass to look out.

I twisted back around in my seat and tapped my hand on the table to get Niko's attention. "I'll be back in a little bit."

Carol looked lonesome sitting all by herself on the long couch across from us. She rested against the leather backing on the left and hugged her knees to her chest.

I plopped down on the other side and mirrored her position. "Is this your first time on a train?"

"Uh-huh."

"Me too. I used to dream about hopping on a train and traveling."

"What's wrong with him?" she asked quietly, tipping her head toward Niko.

"He's shy."

"I mean, he never looks at anyone. It's creepy."

"Niko's blind, that's all. He's a nice guy once you get to know him."

She looked over at him again. "But he's got swords."

"And he knows how to use them. Never underestimate someone's abilities. People underestimate me all the time, and it never works out in their favor."

"What's his Breed?"

"Mage."

She twisted her lips and studied me. "And you're the same?"

"Yep."

"What's it like? I mean, I've never talked to a Mage before."

I had no clue how to answer her question. "It's a little scary. You have all these powers you didn't have before, and someone has to teach you how to use them. Everywhere you go, you have to worry about someone juicing your light."

She played with a wave of her hair. "Oh. I kinda thought it would be awesome to be a Mage without having to be someone's Learner."

That was food for thought. When these kids got older, they could sleep with a Mage and become one without the hassle of having a Creator. Would they share the same mark? Would the Mageri allow them to exist without a Ghuardian to watch over them? So many questions. "You would still need someone to teach you all the basics. There's a lot to learn, and training isn't easy. I went five years without knowing how to flash."

"So then why did you choose it?"

"I didn't."

Her eyes lowered. "Oh." After a long pause, she looked up again. There was so much innocence in her eyes. "I think it would be cool to be a Shifter. I like the idea of transforming into something powerful and amazing. To be able to run fast and live free."

"You know, it's not a bad thing being human," I offered. "Sometimes immortality isn't all it's cracked up to be."

"But I'll never really be free," she said glumly. "Not as long as I'm marked. I'm always gonna have to hide."

"Do all the kids in your orphanage feel that way?"

"I ain't friends with a lot of them, so I don't know. Adam and Eve don't want to be Breed, not after being locked up their whole lives. The least the Relics could have done is let us go outside on field trips once in a while. I've lived my whole life looking out a window." She shivered and blew heat into her hands.

"Niko," I called out. "Come here for a minute."

Niko slid out of the seat and stopped at the edge of the couch.

"Take a step to your right and sit down," I said. "We need you."

When the toe of his shoe met the end of the bench, he pivoted around and took a seat between us.

Carol looked a little confused and uncomfortable with his presence.

"It's a little cold in here, Niko. Do you think you could turn up the heat?"

Niko inclined his head. "As you wish."

Within seconds, heat was wafting off him. So much so that it actually lifted the ends of his fine hair as if a draft had blown up from the floor.

Carol's eyes rounded, and she extended her hands to feel the warmth. "Wow! That's so awesome."

"Every Mage has at least one unique gift. Niko's a Thermal. That means he can not only regulate his body temperature but he's also our portable heater." I stood up, the heat a little intense for my liking. "Niko, why don't you two get to know each other? Carol has some questions about Breed, and I'd rather not traumatize her with my stories."

I branched away, deciding that Niko would be able to give her better advice on her future decision than I could. We probably had no business interfering, but it didn't sound like anyone had really counseled these kids. How could they possibly make an informed decision without any real understanding of our world?

I opened the door to the outside room between the cars. Christian was standing on the left by the side exit, gazing out the window. I stood across from him, acclimating to the much colder air. "Having fun?"

He pointed out the window. "Can you see the wolves?"

I leaned against the glass and squinted. "I can't see anything."

"They're on the run."

I drew in a sharp intake of breath. "After us?"

Christian shook his head and leaned his shoulder against the door. "Poachers are after them."

"Poachers? What do they want, their pelts?"

"No. To reduce the Shifter population."

"Isn't that against the law?"

"In the wild there are no laws."

The door to the connecting train opened. Claude and Blue

walked through, not paying us any attention as they entered our car.

Once we were alone again, I snuggled against Christian and gazed into the darkness. I had a sinking feeling come over me. These were just innocent children. *Human* children.

"You shouldn't care about them," he said judgmentally.

"What makes you think I do?"

"I heard you talking to the wee lass."

"You shouldn't eavesdrop."

He lifted my chin with one finger. "Never get close to your work, Raven. It only makes it harder if something happens. Your emotions become a distraction and put everyone in danger."

"Is that what happened with the last woman you guarded?"

A crooked smile appeared on his lips. "She made me realize it was time to retire. Letting your clients in can destroy you. Think of them as cargo."

I drew back. "But they're kids, Christian."

"Aye, and you are their protector, not their friend. The dangerous world you lived in before Keystone hardened you. Don't let go of that quality, lass. You can't do this job with a tender heart. Even Viktor knows it, and that's why he keeps his distance."

"Why are you telling me this?"

He stroked my cheek. "I've got years of experience as a guard. Not everyone in that room does. Will you not learn from me? I have more to offer than just blood and kisses."

I reached for his hand and held it. "I'm listening. Even when it seems like I'm not, I am."

He jerked his arm, and the outside door suddenly opened. "Do you trust me?"

The roar of the train against the tracks filled my ears. "Not if you're going to break up with me by tossing me off a train."

He winked, gripped the top of the door, and literally flung himself upward. There was a moment where Christian looked like a pool of black water before he vanished.

My heart raced as I approached the open door and looked out. His hand appeared overhead.

"This is the dumbest thing you've ever done," I muttered, grabbing his wrist.

With a hard yank, Christian didn't just pull me up, he swung me right out the door and onto the roof. I might have actually screamed before he rolled on top of me and pinned me with his body.

"You all right?" he yelled over the roar of the wind.

It felt as if I might slide right off the train. The ridges of metal pushed against my back, and I gripped them for balance.

"Are you ready?" he asked against my ear.

Christian slowly pulled me to a sitting position. The wind blasted all my hair forward. Once I got my balance, I turned around. Hills and trees moved past like slow-moving shadows, and my Vampire eyes allowed me to see much more from this vantage point. I had always dreamed about riding a train, but never like this.

Sitting on my knees, I felt the cool wind rushing against my fingers. I threw my head back and howled like a wolf, my arms wide.

Christian wrapped his arms around me, his lips to my ear. "I knew you'd like it."

I didn't care how cold my face was. I didn't even care how I was going to get down. This was the most spectacular gift anyone had ever given me.

When I leaned my head against his shoulder, he turned so our lips met. We fell into a deep kiss, one so hot and erotic that I might compare all future kisses to it. His tongue swept over mine, and I felt him moan against my mouth. Christian's hand roamed over my breast and stomach before cupping between my legs.

It could have led to sex on a train. Christian was like an untamed horse, and I loved his wild soul. We could have met those primal needs with absolute privacy and complete danger. But instead, we kissed for an eternity.

And that was enough.

I combed my tangled hair with my fingers, still coming down off the high from the train surfing. Christian shut the outside door.

"I remember you telling me you did that once," Christian said, straightening out his own hair.

"It was a freight train and not anywhere near this fast. That was amazing."

He took my hands to warm them. "The ride or the kiss?"

"You need to stop with all the romantic gestures."

"And why's that?"

I put my hoodie over my head. "You're making me look bad. I haven't given you anything."

He wrapped his arms around me and growled in that sexy way he often did late at night in bed. "You give me more than you think, Precious."

"Don't tell Viktor we did that. He'll fire us on the spot."

"I can keep a secret if you can."

Christian was good at secrets. Too good.

He put distance between us and tucked away a rogue lock of hair that had fallen in front of my nose. "Better get the kids to bed. We don't have long before our next stop."

"Thanks for the date, Poe."

"You're the only woman I know who would call something that dangerous a date and do it with a smile."

Once inside our car, I headed to the main room and looked around at the kids. "Everyone, go to bed. If you're not sleepy, shut your eyes and rest."

To my surprise, all three got up and dragged their feet to the bedroom. They must have been used to taking orders, because I didn't have to herd them in there with threats.

"What are you looking for?" I asked Blue.

She closed a lower cabinet beneath the bar and stood up. "Shifter craving. It's nothing."

I drew back my hood. "What's your craving?"

Blue gripped the lapels of her cloak and sighed. "Green olives. I thought they might have some in here with all the alcohol. No such luck."

"We're in the luxury car. That means we can order anything we want."

"Is that so? Maybe I'll have Viktor call and see if they have any in the dining car."

"How was your flight?"

"Not bad. The view is amazing." She traced her finger along the smooth surface of the bar with a grim look on her face. Blue looked naked without her trademark feather earrings, but given the circumstances, she probably didn't want to fool with that kind of thing. "I really hope we're heading to another big city. I don't like the idea of hiking around in the wilderness. It's too treacherous out there for these kids."

"I feel the same. I'm not a nature person."

She pursed her lips and looked at me for a spell. "What happened to your hair? It looks like you went through a wind tunnel."

I tried to straighten it again. "Christian opened the door and threatened to toss me out."

She raised a brow and looked away. "Typical Vampire humor."

Viktor entered the room, the phone pressed to his ear and his face as white as a ghost. We both watched him make a quick trip to the back of the train near Shepherd, who was finally waking up from his nap. Moments later, Christian walked in. He didn't look like himself. His spine was arrow-straight, his eyes intense.

"Something's wrong," Blue said, staring at Viktor's reflection in the rear window.

"That is not acceptable!" Viktor snarled.

Claude sat up in his seat, his nostrils flaring.

Viktor lowered his head. "I cannot."

Niko rose from the couch and found me. "This doesn't look good. His light is going dark. Does anyone know who he's talking to?"

Only Christian could hear the full conversation on both ends. My heart was in my throat as I waited anxiously to find out the news. Was there an ambush waiting? Had someone canceled our assignment? Did our final destination change at the last minute?

Viktor lowered his arm, the phone clutched tightly in his

hand. When he turned around, you could have heard a pin drop. The next words he spoke were succinct and yet powerful enough to split a soul wide open. "Gem's gone."

Chapter 9

GEM WAITED A COUPLE OF hours after dinner before putting on her swim gear. Her aversion to bathing suits had to do with the way they amplified her petite body. She'd become a Mage at twenty-three because there was no point in waiting for her body to grow any larger. She was as tall as she'd ever be, and her fast metabolism kept her from gaining additional weight. Anyhow, a bikini for a night swim seemed gratuitous. People wore those to tan their skin, and Gem didn't exactly need a moonburn. She had a few simple gowns, and tonight she chose the red. Something about the way it lit up in the water like a blossoming flower appealed to her romantic side.

On her way to the staircase, she passed by the billiard room and overheard Wyatt and Switch playing games and being rowdy. Kira had already put Hunter to bed and was probably snuffing out candles and replacing them throughout the mansion.

As Gem floated down the stairs, her blue kimono opening in the front, Switch called out from above.

"Hey, Gem. You want company?"

She grimaced and stopped in her tracks. "Not to be rude, but swimming is the one thing I like to do alone."

"I get it. Just thought I'd ask. Maybe some other time?"

She drifted down a few steps. "Viktor has me really busy, but maybe." Gem paused, her hand on the stone handrail. "If you look out the window and see me floating, don't panic. I'm not dead. Shep made that mistake once when he first came here. He dove right in after me and created a scene. I just like to float."

"For a morbidly long time," Wyatt added as he joined Switch's side. "Enjoy it while you can, buttercup. It'll be mosquito season soon."

She simpered and waved her fingers, light leaking from the tips. "Don't you know? I'm a live bug zapper." She flashed away, their laughter fading in the distance.

Silly boys.

The night air nipped at her skin as she padded across the wide patio that led to the pool. The lights were easy to change colors, but Gem preferred blue and green. She let the kimono drop to the concrete as she walked down the steps of the shallow end. A thin veil of steam hovered just above the pool, and she let her fingers skim across the surface. Nothing made her feel more alive and in touch with the universe than floating on water. If she were a Shifter, she'd be a dolphin.

After she waded farther in, the water quickly reached her shoulders. Gem didn't have to walk far in a pool before that happened. She kicked off the bottom and waved her arms, finding her center as she drew in a deep breath and raised her body to the surface. When the water filled her ears, a peaceful *in utero* effect took hold, and she was surrounded by warmth with only the top of her body exposed to the cool night air. She marveled at the heavens. The sky looked like a black pincushion filled with shiny pins. On some nights she glimpsed shooting stars.

As she often did in quiet moments, Gem thought about work-related obstacles. Ancient languages swirled through her head like a kaleidoscope. She fluently spoke sixteen languages. All other languages she understood on paper and kept the words stored in her head. Many belonged to extinct Breeds long forgotten.

She closed her eyes when the patterns overlapped and whispers from her Relic ancestors guided her thoughts back to the new book she'd recently acquired. It wasn't often she found direct translations written on the page, but what exactly was that language? It seemed strangely familiar but completely foreign. Just when she was on the cusp of an idea, something jerked her underwater.

Gem's arms sliced through the water as she tried in vain to

resurface. Someone was pulling her down to the bottom by her dress. An arm snaked around her waist, and Gem's heart galloped in her chest as she was pulled to the bottom. What kind of sick joke was this? If this was Switch's idea of a prank, it would be his last day on the job. She'd make sure of that. A pocket of air escaped her lungs in large bubbles that ascended to the surface.

When her feet touched the bottom of the pool, she writhed and struggled to break free, only managing to turn herself partway around.

Gem was face-to-face with a complete stranger, an Asian man with shaggy hair.

Dry hair.

She could feel the energy sphere encasing his body, keeping him dry and able to breathe. The shield didn't include her, and her lungs began to spasm. Gem tried to wield an energy ball, but the sparks quickly died in the water. That was the moment true panic set in. She elbowed him and clawed, her lungs squeezing tight as the need for oxygen overrode all rational thought.

Another breath escaped her lungs, and the urge to breathe intensified.

Let me go! she screamed in her head.

No matter how hard she struggled, no matter how hard she tried to kick underwater, his grip was iron, his smile never wavering.

Not like this. Not like this. Please, somebody… anybody!

If only Niko or Raven were here, she could flare and make them realize something was wrong. So many things flew through her mind. Why hadn't she just allowed Switch to join her? Who would finish all her work in her study and care for those books? Would anyone miss her?

She couldn't even cry out for help.

The terror of taking a breath was agonizing, the urge so strong she could no longer fight it. She tried again to swim upward, but the man wouldn't let go.

Of all the languages she knew, the only word that came to mind in those last moments was *why.*

Why?

Water snaked through her nose and gushed down her windpipe as she took a deep breath. Her lungs filled, but there was no relief. They burned like liquid fire, and she suddenly couldn't move anymore. It was as if with that final reflexive jerk, all her limbs turned to stone, and she became one with the water around her.

Gem was truly floating.

"Now you're just showing off," Wyatt grumbled. What he wouldn't give to wipe that cocky smile off Switch's face.

Switch looked over his shoulder. "I learned that trick when I was seventeen."

Wyatt grabbed his beer and plopped down in a chair. He flicked a glance at the dart, which had struck the bull's-eye on the dartboard from Switch's blind throw. "I'm just letting you win, being that you're the new guy and all." He put one foot up on the footrest. "Don't get too full of yourself. You haven't seen Niko play. He never misses."

Switch lifted his beer with two fingers and ambled over to the chair across from Wyatt. He sat down and shook his long brown hair away from his face. "Isn't he blind?"

Wyatt snorted. "Blind or not, he's the best I've ever seen."

"I doubt that."

"O ye of little faith." Wyatt took a swig of his beer. "Say, what's the scoop on you and Raven? Did you two ever hook up? Is that why she wants you in the house?"

Switch nearly spit out his beer. After he wiped his mouth, he set the bottle between his legs and brushed his hand down his tattered shirt with a bar logo on it. "Do you really think I'd roll up in here like some kind of home-wrecker?"

"I don't know you from Mr. Magoo."

Switch tilted his head to the side. "Not that I think that toothy little Vamp deserves a woman like her, but that's not what I'm about. Raven and I are just friends, nothing more."

"Even if they split up?"

Intriguing. Wyatt noticed how Switch's eyebrows sank a little as if he was giving it measured thought. Wyatt had been around the block a time or two, and he gathered that Switch had once had a thing for her. Sometimes old feelings were hard to bury, especially when the other person had undergone too many life transformations. Raven was pretty in a black widow kind of way, but she was batshit crazy. Wyatt didn't feel any attraction to her; she was the worst kind of woman for a Gravewalker to hook up with. Rule number one: never *ever* marry a killer. That was his motto.

Especially now that the mansion was spook-free.

Well, all except for Niko's buddy. Seeing him show up had taken Wyatt by surprise, but the ghost never bothered him like the others had. Never came in his room, messed with his lights, scared the bejesus out of him at three in the morning, or crawled into bed with him and threatened to stay there unless he did them a favor. Wyatt hadn't really seen him since the blackout.

Not until last night. For a split second, he could have sworn he saw the specter floating out the door when Shep had left to pick up a new satellite phone from one of Wyatt's contacts. Of course, Wyatt had been up all night, and hallucinations after six cans of soda were often the norm.

Switch polished off his beer and belched loudly. It was the no-holds-barred kind of burp that men only felt comfortable doing in the presence of other men. "Is this what you guys sit around doing all day?"

Wyatt yawned. "I wish. I spend most of my time in my computer lair, working on assignments."

"What's your job?"

"Resident computer hacker extraordinaire. I'm the intel guy—the brains in this operation."

Switch arched a single eyebrow. "You think highly of yourself."

"Someone's gotta do it." Wyatt looked Switch over. He didn't seem like the kind of guy Wyatt imagined taking care of kids. "So, Mary Poppins, how did a biker like you get into the nanny business?"

"Been doing it since forever. I used to watch the kids in my first pack, and when I was old enough to move out, I just expanded my services. It started out as babysitting, but I mostly teach now. Age doesn't matter. Kids need structure, especially in a large pack where the house can be chaotic. Everyone has different schedules, different jobs." When Switch spoke, he waved his hand slowly as if he were stretching the muscles in his wrist. "When their parents are gone, it's better if they hang out with the same person instead of getting passed around."

"You got your hands full with Hunter. Kira's always losing track of him. He likes to run off when he gets bored, and because he doesn't talk, he won't yell out where he is. We have to go find him."

Switch stroked his lower lip, his eyes pensive. "Maybe we should give him a whistle."

"Not a bad idea. We've tried keeping an eye on him, but some of us have work to do. You turn around for one second and"— Wyatt snapped his fingers—"poof, he's gone."

"Kids do that when they don't have responsibilities. He's at a good age for a few chores. Just something to make him feel good about himself, like he has a place in the house. Once we start lessons, I don't think he'll be pulling any disappearing acts. If he does, my wolf will find him." Switch tapped his nose. "The benefits of being a Shifter. You can run, but you can't hide."

"True words, my friend. Especially with Blue. She can't smell you, but she's got eagle eyes."

Switch set his empty bottle on a table next to him. "What's her story? Did she get kicked out of her tribe or something?"

"Nobody knows, and we like it that way. You're new, so I'll fill you in on the unspoken rules. Once you enter Keystone, you leave your past outside the door. I'm a little more open about some things, but people here don't like questions." Wyatt stared at the ink on his fingers. "And don't bother wagging your tail around Blue. She's hot to look at. Nice breasts, long legs, and you should see what she can do with that tomahawk. But that girl's not interested."

"In me?"

"In anyone. Viktor's the center of her universe. Kinda sad."

Wyatt rubbed his chin. "I love Keystone, but I don't love it enough to be celibate. A man has needs."

"Maybe she has those needs filled when you're not around."

Wyatt snorted. "I doubt it. You start to notice a person's habits when you go out drinking at the bar. She keeps to the pack, so to speak."

"Maybe she's asexual."

Wyatt stood up and stretched, the pain reigniting in his ass. "That's a therapy session I ain't got time for. Feel like crashing the pool party?"

"Gem said she wanted to be alone."

Wyatt's lips sputtered in a noisy retort. "Don't let the girl fool you. She's a people person. Maybe we can take our beers to the hot tub."

"You have a hot tub?"

"Follow me." Wyatt headed down the hall, Switch not far behind him as he descended the stairs to the first floor.

A born night owl, just thinking about a hot tub party was giving Wyatt the munchies. Maybe while the tub was heating up, he could forage for snacks. What he needed to do was go grocery shopping and buy a giant bag of tater tots and french fries. Kira liked making everything from scratch and cooking it the healthy way.

God forbid the woman deep-fry anything and serve it with cheese. To Kira's credit, she tried. Wyatt had Viktor translate recipes, and she'd become less restrictive than when she first moved in. But Wyatt still had to buy his own soda and snacks.

"This is the easiest way to the pool," he said, approaching the courtyard door. "There's another one down the hall that leads directly to the hot tub. You'll get used to this place. It's like a castle."

As soon as Wyatt opened the door, he could smell the chlorine. "Hey, Gem. Company!"

He stepped over her kimono and approached the edge of the empty pool. "Where the Houdini is she?"

"Maybe she's in the hot tub."

Wyatt looked down the veranda to the dark spot where the hot tub was. There were no lights on, and the cover was still in place.

"Gem? Come out of the bushes, it's just us." He circled to the other side of the pool. "Maybe she had to pee."

"Look at this."

Wyatt turned around and wondered why Switch was kneeling.

"There's a lot of water here. A pool of it." His eyes followed the water trail that led toward the other side of the dark courtyard. Switch stood up. "Something's not right. There's too much water."

Without warning, he shifted into a wolf.

Wyatt jumped back and almost fell into the pool. He windmilled his arms, regaining his balance before getting the heck away from that mongrel. The last thing he needed was to get his ass chewed up by that dickish wolf. Viktor said he'd deserved to get bit after tugging on Switch's tail and cracking a joke, but people needed to lighten up.

Switch's animal raised his head and drew in several quick inhalations before sniffing the ground. In a blur of movement, he took off down a trail that cut between clumps of New England asters.

Wyatt peered into the pool as if Gem might be hiding at the bottom, but the lights exposed every corner. She could have gone to the bathroom, but it wasn't like her to leave her robe lying on the ground, and she would have locked the door behind her.

On the plus side, he didn't see her ghost wandering around. As a Gravewalker, Wyatt had a different view of death than most people. When you saw with your own eyes that there was another realm with more destinations to come, it took the fear out of finality. It made it easier for him to not get emotionally attached to life. Dying was dying, but it wasn't the end.

When Switch's wolf came barreling toward him, Wyatt stumbled backward and crashed into the pool. Wyatt sank right to the bottom. Something caught his eye, and he picked it up before kicking toward the surface. Switch grabbed his hand and hauled him out. Soaking wet, Wyatt crawled in front of Switch, who was buck naked. That was the one thing he loved and hated about Shifters.

Loved it about women, but he took a hard pass on all the male nudity.

He flipped back his wet hair, and a spray of water arced over his head. "What did you find?"

Switch reached for his clothes. "My wolf picked up two other scents on the property. What's that?"

Wyatt stood and held up the coin. "I don't know. Never seen it before."

"I'm gonna search for a trail. You better call your boss."

Chapter 10

SECONDS AFTER VIKTOR BROKE THE news about Gem, Claude's eyes went black, and he flipped his switch. To prevent him from running wild through the train, Christian pinned him to the floor. Claude stayed that way for a long while, even after Viktor explained that Gem was missing and not dead. He couldn't fight his Chitah nature, the primal part of him that emerged when a woman, child, or someone he cared about was in danger. And this wasn't just anyone; it was his partner.

We were blindsided by the news, and the details made little sense. Wyatt said that she'd gone for a swim, and when they went to check on her, she wasn't there. Switch's wolf detected a strong scent of intruders within the courtyard that ended by the back wall. Outside Keystone, the scent trail went all the way to a distant road before it disappeared. Gem never went off on her own. Not at night. Not alone. That wasn't like her. She stuck close to the house and mostly went out in the daytime.

"We have to go back," Niko insisted. He pounded his fist on the bar, refusing to sit down with the rest of us.

Viktor put his head in his hands as Shepherd, Blue, and I watched from the curved breakfast nook where we were sitting. "We cannot," he said, his voice pained. "These children depend on us. We put their lives at risk if we go back. There are spies who know what these children look like and where they stay. They are high-risk, and that is why we are transferring them. It was very difficult to orchestrate a plan to get them out."

"We can't abandon her!"

"We have no choice," Blue fired back. "Viktor's right. If something happens to these kids because we called off the mission, what did we accomplish? Our job has always been to protect the innocents, putting *their* lives above our own."

From the sofa, Christian had his arm around Claude as if they were a couple. Christian wasn't offering moral support; he was staying close in case Claude decided to go primal again.

I pushed up my sleeves and folded my arms across the table. "What do you think happened, Viktor? How could someone have broken into the house without them knowing? We keep everything locked up tight."

Viktor sat back and waved away the smoke from Shepherd's cigarette. "Wyatt saw no evidence of a break-in." Viktor drifted into Russian before Shepherd poked his arm. "Apologies. Gem is usually the one who corrects me." He rubbed the deep lines in his forehead.

"So how did they get in?" I pressed. "Did they fly?"

Christian shook his head. "Don't be daft."

I cut him a sharp glare. "Then explain it. Most of the outside windows are lattice and not the kind you can easily jump through. Our doors have bolts. No one heard her screaming for help? Gem would have screamed. She would have blasted them with an energy ball."

Claude leaned forward and buried his fingers in his golden locks.

"What would be their motive?" Blue pondered from her spot next to Viktor. "Why Gem?"

Viktor sat back. "Where is my phone?"

I stood up. "I'll find it."

Viktor had tossed it somewhere during the melee. I scanned the seats and floors as I walked toward the back where the kids were hanging out. When I reached the corner, Carol peered up at me with wide eyes. Her knees were drawn up, her face illuminated by artificial light.

"Sorry." She swiped her finger across the screen. "I was just playing a game."

"You should go back to the bedroom while we talk. No sneaking out for snacks."

Carol had a doll-like face, but instead of a smile she wore a look of apprehension. She sprang up and hustled to their room, the twins following close behind her.

I handed Viktor his phone.

"Spasibo."

We listened while Viktor called Wyatt for an update and gathered more information. Wyatt must have had more to say than Viktor, because there was a lot of silence on our end.

"That's a good plan," Christian remarked the second Viktor hung up.

Blue scooted closer to him. "What did he say?"

Viktor set his phone down. "Switch was concerned about Hunter's safety, so he called Raven's father. Mr. Graves made a few calls, and I trust that he will do everything in his power to secure our people."

Shepherd stubbed out his cigarette in an ashtray. "Who did he call?"

"The cavalry." I turned my head to look at Shepherd on my right. His eyes were darting around, and he couldn't seem to stop fidgeting. "You don't have to worry about Hunter from here on out. If my father asked his buddies to defend our property, they'll do it with their lives. They're good people. Crush never calls on favors, so I'm willing to bet a lot of men stepped up for this one."

Claude attempted to stand, but Christian yanked him down by the back of his shirt. "What about Gem? How did they get in the courtyard? Even I can't climb those walls."

Viktor wrung his hands. "Scaling a wall is a bold move and requires equipment. Whoever did this is determined and skillful. They would have been caught if we were there. I took careful steps to make sure nobody knew we were leaving."

I sat back and felt my blood run cold.

Niko stepped away from the bar behind me and approached the table. "Raven, what troubles you?"

"Maybe nothing. A few weeks ago when we had the last snow, I noticed footprints on the roof."

"Aye, I remember that," Christian said.

I looked toward him, my gaze distant. "I thought they were yours or maybe Niko's. Sometimes you guys follow me up there. It never once occurred to me that they might belong to someone else. The walls are so damn high. You'd need rope with a special hook on the end."

Niko lowered his head. "It wasn't me. I don't climb onto the roof unless I notice you out there."

"I just didn't think it was worth mentioning," I tacked on. "I should have asked around, but you guys are always spying on me or playing jokes, so I forgot about it." I fell silent for a minute and looked at Viktor. "Did they leave behind footprints? Any clues?"

"Wyatt mentioned a coin at the bottom of the pool, but it could belong to anyone."

Niko canted his head. "What kind of coin?"

"Something old."

"Did it have strange writing and uneven edges?"

"Da. He said if Gem were there, she would know what it was."

Niko drew in a deep breath and sighed. It was audible, the kind of sigh a parent might give when they've had enough of their child's bad behavior. "Viktor, you need to send me back."

"I need you here."

"There are enough of us to protect the children. I will only slow you down."

"Nyet. You are a Healer. You can see energy."

"Shepherd is a competent medic," Niko argued. "Everyone else can more than compensate for my absence. You're still a team of two Shifters, one Chitah, a Sensor, a Vampire, and Raven. That's more than enough, and you know it."

"I'll go," Claude insisted, knocking Christian's arm away as he stood up. "She's my partner. Viktor, send me instead."

"No," Niko snapped, his features hardening. "I think I know what this is about. Unless you want Gem to die, I'll be the one making the journey home. If the person behind this is who I think it is, he won't deal with anyone but me."

Claude's eyes briefly flickered from gold to obsidian as he flashed his fangs. "Then why would he steal Gem?"

"He doesn't want Gem, but he knows she's important to us. He's trying to get my attention. Better I go, or he will do something heinous."

Viktor rose to his feet, his eyes fixed on Niko. "So *this* is what he was waiting for. Our absence has created an opportunity."

They were talking about Cyrus.

Niko inclined his head. "He used to leave coins behind at the scene of a crime. No one ever asked him why. Perhaps he didn't want to anger any spirits. He placed the coin where we would find it. He wants me to know it was him."

Blue looked up at Viktor, her eyes brimming with concern. "Can we do this without Niko?"

Viktor stroked his silvery beard a few times and finally nodded. "I will have Wyatt arrange for a flight back. You will be on your own at the airport, Niko. No one to help you navigate to your terminal, so you will need to ask for assistance. Wyatt is too busy gathering surveillance data and monitoring the black-market website to pick you up from the airport."

"I'll take a cab. Viktor, you know I would never leave a mission unless absolutely necessary. If we do nothing, Gem will die, and I cannot promise what will happen next."

I stood up to let Shepherd out.

He gripped Niko by the shoulders. "When you get there, look after my son. Make sure they're protecting him." Shepherd cursed under his breath. "Jesus. What if Hunter had been outside?"

Niko touched his hands. "I'll do everything within my power to ensure that this man never goes near your son. No matter what. You have my word."

Viktor looked at his watch. "We have one hour before the next stop. I must call Wyatt to make arrangements."

I stepped back, still unnerved that we were down a teammate at home and another one was leaving us. On top of that, Crush had sent in his buddies. Now I had my father to worry about. What the hell was going on back at the mansion? Was he there? Knowing Crush, he was there.

Viktor clapped his hands together. "Everyone, collect your things and ready yourselves. With Niko leaving, I need everyone at their best. It's midnight, so if you require a short nap, take it now before we stop."

Blue got up and handed Viktor his phone. She snatched her boots off the floor and put them back on while Shepherd searched the car from back to front.

I gathered up all the empty bottles and tossed them in the trash, cleaning away all evidence that Keystone had been here. "Viktor, where are we going? I think we've been in the dark long enough."

He folded down the collar of his grey turtleneck and almost dropped his phone. "There is no point keeping it a secret since Claude overheard a passenger mention our next stop is Virginia. We will be traveling in an RV to West Virginia from Roanoke."

I sat down and rummaged through my backpack in search of my phone. After a quick check of the weather, I decided my hoodie was fine. The low was in the forties, but the humidity made it seem warmer. Not to mention tomorrow's high would be sixty-five and sunny.

West Virginia. What the hell did I know about West Virginia aside from the fact it was in a John Denver song?

If we were traveling in an RV, that meant we weren't going to a big city. Otherwise he would have rented a bus or large van—something that would blend in with our surroundings. The last time I ventured into the woods, I was jumped by Shifters. Nope. There was no way I was stepping off this train unarmed. I put on my belt so I could hook the sheaths on the back and side. My buckle had a miniature knife, but the full-length dagger would do more damage. Better I wait till we got to the RV to strap that on so I didn't get myself arrested. Then again, maybe country folks wore their weapons with pride. I didn't know the laws in Virginia or West Virginia, so I tucked the large knife back in my bag.

"Viktor, how are we going to rent an RV at night?" I asked. "Everything's closed at this hour."

He was busy on the phone.

Christian joined my side. "He's already arranged everything."

"I hate that you can hear all the phone conversations."

He lifted my chin with the crook of his finger. "Jealousy doesn't suit you."

"I think you should tell the kids to get their things together."

"Jaysus, no."

"Why not?"

"Did you not see the way the wee one looked at me earlier? I thought she would flee for her life. That's why I kept the sunglasses on after dark."

"You look like Ray Charles in those things."

"Great men dress alike."

Walking the streets after midnight in an unfamiliar town added a new layer of danger, especially when I didn't know anything about the Breed culture and districts in these parts. Those of us with hoods kept them on, and I concealed my light while we waited inside the train station. It was enclosed and heated, benches in the middle and bathrooms close to the front. The café was closed, the lights dim, the floors shiny, and the benches empty.

Christian went outside with Niko to wait for the cab. Being the only Mage, I had the advantage of sensing Mage energy from someone who wasn't concealing. But this place wasn't exactly bustling, so I leaned against the wall and thought about Christian and me on top of the train.

Viktor and Shepherd flanked the kids, who looked bored out of their minds.

An hour later, a second train rolled through. I was surprised at how many people were traveling at this hour, but everyone had somewhere to be, and the crowd quickly dispersed as tired travelers dragged their luggage behind them and left the station.

I wandered over to Viktor, my thumbs hooked beneath my backpack straps. "How much longer?"

He glanced at his watch. "Not much."

"I have to go," Carol announced, inviting no argument as she hopped to her feet. "The bathroom's right there." She held her stomach with a look of embarrassment. "I'll be back in a few minutes."

Viktor glanced around at the empty building, which we had secured, and waved his hand for her to go.

Adam flourished a couple of bills. "Get me a soda, pipsqueak."

The vending machines were toward the front, and she skipped off with the money in hand.

Shepherd stood up and struck a match to light his cigarette. The soft glow of the burning paper illuminated his stubbly jaw. It sure didn't take long for his facial hair to grow out. I bet he went through razor blades like Wyatt went through french fries. Claude stole his spot and turned around to chat with Blue, who was sitting on the bench behind them.

"Sir, there's no smoking in here," a man barked from the ticket window.

I grabbed Shepherd's sleeve before he started an argument. "Let's go outside. It's too stuffy in here anyhow."

He threw a dirty look at the ticket attendant as we passed by him. Once we were outside, I scoped out the parking area. There were cars parked off to the right, sufficient lighting, and not a whole lot to look at beyond the station. The road curved in a U shape, and it was dark up ahead, no city lights that I could see. Shepherd puffed on his smoke while I studied the building. The paint looked fresh and the concrete recently poured. Part of the sidewalk to the left had construction tape around it.

Orange embers jumped off Shepherd's cigarette and danced in the air before disappearing.

"I don't like this one bit," he confessed.

"About Gem?"

"That too." When he straightened his shoulders, his leather coat creaked. "Did you know this is Shifter country? The deeper in the woods you go, the more Shifters there are. Some of them run with groups—like packs—but the other fuckers are rogues."

I glanced over my shoulder. "Should we be standing out here?"

"The building's empty, so the kids are safe in there. But some of us should spread out. I don't like being clustered up in there. Let Viktor know I'll keep watch of everyone coming and going. Looks like Christian took off."

"Probably picking up litter."

"Or drinking someone." Shepherd shifted his stance and cocked his head to the side. "Tell me, is drinking another person's blood considered cheating?"

I pinched my chin and thought about it. "I don't know what the Vampire rules are about that kind of thing, but if I find out he's penetrated anyone with either his cock or his fangs, I'll make him regret his own birth."

"Amen to that. But what if he's dying and the only way to survive is to drink someone's blood. Is that infidelity?"

I turned on my heel and headed toward the door. I didn't have time to entertain imaginary scenarios that would only piss me off.

"What if the only vein she had to offer was between her legs?" he called out, choking with laughter as I entered the building.

When I didn't see Carol by the group, I swung left toward the bathrooms. Sometimes a person needed privacy when doing their business, but I was a little concerned. She was human, and the train movement had made even me a little queasy.

"Hey, Carol? You feeling okay?"

I pushed a stall door open and found it empty. "If you're nauseated, we can probably find some medicine. Some people get travel sickness; it's no big deal. Shepherd might have something in his bag. He's our medic."

When I knocked and opened the next door, that stall was also empty. So I bent down and peered underneath the remaining partition to look for her feet.

And didn't see any.

I hurried out and headed toward Viktor. "Is Carol with you?"

His brow furrowed. "Nyet. She went to the ladies' room."

I set down my backpack and heaved a sigh. These kids knew how serious this job was, yet they didn't seem to have an ounce of sense. I thought we could trust them to stick close, but that was naive thinking on my part considering these were teenagers. I forgot how rebellious they were. And sneaky.

God, I was beginning to understand what my old man had gone through.

"I bet she wandered off to look around. Can you watch my bag? I'll go find her."

Blue peered over her shoulder from the other bench. "Where's Shep?"

"He thinks it's a better idea if we're not all clustered together, so he's guarding the front. This place is a ghost town outside, so I guess we came at a good time."

Viktor gave Adam and his sister a scolding glance while wagging his finger at them. "I do not want either of you wandering off, do you understand me? This is not a vacation. I know this adventure has you curious, but this is not the time for you to go exploring."

As Viktor proceeded to lecture our rebellious little teens, I ventured onto the platform in search of the blond-haired pixie.

While my Vampire vision was good, it was too difficult to see anything beyond the bright lights directly above. I walked to the side of the building and searched for a way up since the roof would give me an ideal vantage point. This wasn't a big train station by any means, so it wouldn't be hard to find a good climbing spot.

An elderly couple sitting on a bench watched me like a hawk, and the woman clutched her purse a little tighter. I skirted around the side of the building, searching every dark corner. Carol was small and easy to miss, especially with her black jacket and hood. She might have slipped out to smoke a joint. I really didn't know a damn thing about these kids or what kind of life they led. I hopped onto a large air-conditioning unit and jumped until I caught the edge of the roof. My shoes gripped the brick wall with ease as I pulled myself up.

When I reached the other side of the roof and looked down,

I spied a couple facing each other. I almost turned away until I noticed that neither of them had luggage.

"Carol?" I shouted.

When they looked up, the lamppost illuminated a young man's face. Next to him, a familiar young teen with a ghostly-white complexion and a crown of blond hair. Carol looked like a deer caught in the headlights.

"Get away from her!" I growled at the man. "Carol, go inside," I said, emphasizing every syllable. "Christian, if you can hear me, I need you on the west side of the building. Carol's out here with some random guy."

Fearing this joker might grab her and run, I assessed the edge of the building and decided that risking a broken leg by jumping wasn't an option. Not at night, and not when Niko wasn't around.

"Dammit."

The only way down was to aim for the tree branch. It wasn't very thick, but in my experience, even thin branches were strong.

I squatted and measured the distance in my mind. The branch was a few feet lower but close enough that I could land on it. I'd scaled trees all through childhood, so not having a fear of heights always worked to my advantage. When I jumped, I felt like a cat leaping out a window. I scrambled for the branch, landing on it so hard that it snapped but didn't break in two. It merely hung like a floppy arm, taking me with it.

I hit the sidewalk and went rolling into the dirt.

"That one likes to roll in the mud like a pig," I heard Christian say.

I dusted myself off and stood up. "What are you doing out here?" I gave Carol a scolding glance.

Christian had a grip on her jacket, and she looked startled by the sudden turn of events.

Her breath frosted in the cold night air, and her cheeks turned bright pink. "I just wanted to see where we were."

I looked around, but the man was gone. "Who was that guy? What did he want?"

Christian nudged her toward me. "Romeo took off into the parking lot. Want me to go get him?"

I looked over my shoulder and sighed. "No. Viktor doesn't want us running off." I straightened Carol's black hood and tucked her hair inside. "Are you okay?"

"We were just talking," she said.

"You need to stick with us. Got it? I know you're curious about the outside world, but right now it's dangerous. Viktor doesn't want you guys wandering off. And no talking to strangers. Even cute ones."

"If he had kidnapped me, would you have gone looking? Or would you have finished delivering Adam and Eve?"

She looked a little dejected, so I put my arm around her and led her to the platform as a train whistle sounded in the distance. "There's no way anyone's taking you from us. Think about it. We've got a Vampire, a Chitah, a Mage, a Sensor, two Shifters—you couldn't be in safer hands. And if someone did snatch you, they wouldn't get far. Claude owns your scent."

"Ew. What does that mean?"

"You probably didn't notice him doing it on the train. Chitahs can pull in a person's scent and put it to memory. Forever. It's why they're excellent trackers. No matter how many years pass, anytime he catches even a whiff of your scent, he'll know and he'll find you. Just stay close to the herd from now on."

She glanced over her shoulder and then tucked her hands in her jacket pockets. "How long is this trip gonna last?"

"I don't know."

"Is that Vamp your boyfriend?"

"He's my partner. Why would you ask that?"

Christian and I had been careful about not displaying affection in front of the kids.

Carol met eyes with me in our reflection on the glass door at the rear of the building. "Because he looks at you like he would die for you."

I smiled as we went inside. "He almost has."

She stopped and peered up at me with earnest eyes. "That's

when you know it's true love. When you care about someone else's life more than your own. When you'd do anything to be with them."

Kids and their romantic notions. Someday Carol would learn that love was more complicated than that.

Viktor beckoned us over to the front doors. Everyone had gathered up their gear and was waiting for us. We hustled across the room until we caught up with the group. Blue passed me my bag, which was light enough to toss over my shoulder with ease.

Viktor glowered at Carol. "And where did you go off to?"

She gave him a sheepish grin and shrugged. "I dunno."

He palmed the back of her head and nudged her toward the other two. "Kids always know everything. But when you ask them a question, they suddenly don't know anything."

As soon as we poured outside, the squeals of excited teenagers filled my ears.

Eve hopped in a circle, clapping her hands. "Is this ours?"

"Whoa!" Adam walked along the camper and let his finger glide across the surface. "Sweet!"

How were we all going to fit in that thing? I'd grown up in a single-wide trailer and knew how long people could comfortably dwell in a confined space before they wanted to murder each other. It wasn't one of those luxury bus-sized motor homes but an RV with a standard front end that resembled a van or truck. I guessed the vehicle to be about thirty feet long.

Viktor and Shepherd formed a huddle.

Shepherd finally patted the front end. "Let's roll."

He rounded the front to the driver's side and got in. Viktor pulled out his wallet and tipped the delivery driver before the man and his buddy sped off in a small Toyota.

When Blue opened the door, the kids piled in first. She turned and noticed the look of concern on my face. "If it gets too crowded in there, I can always fly. It just depends on what Viktor says and how long our trip is."

Once inside, I noticed the front cab was sunken down and had a sleeper over it. The small built-in sofa in front of the door was beige vinyl, and the stench of stale cigarette smoke lingered like a bad memory. The second sofa to the left curved around with two seats on either side. It probably had a pullout in the middle that converted it into a bed.

Carol sneezed and headed to the rear bedroom. Adam kept himself busy flipping all the light switches while his sister followed Carol. The sleeper above the cab had a privacy curtain and a TV. Two kids could easily fit up there and keep busy, which gave me a bit of relief that this might not be such a bad ride after all.

"I could live in one of these." Blue surveyed the kitchenette, hands on her hips. "Sink, stove, fridge, cabinets—everything a person needs. Look, there's even a microwave."

Adam jogged to the back.

I sat on the sofa and stared at the open door. "I forgot to bring the popcorn."

Blue opened one of the overhead cabinets. "Someone left a few potato chips in here if you're hungry."

I snorted. "Don't say that too loud. The kids will eat it up in thirty seconds."

"They're probably expired."

"I doubt they care."

When Claude entered the trailer, he had to tilt his head to the side to keep it from touching the ceiling. "Looks like I'm sleeping on the floor."

I smirked at him. He looked like a tall man trapped in a short man's world. "We could always strap you to the roof."

Christian was the last in and locked the door behind him. "*Jaysus wept.* Will you take a gander at this obscenity? I still remember when people traveled in wagons." He scanned the room and looked displeased with all the modern conveniences. "At least the fridge is big enough to fit a body in."

I crossed my legs. "Do you mean dessert?"

He flashed his fangs at me in jest.

Claude plopped down on the U-shaped couch to my right. "In my day, trains were the only way to travel in style."

Adam stood in the hall and opened a frosted-glass door. "Is

this the bathroom? I'm not showering in the hallway. If I have to take a piss, we're pulling over."

Eve peered into the bathroom. "I hope nobody ate any beans."

Viktor climbed into the passenger seat and slammed the door. "Drive."

Since the engine was already running, Shepherd put it in gear and headed out. The jolt from him hitting the gas made Christian lose his balance.

Carol ambled from the rear of the camper and yawned as she unzipped her black jacket. "Are we staying in here the *whole* time? I get claustrophobic. I need to walk around in an open space and use a real bathroom. When's our next stop?"

Adam knocked into her as he jogged toward the sleeper. "Is that a TV? I got dibs!" He hopped over my legs and put his hands on the bunk. "How do you get up?" Without waiting for an answer, he stepped on the couch and climbed up the incorrect way. Then he dropped a ladder over the edge. "Hey, Eve, check it out. We can watch TV."

As soon as she climbed up behind him with their bags, they slid the privacy curtain closed, and the sound of an old movie blared, followed by bickering.

"Turn it down," Viktor ordered, knocking his fist on the roof. "I cannot hear myself think."

Carol opened the fridge and found a can of root beer. "Can I have the bed?"

The four of us looked between each other. Christian and I didn't need to sleep, so it was up to Claude and Blue.

"I'll go with you," Blue said, rising to her feet. "I could use some shut-eye."

"You're wearing an axe," Carol said, eyeballing the tomahawk.

"File a complaint." Blue patted her shoulder as she walked past. "Kid, the axe stays with me at all times. But I'll take it off. Come on. We've probably got a long drive ahead."

Claude found the cushion for the center of his sofa and was attempting to curl up and get comfortable. That didn't leave anywhere else for Christian to sit except beside me.

He took a seat to my left and put his arm across the back of the sofa. "Maybe Viktor will let you ride on top later on if you ask him nicely."

"You only live once."

"Aye, but when you're an immortal, you can die a thousand times."

Viktor turned in his seat and handed Christian a map. "I cannot see the tiny print. How far until we reach Interstate 77?"

Christian didn't need anyone to turn on a light to see the map. He gave it a firm shake and held it up. "Wouldn't Route 460 be faster?"

"My contact specified we not go that route. There is a band of rogues who know that Potentials are smuggled across state lines on that highway. They do not know where we take them, but they ambushed the last group and kidnapped the children. No one survived. We do not know how they found out, only that someone on the last team must have leaked information. That is why I've taken every precaution."

Christian straightened the map and studied it. "If I had to guess, two hours. And where do we go from there?"

Viktor twisted around in his seat. "The less you know of the specifics, the better."

I glanced at the map and quietly spoke to Christian. "It's not a big state. If we're there in two hours, we could probably drive all the way across the state in less than four hours. That means we'll be wherever we're going by morning."

He folded up the map. "Unless there's more to the trip."

"Why do you say that?"

"Did you ever wonder why he chose a camper?"

"So we'll blend in with all the tourists?"

"It's a little early in the year for camping, and we don't exactly pass for hunters."

"We can always buy some flannel and camo at the next gun store."

Christian reached behind us and pulled the shade out so he could see the road.

I just didn't understand why anyone would go to great lengths to get their hands on these kids. Then again, people who lived outside the law did all kinds of crazy shit. My stomach turned when I thought about the last caravan transporting children to this location.

Not a single one had made it through alive.

Chapter 11

G EM'S LUNGS ACHED AND BURNED as she coughed up water. She gasped for air, but the process was like breathing for the first time. Now she knew why newborn babies cried. Expelling every drop seemed like an impossible feat, as if the water lived inside her. With her face to the floor, she retched. Water gushed out, throwing her into another coughing fit. Her throat hurt, her nose burned, and all she could do was sit there and tremble.

"You were out a long time," a man said.

She peered up through her stringy hair. A man with a broad chest was sitting on a short stool, peeling a red apple. The tattoos on his biceps looked Polynesian, but his features weren't of that origin. Gem had spent many years researching cultures, and she even knew how physical features evolved through the centuries among a people, especially as strangers began migrating to new lands. His eyes were narrow and unkind, and when he sneered, he revealed gaps between his teeth. Something about his features felt distinctly Mongolian or perhaps Tibetan. His bronzed skin was aged by hardship and not time, so she couldn't discern how old he was.

She lowered her head, palms on the ground, and coughed up more water.

"Unpleasant, isn't it?" He gave a haughty laugh. "Young immortals know nothing about survival. You are so ill-equipped and weak that you would have never survived in my time."

Gem sat back and shuddered. The last thing she remembered

was struggling for air in the pool, but this wasn't the same man who had held her down. She tried to speak, but the undulation of her fragile throat muscles forced out another cough.

The man ate a slice of his apple, watching her with great amusement. "Who am I? Where are you? Right? Let us start from the beginning. My given Mage name is Cyrus, but it is not my birth name. I was once part of a nomadic tribe under the rule of Genghis Khan. We fought many great battles and earned the right to inherit this world. Even as mortals, we refused to die. We drank the blood of our horses to keep from starving. I was a good hunter, but I was an even better warrior." Cyrus studied his knife for a painfully long moment. "My Creator forced immortality on me, but I turned that curse into a gift. You see, white men know nothing of the seeds they sow with their wickedness." He sliced off another wedge of apple and savored it. "One day, they will reap everything they deserve."

Gem tried to figure out where she was, but the room provided no clues. Cyrus was sitting with his forearms resting on his knees. She briefly eyed the sharp blade in his hand before averting her gaze to the four walls. Lanterns hung from them, so this was probably his perverted dungeon in the city. Unless they were in the Bricks. Just the thought of it gave her the heebie-jeebies. That would make escape impossible without fighting off other rogues, especially if this dwelling was underground.

"Nikodemos hasn't told you about me, has he?" Cyrus inquired. "Very sneaky, that one. He is loyal to no one but himself. Always keeping secrets, even from those with whom he breaks bread. I know this all too well, for Nikodemos once betrayed me."

Gem swallowed hard and curled her legs beneath her red gown. She couldn't shake the cold, and her skin looked ashen. "Why am I here?" she managed to say.

Cyrus kept his eyes on the apple he continued slicing. "You're not a good listener, are you? Arcadius—the man who captured you—has a special gift that allows him to use his energy to breathe underwater. Like a Mage scuba suit. Is that what they call those contraptions around their heads? The only way to capture you quietly and efficiently was to render you unconscious. Lucky for us, you're a creature of habit. Though you haven't been sticking to your routine these past few weeks, have you?"

Gem thought about her nightly swims. Had this man been watching her? "You drowned me."

He studied his knife. "Drowning is an illusion to a Mage. Your core light simply won't allow it. But I can see you've lived a sheltered life. Ancients like me have tested the boundaries of our own existence. We've been hanged, shot, disemboweled, drowned, and even partially burned." Cyrus sliced off the last chunk from his apple and ate it.

Gem scooted away from him in case he had a mind to use that knife on her.

"The one thing you can't do without is your head," he pointed out. "Just ask that man of yours with all the lip rings."

Her stomach dropped. "Hooper?"

"I cannot respect a man who grovels and begs for his life."

Gem's rage circulated through her body like a fiery cyclone gathering speed. "*You* killed Hooper?"

Cyrus set the knife down and nibbled on the meat of the apple around the core. The smile in his eyes tipped her over the edge.

Gem cupped her hands to form a destructive ball of energy and drew back her arm as if she were going to pitch him a baseball. But nothing happened. Then she noticed the absence of light from within. She felt as cavernous as the Grand Canyon. "What did you do to me?" Horror swept over her when she thought about Raven's gift as a Stealer. Had this man rendered her mortal by removing her core light? He couldn't be using his Mage gifts to suppress her energy. That would be impossible since she was a Blocker and immune to such gifts.

Cyrus tossed the apple core on the ground and spit out a seed. He studied her for a long moment. "I wonder what you might do with that hand if you had your power. Hmm, little Mage?"

She clenched her fist and stared defiantly at him. "My friends will come for me, and when they do, you'll be sorry."

Cyrus tossed back his head and laughed. "You watch too many

movies. You're starting to sound like one of those pathetically hopeful characters who believes goodness always prevails."

Gem stared at the floor and squeezed her eyes shut. *This* was the man who'd taken Hooper's life? Was his heartless laugh the last thing Hooper had heard? She'd never wanted to kill someone with her bare hands until this moment. Just when she thought she'd let go of the pain, his confession had reawakened it on a whole new level.

"See that cuff on your ankle?" he asked.

She glanced at her feet. Sure enough, there was a silver link around her right ankle. Gem reached back and turned it, unable to find the opening. It fit snugly against her skin with no wiggle room.

"They are so rare to find on the black market," Cyrus informed her. "So very rare. And this one is far superior to the one they sell for the wrist. You'd be surprised how a determined person will break their fingers and cut through skin to remove them. Not so easily done on the ankle, I'm afraid. And if you manage to sever off your entire foot, good luck escaping."

"What do you want from me?"

He laced his fingers together. "Our Nikodemos has been very uncooperative."

"How do you know him?"

His gaze drifted off. "We go… way back." Cyrus slapped his knee and stood up. "Who knew that he would lead us on such an expedition across the globe? The greatest quest of all time and led by a blind man."

She tried to be concise, but none of his answers gave her any inkling of what he wanted. "What do you want from Niko?"

"So much, little Mage. He's a conniving thief who absconded with my greatest treasure many centuries ago. He broke my trust, and I want my book."

A book? What would Niko—of all people—be doing with a book? "He can't read, let alone care for a fragile book that would have fallen apart and decayed from improper care through each passing century. It's impossible."

Cyrus spun on his heel and looked at her with sudden interest. "What would *you* know about such things?"

With all the strength she could muster, Gem pushed herself to her feet to face him. "I study language, and part of my interest involves books."

"Ah, so you're a scholar."

"Not exactly."

"A studious woman is a blight that insults the gods."

Ignoring his ignorance, she went on. "You say the book you're looking for is hundreds of years old? I'm assuming we're talking about a book and not clay tablets," she said with derision. "Without proper care, it wouldn't have survived in the hands of a blind man traveling the globe. Books decay when stored in an attic or garage for a long period. Even parchment buckles with humidity. Books that survived the ravages of history were cared for, kept in libraries or churches. Many didn't survive fires and floods. Do you really believe a blind man traveling on foot could have kept it from sunlight, water, or thieves?" Gem huffed and shook her head. "Why kidnap me when I'm not even the one who has what you're looking for?"

Cyrus tipped his head to the side. "Friendship is a bond that is rarely tested, and when it is, it often crumbles. Nikodemos has proven this theory, but I am fortunate that my other brothers are loyal. Even in death. Do you know why? Fear. That is the strongest influencer of all. Except for love, perhaps. Funny how humans romanticize such a fleeting emotion when it is the very thing that brings them to ruin. Love makes men weak. But it can also be used as a weapon. I can manipulate anyone I want simply by threatening to destroy what they love." He gave Gem an oblique grin and turned toward the door. When he reached for the knob, he looked over his shoulder and studied her for a moment before turning to face her. "You don't know what I'm talking about, do you? Let's take that little boy, for instance. Everyone loves a child, am I right? It's automatic, even when he's not yours. If I told you that I would murder that boy if you escaped, what might you do? Save yourself and let the boy perish? Do you think you could protect the child from my reach forever and ever? Do you think I wouldn't follow through with my word?"

Chills rippled down her spine at the thought of anyone hurting Hunter. Now she couldn't escape—not if it meant this maniac going after a little child.

"Isn't love a fascinating emotion? That which makes you feel invincible actually renders you powerless." Cyrus opened the door and gave her a baleful look. "I do not enjoy listening to the wails of a woman, fists pounding on the walls, or having to sleep with one eye open. No doors will be locked. You are free to walk about. You are also free to escape… should you feel so inclined." Cyrus bowed his head and left the room, leaving the door wide open.

Chapter 12

I DREAMED OF FALLING DOWN a hole that tunneled through the center of the earth. The walls around me were made of beautiful crystals, but each time I tried to reach for them to slow my descent, they would slice my hands.

"Raven, wake up."

I gasped and rose to my elbows. Out of breath, I stared into Christian's welcoming eyes, but part of me still felt tethered to the dream world as the road hummed beneath the tires of the RV.

"Are your nightmares back?" he asked quietly.

I relaxed my shoulders. "No, it wasn't one of those. I felt helpless, and I think I know why. Any updates on Gem?"

"No word on anything new."

"I can't believe someone took her. I hope Niko finds out who it was and puts a dagger in their eye."

"That man can find a needle in a haystack. You want a glass of water? Perhaps with a splash of blood?"

I glared at him.

"Don't be giving me the evil eye. A tiny drop will calm you down. It's not enough to cause any problems, but it's just enough to smooth out the rough edges."

"No thanks, Poe. You're the one who told me I shouldn't drink on the job."

"It's hardly a drink."

"Have you ever transported Potentials before?"

Christian shook his head. "They've always been an urban

legend, but the ancients know about their existence. People choose what they want to believe."

I scooted up and swept my tousled hair away from my face. "They'll never have normal lives."

"Unless they become Breed. Private organizations do what they can to protect the children until they're old enough to make a choice. It's a dark world we live in, Raven. There's wickedness the likes of which you've never seen."

I peered over at Claude, who was fast asleep on the adjacent couch. Though it was still dark outside, I reached in the backpack at my feet and found a T-shirt to change into. The cabin felt uncomfortably warm and stuffy. When I took off my hoodie, Christian stretched his legs and put his hand over his growing erection. His hot gaze slid down my body, giving me a little tingle between my legs.

After dressing, I folded my hoodie and stuffed it in my bag. "You better watch yourself, Poe."

Carol appeared from the back room, feeling her way around the dark cabin.

Christian shot out of his seat and approached the kitchen cabinets. "Are you hungry?" He turned on a dimmer switch.

"No, I just need to…" She sneezed and quickly covered her nose.

Christian handed her a paper towel, and she blew into it.

"I can't sleep with that lady lying next to me." Carol handed Christian back the paper towel, and I could have sworn I saw him shudder. She moved past him and peered out the door window. "Where are we going? Is it like a prison with security bars and electric fences?"

"I doubt they're sending you to Jurassic Park," I said, trying to be a voice of reason. "I'm sure it'll be nice. I've heard it's new and the best of its kind."

She rolled her eyes. "Jail is jail. Can we please stop at a gas station before we get there? My head's stuffed up, and I need some nasal spray."

I leaned toward the front cab. "Shep, do you have anything for a cold?"

"Negative."

Carol plopped down next to me, her jacket still on but unzipped. "I bet they don't have any good medicine where we're going. They didn't at the last place. I just had to suffer."

"Aren't they supposed to take care of you?"

She shrugged. "They're supposed to hire Relics that know about humans, but they hardly ever gave us medicine when we were sick. I think their job was just to make sure we didn't keel over and die or something." She studied her fingernails. "I've got money saved from working in the kitchen. I can buy the nasal spray. I'm not a drug addict, if that's what you're afraid of. But I can't breathe." She pinched one nostril closed and made an attempt to breathe through the other one. It made an awful sound before she sighed.

"I'll see what I can do," I promised her.

Christian moseyed to the back where Blue was sleeping.

"How long have you lived under protection?" I asked.

She crossed one leg over the other and picked at the thick treads on the bottom of her black shoe. "My whole life. My mom—or whoever—left me at a fire station when I was born. Someone must have seen the mark on me, because they never sent me to foster care or anything like that. I went right to the Breed facility."

"Does anyone get adopted from that place?"

"Are you kidding? It's not an orphanage, so getting a family isn't an option."

I leaned back. "At least you got to grow up with the same kids, so it was like having siblings."

"Not really. Sometimes they shipped kids out in the middle of the night, and nobody got a chance to say goodbye. Why bother making friends? I think they only kept me around because I did a lot of work in the kitchen. Not everyone there worked for money. I like having personal stuff that's mine, but I had to leave it all behind," she grumbled. "They didn't even give us time to pack because they were afraid we might tattle or try to escape. The only time there were runaways was during a transfer. You get attached to your friends, and it's the only home you know." She sighed and put her foot down. "I wish they'd never found that mark on my back. I would have had a normal life in foster care."

"Trust me, kid, you're better off. I knew someone who grew up in foster care, and it was no picnic. She told me stories about how they were bounced around, neglected, and sometimes abused. You're lucky if you can get through the system unscathed."

She sprang to her feet. "Do I look unscathed? I don't have any family, I'm not allowed to go outside by myself... like ever, and now I'm being kidnapped and taken to some top secret location that no one will tell me about."

"Shhh." I pointed at the sleeper above where Adam and Eve were.

"Don't bother," Adam said from behind the curtain. "She whines about everything."

Carol wrinkled her nose and stared upward. "At least *I* want something better in life."

Adam ripped open the curtain and scowled at her. "You gaze out the window all night like some kind of lunatic. That's not even your real accent."

"It is too!"

"Nobody in the northeast talks like that. You sound like a hillbilly. At least I live in the real world."

I stood up and yanked the curtain closed. "Go back to sleep."

"Whatever," he grumbled.

If I had to listen to these kids bickering for the next twelve hours, I was going to need a whole lot of alcohol. I gripped the back of Shepherd's seat and noticed Viktor snoozing on the passenger side. "We need to pull over at a convenience store and pick up a few things."

He looked at me in the rearview. "Later. I'm only making one stop, and that's to top off the gas."

"Fine, but we're stopping for medicine."

I went to the fridge to get a drink.

"He don't know nothing," Carol whispered loudly.

"Who, Shepherd?"

"No."

"Oh, you mean Adam."

"This *is too* my accent."

I filled the glass, and after I took a drink, I set the plastic cup in the sink. "But if you were raised in that orphanage—"

"Prison," she corrected.

"Semantics. Nobody in Cognito sounds like you."

"On the contrary, people have all kinds of accents. Even him," she said, pointing to the back room where Christian had gone.

"But he wasn't born here. You were. How did you end up with yours?"

She looped her finger around her gold necklace and leaned against the counter. "When I was a baby, there wasn't anyone else my age. Just a few older kids who were like teenagers or something. So an elderly lady took care of me. She taught me how to talk and read and... well, I guess I learned to talk like her."

"Did you at least get to say goodbye to her when you left?"

"I said my goodbyes a long time ago. She died. She was kinda old. Relics don't live that long, you know. Just as long as humans, and they can get diseases and stuff." Carol fished a piece of gum out of her pocket. "My last one."

"We'll stop somewhere a little later. You can buy gum and cold medicine then."

Her eyes lit up, and she pushed away. "Awesome! If I fall asleep, wake me up, okay? I don't want to miss it. Hey, can I sleep in the back by myself? It's weird having people in there."

"You can sleep here on the sofa."

"I can't sleep with y'all talking all the time. Can you please ask that lady to leave?"

I journeyed down the hall and opened the doors. Blue was facedown on the bed to the left, her arms and legs spread wide. I stared at the open window straight ahead and then to Christian on my right, who had wedged himself on a counter between two storage closets.

"Clear out," I said. "Carol wants to sleep."

He knocked the heels of his shoes against the lower cabinet

and nodded at Blue. "Good luck waking up that one. She sleeps like the dead."

An hour or two after Carol had gone to sleep, the RV entered a long tunnel. Claude shared his sofa space with Blue, and every so often, he'd start purring, only to be silenced by Blue slapping his chest. The twins had finally gone to sleep, the television now off.

Christian unwrapped what looked like a Jolly Rancher and tucked the plastic wrapper in a trash can beneath the sink.

"You can sit next to me," I offered, thinking he couldn't be comfortable on the floor.

Christian patted the floor, his knees bent and his back against the counter. "And you can do the same. There's plenty of room down here," he said with a naughty wink.

"You can't be trusted."

He lowered one leg and rested his hand over his crotch. "To be sure."

I stood up and stretched. This trip was dragging like molasses. It was still dark outside, and we had hours left to go. I squatted behind the two front seats and looked for the end of the tunnel. "Are we there yet?"

Shepherd gave me a peevish glance over his shoulder, a cigarette wedged between his lips. "Whenever you two are done eye fucking back there, can someone look up the weather report?"

"No rain in the forecast," Christian piped in.

Shepherd blew out a puff of smoke. "Yeah? How do you know that?"

"Me bones don't hurt," he said, his humor lost to the boredom in his voice.

I took out my phone to search for the weather report. "How long is this damn tunnel? I'm not getting a signal."

Viktor snored loudly when his head rolled the other way. That man could probably nap through an asteroid collision with Earth.

Lucky for me, I didn't require the same amount of rest as everyone else, but it made time crawl.

When we emerged from the tunnel, everything went dark again.

Shepherd steered his head back toward me. "How about now?"

"Maybe you should call Wyatt for the weather forecast. I don't even know what zip code we're in."

"Spooky asks too many questions on the phone. Nobody's got time for that."

I looked up ahead. "What's that?"

Shepherd turned his attention back to the road and gripped the wheel. "Jesus fuck!"

We jerked left. Then right. My shoulder hit the side of the trailer, and I fell back. Eve squeaked from above, and the loud thump of a body hitting the floor sounded from behind. The tires screeched when Shepherd hit the brakes.

He barked out a curse, and everything tipped on its side. The children screamed. I hit my elbow on something, objects went flying, and the sound of grating metal filled my eardrums.

When everything stopped moving, I realized that the trailer was on its side. What I thought was furniture on top of me was actually Christian. Somehow during the chaos, he'd sailed up from his spot on the floor and cradled my head.

My heart thumped against my rib cage. Out of breath, I sat up and surveyed the damage. One of the cabinets had vomited Tupperware everywhere.

Shepherd crawled over his seat, the cigarette still wedged between his lips and a long ash miraculously hanging from the end. When he spoke, it broke off and fell to the floor. "Everyone okay?"

Claude sat up holding his head, a small sliver of blood trickling between his fingers. His eyes suddenly widened, and he climbed over the wall and toward the back where Carol was sleeping.

Viktor looked startled when he finally unbuckled himself and fell toward the driver's seat.

The overhead curtain had opened, revealing the two siblings who were wrapped together like pretzels, their legs hanging out. The sleeping cab now looked like a standing closet.

"What the crap?" Adam said as he climbed over me and tripped on the shutters.

Christian stood on the end of the sofa and reached up to open the door overhead.

"What happened?" Viktor wedged himself between the seats to join us.

Shepherd flicked his cigarette butt out the door once Christian climbed out. "Detour."

Blue's disheveled hair obscured most of her face. "Everyone okay? Kids?"

Eve swept her hair back, her eyes glittering with tears. "My elbow hurts."

"You could have internal bleeding," Adam pointed out. "We should go to a hospital."

Eve blanched.

"This is not an option," Viktor said. "Everyone out. Shepherd will examine you. Blue, find his bag."

Adam reached for the door. "Oh, you mean the guy who almost killed us? Yeah. Sounds like a plan."

I gave Eve a boost before following. Once outside, I walked to the back of the trailer where Christian and Shepherd were standing. I spotted a dead deer beneath an overpass, but that wasn't what they were looking at.

"You got a spare?" Christian asked.

"In the back." Shepherd leaned over. "Son of a bitch."

I leaned over and saw that the tire had blown out. "Forget the tire. The trailer flipped over. We're not going anywhere."

Christian swiveled around and arched his brow. "Is that so?"

He stepped off the edge and dropped to the ground.

Adam had already jumped onto the road and was standing with his arms out, waiting for his sister.

Eve sat on the edge and jumped when the undercarriage popped. "Don't drop me!"

"Don't be a drama queen. It's like eight feet from the ground."

"But I can't see anything."

"Come on already. The gas line might be leaking, and the whole thing could blow."

Shepherd grinned. "That kid watches too many movies."

"Viktor wants you to check them over and make sure they're okay."

"If they're walking and talking, they're fine. I'll look at them after we get the tire on."

I knelt down and hopped onto the road. On the opposite side, across a grassy ditch, an eighteen-wheeler went flying by. Trees surrounded the road, and four of the streetlights were out, putting us in a dangerous spot.

On top of the trailer, Claude stood with Carol in his arms. He looked fierce, unlike the gentle giant I was used to seeing. His nostrils flared as he took in the scents around us, but any scents were likely masked by the smell of burning rubber and metal. He jumped to the ground, his knees bending with the landing as if they were shock absorbers. Carol hopped out of his arms and staggered backward.

Blue appeared next. "We need to hurry up before someone calls the state police."

Viktor sat on the edge and judged the distance before jumping off.

The RV rocked.

"Not until we're off!" Blue yelled.

"Jaysus wept. Hurry your arse up. I don't have all day."

I walked around to the other side and my jaw slackened when I found Christian squatting on the ground. "You can't lift this thing. Vamps aren't that strong."

"I'll thank you not to use that word again."

"Which one? Vamp or can't?"

Shepherd moseyed around. "Need help?"

"Unless you want to know what it feels like to be roadkill, stand aside and give me room." Christian cupped his hand around his mouth and shouted to the other side. "All clear?"

"Yeah!" Blue yelled back.

Christian anchored one knee on the ground and lifted the

trailer with a Herculean effort. Veins I'd never seen were protruding from his forehead as the RV began to rise up off the concrete.

"Better hurry," Shepherd said. "Someone might see you."

"It's dark, you eejit," he grunted out, his arms trembling as he tried to push it over. When it reached the height of his elbows, it began lowering. Christian jumped back as it hit the concrete.

I folded my arms. "What did I tell you?"

He bent over, hands on his knees. "I just needed to test how heavy it was."

I patted Shepherd on the arm. "Can you give us a minute alone? Make sure nobody slows down to help. I doubt they will, but if they see the kids they might have a bleeding-heart moment or something."

Shepherd shrugged and headed off.

"Don't let your ego kill us all," I said to Christian. "You can't lift a trailer. Don't waste Viktor's time—he needs to make other plans."

Christian shot me a baleful look. "I don't have time to dillydally around. I'll get this fecking thing upright if it kills me."

I gripped his shoulders until he stood up straight. "There's another way."

"And what idea could be weaving in that spinning wheel of yours?"

"I know a thing or two about a thing or two." I traced my finger along his jugular until his fangs elongated.

He shook his head. "We can't. A wee drop is one thing, but you're asking for too much."

I tucked my hands inside his coat and wrapped my arms around his warm body. "Lives are at stake. I can help, and you know it." I rose up on tiptoes, my lips to his neck. "Let me have a drink."

He growled low and cradled my head in his hands. "You shouldn't tempt me."

I leaned back and tipped my head to the side. "We don't have much time to fix this situation before someone calls the police and they send out a tow truck. Viktor's on a tight schedule, so we can either play this game of cat and mouse"—I leaned in and ran my fangs along his neck—"or we can lift this damn trailer and get the hell out of here. What'll it be, Mr. Poe?"

Christian didn't like the idea of making this a regular habit, especially given his history with Lenore and the control she'd had over him. But as decadent as his blood was, it had no influence over me. Not that I could tell.

Still, I wasn't going to take without asking.

"Can I drink from you?" I whispered.

He staggered forward and gave me a roguish grin. "Aye, Precious. Take all you need."

My fangs sank into his neck, deep enough to puncture the vein. Warm blood flooded my mouth, and my Vampire nature took over. I pulled hard and drank as much as he would allow. I'd forgotten how invigorating it was, how delightfully sinful. The adrenaline sharpened on my tongue, and the more I drank, the more I felt the connection between us growing. It was as if his blood was binding with my own. My sore shoulder no longer bothered me, and my cheeks flushed with the rejuvenating quality of his power. Beneath his lust, I picked up on other emotions I hadn't expected to find. Like worry.

His erection stirred against my lower belly as he gripped my hair in a loose fist.

"Gross," I heard Adam say. "They're making out."

When I leaned back, Christian locked eyes with me. The connection lingered, and it was as if we shared one mind. I licked my lips, and his eyes followed the movement of my tongue.

"Let's get this show on the road," I said.

He stepped back and bowed dramatically before extending his arm. "Ladies first."

I squatted next to the RV and wedged my fingers beneath it. Christian did the same. We looked at each other and held a silent countdown before putting our backs into it. Up until that point, the heaviest piece of machinery I'd ever moved was a washer. On a dolly. With the help of a neighbor.

The muscles in my arms were so taut that I imagined them snapping beneath my skin. My back strained beneath the weight, and my shoulders felt like they might pop right out of their sockets. But with both of us working together, we lifted that bad boy up to our chins before shifting our hands so the heels of our palms were up.

With my right knee bent, I held another silent countdown with Christian before we shoved with all our might. The trailer sailed forward and made a racket when the tires hit the concrete. For a minute, I thought we'd pushed it too hard and it might tip the other way, but it merely teetered before steadying.

Applause erupted from the other side. I blew out a breath and staggered around to keep myself from falling into the grass. *Did I just lift a thirty-foot trailer?*

"The window's busted," Christian pointed out. "You wouldn't happen to have any duct tape, now would you?"

I rubbed my back. "Ask Shepherd. That man carries the most random shit in his coat pockets."

Once I caught my breath, we joined everyone on the other side. Shepherd was eyeballing the spare tire affixed to the back.

Blue darted inside the trailer. "Where the hell are the tools?" she yelled.

Another car drove by, but this one didn't slow down. Humans were spectators who didn't like getting involved in anything that might put a damper on their schedule. Not unless it was something visually exciting to video and upload to the internet.

Claude mussed Carol's hair and strolled to the door. "I'll clean up inside."

Carol looked around, and Viktor caught her gaze.

"Why don't you children go in and help clean," he suggested. "Better you stay off the street. You might get struck by a car, and then where would we be?"

After a few groans, the kids piled in. Someone flipped on the lights, and the engine fired up briefly before cutting off.

"Engine works," Blue announced, hopping out of the trailer. She strode to the back and rested her arm on Shepherd's shoulder. "Where's the jack?"

"Fuck the jack. I need a socket wrench."

I looked alongside the bottom. "What about the storage area?"

"Jaysus wept. We'll be here a fortnight at this rate." Christian patted the tire on the back. "Let me handle it."

Shepherd poked him with his finger. "Bust that tire, and I'll bust your ass."

"Shut your gob and show me what you need."

"Show-off," I muttered, heading over to Viktor. "Anything I can do?"

He glanced at the woods. "Search the perimeter while they're fixing the wheel. I do not like this location." Viktor snapped his fingers, and Blue darted over. "How well can you see in the dark?"

"Pretty good. I don't normally fly at night though, and the trees are dense."

"Circle the area. Fly back if you see anything suspicious."

She bustled back to the trailer and looked left and right before shifting into a beautiful falcon. After she ascended into the night sky, Viktor collected her clothes and went inside.

To the sound of Shepherd and Christian's curses, I distanced myself from the trailer and traversed the woods. While I already had decent night vision, Christian's blood allowed me to see a smidge better. Perhaps even hear better, but not enough to pick up someone's heartbeat or hear a cricket tap-dancing on a rock.

I used my Mage gift to search for large currents of energy. Twigs snapped beneath my shoes, and a branch jabbed me in the ribs when I circled a tree. I broke it with ease, still marveling over my temporary Vampire strength.

I turned a sharp eye toward a movement in the tree overhead, but it was only an owl rustling its feathers. Nothing looked out of the ordinary. If someone wanted to ambush us, they would have already done it by now. But if it gave Viktor peace of mind, I was willing to get poked in the eye by sticks and step in muddy holes. Just don't let me run into a skunk.

I froze in my tracks when a rumbling growl sounded from up ahead. Bears didn't growl like that. It sounded more like a…

My heart skidded to a stop when I heard it again. Nope. That was definitely a wildcat. Probably a mountain lion. I bet it smelled the dead deer in the road and was waiting impatiently for us to leave.

This was not in the brochure.

"Nice kitty kitty," I sang, backing up slowly. Christian's blood could be unpredictable. Sometimes his strength lasted for hours, but I hadn't tested it every single time to know for certain what the limitations were. What if this thing ripped out my throat before I had a chance to fight it?

I spun around and slammed into someone.

"Miss me?" Christian asked.

I punched his shoulder. "You scared the shit out of me! Hasn't anyone ever told you that you shouldn't sneak up on people in the woods?"

"I've heard you shouldn't sneak up on a bear." He wrapped his arms around me.

"There's a hungry mountain lion nearby. We should probably get out of here."

"Scared of a little pussy?"

"And you're not?"

"Never have been." He snuggled me close to him. "My blood is coursing through your veins, and all I want to do is fuck you."

"There's a hungry animal out there."

His lips touched mine. "Aye. That would be me."

I locked my hands behind his neck. "We could get mauled."

"Not if he's behind you. You'll be the first to go."

"And you wouldn't make the ultimate sacrifice by offering your life for mine?"

He chuckled darkly. "It's not my ambition to wind up on some wild animal's dinner plate if I can help it. A mountain lion can run up to fifty miles an hour. How fast can you run?"

"So while you shadow walk to safety, I'll be nothing but a carcass on the side of the road."

"I'll be sure Shepherd stuffs your remains in the refrigerator. There's plenty of room in there."

I kissed his lips. "You're such a fanghole."

"I'd never leave you behind. Come on. Viktor's impatient."

"He's not the only one."

Chapter 13

NIKO DASHED UP THE STAIRS toward Wyatt's office as if he had wings on his heels but jerked to a stop when he turned the corner and sensed an unfamiliar light in the hallway. He drew his katanas, which airport security had almost confiscated after an hour of questioning.

"Hold up there," a man said gruffly.

Niko studied the light, and there was something familiar about it.

"It's Crush Graves. Raven's father?"

Niko lowered his swords. He'd come close to doing something regretful, and part of it was his lack of focus. Emotions were making him irrational.

"I don't give two shits," Crush growled. "Close the shop. I don't have time to worry about that right now. I'll call you later." After a beep sounded, his silver light approached. "You're probably wondering what I'm doing here."

Niko sheathed his swords, remembering that Shifters were securing the property. "I didn't notice anyone outside."

Crush clapped Niko on the shoulder. "I didn't know you could see anything, friend. Don't worry, my buddies are good about staying out of sight. I've got eyes all over the property. This is a big piece of real estate you got out here."

"Any news?"

"That Gravewalker doesn't tell me jack shit. Got a mouth on him though. Between you and me, I'd knock his lights out under different circumstances. Cocky little son of a bitch. I'm surprised Switch has held it together."

"Where's the boy?"

"Switch is keeping a close eye on him. I don't know where they are. I can't even find the damn bathroom in this place. Maybe I should stay outside."

Niko walked at a sedate pace. "No, you're safer inside. We appreciate your assistance."

"Anything I can do to help. That's a damn shame what happened to your friend. She's a sweet girl, and I hope you guys find her."

Niko rested his palm over a sharp pain that lanced through his chest. Perhaps it was just an energy spike.

Though Wyatt had booked his flight, Niko hadn't been prepared for all the security checks. His swords had to go through as checked luggage, and that required packaging them in accordance with their rules. After the flight, he had to ask an older woman to help him at the baggage claim. The modern world posed so many new obstacles that it made him appreciate the difficulties of his past.

"You're welcome to stay as long as you like," Niko offered. "Kira does the cooking, and she can make you something anytime you're hungry."

Crush's light pulsed. "I don't like other people waiting on me like I'm some kind of Daddy Warbucks. No offense. You got yourself a nice setup here, but I'll fix my own sandwich if I get hungry."

Niko entered the room, and Wyatt's smoky-blue light spun into view from his chair. The room smelled like french fries and peanuts.

"Hey, buddy. Did that cab driver I sent find you?"

"Yes." Niko eased up to the desk, and when he found the edge, he turned and leaned against it. "Tell me every detail of what happened."

A wrapper rustled as Wyatt took a bite of food. "Someone snuck their ass into the courtyard and snatched Gem. We found her kimono by the pool. She doesn't just leave her stuff lying around like that. There was water everywhere, and I swear, we didn't hear a thing. Switch picked up more than one scent, but he lost the trail."

"Viktor said you found a coin."

"Yeah." His chair squeaked, and then he said, "Here."

Niko held out his hand, palm up. When Wyatt gave him the coin, Niko considered the weight of it before feeling the edges and both sides.

"Some weird writing on it. Looks really old."

Niko bit the edge and tasted it with his tongue. He was absolutely certain that Cyrus had left it behind. It had always been his calling card. "What did the security cameras in the city reveal?"

"You're a lunatic if you think I'm going to check every camera in Cognito. We don't live near the human district anyhow. For all I know, they flew out in a helicopter. That's possible, you know. There's a lot of land out there. I once heard of a guy making an escape using one of those antigravity—"

"Stay focused," Niko said, knowing how Wyatt's train of thought often went off the rails.

Wyatt finished what was probably a candy bar as the familiar sound of the thin wrapper drifted into the wastebasket. "Crush showed up with all his Shifter buddies. Look, I know Viktor gave them the green light, but I don't like a bunch of wolves running around the property. Makes me nervous."

"You know what makes me nervous?" Crush asked. "Men who let women go swimming alone at night."

Wyatt's chair squeaked, and his blue line funneled in a circular motion. "Don't try to pin that on me. We come and go as we like around here, old man. I'm not anyone's watchdog. The courtyard is walled in. It's not like we have secret tunnels or doors out there. What are the odds that someone would scale three stories and execute the ultimate heist?"

"A heist is a robbery. What you've got is a kidnapping."

"Stealing is stealing."

Niko rapped his knuckles on the table. "Has anyone called or left a note?"

"A note?" Wyatt snorted. "I doubt any messenger can reach the door with all the wolves running around, not to mention the land mines on the property. Did you know that Crush let them sniff your dirty clothes before you arrived?"

"And if I hadn't let them, they would have torn him apart before he hit the front door," Crush retorted.

"I doubt that. Ever seen Niko use his swords? A man has a right to privacy. I don't want anyone sniffing my dirty drawers."

"I'm all out of fucks to give."

Wyatt had a tendency to get worked up when he was sleep-deprived and full of caffeine and sugar. Cyrus had to be behind this, and the wolves posed a problem. Cyrus would need a way to reach out to Niko with his demands. If he sent one of his men, the wolves would tear him to pieces.

Cyrus wouldn't risk it, which meant he was waiting for Niko to make the next move.

Niko stood up and removed his sword belt and laid his sheathed weapons on the desk. "I'm going for a walk. Crush, can you instruct the wolves to stay away from me? Keep them close to the house but no farther out than a hundred feet."

"I'll try, but they've already marked the territory."

"Is there an alpha?"

"Yep. Good buddy of mine. Don't know how long he'll be able to stay, but he's assigned his best men. I'll go talk to him."

Niko bowed to show his respect. He couldn't reveal too much information since Crush wasn't a member of Keystone. Once Raven's father left the room, Niko lowered his voice. "If Viktor calls, tell him I'm reaching out to the kidnappers. I know who's behind this."

"Now that's a plot twist I didn't see coming. Who? Never mind. That's not as important as why they would snatch Gem."

"They want something from me. Inform Viktor that if anyone calls him looking for me, give that person my number. I don't think that's how he'll make contact, but just in case. Cyrus is a man who prefers dealing with people face-to-face, but he won't come close if wolves are on the property."

"Uh, maybe you should take your weapons. He might want you dead."

"Needn't worry. My death isn't what he desires. I'm afraid the only way to get Gem back is to capitulate. Swords will give him the opposite impression, so I must leave them behind. If he thinks he can't trust me, we may never see her again."

"Holy Toledo. You think he'd really do something to Gem? She wouldn't hurt a fly. Well, except for those people she blasted that time in the Bricks."

Niko turned to the door and froze in his tracks. "Don't come looking for me, Wyatt."

"Just don't get your head lopped off. If you come back as a freshy, I'll kick your kung fu ass."

Niko plodded to the first floor, giving Crush enough time to relay the orders to his friends. Switch's voice reverberated off the walls in the dining room. He must have been eating breakfast with Hunter and Kira. Niko didn't have time for conversation. He didn't even have time to formulate a plan.

He only had enough time to save Gem.

Wyatt rubbed his eyes, struggling to stay awake. He'd zoned out a few times while working on Viktor's route and reviewing traffic reports. Viktor didn't want to get stuck in a gridlock, so Wyatt had to monitor the situation in case an alternative route was needed. As if he didn't have enough to do, Gem went missing. And things really went to shit when he had to work out Niko's travel arrangements on the fly.

Wyatt rolled his chair in front of the vending machine and stared at his reflection. He looked worse than a six-hundred-year-old specter. Without his beanie on, his hair was sticking out in every direction as if he'd stuck his finger in a light socket. Why couldn't it lie flat like a normal person's follicles? Nope. He got the crazy-hair gene.

His stomach growled like a dog guarding its food bowl. How

long had Niko been gone? Maybe he'd changed his mind and gone down to the training room to do all that weird balancing shit. Wyatt had lost track of time. He liked it that way. A window in his workspace would only make him aware of the time, and he couldn't afford to nod off when he had a job to do. It was probably morning by now.

Hell, it was probably November.

In the middle of another yawn, Wyatt stood up and peeled off his T-shirt. After a quick whiff of his armpit, he headed down the hall to take a long hot shower. A man can't work nonstop. It's not good for the brain cells or the pit smells. So long as he kept his computer and phone alarms on, he could take micro naps on the sofa in his office.

When he turned the corner, he couldn't help but wince at the thought of running into a freshy. Even though it had been months since they were cleared from the house, he never got over that creepy feeling that someone might have followed him home. Ghosts were like leaves that tracked in the house. The specter that followed Niko home was proof of that, but at least he left Wyatt alone. The upside of Keystone was that it was secluded enough that the dead wouldn't wander into the house on their own. It was one of the main reasons Wyatt had accepted the job. A Gravewalker would never have peace living in the city; the dead were everywhere.

He started humming the words to "Even the Nights Are Better." Seventies and eighties soft rock had a special place in his heart. It took him back to another time in his life—a time when he'd finally gotten out of the Gravewalker business after his computer hobby had led to a career change.

Dealing with ghosts had never been a cakewalk. Who could sleep with specters wandering around the bedroom at night, asking for favors? Conversing with the dead and making deals was a way of life for his kind, but it took its toll. Wyatt had met many a Gravewalker who'd lost his marbles. Yet he'd begrudgingly accepted his fate for lack of options.

All that changed when Wyatt discovered computers. He was one of the first to get a personal computer after they hit the market in the late seventies. Arcade games had always intrigued him, and he'd even dabbled in designing a few. Computers came naturally to him, and he excelled ahead of others, enough that he did programming and repair as a side job. He didn't make much in the early days, but the internet changed everything. It allowed him to communicate with other Breed and do special research assignments. The higher authority, Mageri, and other organizations were late to the party when it came to the importance of data, so Wyatt was on one of the first teams assembled to hack into government systems and search for any files on Breed. He trained recruits hired by the authorities to use computers so they could get jobs at key companies to monitor Breed activity.

Now it was commonplace. Immortals were everywhere. Planted in the military, hotels, hospitals, border crossings, prisons—anywhere you could think of in order to track Breed.

It had all been going great until he got greedy and wanted more money. There was a cap on how much he could earn with the higher authority, and users on the dark web were offering money to locate people. Wyatt didn't ask questions. He just took the money and passed along the info. Seemed like an easy way to make cash.

Until he found out his contacts were professional killers.

Someone had been monitoring Wyatt's activities and reported him when they discovered that all the people he'd gathered information on were dead or missing. How the hell was he supposed to know what the client wanted it for?

Wyatt fell out of the song as the memories made him livid all over again. It wasn't as if he was doing the killing, but that wasn't how the authorities saw it. After confiscating his money, they made him serve a short sentence in Breed jail. Technically he hadn't broken any laws, so they had to release him. Freedom didn't matter. His reputation was ruined. He'd lost his home, his job, his life savings, the respect of his peers, and eventually his girl. He was no better off than the poor schmucks floating around in the afterlife. At least he could enjoy food and play video games. The dead could only watch.

Wyatt made a fist and looked at the ink on his right hand that spelled out LOST. The tattoos on his fingers were a reminder that nothing lasts forever. That one minute you can be on top of the world, and the next you're nothing but a ghost. Never get attached to a life, a person, money, love, or happiness. Even Keystone wouldn't last forever. Eventually he'd screw up.

Like now.

Viktor had left him in charge, and all hell was breaking loose. Gem was missing, wolves were on the property, and he was almost out of chocolate donuts.

What if Niko got himself killed? The thought made him panicky. He should have never let him go, but Wyatt hadn't had a moment of clarity in twenty-four hours.

When he reached the first floor, he blindly grabbed a jacket from the closet. His thoughts were scrambled as he jogged down the hall on the right.

Just when he reached the painting and turned the corner, he slammed into Switch and pirouetted toward the bright blue windows. "Son of a ghost! Don't sneak up on a guy like that."

Switch frowned. "Is there something you need help with?"

Wyatt glanced behind him and quelled his anger. "Yeah, keep a better eye on the kid."

"Kira's giving him a bath. He's fine." Switch's lips twitched when he noticed Wyatt's jacket. "New fashion style?"

Wyatt looked down at the sparkly silver jacket that barely reached his navel. "It's Gem's. I wasn't paying attention." The sleeves barely went past his elbows, and they were tight. Wyatt tugged at them anyway. "I'm going out to look for Niko."

"I thought you two had a plan?"

Wyatt headed down the hall toward the side exit. "Yeah. *His* plan was to get himself kidnapped, but I'm all booked up on crazy. And if any of your wolf buddies decide to make me into a snack, I'm gonna haunt them from the afterlife."

"They know my scent. They'll stay back."

"What scent is that, Shifter? The scent of toxic masculinity?"

Switch glared down at him. "You seem insecure."

Wyatt liked Switch, but he couldn't help but bust his chops. A guy like that would steal his thunder if they took him out to the bar. Wyatt had always been the guy in their group that the chicks flocked to, and that was saying something considering Claude's good looks. But not everyone loved Chitahs or extremely tall men. If this Switch thing turned out to be permanent, that meant Gaston here was going to serve up competition.

After a brief flash of disappointment, Wyatt glanced down at his chest through the open jacket. *Nah.* There was way too much man here to admire, even if he didn't have all that extra muscle tone and height.

I need a nap, he thought.

As soon as they stepped outside, a black wolf raised his head from a grove of trees up ahead.

"If I were you, I wouldn't look that one directly in the eye," Switch advised. "That's Tank. He was Raven's watchdog for quite a few years. She didn't know it. I heard a rumor that he did barbaric things to some old pervert who was trying to give Raven a ride home one afternoon. Tank's a badass. Nobody fucks with him."

Wyatt's heart thumped in his chest. He didn't fear death—Gravewalkers rarely did—but it was the dying part that kept him on his toes. There are particular ways a man doesn't want to die, and in the jaws of a predator is one of them. Sometimes the dead remembered their last moments, and they liked to talk about the agony and horror of it all. Wyatt had heard enough gruesome stories to give him nightmares in the afterlife. Especially from the guy who was pushed into a meat grinder and—

"You got a shitload of land out here," Switch remarked. "You could build a dozen homes. What do you do with it all?"

"Fly kites."

"Packs dream about property like this."

Behind the house were rolling hills. The Shifters who used to live here must have cleared away a good number of trees near the house to provide more visibility, security, and running room. Wyatt and Switch walked a long distance across the wet grass until they reached the far corner of the property. Wyatt knew where the property line ended based on tree markers, but did Niko? He might be lost.

"Niko has a funny way of blending in with his surroundings like some kind of chameleon, so keep your eyes open," he said to Switch.

"Who needs eyes?"

Switch morphed into a brown wolf, and Wyatt hopped back a step.

"If you put one fang on me, you're toast."

Switch's wolf peeled back his teeth in a grotesque smile before turning his head away and lifting his nose to the air. After a beat, he trotted off and searched the perimeter.

Wyatt grumbled as he trudged through a dense grove of trees. His ass still hurt, and if he didn't have so much work to do, he'd smoke a little cannabis to deaden the pain. Shepherd had taken all the Neosporin and peroxide for his trip, leaving Wyatt with nothing but bandages and alcohol.

He cupped his hands around his mouth. "Niko?"

Too bad they weren't situated near a cemetery. Gravewalkers could pick up on the living in a cemetery, but it only seemed to work around a number of dead bodies. Some had heightened abilities to detect a living body no matter where they were, but usually that wasn't how it worked. It also helped when there were ghosts on-site who could point in the direction of someone who didn't belong. Even the dead were picky about who they wanted in their neighborhood.

"Niko!" he yelled, his voice swallowed up by the open space. A few birds scattered from the trees, and the next time he yelled, he stretched out all the vowels.

Barking snagged his attention, and he jogged toward the sound. Wyatt weaved around thick trees and hopped over twisted roots, the jacket tightening with every step as if reminding him that Gem was missing.

He tripped over a rock and windmilled his arms before regaining his balance.

Switch's brown wolf blended in with their surroundings, so it took Wyatt a minute to spot him.

Wyatt strode up and looked at where Switch had pawed through the leaves. He knelt down and studied the deep mark in the mud, which wasn't a typical footprint. It didn't look like a struggle but more like the heel of someone's shoe digging up the earth as they pivoted around.

Wyatt stood up and shouted with urgency, "Niko!"

Switch's wolf trotted around the area, sniffing everything in sight. When he began barking again, Wyatt hurried over. He lifted a leather hair tie from a small twig poking out of a tree. It was intentionally placed, and it belonged to Niko. Wyatt didn't recall him wearing his hair up earlier, but Niko often carried one in his pocket.

That hair tie was a message that he'd left of his own free will.

"Blast! You just *had* to go and do it, didn't you?" He flicked the tie on the ground. "This is superb. Two people missing, and one of them I let walk right out the door. Niko, if you don't find Gem and bring her home, I'm dead meat. I might as well reserve my spot under the bridge, because that's where I'll be living for the rest of my life. Like a troll."

Switch shifted to human form and gave his surroundings a cursory glance. He didn't seem to recall the shift. "What happened?"

"Niko's gone, that's what happened. Gone. Poof. *Sayonara.*"

"How do you know?"

"I found one of his hair ties over yonder," Wyatt said, pointing at the tree.

Switch gave him a skeptical look and pursed his lips. "You did, huh? All by yourself? That's amazing. One tiny hair tie in all this forest, and you happened to—"

"Do me a favor and shift back. Nobody wants to see all that," he said, waving a hand at Switch's privates.

Switch ignored him and pulled a leaf off a tree as they kept walking. "Are we outside the property line?"

"Yup. And your wolves didn't rescue him."

"They were instructed to stay away. Did your friend go willingly?"

Wyatt jumped ahead of Switch. "Why don't you send a few of your friends to track them down?"

"No can do."

Wyatt turned and cast him a sharp glare. "And why not?"

"News flash—you have a child in that house and a helpless woman. Whatever Viktor has planned for you is nothing compared to what Shepherd would do if his kid went missing."

Damn, he had a point.

Switch halted and looked skyward. "You hear that?"

Wyatt cocked his head and turned. The wind carried a faint sound that didn't belong in these woods. A repeated buzzing.

They both jogged back to where they'd just been.

Wyatt shielded his view of Switch with his hand. "It's even worse when you run."

Switch shifted to wolf form and sprinted ahead of Wyatt.

Out of breath and his ass throbbing, Wyatt slowed his pace when he caught Switch nosing around where they'd found the hair tie. "I'm fixin' to take you to the vet and put you in that cone of shame."

Switch pawed at the leaves.

Wyatt bent down and spotted Niko's phone. Niko didn't use the newer models since they would require him to use voice command, which wasn't allowed for privacy reasons. His was a simple one with push buttons.

The phone vibrated again, and Wyatt cringed when he saw the number on the display.

He pushed Talk and steadied his breath. "Hi, Viktor. Don't kill me, but we've got another problem."

Chapter 14

I PEERED THROUGH THE BROKEN SHUTTERS—NOTHING but sunshine and rolling hills as far as the eye could see. We'd finally hit a few small towns, the roads bordered by telephone poles and old homes. "I've never seen so many trees in my life."

Claude looked at me from the adjacent sofa, his arm resting on the back and his face turned my way. "You sound disappointed. Miss the smell of garbage bins and pollution already?"

He rubbed his bright-red nose and zipped his coat all the way up. The window next to him had been smashed during the accident, so outside air was roaring against the shutters and cooling the interior. Shepherd had briefly pulled over to a secluded area so he could give the tires and engine a closer inspection, but Viktor didn't want to make any more stops until after sunrise, so we pressed on.

We killed time talking about great inventions and history. Blue sat quietly beside me, listening to Christian and Claude reminiscing about the good old days of horse-drawn carriages. Adam and his sister had gone back into the sleeper, and Carol was in the back. The kids needed to rest up as much as possible. I noticed that Claude kept checking on Carol. Maybe he felt sorry for her because she didn't have anyone, but he periodically walked to the back and sniffed the door. Creepy, but Blue explained that it was Claude's way of looking out for her. I simply didn't get Chitahs and all their strange customs.

When the RV slowed down, the chatter stopped and everyone looked out the windows.

Viktor put on his aviator sunglasses and turned his attention to the group. "People in small towns ask questions. We are on a family vacation. I am the grandfather and do not speak since my stroke."

Claude laughed. "A stroke?"

A comb appeared in Viktor's hand, and he began styling his hair and beard. "I cannot speak with this accent. It is one that makes me easy to remember, and not one that many people trust. Christian, you should also refrain from speaking."

Christian made me jump with surprise when he answered in a Southern accent just as sweet as Southern tea. "Don't you worry, Grandpappy. I fit in just fine with the locals."

I smiled at him. "That's a nifty accent you got there, Farmer Poe."

He pretended to tip an invisible hat on his head. "Comes in handy."

Blue stood up and stretched. "You almost sound like someone I could like."

I looked out the window at a few buildings along the two-lane road. A community bank, some houses, a chapel, and a backdrop of rolling hills. "Something tells me they don't have a Walmart."

Shepherd pulled the camper into the parking lot of a tiny gas station. It looked like we were on Main Street of a small town.

I quickly hopped out of the trailer and soaked up the morning sun. There was a Dairy Queen down to the right and a McDonald's to the left. "Food run. Anyone hungry?"

"Me!" Eve shouted as she emerged from the trailer.

Adam followed sluggishly behind her, his complexion as green as his shirt. "Do they have a bathroom?"

"There's one in the trailer," I reminded him.

He shook his head. "I need to be alone."

Shepherd clapped him on the shoulder. "Come with me, kid."

Eve sidled up and giggled. "He's carsick. He also doesn't like pooping around people. He got in trouble a lot because he'd sneak off and go up to the top floor. Nobody ever went up there, so the bathroom was always empty."

"Too much information," I said, pivoting on my heel and

assessing the trailer in daylight. It had definitely taken a beating, but somehow that made us stand out even less.

Eve's teeth chattered. "I'm going back inside."

"Stay inside. I mean it."

Christian stepped out of the trailer, looking dapper. He'd changed into jeans and a chocolate-brown Henley.

"You want to come with me?" I asked.

"Better I stay here. Shepherd has a tendency of getting himself in trouble. He hasn't quite mastered the skill of friendliness, and we still have a window to patch up." Christian slid on his sunglasses. "Don't you want your coat?"

I straightened my charcoal-colored T-shirt. "Nah. I'll warm up once I start walking."

Blue appeared, her straight hair shining like silk in the sun. She had on green cargo pants with her soft brown leather jacket. "Where are you going?"

"McDonald's, I guess."

She frowned at the building nearby. "What's Hardee's?"

Carol jumped out and bolted toward the convenience store. Claude chased after her. "Hold up!"

Blue joined my side as we ventured up the road. "It's pretty here," she said. "You forget what quiet sounds like until you're out of the city. It's one reason why I like living at Keystone."

We cut through a parking lot since there wasn't a sidewalk. A few cars drove by and slowed down, no doubt locals getting a gander at the tourists. Hopefully we looked like tourists instead of mercenary killers.

"Why do they keep staring?" I asked. "They act like they've never seen a woman before."

"Maybe it's the dagger strapped to your leg."

I looked down. "Shit. I forgot." After unlatching the strap, I tucked it in my jeans beneath my T-shirt.

"Don't worry. I'm sure there are a lot of hunters out here. But maybe they're not used to seeing a woman walking around this early, fully armed." Blue chuckled, and I noticed the axe affixed to her side.

"Don't you want to hide that?"

"No. I'm good."

"They're going to kick you out of McDonald's."

"Not exactly a travesty." She took off her jacket and tied it around her waist so it covered the weapon. After adjusting her tank top, she squinted at the buildings ahead. "There's a grocery store up there. Viktor might need supplies." She stopped and sent a text message.

I neared the door to the fast-food place. "Adam probably needs a quart of the pink stuff. He's got stomach issues."

She continued staring at her phone. "Viktor wants duct tape and plastic bags for the broken window. You good here?"

I laughed and headed inside. Duct tape and plastic bags. Nope. Nothing suspicious about that.

Inside, only two employees manned the register. Not a single customer to be found.

When I approached the counter, my hair stood on end. Someone in or around this establishment was a Mage. Their energy was carelessly swirling around me like air hissing out of a flat tire.

"What can I get for you?" the lanky man asked. The name tag on his dark shirt said "Willie."

I shielded my light. Willie had light eyes and crooked teeth, and he stared at me for a long while.

"Are you new here?" he asked. "I'm new. Second week on the job. But I've tried everything on the menu. The sausage biscuits are good."

"I'm sure they are, Willie. I'm just suddenly not hungry anymore."

He frowned. "Thirsty? We got orange juice, coffee—"

"No, never mind. Sorry to bother you."

He waved as I backed up toward the door. "No bother at all. Hope to see you around."

The woman in the back was staring at me, and I didn't like it.

Once outside, I glanced at a car in the drive-through and hurried toward the road. We needed to get the hell out of here. Especially since we were carrying special cargo. As I turned to head back, a silver truck pulled out of the gas station next door. When he turned left, it forced the oncoming car to hit the brakes.

I looked at the windshield of the car and froze.

Is that Carol?

Without thinking, I jogged into the road to get a better look. I fully expected it to be the sun playing tricks on me, but hell no, that was Carol sitting in the passenger seat. The driver's eyes widened when he saw me staring daggers at him. When Carol shouted at him, he turned the wheel and almost ran me over as they steered into oncoming traffic. Luckily there was no traffic this early.

"Carol!" I ran toward the car and slapped the trunk as it sped off.

This was a hot mess. I had no time to dial Viktor or get Blue when we had a kidnapper on our hands.

"Feet don't fail me now." Taking a quick glance around for witnesses, I flashed after their car.

It didn't take long before I reached the bumper. The driver steered around a curve, and instead of following, I cut straight across the grass to head them off. Without missing a step, I jumped onto the hood of the white car and nearly rolled off before gripping the windshield wiper. When it snapped, I tucked my fingers inside the top of the hood. A police station flew past my view.

"Stop the car!" I pounded on the windshield.

Since I was blocking his view, he leaned over to see around me.

Carol frantically grabbed his arm and tried to pry his hand off the steering wheel. Then she gripped her seat belt and screamed, her eyes as wide as saucers. The drive got a lot bumpier when the road abruptly ended and we sped onto the grass. My only goal at this point was to save my ass from sliding off and falling under the tires.

I ran over the roof, jumped on the back, and rolled safely to the ground.

A loud crash exploded behind me, and I staggered to my feet.

The car had smashed into a dense thicket of trees and bushes. Smoke hissed from the engine beneath the crumpled hood.

"Carol!" My heart lurched at the sight of it all.

I skidded down the hill to the driver's side and yanked the door open. An involuntary shriek escaped my lips when a large mountain lion tackled me to the ground. I blasted him with energy seconds before he went for my throat.

I scuttled backward, pulled the dagger from inside my jeans, and unsheathed it. As I crawled on my knees toward the animal, Carol fought her way through the airbags.

No way in hell I was letting this bastard get away. I raised my arm to jam the blade into his heart.

"No!" Carol screamed, spilling out onto the grass. "Don't hurt him!"

She shielded the mountain lion with her body, her thin arms wrapped around him and tears welling in her eyes.

I lowered my weapon.

She knew him.

This wasn't a kidnapping by some crazed rogue. Carol knew this guy, and they must have been planning her escape.

Lights flashed behind us, accompanied by the intermittent sound of sirens wailing.

Disastrous.

"This is gonna get ugly," I promised her. "That cop won't blink twice about shooting a wild animal. If you know this guy and care what happens to him, don't let him get up."

Worry pooled in her green eyes as she whispered in his ear.

"Drop your weapon," the cop shouted.

I rolled my neck around as the urge to defend myself came on strong.

Not here, Raven. Not now.

When the dagger fell from my hand to the grass, I slowly raised my arms and tried to keep my cool.

The cop approached, his shiny black shoes rustling in the dewy grass.

"There's a mountain lion." I pointed to the animal. "I was just trying to protect myself."

"He's unconscious," Carol said, still clutching the animal. "Don't hurt him. He didn't do anything."

If this guy shifted in front of the cop, we were dead meat. I'd have no choice but to attack a cop and pin him until Christian could scrub his memories. I had a soft spot for humans, especially ones who were just doing their job.

"Don't move," he said, inching in closer.

I peered over my shoulder and saw he had his gun drawn.

"Sir, the animal caused the accident."

"And I suppose you jumped onto the hood of a moving vehicle for what exactly?"

He lifted my dagger and pricked his finger with it. "A stunner, huh? We don't like trouble around here."

My mouth fell open, and I shifted around to get a closer look.

The cop, who could have been a stunt double for Burt Reynolds, put his gun back in the holster. "You're a little far from home, aren't you?"

When I furrowed my brow, he pointed at the plates on the car.

"It's a long story," I began. "We didn't mean to crash the car; we were just, uh, goofing around."

He looked at Carol. "Your Shifter friend there better change before someone else comes along." When I started to get up, he touched his gun. "Did I say you could stand? Stay right where you are."

"I'm not a threat," I assured him, choosing my words carefully.

"I beg to differ. You flashed down the road in broad daylight, you jumped onto a moving vehicle, and you attempted to murder a Shifter."

"Attempted isn't the same as doing it."

He gave me a probing gaze. "You still flashed in public view. That's a Breed violation, and I'll have to take you in."

Going to Breed jail wasn't an option. "You're kidding me, right? We're in the middle of nowhere."

When the mountain lion transformed to a man, Carol shielded her eyes and reached in the car for his clothes.

"I'm not looking," she announced. "Put your clothes on, Joshua. There's a cop."

Joshua sat up and glared over his shoulder at me. While he had mannish features, the twinkle in his eyes was that of a boy. They didn't look related, not with his shaggy black hair and dark eyes.

"How old are you?" I asked with derision.

He put on his jeans and stood up to button them. "Sixteen."

"You do realize she's only fourteen."

"And I just turned sixteen. We're *both* minors. Your point?"

"You don't look like a minor," I grumbled, noting his broad chest and height. Maybe I was getting so old that I couldn't tell a person's age anymore, but they sure didn't have boys like that in my old high school.

"I got my dad's genes," he said, arms folded.

"You look like you play professional football."

He narrowed his eyes. "Maybe I should."

Definitely a teenager's attitude.

"If you're only sixteen, do you even have a driver's license?"

"Do *you*? Last I checked, none of us were allowed to take a written exam. Everyone has a fake ID, and I can pass for driving age."

"You can pass for drinking age."

"I'm Officer Barnes," the cop interrupted. "Are you two kids okay? That's quite a spill you took."

Joshua glowered at me. "This crazy woman jumped on my car and scared the shit out of me. I lost control."

Carol looked back at the damaged car and paced. "We have to go."

"You better not move an inch," I said to her. "You have no idea how much trouble you're in."

Officer Barnes kicked my foot. "Keep quiet." He crouched behind me and forcefully grabbed my arm, slapping a handcuff around my wrist. "You're under arrest."

"For what? I didn't break any laws."

"You want to look at it from my point of view? I catch you violating Breed law and flashing down the road, causing this car to speed off the road and nearly killing these kids. Then I catch you about to put a dagger into that boy. We got a special place for people like you."

The way he said it put a knot in my stomach. I had to find a way to stall long enough for Viktor to locate us and get Carol away from this bozo.

I swung my eyes up to a screeching falcon. Blue's bird was easy to identify, and she surveyed the scene before flapping away. Carol noticed her too, and her expression quickly switched from panic to defeat. It wasn't as if they were getting far with a wrecked vehicle.

After Officer Barnes cuffed my wrists, he stood up. "Do you two kids have someone you can call?"

Carol shrugged and leaned against the car. "We're kinda here with someone. They'll probably be here any minute now."

Joshua cursed and turned his back to us, hands on his hips. What in the world was a Shifter doing with Carol? And why would she run away with some guy when he could never offer her the kind of protection the higher authority could?

Officer Barnes yanked me up. "Good. Are you sure you kids are all right? We don't have any Relics in town, but I can always call one in."

Yeah, don't mind me. I was almost eaten by Carol's boyfriend, but sure, ask how they're doing.

Carol reached in the car and pulled out her bag. "I'm sorry about your car, Joshua."

He prowled toward her and cupped her face. I tensed when I thought they were about to make out in front of me, but instead he simply rubbed noses with her.

"Nothing's your fault," he said.

I stumbled as the policeman dragged me to his vehicle. "Where are you taking me?"

"Breed jail."

Chapter 15

O FFICER BARNES DIDN'T BOTHER TO wait for my team even though I asked him to. This man didn't give a damn about anything other than locking me up. In his eyes, I was a menace to his small town. After driving down a dirt road, we finally reached a red brick building. There were no windows or parking spaces, and there was certainly no sign out front indicating that this was an official police station. It also didn't look like a legit Breed jail. Those places were large with multiple stories.

"What is this, redneck hell?" I shivered from a cracked window blowing air into the back.

He shut off the engine. "You might be able to get away with flaunting your gifts in the big city, but out here, people pay attention. I'm the only officer in this town who knows about Breed, so it's my job to take care of people like you. It's bad enough I gotta deal with all the Shifters running around and getting into territorial disputes."

"Don't they have a Council out here?"

He snorted and opened his door. "Honey, this is West Virginia. You might have Councils in the big city, but when you're a stone's throw away from tens of thousands of acres of national park, a Council is pretty damn useless."

Officer Barnes stepped out of the vehicle and opened my door. I reluctantly slid out and followed him to the building, my hands still cuffed. He used a key on his ring to unlock the heavy door, and once inside, he switched on a light.

The steel door ahead had a small opening wide enough to peer through but not to poke your hand through. It was nothing more than an additional barrier between the prisoners and freedom. The room we were in didn't have any furniture except for a giant locker on the left.

He patted me down and removed the small push dagger strapped to my belt.

"Wait a second," I said, thinking about the isolation of this place. "You're not gonna leave me here by myself, are you? Don't you have a secretary or deputy?"

He snickered and opened the heavy door. The next room was pitch-black. Light poured in from the front room and spotlighted the jail cells. There were a total of six, each with bars in the front and walls between.

Each cell had chains attached to the far wall.

Fight or flight kicked in, and I came to a hard stop.

Officer Barnes caught the direction of my stare. "Don't worry, those are for the Shifters. Some are less likely to shift with a cuff attached to their ankle or neck. I had a problem a few years back with a boa Shifter. Slithered right out of his cell. The chains keep them in line. Nobody wants to break bones or strangle themselves."

I let out a nervous laugh and stepped into the cell after he opened it. "What do you do about Vampires?"

He slid the door shut. "Turn around."

When I did, Barnes unlocked my handcuffs. If they chained Shifters to keep some of them under control, they probably staked Vampires to keep them from breaking the bars. Hopefully this guy didn't get any ideas to put a stunner in me.

An incessant pounding came from the outside door.

"I take it those are your friends?"

I gripped the bars anxiously and watched him exit the room. Since the door was farther to the right, I couldn't see anything.

But I didn't need to see.

I heard.

"This is a real dandy little setup you've got here," Christian said, not holding back on his annoyance. "And what would the other guards say about your kidnapping innocent people?"

"Innocent? Your friend here broke the law. We don't allow public displays of Breed gifts, and she was flashing down the street."

"It's only a crime if there were witnesses."

"I'm a witness."

"You hardly count, you insipid little man."

"My friend does not mean to insult," Viktor cut in. "Can we speak for a moment?"

Footfalls overlapped, and I moved to the corner of the cell to try to catch a glimpse.

"You're gonna have a hell of a time backing that RV outta here," Officer Barnes said.

Christian briefly appeared in the open doorway and regarded me for a moment before steering his attention away.

"Don't get any bright ideas, Vamp," the cop warned him.

Christian's gaze drifted down. "Do you have a holster for those too?"

Barnes was either holding impalement wood or a brass set of balls.

"There has been a misunderstanding," Viktor said, doing a magnificent job at keeping his cool. "She was merely following my orders. One of our young ones disappeared with a boy. Not acceptable. Raven was only bringing her safely back to me. Come outside. You can speak with her yourself."

"I don't like to get involved in personal affairs," Barnes replied. "Everyone's got an excuse. But around here, I've gotta keep the peace. I can't afford to have the locals exposed to your shenanigans. You and I both know that the higher authority wouldn't approve, or in this case, the Mageri. She can either serve out her sentence, or I can call the Mageri and ask what *they'd* like me to do with her."

My eyes rounded, and I vehemently shook my head at Christian. I'd rather do my time than be handed over to the Mageri. While Viktor had secured my position with Keystone, the Mageri still scared me. They held absolute power. What would they do if they found out I was a crossbreed? What would they do if they found out about my past crimes?

Christian folded his arms. "Can we not make this worth your

time? I'm sure it'll cost precious taxpayer dollars to feed and care for this one. We can work something out."

"I don't feed my prisoners, so it ain't costing taxpayers jack shit. And you better think twice about bribing an officer of the law, especially one assigned this post by the higher authority. I want the names of all of you so I can report it to my contact."

"This is not necessary," Viktor insisted. "I will call someone and settle this matter."

"Are you trying to outrank me?" Barnes asked in a huff. "My contact keeps your info in case you decide to bust your friend out of here. If that door is open when I return later, I'll know who did it. It doesn't matter who your connections are. She broke the law, and I represent the higher authority out here. I *am* the law."

I watched Christian narrow his eyes.

"Like it or not, this is how we keep the locals in line."

"Aye, but we're not local," Christian pointed out.

Barnes appeared in front of Christian's face and didn't look away. "I don't care if you're passing through. If you're not smart enough to respect the laws in one town, what's to stop you from breaking them everywhere you go? Better your friend learn now what's permissible. She might wind up in another small town that isn't so forgiving."

"Is there no bail?" Viktor inquired. "We will be more than happy to face any sentencing or punishment. I can provide you with our names and information, but can you release her on bail and schedule a hearing or sentencing date?"

Barnes turned sharply and groomed his mustache. "She stays. We don't have any hotels in town, but seeing as you have an RV, you shouldn't have a problem sticking around until her sentence is served."

Christian dropped his arms to his sides and clenched his fists. "And how long is that?"

"Fifteen days."

"Without food?"

"Yep. You're lucky I don't put a stunner in her, but she's been cooperative. As long as she stays that way, I won't have to take drastic measures to keep her subdued."

"Can we see her?" Viktor asked, the disappointment in his voice thinly veiled. "Please allow us a chance to speak with her."

"Be my guest."

Viktor and Christian shuffled into the dark room and approached the bars.

I couldn't look him in the eye. "Viktor, I'm so sorry. I thought that guy was kidnapping her, and there wasn't time to do anything else."

"He *was* kidnapping her, but not against will. Claude was using bathroom when girl escaped."

Despite his cool façade, Viktor was upset. He was dropping words from his sentences left and right.

Viktor took a calming breath and shook his head. "Had you not chased her down, it would be Claude in here instead of you. I am not letting children out of sight again. If not external dangers, we have to worry about children running away. Children become afraid when moving locations, but I did not sense they would be a problem."

"So her boyfriend, what happened to him?" I asked.

"You're not the only prisoner," Christian replied coolly. "We can't let the arseface go free."

"Scrub his memories," I suggested. "And make him believe he's a sheep Shifter."

"That was my idea. The erasing, not the sheep. But I like where you're going with that."

Viktor shook his head. "We will do no such thing. He is a child, and we will turn him over to his family or Council."

I leaned back, still gripping the bars. "So you're taking him where we're going? Isn't that a security breach?"

Viktor sighed and tugged on his turtleneck collar. "I have not planned that far ahead. I cannot release him since he knows too much, and we have not completed our mission. It would also be remiss of me to set free someone who could follow and bring even greater danger. I have no choice. Perhaps the compound will take him in."

"Against his will? If he escapes, he'll know too much."

"We must tread carefully when it comes to children," Viktor cautioned me. "Breed laws protect all children under the age of eighteen. If he were just a few years older, we could take any action necessary."

I lowered my head, frustrated that I couldn't go with them.

"Do not blame yourself, Raven. Your sacrifice saved a child. One must prepare for the unexpected, and this is why I included so many on this mission."

"For feck's sake, Viktor. We can't just leave her here to rot."

"I have no choice," he said matter-of-factly. "The children come first. It is only for fifteen days. I know you two are in relations now, but we had an understanding. If you cannot perform your duties because of separation, I have no place for you on my team."

I let go of the bars. "Viktor's right. I'll stake you myself if you stay. And who knows? Maybe I'll get on his good side and Barnes will let me out on good behavior."

Christian tipped his head to the side. "And maybe unicorns will fly out of my arse."

Viktor reached through the bars and gripped my shoulder. "I will call my contact and see what I can do to release you. But we are going to an area where our phones may not work. I have a satellite phone to keep in touch with Wyatt, so if you are released early, call him. He might be able to give you directions if I think you are close enough to rejoin us. But be prepared to go home." Viktor withdrew his arm.

"It's fine. I don't want to hold you guys up. Just keep an eye on Joshua. If they tried running off once, they'll do it again."

"Claude put fear into the boy. No one wants an angry Chitah tracking them. I will try once more to speak with the officer." Viktor shook his head, looking conflicted. "I have no choice."

"I understand," I said convincingly, even though deep down, I wanted them to break me out of here. But that would bring a hell of a lot more trouble, not to mention jeopardizing the mission.

"Fifteen days isn't that bad. I've got a roof over my head and all the privacy a woman could want. I'm just glad we got Carol back."

Viktor nodded and disappeared out the door.

Christian gripped the bars and rested his forehead against them. "I could break these into a million pieces."

I sidled over and put my hands on his. "Don't even try it. That cop will stake you and put you in the next cell. Look, I'll be fine. Probably a lot safer than you guys. Viktor needs to know we're serious about this job, so you have to stay focused."

"I'll have you know this ruins my plans to flatten you on top of the trailer while going sixty down the highway."

I stood on my tiptoes and wanted to touch noses with him like I'd seen Carol and Joshua do, but all I could do was rest my head against the bars. What was fifteen days? Eventually Viktor would send one of us on a three-month assignment. We couldn't let separation divide us, no matter the length of time.

But damn if it didn't feel like an amputation of my heart. I wanted to be with him, protect him and help the team.

"I can scrub his memories," Christian offered on a breath, his eyes closed. "He'll never feel a thing."

"Stay out of trouble. I'll figure something out."

"That's enough," Officer Barnes snapped from the doorway. "Get a move on. I've got work to do."

Christian's eyes locked with mine, and he kept holding the bars as he stepped back. I knew how devoted this man was to me. He'd tattooed a raven on his body, for crying out loud. But the look on his face—it reached deep down into my chest and seized my heart.

It was that feeling that he was mine, and I was his.

When he left the room, I heard him say, "If you mistreat her, I'll hunt you down and remove your spine."

That's my Poe.

When they left, Officer Barnes reappeared and smoothed out his black mustache with two fingers. He tossed my oversized backpack toward the bars. "I believe that's yours. Don't get your hopes up; I already searched it and removed the weapons. Good thing you packed a lot of panties. We ran out of toilet paper two years ago."

I mashed my lips together as he shut the door, leaving me in the dark with only a sliver of light shining from the outside room.

I reached through the bars and searched my gear to see what he'd confiscated. My jacket and clothes were stuffed in a wrinkly wad, so I carefully folded each item as a means to pass the time. At least he hadn't taken away my peanuts or toothbrush.

Once I'd put on my leather coat and fingerless gloves, I stood up and looked around. Officer Barnes had done his best to make this place so uncomfortable that a person would never commit a crime in his town again. No vents meant no heater. The cell didn't have a bed, only a toilet and sink. Luckily both worked. I sat on top of my backpack and wondered if I could have done anything differently. I replayed the scene in my head, trying to spot mistakes. Carol and her boyfriend would have gotten away had I'd gone back to the RV or called Viktor. I'd thought her life was in danger, and my only goal was to kill the asshole who'd taken her.

After thirty minutes of sitting in near darkness, someone entered the building.

"Get inside!" Barnes growled.

Oh shit. That better not be Christian.

When the door opened, a cuffed man staggered in naked. He lifted his chin defiantly, and when he charged backward, Barnes threw his hands out and blasted him. The man crumpled to the floor, moaning like a wounded moose.

"I'm a Mage, dumbass. Don't try that again."

The prisoner passed out.

As Barnes grabbed his feet to drag him into a cell, the man's head rolled to the side and I got a good look at his face and buzz cut.

Holy crap. That was one of General's brothers.

I'd know their faces anywhere. General was the loan shark who had attacked my father and swindled me out of a million dollars. What the hell was his brother doing out here?

"Major, huh? Is that the only name you're gonna give me?"

Barnes locked chains in place and then slammed the door. "Major pain in the ass."

I rushed to the bars and pressed my face between them. "What did he do?"

Barnes dusted off his uniform. "Shifted in the middle of the damn street. Good thing I carry a tranquilizer gun." He gave me a cross look. "Two incidents in one day. That's a record. They say trouble always comes in threes." Then he pointed at me. "You better behave."

As he locked up, my blood chilled. This wasn't a coincidence. I thought General would back off after what we'd done to his family, but he must have had other ideas in mind.

I searched my bag for my phone, but it wasn't there. Barnes or Viktor must have confiscated it.

"*Shit, shit, shit,*" I hissed. How was I going to warn Viktor that General was gunning for revenge?

Or maybe he just wanted me dead, and Major was here to take me out.

Uncertain, I sank back into the shadows and waited.

Chapter 16

"WHAT TIME IS IT?" GEM asked.

She didn't really want to know. It was the only way she could indirectly protest Cyrus blocking her gifts with the ankle cuff.

Cyrus continued playing a game of Go with one of his brothers at a short table in the corner across the room. He set a black stone on the board next to a white one before sitting back on a floor pillow. "Foolish girl. Do you think you can annoy me and I'll remove the link? If a fly pesters me, I swat it. Do you want me to swat you?"

Gem remained in her wooden chair and pressed her lips tightly together.

What a barbarian.

She'd been eying the unlocked door for hours but didn't dare walk out. Not if it meant Cyrus and his men putting Hunter on their hit list. How could she possibly protect him against these men when she couldn't use her Mage gifts? She wasn't even sure how many men there were in this outfit. Cyrus had made two calls. The first one, he spoke using a dialect similar to Moghol, which to her knowledge was now an extinct language. There were variations she couldn't quite pick up on, and when he noticed her listening in, he finished the call in another room.

The man sitting across from Cyrus wasn't the same one who had drowned her in the pool. She felt sick to her stomach at the thought of seeing Arcadius again.

A large tapestry hung on the wall behind them. It was primarily beige with elaborate images of animals, plants, mountains, and Mongolians on horseback. Some were wielding swords. The room also had a wide Chinese tea table with flat cushions on every side. There were no artificial light or windows, only oil lanterns and candles to illuminate the wood floor and green walls.

Cyrus wore loose black trousers and nothing else. His husky arms were heavily inked with a unique design that stretched from his elbows to his shoulders. It looked like armor. It wasn't the style of the time he lived in, so he must have acquired it later in life.

Stop overanalyzing everything, she thought, rolling her eyes. What else did she have to do? Gem wasn't exactly an idle creature, and she had no desire to engage in conversation with Cyrus.

Begging for her freedom was a waste of breath. Could she outwit this man? Did he really think that Niko would give him something valuable in exchange for her life? If Niko had kept a book away from Cyrus for centuries, he wasn't going to give it up for anything or anyone.

If only she had a blanket or something to wear. Her red nightgown had finally dried, but it barely covered her knees. Gem cupped her arms and crossed her feet at the ankles.

"I offered you hot tea," Cyrus said without looking at her.

After watching him pour one cup after another down his gullet, she had no desire to accept anything that he offered.

"I'm not thirsty."

"Suit yourself," he said indifferently. "Lykos, you sneaky devil."

Lykos sat back and grinned. He didn't look anything like Cyrus, but Cyrus had called him his brother on more than one occasion. They must have had the same Creator. Lykos was leaner and also Asian, but his features were traditional Chinese. Cyrus was bigger, tanner, and had a barely-there mustache beneath his broad nose. He didn't have a kind expression. His smile revealed gaps between his teeth, and his eyes were malevolent beads.

Gem glanced across the room at the folding screen in the right-hand corner. Behind it was a tiny kitchen with only a stove, a small refrigerator, and a sink. Ancients were peculiar. They turned their noses up at television and technology, but they had no problem incorporating kitchen appliances in their home. There was nothing inherently offensive or evil about soap operas and a little music.

Someone pounded against the door.

Cyrus rose from his seat and pointed at the hall. "Leave."

She blinked up at him in surprise. "I thought I could walk around freely?"

He lowered his chin, acknowledging the promise he'd made. "Once I have greeted my visitor, you may come out. Now go, unless you wish to upset me."

His words sent a shudder through her spine, so she hopped to her feet and padded down the hall. Gem had learned a long time ago that mouthing off to a person with a volatile personality would accomplish his goal more than yours. One had to be craftier than that. She slipped into the second room on the left and pretended to shut the door. After a few seconds, she slowly let go of the knob and leaned into the crack to eavesdrop.

"Come in," Cyrus said cordially, as if he were hosting a dinner party. "I've been expecting you."

"Where is she?"

Gem gasped when she recognized Niko's voice.

"Safe," Cyrus replied. "Heed my warning, Nikodemos: if you attempt anything foolish and Kallisto doesn't receive a call from me, he's been ordered to strike."

"And who is the target?"

"Do you really wish to find out? Test me, boy."

A blanket of silence fell, and Gem widened the door to poke her head in the hallway. Unfortunately, they were standing out of eyeshot.

"I don't see my book," Cyrus griped.

Gem crept into the hallway, her back to the wall as she slowly sidestepped toward the main room.

"You and I both know you're a man who bargains face-to-face," Niko replied. "I cannot barter without knowing."

"You wanted to see the girl with your own eyes?" Cyrus laughed haughtily.

"I see your sense of humor hasn't changed."

"You were always too sensitive about your handicap. That was what made you weak to begin with."

"Where is she?"

Gem held her breath when she heard someone rustling around.

"She's here. I give you my word that I haven't harmed her. So… are you ready to negotiate? You know what I seek."

"Indeed. I find it remarkably uncharacteristic of you to sink this low. Why not come after me?"

Cyrus's voice tightened. "I have been coming after you for centuries. You try my patience, boy."

"I'm no longer the boy you remember."

"Is that so?" Cyrus chuckled. "Let me pour you some sake. I bought it especially for you, my half-Japanese friend."

"No, thank you."

"You never could hold your liquor. But nothing was funnier than a drunk blind man. Remember how clumsy he was, Lykos?"

Their laughter overlapped, and Gem clenched her fists. She inched closer, realizing that the voices were coming from the right. She peered around the corner at the group. With his back to everyone, Cyrus stood before a long table and poured alcohol into cups. Niko was also turned away, but the sight of him brought her such relief.

That feeling vanished when she noticed a third man sitting on the floor, examining the pieces on the game board. Gem would never forget that face as long as she lived. That brute had held her down in the pool and drowned her. His was the last face she'd seen before water rushed into her lungs and she lost consciousness.

Cyrus half turned and handed small white cups to each brother. Lykos must have been standing near the kitchen, because Gem couldn't see him. She slowly leaned back, careful about how much time she spent peering.

When Cyrus spoke, all civilities in his tone were gone. "Let us get straight to the matter. I want that book, and I will accept nothing less in exchange."

"You have given me no reason to trust you. If I hand over the book, what is to stop you from harming her out of spite? Your word? You harbor much resentment, and I would be a fool to believe you wouldn't retaliate."

Gem held her breath and peered around the corner again. Where were Niko's swords? Had they taken them?

Cyrus turned away, hands clasped behind his back. "So what do you offer me?"

"My servitude."

Cyrus looked over his shoulder, his eyes wide with surprise. "You jest."

Niko bowed. "On the contrary."

"But it's not you I want; it's the book."

"Are you not wise enough to see that if you have me, you will eventually have the book? If you harm the woman or anyone else, you'll never see it. My anger is not an emotion to dismiss."

Cyrus turned and gave a disparaging sigh. "I could torture her."

"To what avail? Set her free, and you may have my life in exchange. You can win my loyalty back or torture me until I have no strength left to resist."

Cyrus looked at him with measured interest before swinging his gaze up at the ceiling.

"You tried this hostage tactic once before," Niko said. "Remember how that turned out? Do not make moves that will set you farther away from what you desire most."

Cyrus turned his gaze to the Go board, which Arcadius was still studying. "Lykos, bring me the box."

Gem scurried into the nearest room and tucked herself deep in the shadows. Lykos cruised past the doorway to a different room. After a moment, she glimpsed him walking past with what looked like a tall hatbox. Curious, she waited until he was out of sight before she tiptoed back to her vantage point.

Lykos handed Cyrus the box and then stepped out of her line of view.

"Strip out of your clothes," Cyrus ordered him.

Niko went rigid. "For what reason?"

"You offered yourself as a servant, and I accept. But a servant cannot serve if he is in attire equal to his master. This is a long-standing tradition, and you know it to be true." The box top fell to the floor. "I held on to your clothes for many years, but the material rotted away. So I bought a replacement."

Niko's disgust was thinly veiled. "Why would you have kept them?"

"I needed a visual reminder to help me sleep at night—something to give me the motivation to find you again."

"You have me. There is no need—"

"Silence!"

Gem froze as Cyrus's command came with a ripple of Mage energy that crackled against her skin.

"You were an insolent boy. Time for all that to change." Cyrus tossed the garb to Niko's feet. "Dress."

Lykos snickered as Niko slowly removed his shirt. Cyrus merely watched, and Arcadius had no interest in any of it. Gem watched in stunned disbelief as Niko gave his freedom to these men.

He could have gone back for the book, but Cyrus wouldn't have let her go. She already knew firsthand how willing they were to end her life. But why would Niko do this? Was it a trick? Did he have blades hidden beneath his trousers?

The same trousers that quietly dropped to the floor.

Gem had seen Niko's bare chest on numerous occasions. He was the perfect specimen of the male form, thanks to all the strength training he did in the gym. Sinewy, muscular, and with perfect posture.

His silky long hair draped down his back. Gem had never seen his bare legs, and they were strong, his muscles taut. Her cheeks heated as she admired his bare behind, so perfectly shaped and the same golden hue as the rest of his body.

Cyrus threw back his head and laughed. When her gaze flicked up, she realized that Cyrus had seen her gawking.

"It looks like you have a captive audience, Nikodemos. I think she likes what she sees."

Niko turned his head toward her, revealing his profile. It felt like a punch to the gut when she saw the shame on his face.

Gem whirled around. Her knees weakened, and she slid down to the floor.

"No use hiding, girl." Cyrus gave a throaty chuckle. "You've gotten more than an eyeful."

After a deep breath, she mustered the courage to stand up and confront him. Gem marched into the room, ready to start a war, but her plan backfired when she caught sight of Niko in his new attire. He might as well have been wearing a potato sack. His tan pants were tattered and frayed at the ankle, and when he turned in her direction, he resembled an impoverished commoner. His bare feet weren't dirty, but his shirt had stains on the wide sleeves. The tunic reached his knees, and there was nothing embellished about it.

"You like?" Cyrus asked. "I bought it off the black market. Genuine slave attire. Not the kind we wore in our time, but fitting nonetheless. There are still bloodstains if you look closely."

Gem seethed. "If his clothes didn't last through the centuries, what makes you think he saved a book?"

Cyrus grinned. "Because he's here."

"Are you hurt?" Niko asked, ignoring Cyrus's snide remarks.

Gem steeled her voice. "I'm fine."

He tilted his head and studied her light. "Did they hurt you?"

Her energy must have revealed something, because his expression tightened.

Cyrus scoffed. "Cast your worries aside, Nikodemos. You'll find her unsullied. I have never and will never bed a white woman. Especially one so ugly."

Gem steadied her emotions to put Niko at ease. "I'm not hurt."

Cyrus's grin vanished. "Niko, fetch me a glass of water."

Niko's height shrank when his shoulders sagged. "I'm not familiar with your home."

"Then learn!"

Lykos strode up and shoved Niko. "I also want a glass."

"Me too," Arcadius said, finally looking up.

While Lykos collected Niko's clothes, Niko walked alongside the wall by the door. With his arm extended, he learned the shape of the room, including every item that was within a few feet of the walls. The hand-carved wooden sofa and silk pillows seemed more for pageantry than comfort. They were probably from the Ming Dynasty if she had to guess. When he bumped into a chair, the men laughed again.

Gem pivoted around. This was too insufferable to endure.

Niko reached the corner and turned again, heading toward Gem. His hand lost connection with the wall when he passed in front of the hallway. He snapped his fingers and cocked his head before reaching Gem.

"Do nothing to upset them," he said quietly.

"Are you really giving yourself to them? Niko, if you're hatching an escape plan, I can't help. My powers are gone."

Confusion flickered in his eyes, and his eyebrows slanted. "What do you mean?"

"Hurry up, Nikodemos. You try my patience."

"Do nothing," Niko repeated before continuing his process of memorizing the dimensions of the room. When he reached the kitchen entryway, he snapped his fingers and went inside.

He must have learned how sound waves bounced off objects, and maybe he could tell how long a room or hallway was. She wouldn't be surprised if he'd developed sonic hearing over the course of fifteen hundred years.

"I've missed this." Cyrus's words were thick with nostalgia and self-satisfaction.

Arcadius rose to his feet and bowed. "A strong leader deserves those who will serve him. But he proved once he couldn't be loyal. What can you gain from this?"

Cyrus folded his arms. "Satisfaction."

Niko entered the room, three glasses of water perfectly lined up on a tray. He slowly moved toward the men and then stopped.

"Do it right," Cyrus commanded.

Niko shifted his eyes toward Gem but quickly knelt, the tray raised high. All three men collected their glasses and made a toast.

Gem wanted to rush to Niko's side, but she heeded his warning. He knew these men better than she did, and Gem trusted his judgment, even though it hurt to see him dominated by a narcissistic jerk.

When Cyrus set his empty glass on the tray, it slid off and shattered on the floor.

Cyrus kicked Niko's shoulder and knocked him onto his back. "Fool! Have you forgotten the simple task of holding a tray properly? Do you want to know why I never treated you as an equal? Besides your obvious defect, you're a mongrel. I don't trust white men, and you're half. That means I can only trust one half of you, and I never know which half I'm dealing with." Cyrus kicked a shard of glass, and it skittered across the floor. "Clean up this mess."

The brothers exchanged a look of satisfaction, and Gem could watch no more. She retreated to her room. Aside from the wooden stool, the only other furniture was a mattress on the floor. The lanterns on all four walls had dimmed, so she lengthened their wicks to brighten the glass globes. It gave her something to do—something to distract her mind from ruminating over this awful situation.

Had she one ounce of her Mage power, she would have blasted Cyrus and his men with an energy ball like he'd never seen.

When the door opened, she reared back and clutched her gown.

"Niko!" She rushed to Niko as he closed it behind him. "Why did you come? What's happening?"

He reached out and clasped her wrist. His hand moved up her bare arm until he felt the strap of her gown. "Did they not clothe you?"

"It's my swimming gown." She peered around him at the door. "They might catch you."

"I'm permitted to learn the house."

Her shoulders sagged. "Why didn't you fight them? I've seen you fight. You could beat them."

He slowly shook his head. "At least one of them is armed, and I don't know where they store their weapons and how many there are. And… you're still here."

"So?"

"As long as you're still here, they can use you to thwart any plans I might have to attack. A wise man doesn't fight against impossible odds. He must wait like the serpent in the grass and only strike when he's certain of victory."

She whirled around and stalked off. "This isn't the time for proverbs."

A moment later, she turned and watched him feeling the wall with his hands. Each time he reached a lantern, he sensed the flame as if he could see it.

"The bed," she blurted out just seconds before he stumbled over it.

Niko kicked the mattress. "Did he at least provide you with blankets?"

"Alas, I'm too traumatized to sleep."

Niko bent down and touched the bed before lifting a blanket. "Wrap this around you."

Gem sighed and did as he asked. Once the blanket covered her shoulders, she sat on the mattress. "I can't believe I let this happen."

Niko sat beside her. "If not you, they would have chosen someone else."

She couldn't get used to his ragged clothes and focused on his face instead. "What's this book they want?"

He drew in a deep breath, his crystal-blue eyes holding so many secrets. "Long ago, Cyrus was a master thief. It was how he acquired a small fortune. He would steal and resell items, only to discover that objects are worth more to their owners than anyone else. So he changed his method by targeting wealthy men and finding out what precious things they treasured the most. People will pay most anything for sentimental or rare objects. Then he tried taking people, but that didn't always turn out well for him in the end."

"Like he did with me."

"Yes. Cyrus knew taking you wouldn't guarantee an exchange, but it would force me to listen to him. I have been avoiding him since he found me last year." Niko folded his arms over his knees. "One day he stole a book. It contained symbols and images that

Cyrus didn't understand, but when the owner was willing to pay anything for it, Cyrus tested him. The man did everything he asked. He stole horses for us, burned down a temple, even killed his wife. That was when Cyrus realized the book was far too valuable to let go, if only he knew what was inside the pages. He tried bribery, hoping the man would translate it for him, but the man refused."

"Was he a human?"

Niko turned his head as if looking at her. "No. He was a Relic. Not someone who could fight against the six of us. Well, five of us now that Plato is dead," he said absently.

Gem didn't like the way he kept saying *us* and including himself in the count. "How could you have been involved with someone like Cyrus?"

"He is my Mage brother, and we were on the run. He offered me protection in return for my loyalty. I wasn't the same man you see before you now. I was weak and unfamiliar with my gift of sight." Niko tugged at his worn sleeves.

"What's in the book?"

"Death. Life. Power. Magic."

She furrowed her brow. "I don't understand."

Niko raised his head and stared vacantly at the closed door. "There is power in this world that you cannot understand as a young Mage. Power that existed many lifetimes ago. A Mage with a unique gift put power in the words, and those who read them can manipulate energy in ways never imagined."

Gem let the blanket fall away from her shoulders. She wasn't cold anymore. Heat radiated from Niko as if he were the sun. "Like a spell book?"

"Exactly. Only this one holds true power. In my lifetime, I've heard of such books. They were destroyed along with their owners, who were accused of witchcraft."

"But they weren't witches."

"Yes, but our kind was hunted and executed by humans who knew of our existence. They feared our gifts, and the only way to persecute us was to label us witches in league with the devil. That allowed them to reduce our numbers while also controlling humans using fear that they too could receive the same sentence if they didn't abide by their laws."

"If the book is so powerful, why didn't you just destroy it?"

Niko rose to his feet, his hands clasped behind his back. "Because I don't know how."

She chortled. "How about a match for starters?"

"The paper won't burn. The ink won't smudge. And the pages cannot be torn."

Her jaw slackened.

"I cannot fathom what it takes to destroy this object. The rumors I heard on other similar books never mentioned their indestructibility or how they were destroyed. If a man like Cyrus gets his hands on it, there's no telling what he might be capable of doing. It's been in my possession for centuries. Cyrus foolishly entrusted me to guard the book, knowing I couldn't read it. Perhaps that is why I'm the ideal guardian."

"Oh, Niko. Why did you give yourself up?"

Niko approached her and dropped to one knee. His face was the same, but something was different about him. Not his strong bone structure nor the Mage light that sparkled in the depths of his almond-shaped eyes. Gem didn't know this man, and that revelation was staring her right in the face.

"Why did your light change when I asked if they hurt you?"

She blinked rapidly and gathered up the blanket. "It's nothing. He put a cuff on my ankle that suppresses my gifts. It's like I'm mortal again."

"That's not what I meant." He leaned forward like a knight kneeling before a queen. "Don't lie to me, Gem. I can read the deception in your light."

She tugged the blanket onto her lap. "He drowned me in the pool."

"Cyrus?"

"No. The other one. The one who came in with you."

Niko glowered. "Arcadius."

"I guess it was the only way to keep me from flashing away or screaming for help. He lets me go where I want, but if I leave, he'll hurt Hunter. I can't, Niko. I just can't have that on my conscience. Not unless they're all dead, and I think he's got more friends on the outside."

"Indeed. Kallisto is unaccounted for. But if he plans to storm Keystone, he'll have wolves to contend with."

"What wolves?"

The door was kicked open, and Lykos appeared. "Cyrus demands your presence, Nikodemos. *Now*."

When Lykos walked off, Niko spoke quietly. "Comply with his wishes, Gem. Stay out of sight, and do not meddle in his conversations or business. Cyrus is unpredictable and merciless when provoked."

"What's your plan?"

"I have none."

She shot to her feet and gave an exasperated sigh. "If you won't give him the book, then why did you come? Why did you give yourself over to him as a slave, knowing he wouldn't release me?"

Niko stood up and bowed before turning away to leave the room. "To protect you."

Chapter 17

CHRISTIAN BRISTLED WHEN HE THOUGHT about Raven in that jail cell. Not only was Keystone a man down, but they'd left her behind. Fifteen days was a blink of an eye, and they would probably be done with this mission long before that. But it still vexed him.

Viktor had banished the twins to the bedroom in the back, but Christian heard their ears rubbing against the door. He tuned out all the childish whispering to give this shitebag kidnapper his undivided attention.

Carol and her so-called boyfriend were sitting on the sofa behind the driver's seat, her hand clutching his. Shepherd focused on the road, but Blue was watching them with a hawkish stare from the passenger seat.

Christian nudged Viktor, who was staring at the wee lass like a disappointed father put in charge of punishment. "If I can't scrub the eejit, at least let me charm him for information."

"I said I'll talk," the boy grumbled. Boy. Now *there* was a word that didn't seem to fit. Shifters often matured quickly after their first change, so the ones capable of shifting were easy to spot. "I have nothing to hide."

"No, you just have something to steal," Claude said from the seating area adjacent to him. He sat on the side facing the kids, his arms folded and feet resting on the opposite bench. Christian didn't usually see Claude with such a baneful disposition. Shortly after recovering the pair on the side of the road, Claude had pinned the lad to the floor and threatened to disembowel him. Once he found out the kid was only sixteen, he backed off.

Reluctantly.

The plastic cover on the broken window rattled from the rushing wind outside. Blue had secured it with duct tape and shut the broken blinds to keep the vehicle warm. Apparently Viktor hadn't secured one with good heating.

Viktor glanced at his watch. He looked like a Russian agent in his black turtleneck and cargo pants, which he'd changed into shortly after leaving the jail. Christian had never seen the man in pants like that, not to mention the hiking shoes, so he had a feeling they would be ditching the RV soon.

"What is your name?" Viktor asked.

"Joshua Salsbury."

"Like the steak?" Shepherd asked, an unlit cigarette wedged between his lips.

Joshua swung his dark eyes to the front. "No. It's spelled differently."

He definitely acted like a child, despite his furtive look and brawn.

"What if he's not sixteen?" Christian pondered as he stroked his beard. "What if he's only saying that to save his arse?"

Joshua reached in his back pocket and slapped his wallet on the floor. "My alias ID shows my age. You can look it up if you want."

Christian lifted the wallet and thumbed through the pockets. He didn't give a shite about the kid's ID; he wanted to see if there was a condom in there. Obviously they hadn't done anything yet or else Carol would be licking her paws, but Christian didn't quite know how it worked with Potentials. Sex made them become the Breed of their partner, probably through bodily fluids, but did it work when there was a barrier?

When all he found were a few twenties, ticket stubs to a concert, and a penny, he tossed it back in Joshua's lap.

"How much do you know?" Viktor asked.

Joshua shook his dark hair away from his eyes. "That you're kidnapping people."

"We have done no such thing."

"Oh?" He snapped his head toward Carol. "Do you want to be here?"

Her shoulders sagged. "No."

Satisfied, Joshua met eyes with Viktor. "See? Kidnapping. Against her will."

"We are protecting them," Viktor fired back, his patience tried.

"From what? Life? Look, I know what she is. I know she's a Potential. But that doesn't mean you can hold them against their will."

"Children cannot protect themselves," Viktor stated flatly. "Especially human orphans. Would you like me to tell you a bedtime story that will give you nightmares about what happens to young Potentials taken by the wrong people? Shall I tell you about perverse men who want child brides, or perhaps you would like to know about the ones who are held in captivity and tortured in order to make them submissive? Or would you like to hear about a breed of Australian cat Shifters who were going extinct because all their women died, and they kidnapped a twelve-year-old girl to mate with every single one of them to produce more children? Or a young boy of seven who—"

"That's enough." Joshua cleared his throat, his eyes downcast. "I get it."

"I have no time to finesse the truth. Following us was foolish," Viktor fumed, not giving the kid any leniency. "You put all our lives at risk, and you could have killed her crashing the car!"

"I say we leave him on the side of the road," Claude suggested, his canines still out.

Christian expected the kid to promise how he wouldn't tell anyone, but he pressed his lips into a mulish line.

"Nyet. He knows too much. He has seen our faces and knows how we're traveling." Viktor turned his attention back to the kids. "How did you follow us this far? We were careful."

Joshua bit his lip.

"I called him," Carol confessed.

Viktor jerked his neck back. "With what?"

She looked up at him with wide green eyes. "Your phone. I had no idea we were going to a train station, so I got scared. When you left your phone on the floor, I sent him a message to let him know what was happening. I guess he found out from someone at the train station where all our stops would be and sped the whole way. I couldn't believe it when I saw him at the station. He was gonna take me then, but that black-haired girl caught us."

Viktor's neck turned red, and Christian noticed a little vein appearing on his temple.

Christian furrowed his brow. "And tell me how it is the fella knew you were leaving to begin with? You don't have phones, and he's not a Potential."

"Joshua and I made a promise to each other," she explained. "They always sneak the kids out in the middle of the night during a transfer, so I said if something ever happened, I'd put a snowman in the window. It's one thing I saved my money for. It lights up blue and red and green. Joshua lived across the street. We used to just look at each other and wave, but one night he climbed the fire escape to my window. After that we'd meet up on the top floor where nobody's supposed to go."

"And why didn't he take you then?"

She shrugged. "I wanted to, but he said I only had a few years left to go before they released me. As long as we could see each other, it wasn't a big deal."

Viktor rubbed his hands together before stroking his beard. "You leave me with no choice. Go in the back until I call you out."

"Please don't hurt him," Carol pleaded. "Please don't erase his memories. You can't! It ain't fair. We didn't mean to hurt nobody." Tears welled in her eyes.

"Spare me the crocodile tears," Christian said, knowing how clever children were at manipulating adults. "Your infatuation put one of us behind bars."

Viktor snapped his fingers. "Both of you, go."

Joshua stood first and helped Carol to her feet. He clutched the pixie-sized girl tightly to him as they made their way to the back of the trailer and closed themselves up in the room with the twins.

Viktor crossed the room and took a seat in their place.

Without missing a beat, Blue got out of the passenger seat and dutifully sat beside him. "When's the last time you had anything to drink? Christian, get him some water."

He patted her hand. "What would I do without my Blue?"

Christian filled a plastic glass and handed it over.

After Viktor quenched his thirst, he set the empty cup on the divider between him and Claude. "One of you must stay behind and watch the boy until the mission is complete. If we set him free, he'll either follow us or try to get help. Someone might get information from him or charm him. We cannot afford to make any mistakes, and he is a liability."

Blue raised a finger. "I'll stay."

"Nyet. I need your eyes. And I need Christian's ears and Claude's nose."

Shepherd tucked the unlit cigarette behind his ear. "I guess through process of elimination, that leaves yours truly."

"But we won't have a healer." Blue looked between all the men. "Niko's gone, and if something happens to one of the children, Shepherd's the only one who knows emergency medicine."

Claude raised his finger and cleared his throat. "I can heal superficial wounds."

She raised her eyebrows. "Superficial isn't what I'm worried about."

"If Raven were here, I'd have her stay with the boy," Viktor said. "But I cannot afford to spare any of you on the last part of our journey."

"But you don't need my eyes. We're driving."

Viktor averted his gaze and fell silent. Evidently, he had more in store for them. By the looks of the rugged terrain, probably hiking.

She leaned away and put her hands on her lap. "I'll do as you ask. You're the alpha of Keystone."

Viktor wasn't an alpha wolf by birth, but he had formed a group and led it with as much authority as any Packmaster would. Calling him an alpha was the biggest compliment you could pay to a beta wolf.

Christian climbed into the passenger seat and stared at the open road before them. He needed to forget Raven and keep his mind on the mission, or someone might die under his watch. It felt like an act of betrayal, but he'd seen many men make foolish choices in the name of love. Viktor had smartly included most of the team on this mission to prepare for the unexpected, including the loss of members.

Nevertheless, it wouldn't stop Christian from paying a visit to that redneck gobshite someday and delivering a little payback, perhaps charm him into believing he's a circus monkey instead of a cop.

Revenge was not only a dish best served cold, it was one served in the middle of the night, five years in the future.

Chapter 18

MY INTERNAL MAGE CLOCK TOLD me it was late afternoon. I had given up on concealing my presence from General's brother, but I didn't speak to him. I used the toilet, drank water from the sink, and stuffed my coat back in the bag, putting the hoodie over my T-shirt instead. Cold leather against my arms just wasn't cutting it.

I wonder where they are? Have they made it to their destination? Probably not. Has Niko found Gem? Why the hell would Niko's nemesis have taken her to begin with? Ransom?

We were stronger as a group, and the more divided we became, the more vulnerable. Hopefully nothing else had happened, like Carol escaping with that boyfriend of hers.

I jumped to my feet when I heard the outside door open. Someone whistled a melody out of tune while they unlocked the heavy door to the cells. A skinny man stepped in, silhouetted by the light in the front room.

I squinted and recognized the man. *What the hell?* It was Willie, the server from McDonald's earlier that morning. The door swung wide and showered the room with light.

He walked jauntily in and headed toward Major's cell. "So what did you do?"

"Fuck off."

"Don't you want a french fry? Why are you naked? Are you a Shifter?"

A scuffle ensued, and I cocked my head to discern what might be happening.

"Try all you like, it's not like you're going anywhere," Willie said. His footfalls approached until he appeared in front of my cell, a sack of food in his hand. "Hey, I remember you. Maybe if you had ordered something, you wouldn't be in here. What did you do?"

He reached in his bag and ate a french fry. While amiable, this guy seemed to get off on questioning criminals.

"Why are you here?" I asked quietly.

He ambled up to the bars. "My uncle owns the building."

"The cop?"

"Yes'm."

"Isn't he a…"

I didn't dare say the word.

"Mage?" Willie finished. "Uncle Al doesn't like me here, so I made a copy of the key when he was drinking one night. They have those neat little key machines at Walmart, you know."

This kid seemed to be a few cards short of a deck. "You're a rebel, aren't you?"

He grinned, revealing a mouthful of crooked teeth. He was a gangly-looking guy, probably eighteen or twenty if I had to guess.

Willie wiped his greasy fingers on his dark work shirt. "My uncle got me the job at McDonald's and invited me to stay here, but he doesn't trust me. It's not fair that he doesn't let me work here. I could be a special deputy."

"You sure could." I took a seat in front of the bars so that we could talk more privately.

Willie had a thumbprint of hair below his lower lip that wasn't well groomed. "Want some fries?"

"Sure." I reached through the bars and pulled out a couple. I wasn't hungry, but this wasn't about hunger. I was playing a game, and the object was to get the hell out of jail. "So you're a Mage too, huh?"

"No," he said, acting like a teenager who didn't get what he wanted for Christmas. "The Mageri doesn't like nepotism and turning family. I'm just a human."

I ate a second fry. "I thought humans weren't supposed to know about us?"

"He got approval to make me a trusted human. I guess 'cause he's law and all. My dad died a few years back, and I didn't have any other family to take me in. I was already sixteen, so I guess they didn't think it was a big deal. That's why we moved to the middle of nowhere."

"So you wouldn't have any friends to tell?"

He reached for a small sandwich and unwrapped it. "Do you really want to know? Nobody ever asks me questions."

"Sure I wanna know. You're the most interesting person I've met in this town."

He sat up a little straighter and chomped into his chicken sandwich. "I grew up in Parkersburg. My uncle thought it would be safer if we lived somewhere that didn't have a lot of Breed. I guess he didn't take into account all the Shifters. It keeps him busy. We could have moved since I'm over eighteen now, but he likes it here."

"If you're not a Mage, how come I felt energy when I went into the restaurant?"

"Uncle Al was in the drive-through. That's how he gets when he's hungry and has to wait for us to cook up his order. He flares his anger like some kind of food demon."

While Willie was yapping about his job, I took notice of his pockets and belt as I searched for keys. The ones that opened these cells were different from the key that opened the main door.

"What do you do around here for fun?" I asked.

He shrugged. "I don't know. Rainelle is only a thousand or so people, and I ain't got any friends. That's why I like to come up here and visit the prisoners. Uncle Al doesn't usually lock up that many people. Mostly drunk Shifters, but once he busted a Vampire sipping from one of the ladies who works at the thrift store. I still come up here every day after work. It's my excitement. Tonight's a busy night! Two of you. Are you together?"

I shook my head.

"What did you do?"

"Public display of gifts in the middle of the road."

He cackled and finished the rest of his sandwich. "I bet I can guess what that was. What's your name?"

I wasn't sure if Major could hear us since he was several cells down, and I also didn't know if he was aware that I was locked up in here. I decided to play it safe. "Jonie."

"I'm Willie."

"I know." I gestured to his shirt.

He glanced down at the name tag. "Oh, yeah. Duh."

I leaned forward. "If your uncle doesn't know you come up here, why don't you let me out? I can't sit here for fifteen days."

"Don't worry about food. I can bring you some."

I realized that Willie probably liked having the company and wouldn't object to my serving the full sentence. I worried my lip and came up with a different approach. "I can give you something in exchange. Something very… special."

His eyes lit up. "What?"

"I can't tell you."

He glanced at my backpack. "What is it? Come on. Tell me."

"You have to promise to let me out. I won't cause any trouble, and I'll be on my way. Your uncle will never know. What do you say, Willie? Haven't you ever wanted to do something crazy in your life? Why should your uncle have all the fun? You're an adult, and you can make your own decisions."

He sat back and rested on his palms. I knew enough about kids his age to guess what they wanted. Sex wasn't on this guy's radar, but he seemed aimless. Like a guy who just got stuck somewhere but didn't have a quest or a purpose in life.

"It can be a secret mission," I continued. "What fun is it having kids and grandkids if you don't have stories to tell them?"

He tipped his head to the side and then shot forward. "Okay. If I promise to let you out, what do I get?"

"Besides an adventure to tell your grandkids? I'll give you a Breed weapon."

I hated to give up one of my daggers, but Shepherd had access to an arsenal.

He glanced at my backpack. "Uncle Al would never let you keep knives in your bag."

"No, but I bet it's in the front room. I know you wouldn't just steal it, because you're not that kind of guy. Besides, if I'm still in the cell, your uncle would figure out it was you. It's my best one," I said as if the offer were going fast. I stood up and turned away while scratching the back of my neck. "On second thought, maybe this isn't such a good idea. I'm not sure if I should hand over such a prized weapon to a human."

He shot to his feet. "You can't take it back. A deal is a deal."

I turned around. "This is too dangerous. I shouldn't have made an enticing offer like that to a human. You should go home. This isn't a place for a sweet kid like you."

Willie kicked the empty sack and marched out of sight.

I held my breath. Had I misread him?

A minute later, he reappeared, a key ring orbiting around his twirling index finger. "Too late to back out of a deal. The dagger's mine."

I sighed and gave him a reluctant smile. "All right. You win." I ambled toward the door when he opened it. "Are you sure about this, Willie?"

He walked out of the room with his chin high and a self-satisfied swing in his step. I followed behind with my bag and obscured my face from the other prisoner, just in case he could see me from his cell.

After shutting the heavy door, Willie hurried over to the locker and tugged at the handle. "Holy crow! Are all these yours?"

I stepped close and peered over his shoulder at the daggers lined up on the middle shelf. "Yep. But the big one—that's yours."

His eyes lit up, and he grabbed it immediately. It was still in its sheath and attached to the leg holster. It wasn't my favorite; I was more attached to the smaller push daggers that fit in the palm of my hand. Those little blades were my go-to weapons. I put two back in the sheaths on my belt and the rest in my backpack along with my phone.

"Be careful. I recently sharpened it," I cautioned him as he pulled it free. "It's a genuine stunner. If your uncle or Breed catches you with one of these, it would be bad news."

"They're not illegal," he argued.

"No, but humans aren't supposed to have them. Don't you know?"

While he stabbed thin air and reenacted a fantasy where he was the greatest warrior alive, I pondered my situation. I was officially out of the mission, and while I felt compelled to return home and help Niko, I couldn't bring myself to leave without knowing what Major had planned. Was he here alone, or was General around?

I glanced at the pile of clothes in the bottom of the locker and then to the keys hanging from hooks at the top. There were four, the fifth key still in Willie's hand.

I turned away, and an idea sprang to mind. "Say, Willie, how would you like something else besides the dagger?"

He turned around and sheathed the weapon. "What do you mean?"

I jerked my chin toward the inside door. "Do you know what the most valuable commodity is in the Breed world? Even more valuable than weapons?"

He chewed on his chapped bottom lip and looked up. "Money?"

"No. Favors. It's like a rule everyone follows—even criminals. If we didn't put so much value in them, most of us would be dead. If you let that guy out, he'll trade you a favor. You can stage the escape to look like a break-in. Guys like that always have friends on the outside, so your uncle will never suspect a thing. Favors are a big deal. You can hold them in your pocket for as long as you want and then ask for anything you need."

Willie gave me a skeptical look, his light eyes narrowing. "Anything?"

"Within reason. It usually has to be the same value. Granting a man his freedom is big. I bet he'd agree."

Knife still in hand, he folded his arms. "Like... what could I get?"

"That's up to you. Maybe down the road someone denies you a loan. All you'd have to do is call this guy up on the favor, and he'd find a way to get your loan approved. That's how it works. Or maybe you're in jail or some other sticky situation, and you can't get out. Or hell, maybe you just wanna become Breed. I bet he could arrange that."

"You think? My uncle said the Mageri don't want a minimum-wage worker. I have to be someone special or have some great big job." Willie shook his head and huffed out a breath. "What do they know?"

"Maybe they're right. Your uncle's just looking out for you. I should probably just keep my mouth shut. Nobody wants to be a Mage. Sure, we can run super fast and have all these magical gifts, but who wants to live forever? Long after you're dust in the graveyard, I'll still be walking around. And I know you wouldn't want to be a Vampire. They have all that sonic hearing, and that could probably get annoying. Not to mention night vision and never having to sleep. Though I once saw a Vampire lift a thirty-foot trailer. But people don't trust them anyhow."

Willie struck me as the kind of guy who had to think that everything was his idea if he was going to go along with it. Maybe his uncle had made too many decisions and this kid just wanted to feel like he was behind the steering wheel for a change. I almost felt bad I'd be getting him into trouble. But he was an adult now, and maybe this blowout with his uncle needed to happen so he could live his own life.

I pivoted on my heel. "Forget I said anything. You probably don't need any big favors. You've got a steady job, live in a nice town… Anyhow, thanks for letting me out. Take good care of that dagger. She's been in a lot of battles with some of the toughest criminals alive. Well, most of them aren't alive anymore. See ya!"

I swung my backpack over my shoulders and jogged out the door and past Willie's car. A thin sheet of filtered sunlight shone through a heavy blanket of clouds. I flashed down the road to find a good hiding spot. If Willie was tempted by my suggestions, Major would come out this way. Maybe his brothers would be waiting for him, but I still couldn't be sure if this guy had company or not.

Amid all the forest green and timber, a silver object caught my eye—a sedan parked in an open patch to the right. When I opened the door and peered in, I took note of the keys in the ignition and a metal lion's head dangling from the rearview mirror.

"This is too good to be true."

By the looks of all the tire marks, Officer Barnes used this clearing to store the cars of the men he locked up in his Breed jail. This had to be Major's vehicle. A quick search yielded nothing except for a map of Cognito, an ice scraper, and napkins. I popped the trunk and walked around to check things out. The trunk was empty, but suddenly I remembered something that Wyatt had mentioned. After looking around, I located the emergency trunk release.

"This couldn't be more perfect."

Worst-case scenario, Willie wouldn't take the bait, and I'd have to get out of the trunk and steal the car. Either way, it was a win-win in my book.

"Worth a shot," I muttered while climbing in.

I curled up in a fetal position and stared at the trunk release. Fifteen minutes must have passed before I finally heard something outside. It wasn't a car, so that was promising.

Even though Major was a Shifter, I concealed every drop of my light to be on the safe side. No sense taking any chances. Some people were more sensitive than others to electrical impulses, which could spike with adrenaline. When the car jostled and the door closed, I held my breath.

"It's me," I heard him say. "No, just some jackass cop. It's under control. Where are you?"

I turned my head so I could hear him better.

"You're shitting me. They're on foot? That's like shooting fish in a barrel. … No, that's not far at all. What happened?" He laughed. "Mechanical issues, huh? Four hours? I can make it there in two, but I don't see the rush. It's almost dark, and they'll set up camp. Look, if we lose contact, I'll shift and pick up your scent. Just mark a few spots for me." He cleared his throat and went quiet again. "The cop has some jail set up in the woods. Well, fucking hell, General! I thought you guys were taking off without me."

There was the faint sound of an angry voice, but it was too muffled to hear.

"I think she's out, but you don't have to worry about her. There's no way she can flash her ass all the way out there. It's a four-hour drive."

Four hours? I considered the timeline. Keystone had left that morning, but my arrest staggered the trip. Mechanical issues. I wondered if that meant they'd had the trailer serviced or maybe a wheel rolled off. In any case, four hours left me with enough hope that I could catch up.

"Did that blonde get away?"

My eyes widened.

"Three is better than two. You'll get a lot for them." He paused for a minute. "I *told* you the deer was a good idea. Now we know what we're dealing with. … Okay, will do."

My pulse rocketed when the engine started up. They were after the kids? How could they have known? General could have easily ambushed us when our trailer tipped after dodging his trap, but it sounded like they were investigating how many of us there were and perhaps what Breed. We had slaughtered two of his brothers in lion form and almost a third, so this guy was taking his time formulating a plan. I remembered the growl I'd heard in the woods.

Once we began moving, I quietly unzipped my backpack and took out my phone. I changed all my settings to make sure the sound and vibrations were turned off. Instead of calling, I sent Viktor a text message that someone was following them. Just in case his phone was off, I sent the same message to Christian. When neither man replied, I remembered Viktor mentioning his satellite phone. They probably weren't answering because they were out of range of cell phone towers.

Great.

On the upside, the empty trunk assured me that Major would have no reason to come back here and discover his stowaway.

The downside?

It was going to be a long drive.

Three hours later, the muscles in my neck felt like a box of Cracker Jack that had all stuck together. The trunk wasn't airtight, so at least I didn't have any trouble breathing.

What I *did* have trouble with was listening to an hour's worth of Michael Jackson. When "Beat It" went on continual replay, I wanted to beat Major with a tire iron.

Eventually the ride got extremely bumpy, and we hit steep inclines that had me smashed against the back end of the trunk. When the car finally stopped and Major got out, I listened closely for other voices. After several minutes of silence, I pulled the release and slowly raised the lid.

Darkness surrounded me. An owl hooted from a nearby tree, adding to the unsynchronized symphony that swelled within the wild woods. Frogs were croaking, crickets chirping, and a strange bird squawked from afar.

Without raising the lid all the way up, I climbed out and quietly closed the trunk. While crouched low to the ground, I peered around both sides of the car to make sure I didn't have company. Then I used my Mage powers to sense any energy in the area, but I felt none.

I shot to my feet and pivoted. Major had parked the car off what appeared to be a dirt road. Using my mediocre Vampire vision and what little moonlight filtered from the clouds, I spotted a neon-orange piece of material tied around a tree, something General must have left behind to mark where to pull over. Major hadn't made any other calls that I'd noticed, but they could have been sending messages.

I marched through high grass toward a path that cut between overgrown bushes. "I'm gonna get covered in ticks."

Major had probably shifted so he could track his brothers, and that posed a danger. If his animal caught wind of me, my plan might backfire.

On the other hand, if I didn't do something, they were going to ambush Keystone.

After securing my backpack, I moved through the woods and focused on picking up on energy. When I detected a significant current and heard a loud roar, I fell back a step but stayed on his trail. The full moon kept peeking out from behind the clouds, providing me enough light to see far ahead in the distance. The animal moved with grace, not running or stopping to look over his shoulder. He must have been following a scent trail that led to General.

Running through city streets, climbing buildings, and hopping subways had nothing on wilderness exercise. It didn't take long before I was winded, sweating, and regretting my life choices. Steep hills went on forever, limbs and bushes were like spears, and if I wasn't sliding on leaves, I was twisting my ankle on a root or stepping in a hole.

When the lion's energy intensified, I knew he'd stopped to rest. It gave me a chance to catch my breath and focus. I'd never been in woods like these—I was out of my comfort zone. I was a city girl born in a trailer park, so the idea of snakes and getting lost in the wilderness was petrifying.

Major's lion didn't rest for long, and before I knew it, I was hot on his trail.

After what seemed like an hour, I struggled to keep up. The bushes were dense, the ground uneven, the moon barely made an appearance, and my heart was pounding against my chest. The steep terrain made it impossible to flash after him to keep up.

Sweat trickled down my brow. My sweatshirt felt like a torture device, yet it was the only protection I had against the branches that were clawing at me like Satan's minions. At least it wasn't summer. Hopefully all the mosquitoes were still in hibernation.

Panic set in when I couldn't sense the lion anymore. I held my breath, listening for the sound of its heavy paws trampling across the forest leaves. I searched the ground blindly for paw prints. There were too many dead leaves, and my Vampire eyes weren't helpful with the moon hiding behind clouds. After turning in a short circle, I kept following my inner compass in the direction that he'd been heading.

After five minutes, I finally accepted that I'd lost him.

One-way train to panic town, all aboard!

I thought about wild packs, but maybe they weren't half as threatening as the idea of a real animal. The kind whose sole purpose was to stalk its prey and eat them.

One minute I was jogging through a break in the trees, following what looked like a trail. The next, I was falling into an abyss when the ground disappeared. I slammed facedown into a dark pit, the air whooshing out of my lungs.

Disoriented, I lay there for a minute, doing a mental check on what bones I might have broken. When I opened my eyes, I was staring at a metal spike just inches in front of my face.

I sat up and swayed. A pinch of moonlight revealed two more spikes protruding from the ground, and luckily I'd missed those too.

I rubbed my sore elbow and assessed the situation. Long sticks and slender branches that must have concealed the trap were scattered about. Is this what hunters built to catch animals? After wiping dirt out of my eye, I stood up and measured the distance with my arms. The edge of the hole was too high for me to reach even when jumping, and the walls were too far apart for other creative ways of escape. Climbing was impossible and only brought down chunks of cold mud. I found a root and pawed the earth to dig a little more of it out, but when I tried to use it to hoist myself up, it broke. I flew backward, and my life flashed before my eyes as I came inches from impaling myself on a spike.

I scooted against the wall. Climbing out was a game of roulette that I wasn't willing to play. But what exactly were my options? To die in a pit, that's what.

"This wasn't in the brochure."

After taking off my bag, I pulled out my phone and cursed. No signal bars.

"Great. This is just great."

The hole must have been twelve feet deep. I stood up and kicked one of the spikes, but it didn't budge.

Dying in a hole wasn't an option. If I couldn't climb my way out, maybe I could slowly dig my way up at a slant. I took out my push dagger, suddenly wishing I hadn't given Willie the big knife.

"Now I know what it feels like to dig my way to China," I muttered, cutting at the wall and pulling away the dirt.

"I wouldn't do that if I were you."

I froze at the sound of a voice that clung to my spine and made me shudder. After releasing a breath, I steered my gaze up at a formidable man standing at the edge of the hole. I couldn't see much, only that he appeared as tall as the trees and full of shadows.

Had General caught me?

The figure knelt down and clucked his tongue. "What have we here?"

That wasn't General's voice. I tightened the push dagger in my palm, the three-inch blade protruding between my fingers. If he was a Shifter planning to jump in for a meal, he was in for a surprise.

The moon glinted off a metal object in his hand, and I braced myself. A piercing light suddenly blinded me from an LED flashlight switching on, and I shielded my eyes. His light shone on the spikes behind me.

I kicked one of them. "Is this your trap? You missed."

"Yes," he said, as if contemplating his mistakes. "Perhaps I need to arrange them differently or add another. Which way did you fall?" He swung the light upward and tapped his chin with it. "Never mind."

This guy looked like he'd been living in the wilderness for a thousand years. His dark brown hair was unkempt and touched the ground where he knelt. His beard was long, and his eyes were light. One problem? This guy was definitely Breed. Humans had weak energy in comparison. At least he wasn't a Vamp.

"Is this your hole?" I asked him.

A chuckle rolled around in his throat before he threw back his head and laughed.

"Look, I need to get out of here."

The laugh died. "Why? So you can catch up with your lion friend?"

"Who?"

"I don't like trespassers in my territory."

"I'm not trespassing on purpose. I was hiking and got lost."

He twirled the flashlight.

"And what are you talking about with lions? There aren't any lions around here. This isn't Africa."

His eyes narrowed.

"My mom's probably worried I haven't called her. Just help me out so I can go back to my car."

The light settled on me. "There isn't a road for miles."

"I got separated from my camp."

He turned around and sat down so all I could see was his back.

"Please!" I cried. "Help me out."

The man shined the light on the trees above. "When you tell me the truth, I'll let you out. But if you continue the charade, you'll be in there for a long time."

"You're really scaring me!"

He looked over his shoulder at me. "You try my patience. Admit you're not human."

I folded my arms. "Fine. What gave it away?"

He got up and circled around. "Your shoes aren't practical for walking in these woods. And I haven't seen a gimlet in many years."

"A what?"

He shined the light on my dagger. "It's very small, and you have another on your belt. Why would a hiker need such weapons?"

I kicked at the wall. Who did this guy think he was?

When I heard a chain rattle, I staggered to the center and looked up. The man had moved out of sight, and I listened anxiously to a metallic tapping sound, like a hammer hitting a spike. Moments later, a chain ladder rolled into the hole. Not all the way down, but low enough for me to grab. I put on my backpack and reached for it.

"Hold on tight," he said, pulling me up with impossible strength.

I tried to use my feet, but there was no footing. Once out, I crawled past where he'd spiked the ladder into the ground.

"Do you normally carry that around with you?"

He crouched in front of me. "When I check my traps, I do. How else would I get out?"

I lifted the flashlight and shined it on his face. He didn't just have light eyes; they were yellow. His tattered clothes were layered, the long sleeveless coat made from real animal fur of different colors. When he stared at me, he really stared at me. My hair stood on end, and I knew right away he was a Chitah.

"Is my dark hair unsettling?" he asked.

"No more than the Overlord's."

His brow furrowed. "What do you mean?"

"You're a Chitah, right?"

He dipped his chin.

"Then you know the Overlord."

"No leader would have dark hair like mine. It would be an abomination."

I huffed out a laugh. "How long have you been living off-grid? It's rare, but for whatever reason, you guys voted for a dark-haired leader."

"They don't vote," he replied matter-of-factly. "It's a challenge. Do you mean to say that a defect won the title of Overlord?" His gaze grew distant as he processed the idea.

I really didn't have time to swap stories with this guy. "Thanks for your help, but I've got a lion to track. Do you know which way he went?"

"You'll never find him on your own, female. My name is Matteo Leone. Come with me."

Chapter 19

ATTEO FILLED MY CUP WITH more water before sitting across the table from me. "It'll get cold."

"I'm not hungry," I said for the fifth time.

He glared at my bowl of tomato and fennel soup. "Is it not to your liking? I grow everything myself."

Matteo's home was rustic but spacious. The entire cabin was constructed of wood, and he probably had a massive garden in the back. This homestead wasn't just a getaway; this man had lived here for a very long time. Contrary to my first impressions, Matteo wasn't a filthy mountain man. He didn't have any kind of relationship with razors or trimming shears, but he was strong and looked like he took good care of himself. He obviously ate well.

I sipped the soup to be cordial. "It's good."

When he smiled, only one side of his mouth curved up. "I've often wondered if the food is good or I've just gotten used to the way I cook it."

I noticed a shelf filled with carved wooden figures. "Lived here long?"

He hooked his arm over the back of his chair and stared at the candles on the table. "Eat more."

"You didn't drug it, did you?"

His eyes locked on mine, and I gazed down to the soup. Matteo didn't have any motivation that I could see to poison me, so I ate the delicious meal. What I didn't like was the way he watched me. Chitahs have a thing about cooking for and feeding their mates, but I was neither a Chitah nor his mate, so his long looks made me uneasy.

I set down my spoon. "I appreciate your hospitality, but I can't stay."

"You won't survive the night."

"I've survived hell. One night in the woods is a walk in the park."

"The lions will hunt you."

"I thought you only saw one."

He stood up and moseyed to the kitchen behind me. His house was one large open room with a huge fireplace in the center that you could enjoy from both sides. And it wasn't just for warmth—he'd put my soup in a kettle and hung it over the fire. There was no refrigerator or electricity. The kitchen space had cabinets and tall shelves filled with jars of all kinds of different foods. They were stacked in deep rows from floor to ceiling. Hopefully the large barrels contained something innocuous like rice instead of pickled bodies.

Matteo returned with black licorice in his hand. "Before dusk, a group of men passed through. The leader had a blond mane of hair and walked ahead of the others. I followed them and discovered they were a pride of lions when I saw them marking trees."

"Did you confront them?"

He chewed off a piece of the dark candy. "Do I look foolish?"

I sat back. "They set up camp within walking distance?"

"They were letting their animals out for the night. They'll be hunting for food."

The way he looked at me, he thought I was going to be the food.

"Did you happen to see anyone else hike through here?"

He sucked on the candy, drawing it slowly past his lips. "I picked up several different scents." He reached across the table and tapped my bowl with his licorice. "Finish your meal."

I lifted the bowl and polished off the lukewarm soup so we could put an end to the constant shift in subject. His pupils dilated as he watched me gulp down something he'd grown, harvested, and prepared with his own hands. When I finished, I stood up and appraised his home. My fingers ran across the soft fur coat that hung from the wall close to the fire. "I take it you hunt?"

"Those pelts weren't for meat."

My hand recoiled as if I'd touched a rattlesnake.

Matteo still had his back to me as he nibbled on his candy. "That's what happens when Shifters cross into my territory."

"Is that what the traps are for? Catching intruders?"

"A man has to protect his land from all sides."

Great. Just what I needed. My only two options were sitting here until morning or falling into another death pit and impaling myself on a metal spike.

I glided past embroidered wall hangings. "Nice needlework. Have you thought about buying a television? It's a great way to kill time."

When he spoke, his voice dropped an octave. "You may critique anything in my home except for those."

When I looked back, his body had tensed like a lion about to pounce.

Interesting.

I crossed to the other side of the fireplace. A small bed tucked in the corner had a fur blanket over it, and blankets hanging from rods covered all the windows, insulating the cabin from chilly drafts. "So… you live out here by yourself?"

He grunted an affirmative sound.

When I reached my bag, I quietly lifted it and moved toward the door.

"What's your Breed?" he asked, rising to his feet. He crossed the room in five easy strides and leaned against the door, arms folded, eyes on me but his mind on the bag in my hands.

If a Mage had one natural enemy, it was a Chitah. Just because he'd fed me didn't mean we were pals. Many of my past enemies had bought me drinks or invited me to parties. While Matteo's venom didn't pose a threat, that wouldn't stop him from finding another way to kill me.

"Well?" he pressed.

"A Relic."

His nose twitched. "Lies."

"Maybe your nose is off."

"My nose is never off. I can always smell a lie."

I set my bag on the floor. "Care to make it interesting?"

He turned his head away as if uninterested.

"I'll say something, and you have to guess if I'm lying or telling the truth."

"Balderdash."

"Are you chicken?"

"This is a silly game."

"If I can fool your nose, you have to tell me where the lions are camped."

His golden eyes slanted toward me even though he was still looking away. "And if you can't trick me?"

"I'll... I'll pay you a thousand dollars."

After a beat, he slowly shifted his full attention toward me. "If I win, you wash my hair."

His hair was brown, like the mud on my clothes, and much longer than Niko's. "When's the last time you washed it?"

When he kept staring at me, I realized the request had nothing to do with cleaning his hair. He wanted the intimacy of all that scalp massaging and close contact. I'd rather just dump a bucket of water over his head, but sensing that wasn't what he had in mind, I decided to make the deal before he got specific.

"It's a deal."

Amusement danced in his eyes. "How do you know I won't deceive you to get what I want?"

I stepped closer. "Because you're a Chitah, and your word is your bond."

He inclined his head.

This was going to be a cakewalk. I rocked on my heels and smirked. "I'm a Vampire."

Matteo's nose twitched, and he suddenly pushed away from the door and loomed over me. He stared deep into my mismatched eyes, studied my flawed skin, and yet couldn't seem to figure out why my words smelled like truth. "Say it again."

My smile dimmed, and I repeated myself in slow words. "I am a Vampire."

His canines punched out as he drew in my emotional scent. "You're obviously not a Vampire. How do you do it? How do you say it with such conviction and belief that I can't scent your lie?"

"Years of practice. Well? Time to pay up."

"North," he replied. "The lions are a two-hour walk, just past a stream."

I grabbed my bag and reached for the doorknob, but he blocked it.

"You promised," I reminded him.

That roguish grin appeared on his face. "Yes. I promised to tell you their location, but you didn't ask me to let you go."

I flung my hands out to blast him, but he gripped my wrists and held them tight.

"I can't read your mind," he said, squeezing my wrists, "but I can smell a spike in adrenaline faster than you can blink."

"I'll just wait until you go to sleep. Did you plan on holding me captive forever? It's only a matter of time before we kill each other."

He leaned close and bared his teeth. "I'm saving your life, female. Danger lurks in the dark woods."

"Danger lurks in a woman's anger."

A laugh bubbled in his throat, and when it finally grew too much to contain, he tossed his head back and shook the room with the noise of it.

I turned away and mulled over my predicament. I wasn't blind. Matteo knew the perils in these woods the same way that I knew the dangers of the city. I would probably get lost, and I had no way to fend off a lion attack in the dark. I needed him.

"Be my guide."

Matteo strode away and settled at the table. He lifted his licorice and bit off another piece. "And why would I do that?"

"Because you're a trading man, and I'm sure you can come up with a fair deal." I approached the table and spun my chair around, straddling it. "I can pay you."

He waved his candy in a circle. "What use do I have for

money?" After swallowing his bite, he set down the licorice. "I haven't spoken to a female in a long time. I want your company."

I chuckled. "I'm the last person you'd want to keep you company. I'm not washing your hair, and I sure as hell don't plan on cleaning your house or cooking your meals. Do you want to hear about all the men I've killed?"

With an enigmatic look, he sat back.

My social skills weren't great, so I needed to figure out a way to get this guy to help me. Maybe through small talk. Matteo had long locks, and that made me curious. "I thought Chitahs only grew their hair long when courting a woman."

His piercing gaze forced me to look away.

"If you're lonely, maybe you should move into town. Find yourself a girlfriend."

"I have no wish for a friend." Matteo abruptly stood up and crossed the room. When he reached the cedar chest next to his bed, he lifted the lid and placed a folded quilt on the floor. Then he set a pair of tiny shoes on top of it before pulling out a pair of boots. After returning the shoes and blanket back to the cedar chest, he strode over to the table and set the boots in front of me.

"These should fit you."

I lifted a tan boot and felt the padded lining. They had thick treads for hiking, but they were too small to be his.

"I can give you thick socks if they're too big. It's not good to have your feet sliding around in a boot, but you'll need these. You can burn your flimsy shoes in the fireplace."

I unlaced my sneakers and set them aside. "These are practical in the city for running."

"And those are practical in the mountains for surviving," he countered, easing back into his chair.

I slid my foot into the boot, and it fit nicely. "Whose are these?"

"They once belonged to a remarkable woman." He gazed pensively into the kitchen.

I put on the second boot. "She left you?"

"Not by choice."

I sensed a story. "Did she die?"

"Yes."

"So you locked yourself away in the woods as punishment?"

He shifted sideways in his chair, propping one elbow on the table. "My kindred spirit is gone. What is the purpose of my life without the other half of my soul?"

I walked around and tested out the boots. "Maybe your purpose is to help me out. I shouldn't be telling you this, but I'm on a mission. Those lions are after children, and you don't want to know what they plan to do to them."

Matteo's golden eyes flashed up, and they were volcanic.

"If you help me, you'll be helping those kids."

"Why would you bring young out here?"

I was used to the nuances of Chitah lingo. Many referred to children as young. The trouble was, I couldn't give him a straight answer, so I rubbed at a mud stain on my sweatshirt.

His nose twitched. "Secrets. Everyone has them. Even me." Matteo traveled to the kitchen. He filled a kettle with water and set it on the woodstove, which was still hot from the bread he had baked that was still cooling on the counter. The black pipe funneled the smoke up through the roof. "There's a place in these woods they take little ones. Is that where you're going?"

I swallowed hard. He knew about it? *Nobody* was supposed to know about it.

"I smell your doubt, female." He removed two cups from the cupboard. "I've seen them taking children to this place. I never scented malice, so I didn't interfere. Not my business." Matteo stood up and pulled tea bags from a box. "Perhaps the fates brought us together for a reason."

I sat in my chair to face him and crossed my legs. "What do you know about those kids?"

"Nothing," he replied, watching the kettle. "The world moves around me like mechanical parts moving inside a clock. I'm not part of that clock anymore. I'm just the man sitting in the hall, staring at the face and watching the time pass with every swing of the pendulum."

I'd felt that way before, and it was a dark place to be. The isolation had almost destroyed me. If Viktor hadn't come along, I don't know what kind of monster I would have become.

A handsome smile crossed his expression.

"What's that look about?" I asked, curious.

"I'm not around people much. Only when I do simple trading with a Shifter a few miles from here. I suppose I've forgotten what it's like to be in a room with a person and scent their constantly changing emotions. You say nothing, but you say everything."

Steam blew from the spout on the kettle, and just as it whistled, Matteo lifted it off the stove and filled the cups.

He strode over and handed me a blue cup with a white string dangling from the side. "Let it steep."

I stood up and turned my chair around while he took his seat again.

Matteo lifted the string on the tea bag and dunked it repeatedly. "I'll be your guide." He said it with absolute certainty, as if it were fact.

I tugged on the string that dangled from my cup. "I have to warn you, it could be dangerous."

His dark lashes fanned down. "And now it's you who's worried about me?"

"I just think a man should know what he's getting into before he agrees to something."

Matteo lifted his cup and blew the steam. "I didn't say I would do it for nothing."

"And what do you want in return?"

When he took a sip, his nose glistened from the steam. After he set down the cup, he touched his lips thoughtfully. "I haven't felt a woman's touch in decades. You always think you'll remember the last kiss, but you don't. Not the one that counts."

I got cold feet and sat back. If this guy thought I was going to sleep with him...

"I want to remember the last kiss I ever have. That's all I ask for."

"You want a kiss? Nothing else?"

He pinched his bottom lip, and though Matteo had a

formidable presence, it seemed like he had folded himself up and become invisible. He was lost in his thoughts and didn't answer.

This was about saving lives, and it seemed like a harmless request. Chances were he'd quickly forget about the promise or change his mind and ask for money.

I lifted my cup and let the steam warm my nose. "Be my guide. Take me to the lions, and I'll promise you your last kiss."

His expression softened. "Drink, female. My kiss awaits."

Chapter 20

I scooped up a handful of damp earth. "Is this really necessary?"

Matteo shined his light on me. "If I can smell you a mile away, so will they. Put extra on your armpits and anywhere you sweat."

Still on my knees, I proceeded to rub dirt, leaves, and forest litter on my sweatshirt. Matteo would point to places he wanted me to pay special attention to. It smelled like earth and decay, and I sneezed when dust from the crushed leaves floated up to my nose.

Matteo tossed me a small bottle.

"What's this for?"

"Pour it in your hand and rub it through your hair and neck. I can smell your shampoo."

I popped the lid off the bottle. "What is it?"

He twirled the flashlight. "You don't want to know."

No. I didn't.

"We're close," he said. "Their scent is stronger."

"Ugh! This is *awful*." I wrinkled my nose and flipped my hair forward to rub it all in.

"Where's your jacket? The temperature's dropping."

"It stays in the bag. I'll be damned if I'm getting this pungent cologne of yours all over my good leather." I shot to my feet and scowled. "Happy?"

Matteo was as tall as Claude, a good six and a half feet. He lowered his head and gave me a warm look. He studied me closely. "You never did tell me your Breed."

"Sure I did." I marched in the direction we'd been walking.

He caught up. "You're not a Vampire. Not unless…" He wagged his finger at me. "Clever girl. You got me on wordplay, didn't you? I bet you suck the souls out of your suitors."

I smirked. "You're probably right."

He clutched my arm to stop me. "I need to know if you can protect yourself."

"Would I be chasing a lion if I couldn't? I know you have some instinctual need to protect women, but I've got a job to do. I'm not asking you to involve yourself. Just take me to the lions and go."

"Follow me."

Chitahs had decent night vision, so neither of us needed to use the flashlight as long as the moon kept periodically peeking out. Matteo moved through the woods as if he knew each tree, rock, hill, and fallen limb like the back of his hand.

He abruptly swung out his arm in front of me. After a few deep breaths, Matteo switched on his flashlight and approached a small clearing. The smell of charred wood lingered in the air like a dim memory. His light settled on the remains of a campfire now covered with dirt. General's men had cleared out, but the dirt still held a mixture of footprints and paw prints.

"I thought they were camping here?" I said, clenching my fists.

He walked around the stone circle and rubbed his nose. "I can still smell their excitement."

I wiped my clammy palms on my pants. "They wouldn't attack my group in the middle of the night, would they?"

He delivered a cold stare, his voice flat. "When would you attack *your* enemy? Daylight, when they're awake and alert? Or after dark, when only one person is keeping watch while the rest sleep?"

I released a controlled breath. "This isn't supposed to happen. I thought you said they were letting their animals out."

"They are. For hunting."

"I thought you meant for food, not my friends!"

I kicked a tree and flattened my palms against it. "How far can you take me? Do you know where to find my people?"

"Their scent is all through these woods," he said. "They stopped many times."

I turned around and locked eyes with him. "Tell me which way they went. I'll go on alone."

He took a step forward. "But then I wouldn't get my prize. I promised to take you to the lions." Matteo outstretched his arms. "They're not here, so I haven't made good on my word."

I gripped his wrist and threw as much sincerity and thanks in my words as I could muster. "Lead the way."

Christian finished splitting another thick branch with his bare hands. He carried the bundle of wood back to the campsite. The kids huddled together on flat stones Christian had placed near the fire. He dropped the wood in a pile so they could keep the fire burning until dawn.

"We shouldn't be lighting this," Blue said as she held out her hands and warmed them.

"We're in the middle of the godforsaken wilderness," Christian pointed out. "The only thing that's going to find us out here are the bears." He took a seat on a tall stone, one of many he'd collected and placed at the campsite shortly before dusk.

"People camp in the woods all the time," Viktor said, lying on his side with his head in his hand. "Besides, we need the fire to keep warm. Shifters will stay in their territory. We have seen no signs of trouble all day. This is good news." He briefly closed his eyes when the flames grew brighter. "I wish I had my vodka."

"Do you want another sandwich?" Blue asked. "I bought two loaves of bread, so there's plenty."

"Nyet. I have no room." Viktor patted his stomach. "Save for the children."

She breezed by him and wrapped up the bread before returning to the fire. "You should take food if you're hungry. You won't be any good to us if you're starving to death."

He chuckled and stroked his silver beard. "I am hardly starving, my dear."

Carol raised her hand from her spot by the fire. "I'll take one. Just jelly. No peanut butter."

"I'll get it." Claude stood up and squatted by the supplies.

Christian split his attention between the group and the woods. He was on the opposite side of everyone except for the twins, who were busy speculating where they were going. Christian didn't want to get too immersed in conversation since he was listening for suspicious footfalls, a human heartbeat, or whispering. They hadn't run into any trouble during the hike, so this would probably be an uneventful trip unless they encountered a rogue band of Shifters. As long as the kids kept their jackets on and their birthmarks covered, they'd be okay. Christian had been busy with manual labor, and this was his first chance to sit down. Once everyone went to sleep, he planned to pick a spot in the shadows and stand guard for the night.

After Claude slathered jelly across a slice of bread, he handed the sandwich to Carol and sat next to her. He'd been keeping a close eye on the lass ever since she and her boyfriend had parted ways. Christian had mentioned to Shepherd that the lad might try to escape, but Shepherd said he had plans to add an extra sleepytime ingredient to Joshua's cocoa, which would allow Shepherd to get some shut-eye for the night.

Eve stood up and removed her black jacket. Christian watched while she opened her bag and put on extra layers of clothing. She flipped her dark hair out from the collar and then made funny faces as she tried pulling her jacket on over everything. When it didn't zip, Christian did everything he could to refrain from laughing. Adam pulled out his clothes and copied her plan.

"Sorry, kids." Blue fished out two flat packages from her bag and tossed them on the ground. "We had to pack light. I only have two of these, but they should keep you warm."

Eve ripped open a plastic package and unfolded a silver Mylar blanket. "I don't get it."

Adam added more leaves to his makeshift bed. Their sleeping

spots were farther back from the fire. Probably just as well since the boy's bed was about as flammable as it got. "You wrap it around yourself, dummy. It's supposed to lock in body heat. Kinda like the foil they wrap around hot dogs."

She plopped down on her pile of leaves and spread the blanket over her. "Great. So now I'll look like a juicy hot dog to all the wild animals."

Adam opened his up and showed her how to wrap it around herself. Once they settled in, they lowered their voices and speculated what the new place would be like. Christian had to mute the rattling from the Mylar blankets. These kids weren't about to win any awards for the quietest camper.

When Carol sneezed, Claude took off his brown jacket and put it around her. She set her sandwich on a rock and put her arms through the long sleeves. After zipping it up, she resumed eating.

Claude dug through his bag and found a long-sleeved shirt to put on over his T-shirt. He ran a hand through his curly hair then poked his stick in the fire. "I think I cursed her."

"Who?" Blue took a seat just behind him, next to Viktor.

Claude looked over his shoulder at her. "Gem."

She rolled her eyes. "I doubt that."

"When we were at the pawnshop, I put on a mask. Gem said it was cursed and would bring bad luck or death to whomever you looked at. I can't remember exactly what she said."

"Superstition."

Viktor's head was still propped in his hand as if he were just resting his eyes and listening, but Christian isolated the sound of his heart and recognized the relaxed rhythm it often hit whenever he slept.

Claude's jacket swallowed Carol, covering her entire body down to her feet. Only her head of curly blond hair stuck out. She was a nervous little thing. Eyes always darting around, never trusting. They had to quell her chewing gum fixation after she kept snapping bubbles during the hike and then sticking the pink candy on trees when she was done. When she didn't have gum to keep her mouth busy, they had to endure a steady stream of complaints about how unfair it was that they left Joshua behind.

Young love.

Jaysus.

Christian heard birds rustling in the trees, a small mammal scurrying across the forest bed, and a larger animal moving around. He had already spotted two bears during their walk, but predators usually kept their distance from Breed.

Unless they were hungry.

"Why don't you seal up the rest of that food," Christian instructed them. "And don't leave any crumbs lying around. Not unless you want to wake up to a bear gnawing on your skull."

Carol's eyes widened as she finished the last bite of her sandwich.

Claude's nose twitched, and he gave Christian a loaded glance. "Don't scare them."

Christian shrugged. "Life is scary. Better they get used to it now."

While Blue gathered up the trash, Claude patted Carol on the back and tried to ease her fears. When he started purring, she snapped her head toward him.

"Are you doing that?"

He inclined his head.

After listening to it for a moment, she scooted closer to him. Chitahs purring seemed to have a soothing effect on people. To Christian, it was a chain saw in his ears.

Carol hugged her knees. "Are all Chitahs tall like you?"

"Most."

"And have the same eyes?"

"Some. There are a lot of variations in color, but usually yellow to golden brown."

"What about your kids?"

"I have none."

"Why not?"

Claude's brows drew together. "You ask too many questions."

"I'm not tired. What else is there to do?" She stared into the tall flames. "You got any brothers or sisters?"

Keystone members didn't probe into each other's personal lives, but Christian couldn't help but listen in, wondering if he might learn a little more about the mysterious Claude Valentine. Claude was a good tracker and a courageous fighter, but he was too amiable. How could a guy like that have no family or options other than Keystone?

Claude looked over his shoulder to see if anyone was listening. Viktor was asleep, and Blue had wandered off to bury the trash. "I had a sister, but she didn't look like me."

"Why not?"

"She was a human."

Carol frowned. "How? I mean…" She grasped for words.

"Chitahs have human DNA far back in our ancestry. Nature selects our babies to be born either a Chitah or a human. If they're human, we give them away."

"Why would you do that?"

"Because the Breed world is too dangerous for a human." Claude tapped her nose with his finger. "You above all should know this. When we give our children to the human world, we offer them a chance to live a normal life. They would always be vulnerable in our world, and it's a parent's greatest sacrifice."

"So you gave your sister away?"

Claude shifted on his rock. "No."

Carol rested her chin on her arms. "What did she look like?"

Christian's shoulders sagged. He was kind of hoping the lass would have asked about Claude's parents. Why would they have kept a human child? It was especially dangerous in olden times. Not just because of all the diseases, but it was commonplace for immortals to threaten the lives of mortal children in order to get what they wanted from a Chitah.

Claude cleared his throat. "Yvette had beautiful brown hair and matching eyes. She was not much taller than you are now. In fact, that's how I first learned to do hair. Yvette couldn't leave the house, and she always wanted to have her hair styled like all the pretty ladies she saw from the window."

"Why couldn't she leave?"

He snapped a small twig between his fingers. "Yvette was special. She had what people today call Down syndrome. In my time, they called it something much worse."

"But I thought…" Carol's mouth hung agape, and Christian could tell she was carefully choosing her words. "I thought if you were Breed, you couldn't have children with anything… different."

"That's very true, and they're the exception. Anyhow, Yvette wasn't Breed. Humans in those times put mentally challenged children into asylums with lunatics, sometimes by force. What a terrible fate for those innocent children to be locked away with madmen and murderers. My parents wanted to protect her, so they kept her at home. Had she not been born that way, they could have given her up for adoption, but Yvette had no chance at a normal life. Humans would have put her away, and none of us would accept that fate. My father consulted a Relic who specialized in Chitah disorders to find out how it could have happened. The Relic said it was very rare, but it was likely they could have more children with the same condition. I didn't care. Yvette was my little sister, and I guarded her with my life." He absently touched the stubble growing along his jaw and chin. "She loved to laugh and brought us so much joy. Children like Yvette are nothing but pure love." His smile faded just as quickly as it had appeared. "It angered me that she couldn't be a part of the world."

"I know how she feels." Carol glanced at the twins, who were sleeping. "I wish I had a brother or sister."

Claude gazed at the fire. "I didn't deserve such a gentle and loving sister, but I was a devoted big brother. I protected her for as long as I could and gave her all the love and laughter that the world never would. She should have had a better life, but she was just born in the wrong time."

Christian thought back to his own blind sister. He wasn't lucky enough to have known her more than a short time before he left Ireland, and it saddened him to think of what Cassie's fate might have been. She'd loved her big brothers, and they had all left her behind in search of adventure and money.

"Is that why you don't have kids?" Carol blurted out with the incivility of a fourteen-year-old. "Because you think they'll be like your sister?"

Claude's face heated, and his gaze intensified as he looked at Carol. "*Never.* I would be honored to have a child even half as beautiful as Yvette. Human or otherwise." He stood up and dusted off his jeans. "You should go to sleep. We'll be leaving early."

Claude lifted his bag and turned around, his heart pounding like a drum. He did what he could to conceal his emotions from a young girl who didn't know any better. Claude probably hadn't told that story in a long time, if ever.

A twig snapped in the woods behind Christian. As different sounds forged together, Christian realized that something was running toward them. Just as he turned, a lion emerged from the mouth of the forest and sailed over the fire.

Carol shielded her face and screamed.

Chapter 21

NAVIGATING THE WILDERNESS IN THE dark presented its own unique set of challenges unlike anything I'd experienced in the city. For one, I couldn't flash. Cognito was lit by cars, streetlamps, and ambient light from shops and windows. In the woods of West Virginia, your only illumination was a flashlight and the moon, and Matteo had put his flashlight away after finding a steaming pile of shit.

Apparently we were close.

He swung his arm in front of me, bringing me to a grinding halt.

"If you keep doing that, I'm going to cut off your—"

"Up ahead," he said quietly.

I squinted at the shadows in the distance. The moon had made another appearance, but it wasn't enough for me to make out anything other than slender tree trunks and patches of darkness.

Just then, the shadowy outline of an animal moved up ahead where two hills joined. A long tail swished, the dark tip making it stand out all the more.

When another lion roared in the distance, the creature before us bounded out of sight.

Matteo and I sprinted after it.

I tripped on a thick root but gripped a tree and kept going. Matteo was four paces ahead of me, but neither of us could use our gifts to run fast. Not on this rough terrain, and not in the dark.

"He'll outrun us!" I said, out of breath.

"I got his scent."

I thought about pulling out my dagger and carrying it, but

then I stumbled on a loose rock and decided it might be wise not to slice open an artery by accident. The straps on my backpack tugged on my shoulders, and every so often, a branch would snag it and yank me back.

Matteo clawed at the ground like an animal when he lost his footing.

I fell back a step, uncertain if he'd flipped his switch. I had better things to do than tangle with a confused Chitah in the middle of nowhere.

My leg muscles were on fire by the time we reached the top of a steep hill. The ground leveled out, and there were fewer trees. Our feet were no longer crunching on leaves but treading across wet ground cover like grass or moss. I swallowed, my throat parched and lungs burning.

The lion veered left. Matteo branched away from me and tore after it, but I headed straight.

The smell of burning firewood invaded my nose. There was also a flicker of light in the distance and the sound of another lion.

Out of breath, I stopped for a second and scanned my surroundings. The campsite was within view, but I didn't hear any screaming, running, or fighting.

That could only mean one thing—an imminent attack.

The acrid smell of urine wafted from a nearby tree, and I kept catching a whiff of it from the soft wind that blew from the direction of the campsite. That meant we were downwind, so Claude wouldn't be able to smell the territorial markings, let alone my panic. My boots were quiet against the mossy forest floor.

Since Matteo had gone left, I went right. Part of me wanted to scream out there was an attack, but I didn't know if Christian was anywhere near camp. My yelling could incite the animals to strike sooner.

I scoured the woods and stalked to the right. My breath caught when I glimpsed a lion charging for the camp. His massive paws tore up the earth behind him, and he moved like a bullet shooting through the dark. With level ground, I had a chance at cutting him off, so I flashed at breakneck speed toward the camp. The firelight grew bigger and bigger, but the bodies were indistinct shapes as they blurred into view.

Please, not the kids.

Time slowed to a crawl as the animal and I raced to the group. I spotted a stone at the last minute and used it to propel me into the air. The animal arced over the fire, his massive body glowing like butterscotch.

Carol's scream pierced the silence. Though it looked like the lion was going for her, he was targeting Claude, who had his back turned. I harnessed my energy and slammed into the animal with all my strength.

Before we even hit the ground, Claude ripped Carol from her seat to safety. Energy blasted through my palms as I gripped whatever body part I could on the beast. We tumbled to the ground, and he flipped over before I could blast him again.

Christian grabbed him by the haunches and dragged him away from me. The lion roared, and the sound made every living thing in the woods tremble with fear. When it kicked its hind legs, Christian lost his grip. The lion took off in a flash with my partner hot on its heels.

Claude held Carol tightly to him, his eyes as black as coal. She blanched, and I couldn't tell if she was more afraid of the near-death experience or Claude flipping his switch.

"The lions want the kids," I said, quickly filling everyone in.

The twins stood with their backs to the fire, Adam holding a big stick and Eve clutching his jacket.

Viktor pulled a gun out of his bag. "How many?"

"I don't know. Maybe you should shift."

He loaded a clip into the gun. "I'm a better shot than my wolf is a lion killer. Children, stay close."

I turned my back to the fire so I could scan the woods. "Where's Blue?"

Viktor looked around. "She was just here."

I steered my gaze upward. These trees weren't suitable for climbing, and the kids needed a safe place. If the lions lured us out…

I held my breath. "Shhh."

Leaves rustled in the distance.

"Another one!" Eve shrieked.

I spun in the direction she was pointing and braced myself, but instead of a lion, Matteo appeared. Blood speckled his cheeks and nose, and it coated his right hand.

"Oh shit," I muttered.

Claude was still in beast mode.

"He won't be a concern," Matteo informed me, barely casting a glance Claude's way.

"His switch is flipped. You need to get out of here."

"As long as the child is near him, he won't separate himself from her. He'll shield her from harm. That is the Chitah way."

Viktor delivered a scrutinizing gaze to our guest. The grip on his gun was tight, and I reached for his arm.

"This is Matteo. He brought me here."

In that moment, I suddenly realized how careless that looked. Viktor could have burned holes through my head with his fiery stare.

Matteo drew in a breath. "I'm not the threat."

"I have no reason to trust you."

Matteo straightened his shoulders. "Do you think I don't know who comes and goes in my woods? Your secret's safe with me. You must know that a Chitah's word is his bond. Gather your things and come with me. The lions will return soon."

I snapped my fingers at the twins. "Come on. Get your stuff together. Hurry up!"

Matteo must have scented their fear and approached. "I know these woods better than anyone. You're safe as long as you're with me. If you stay here, you'll die."

That was enough to get everyone hauling ass. Matteo took the position in front, Claude in the middle with the kids, and Viktor and me in the rear. Matteo switched on the flashlight and widened the beam so we could see.

"How could you bring us this danger?" Viktor said, scolding me.

"The lions aren't with me. Remember General, the loan shark

who tried to murder my father? He's behind this, and he wants the kids. I'm not sure how he knew about them, but one of his brothers wound up in the jail. I did everything I could to catch up."

I didn't need to speak Russian to understand Viktor was cursing.

"Don't worry," I assured him. "Christian will keep them distracted. He can shadow walk and follow their sound."

Viktor kept looking back, and I knew it had to do with leaving Blue.

"I'll go back for her," I promised him. "She's probably tracking everyone from the treetops."

That was a lie, but sometimes you need to tell yourself lies to get through a situation. And we were in a big fucking situation. We skidded down a hill, and Eve fell twice. Her brother clutched her to him after the second time.

I kept my eyes alert for any signs of movement.

When a lion roared in the distance behind us, Matteo shouted, "Move it!"

I glimpsed the lion darting between the trees.

I touched Viktor's arm and fell back. "I'll hold him off long enough for you to find shelter."

Viktor gripped my shoulder and gave it a firm squeeze before catching up with the children.

I flashed toward the lion. The Shifters must have communicated their plans to their animals prior to shifting: follow the kids and kill the rest. But animals were also instinctual. Would they follow their human counterpart's advice if a juicy little stray darted in front of them?

As I neared, I let out a shrill scream and veered left. I wanted him to think I was weak prey. I weaved around trees, charged through bushes, and finally skidded down a hill before stumbling into a shallow stream. The ice-cold water splashed my jeans, but the boots Matteo had given me were blissfully waterproof, so I felt light on my feet when I stepped out of the water.

Before I had a second to breathe, a roar filled my eardrums. The weight of the beast blindsided me, and before we hit the ground, I blasted him in the face with what little energy I had left. It knocked him out long enough for me to stand.

Warm blood trickled down my right arm from the tear in my sleeve. Incensed, I knelt down and blasted him again.

"Dammit! If I had my long dagger, I'd gut you from neck to navel."

I pulled the push dagger from my belt and sliced his neck, but his skin was too thick. So much for learning anything useful about animal biology in school. He belly-crawled away and then shifted to human form. The gash on his neck healed, and I looked at his distinctly familiar face and shaved head. It wasn't Major or any brother that I had met, but it was definitely someone from the same gene pool.

When I lunged forward to strike, he shifted back to animal form.

I reeled backward. With too much of my core light depleted, fighting him was a death wish. I climbed a steep ravine covered in decomposed leaves and roots. To keep from sliding down, I gripped slim trees, but my backpack was throwing me off-balance. The lion lunged, clawing his way up behind me, but his weight pulled him back down.

Halfway up, I rested behind a vertical tree with my feet anchored at the base. I needed a minute to think this through. I could drink a man dry in less than a minute, but this was a lion. I'd have to do some serious damage to his neck. My core energy was too low to continue fighting with light, not unless I wanted to end up as lion food. At least I was keeping him preoccupied. If he gave up on me, he might search for the kids again. Had the team reached safety by now?

The animal pounced at me and slid back down. The second time, his massive paws got too close for comfort. I caught my breath as blood continued to stream down my arm. There might have been exposed tendons for all I knew, and the thought of climbing again was agonizing.

"Hold still," Christian said from above. "I'm coming for you."

The lion tried a third time, and his claws snagged the bottom of my boot before he fell back down. He paced back and forth, huffing and growling with frustration.

The next thing I knew, Christian hooked his arm around me and dragged me the rest of the way up. Out of breath and dizzy, I sat there in a stupor.

"The scent of your blood will hold him here for a while," Christian said. "Here."

He didn't offer his vein; he forced his wrist to my mouth. My fangs punched out and broke skin as I made holes large enough to drink from. When they retracted, I drank greedily. The searing pain in my arm turned to prickles and then disappeared, and while my Mage light was still depleted, I felt a different kind of power filling up my well.

Vampire power.

Christian remained kneeling, his eyes trained on the lion below. "I killed one and saw at least three others. Then I heard you up here, offering yourself as vittles. It's not easy to shadow walk in the fecking wilderness," he grumbled.

Tell me about it, I thought to myself.

"I tracked them by sound, but then everything went haywire."

I took one last drink and used the trace amounts of Vampire magic in my saliva to seal the puncture marks. "What do you mean?"

"They put sonic weapons on the trees near the camp but spaced them far enough out that I didn't hear anyone setting them up. When I went after the lion, someone set them off, and I couldn't hear a bloody thing. The deafening pitch forced me to shut off my hearing at close range."

"How did you find me?"

"I had to break them. Did you separate from the group for thrills?"

"That one was closing in on us. Someone had to distract him."

Christian gave me a crooked smile. "That's my girl."

I wrapped my arms around him. It felt good to be in his arms, to feel healed again.

"You smell like a litter box," he muttered, squeezing me tight. "How did you get out of jail?"

"Long story."

He removed my backpack and helped me up. "Do you know where they went?"

"I know the general direction. Matteo had a place in mind. It can't be far."

Christian put his hands on his hips. "Matteo? And who the feck is this you're bringing along?"

"He helped me get here, and we made a deal. I trust him. Well, sort of."

Christian arched an eyebrow. "Sort of? Thank the heavenly angels you only partly trust the man in charge of three children."

I gave Christian a light shove and headed north. "I only trust him because he gave me his word."

Christian snorted. "Are you afflicted in some way? A man's word is as good as a gas station burrito."

"You're not even making sense."

"It's as reliable as a three-legged horse in a race."

I glanced over my shoulder. "Do I know you?"

"If something happens to them, you'll never forgive yourself for being so naive."

"He's a Chitah. You know how they are about their word, and despite all the scumbags I've run into, they're pretty serious about a promise."

"You haven't fallen for him, have you?"

Christian was joking, but something beneath his tone made me wonder. Ah, the smell of jealousy.

"Sorry it had to work out this way, Christian. But after nearly dying in one of Matteo's traps, I realized it was true love. *Of course* I'm not falling for him. He's not my type. He's Claude's height. Not that there's anything wrong with tall men. If he were skinny it might look strange, but he's definitely buff and filled out in all the right places."

"What are you blathering on about?"

"Never mind. I can't trust a man who makes me smell like animal urine."

"Do I even want to know?"

I sniffed my hair and wrinkled my nose. "No, you don't."

When we'd walked far enough to put distance between us and the lion, we crossed the stream. I removed my sweatshirt and washed the blood off my arm. Then I let the stinky garment float away.

"I think as long as we walk slowly and stay calm, they won't be able to track us," I said, shivering in my T-shirt. "Vampires don't have a scent, and I smell like—"

"A toilet," he answered. "If there was ever a test of love, this is it."

"Careful, Poe. I just might want to make out later on after we kill these bastards."

I froze in my tracks when a gunshot erupted, followed by three more. Christian and I tore through the woods in the same direction. The sounds were close, and I knew Viktor had a gun.

Christian shadow walked, gliding through the darkness like liquid. I'd seen him climb a tree that way, but it wasn't as easy with uneven ground. A rabbit scurried off when I jumped over a fallen tree. I was having trouble seeing until the moonlight appeared again.

The fourth gunshot made me duck.

Another fired.

"It's me, you dolt!" Christian yelled.

Confused, I lost my concentration and smacked into a tree.

"Next time fucking announce yourself," Shepherd snarled. "I almost shot your damn head off!"

When I backed away from the tree and weaved around a thicket of overgrown bushes, I saw Shepherd standing with a gun in his hand and a torch light strapped to his head. His leather coat was zipped up to the collar.

"Nice hat," I remarked, not winded at all thanks to Christian's blood. "Where did you come from?"

"You wouldn't happen to have seen a mountain lion running around, would you?"

"Don't tell me. Joshua got away?"

He put his gun back in the holster and shifted his backpack.

"A lion just came at me. I think I got him in the leg. Mind filling me in?"

Christian scanned the woods.

"Remember General?" I straightened my T-shirt. "They ambushed the campsite, and it was well planned. They put those sonic blockers or whatever on the trees so Christian wouldn't hear them once the attack began."

"What do they want? Revenge?" He patted his gun. "I got their revenge right here."

"They want the kids."

He cursed under his breath. "We're in a tight spot. Where is everyone?"

"North, but that's all I know. A local tracker is helping us. He knows these woods, and before you ask, we can trust him."

Shepherd rubbed the whiskers on his jaw, which had ventured into beard territory. "He must know of a nearby house. Only an idiot would pitch another campsite."

I walked past them. "We need to get moving."

"Everyone all right?" Shepherd patted the shoulder strap of his bag. "I've got all my medical gear."

"I don't know. Blue's missing."

Shepherd walked ahead of me, but I could tell he was worn out from all the hiking he must have done. He suddenly jerked his head toward me and blinded me with that damn headlamp. "You smell like—"

"Roses. That's what you're about to say, isn't it?"

He chuckled. "Something like that." After a few more paces, he pointed at some brush. "Footprints. They've been through here." He aimed the light at the ground and moved it around. "This way."

"I hear them," Christian alerted us. "They're not far."

"You can hear again?" I asked him.

"Aye. They only planted the devices by the camp. Guess their plan backfired."

My stomach turned. "I don't know. They thought this through. Maybe this was part of the plan."

"Then why did they not attack us all at once?"

Shepherd wiped his nose. "Because the first rule of battle is to disorient your enemy and force them to a second location. Lions also like to separate the herd. It increases their odds of success. When you keep someone moving on the defense, they panic and make mistakes. They've already managed to separate us, and they're cutting into our sleep time. These guys are playing chess, not checkers. One calculated move at a time."

"It's gonna be a long night," I muttered, ducking beneath a low branch.

After several minutes hiking, we spotted a bright glow up ahead. The smell of charred wood wafted toward us as a huge fire burned at the mouth of a cave. Most wild animals instinctually avoided smoke and fire as a source of danger, so if the lions didn't shift back, it might keep them at bay.

"Don't shoot. It's Shepherd," he called out.

Viktor emerged from the entrance and lowered his gun as he met up with Shepherd. "You're not supposed to be here. Where is the boy?"

Shepherd sighed. "We stayed parked right where we were, just like you instructed. You're right. That kid would have bolted from the door and jumped onto the road if I'd driven back. I drugged his tea to knock him out, but I guess he was onto me. After he nodded off on the couch, I went to take a piss. He must have dumped it when I wasn't looking. Swear I was in there for only one minute with the door open, and when I came out, poof... he was gone. Searched the whole damn area, but I knew which way he was headed."

Christian dropped my bag and raked his fingers through his disheveled hair.

"How did you find us?" I asked, baffled by Shepherd's tracking skills.

"Viktor and I mapped out the path on the way here after talking to Wyatt on the satellite phone. I knew the general area and distance, but the lions and screams led me to the right spot."

I blinked and looked between them. "Where's the phone? Can we call for backup or cancel the mission?"

"Nyet." Viktor led us into the cave. "We have no choice but to follow this through. No outside parties were approved for this mission. I have explicit orders to keep everyone out, and we have already broken that rule with your new acquaintance."

"Speak of the devil," Christian murmured.

Matteo appeared from the woods with an armload of sticks and branches. "We need more wood, but I don't have my axe."

Christian walked assertively up to him, and the two men stared at each other. While Matteo was a good five or six inches taller, Christian had the advantage in looking him in the eye. Matteo didn't chance it and kept his gaze at mouth level.

Christian folded his arms. "And who might you be?"

"Matteo Leone, at your service." He bowed, his long hair falling forward.

"Is that so?" Christian's fangs punched out. "If you do one thing to put these children in harm's way, I'll cast your head to the lions." He snapped his gaze toward Viktor. "Why do we still need him?"

Viktor zipped his coat all the way up. "Because we are lost and lions are hunting us."

I searched the chamber. "Where are the kids?"

"Up here," Carol said.

I swung my gaze up to a narrow crevice and saw her head poking out. They must have used the pile of large rocks below to climb up.

"It's roomy in here, but I'm scared of spiders." Her eyes flicked over to the group and noticed Shepherd. "Where's Joshua? You didn't hurt him, did you?"

"I'm sure he's fine," Shepherd said, easing her fears. "He ran off."

Carol's eyes sparkled with excitement, and she ducked out of sight.

We all knew what she was thinking. But if Joshua was out there with those savage lions, Carol might never see him again, and that scenario was more likely than him whisking her away into the proverbial sunset.

Claude crawled out from a passageway on the right, a flashlight in his hand. "There's a stream in there. We can fill up the canteens and bathe. Without moving large rocks, I can't tell if the water channel is wide enough to create a breach."

Matteo shook his head. "I've been here a dozen times, and it's safe. The water comes in through narrow gaps, and the only way in and out of this cave is through the entrance. The second chamber is big enough if the little ones would rather sleep in there, but I think it best if you keep them in here. You might have to move out quickly."

Christian stared at the sparse pile of sticks before heading out. "I'll gather more wood."

Viktor guarded the entrance while Matteo stoked the fire.

I approached Claude, hands on my hips. "Can I borrow your flashlight? I need to wash my hair."

He wrinkled his nose. "Yes, you do. Want me to help?"

I shrugged and followed his lead.

After crawling through a crooked gap between two massive rocks, we entered a larger room. The ceiling was maybe ten feet high, and while I could hear the constant rushing of water, I couldn't see it.

Claude went left and stood on top of a flat rock with his flashlight aimed at the clear water trickling through. "It's shallow, but maybe I can pull some of the rocks out so we can submerse your head." He handed me the flashlight. "Be right back."

"Bring me my bag."

Claude slipped through the crevice and out of sight.

There was no point in wearing Matteo's camouflage cologne anymore, especially since I'd sweated like a horse and bled like a stuck pig. Eager to ditch my dirty clothes, I stripped out of my T-shirt and flung it into a corner. After taking off the boots and my weapons, I tossed my jeans in the corner with the shirt.

"Holy crap!" My voice reverberated off the chamber walls. The icy water burned my scalp, so I quickly scooped up handfuls of it to wash my arms, torso, and neck.

"Um… maybe you need Christian," I heard Claude say.

"Now isn't the time to be bashful. You're lucky I'm wearing a bra today. Toss me my bag."

The backpack hit the spot behind me, but Claude remained by the door with his head turned. How adorable.

To my dismay, I hadn't packed a full wardrobe. I had clean underwear and sweatpants, which I put on, but no extra shirt. Just my leather jacket. This would teach me a valuable lesson about packing in the future.

"I'm ready for my makeover," I sang. "Hurry up. I'm freezing to death."

When he approached, his eyes swung down. "You should cover yourself."

"I don't have a shirt. Let's get this over with, because this stone is going to be cold as hell against my back." I widened the beam of the flashlight and set it down.

Claude suddenly took off his long-sleeved black shirt and tossed it at my feet. He had a T-shirt on beneath it, but it wasn't enough to keep him warm. "I have another shirt," he said, encouraging me to accept his offering.

"Thanks. Let's wash my hair first so this doesn't smell."

The stone slab against my back was enough to wake me up into my next reincarnation. It numbed my skin, and Claude must have scented my discomfort, because his magic hands were moving faster than usual. He'd also put a dollop of shampoo in my hair that he'd brought in his supplies.

Leave it to Claude. That man would have great hair even during the apocalypse.

My teeth chattered, and I tried to think of warm things like campfires, cocoa, hot summer days, and Christian's hands on my body.

"That's it." He washed his hands in the water and then stood up. "We should mark this spot and draw water from the opening. If anyone has to pee, they should do it on the far right so they don't contaminate the drinking source."

"Why not in a corner, away from the water?"

"Better to let the water carry it out. It's sanitary that way. If for some reason we wind up staying here a week, do you want to contend with a urine pool? The stream moves in one direction, so the source on the left is fresh." He rubbed the spot below his bottom lip with his index finger. "I'm afraid the kids might get sick. This isn't purified water, and we don't have anything to boil it in."

I squeezed out my hair and put on Claude's shirt. "Shepherd probably has medicine. What's the worst that can happen?"

"Three children with diarrhea in a small cave." His nose wrinkled. "That's the worst that can happen."

I laughed. "To you or them?" The sleeves on the shirt flopped around, making me feel like I was five again and wearing my father's clothes. I rolled each one up to my wrists. "We need to hunt down those lions tonight. If they don't attack, they're going to wait until we starve to death."

"We can't abandon the children."

I stepped into my boots. "*You* can't leave the children. They need your protection. But I have to leave. We need to find out what happened to Blue."

He gripped the flashlight tightly in his hand. "I should have picked up their scent."

"They were stalking you with the wind in their favor and doing it at a safe distance. This isn't about what we did wrong; it's about who can outsmart the other. If they haven't already found us, they will. And they'll expect us to stay here and protect the kids as a group. Safety in numbers and all that. Maybe that's our best move, but it's also the one they're probably anticipating." I lifted my backpack and slung it over my shoulder.

"I don't trust him," Claude said, jerking his head toward the passageway.

"Matteo? I know. He wasn't part of the plan, but he saved me."

Claude rubbed his hand down his bare chest, a predatory look in his eyes. "Did it ever cross your mind that he might be a part of this? Perhaps that's why they didn't attack. It was a scare tactic so your friend could lure us to this cave."

I wanted to argue, but I bit my lip and thought about it. "We didn't just bump into each other on the path. I fell into a trap."

He rolled his shoulders back and turned away. "Maybe we all have."

Chapter 22

A FTER NIKO MEMORIZED THE LAYOUT of Cyrus's home, he did his best to keep the tyrant occupied. The more focus Niko drew to himself, the better. Cyrus's obsession wasn't limited to the book but also the power he held over people. His strength was his weakness, and Niko had taken advantage of that Achilles' heel by offering himself to Cyrus. It was the only way to ensure Gem was protected if he couldn't negotiate her release.

After Niko finished heating a kettle of tea, he navigated across the spacious room until he reached the wooden couch on the opposite side. Cyrus had a distinct light that Niko categorized as a bumpy red. Having been blind all his life, Niko didn't have a true frame of reference outside of his own imagination to describe the colors his gift allowed him to see. His sensei had taught him a great deal about his special gift of sight, and Cyrus didn't need to know those things.

Niko set the tray on a raised section designed for holding food and beverages.

"Sit," Cyrus invited him.

Niko reached for a nearby chair before taking a seat.

"On the floor, Nikodemos. You know your place by now."

Niko suppressed his irritation and sat cross-legged on the floor. "Where is everyone?"

Cyrus's clothes rustled as he shifted in his seat. "Lykos and Arcadius are guarding, so don't get any ideas."

"And Kallisto? I regret not meeting him. Has something happened?"

Tea poured into a cup. "That is for me to know. It is a shame you broke my loyalty all those years ago." After a noisy slurp, Cyrus's cup clicked on the surface of the tray. "Plato has shown exceptional loyalty, even in death. He's kept a close eye on your collection of misfits. He followed that woman with the blue eye and her Vampire friend when they were transporting weapons. He mentally encouraged a Mage to stop the traffic lights. Would you believe he went into a nearby vehicle and convinced a man to follow them? He has that gift, you know. Something about being dead allows ghosts to slip into people's heads and give them gut feelings about something."

"To what purpose?" Niko asked.

"To sabotage. To collect information. To do everything in his power to unravel the rug from beneath your feet. He listened in on private conversations your leader held regarding those precious children you're protecting. He followed your friends as they picked up supplies and patiently waited until he had enough information on where they were going and what they were transporting. Potentials… I always thought they were a myth. Only the ancients believe, but even I am skeptical as I've never seen one myself."

"What could you possibly want with innocent children?"

"Innocent?" Cyrus belted out a laugh. "Innocence is an illusion. Worry not, brother. I have no use for them, but I happen to know all about your friend's financial entanglement with the loan shark. You murdered two of his brothers and turned in a third. That's exactly the kind of thing that incites a man to revenge, and I love a man with motives. I passed along the information about your trip to see if he was interested."

"So they could kill me? You're a coward."

Cyrus laughed. "Kill you? The gods have kept you alive for over a thousand years. If they wanted you dead, it wouldn't be at the hands of lions. But perhaps those bloodthirsty Shifters might weaken your team. Or even better, ruin your reputation with the higher authority." Cyrus took another sip of his tea. "Regardless of General's plans, I knew your leader wouldn't take along the child you live with. Someone would have to remain behind, and usually those are the weakest links in the chain."

"Why target Keystone when it's me you want? You're pathetic to involve a child."

Cyrus sipped more tea and set down his cup. "I will always have a hand in Keystone affairs as long as you're with them, but it seems that you're with me now. I hope this isn't a ruse. I cased the Keystone property not long ago. It's not difficult to climb to the roof when you have the right equipment. Remember when we scaled the royal walls? Oh, wait. You weren't there."

Clearly Cyrus was still bitter over Niko leaving him. Perhaps most of that hostility lay with the betrayal more than Niko taking the book. Cyrus craved fealty, and he loved putting someone in their place. But Niko's focus was currently elsewhere—Cyrus had just admitted to disclosing private information about their latest mission to one of Keystone's enemies. Viktor and the team were in danger, and there was nothing Niko could do about it.

Nothing.

Their fate was already sealed.

"If Plato is here, give him my regards."

Cyrus belted out a laugh. "I would, but the Gravewalker I hired instructed him to stay with Kallisto." His light fluttered. "Let's speak openly. Where did you go after you left us?"

"Many places."

"And who trained a blind man to fight with a sword?"

"A master at his craft."

Cyrus sighed. "You test my patience, boy."

Niko's jaw set. "I'm no boy, Cyrus. I'm over fifteen hundred years old."

"And I have the power to destroy a woman you care about."

Niko lowered his head. "I am at your mercy."

Cyrus's tone lifted along with his mood. "That's what I like to hear."

"Let her go. She's no longer of any use to us."

"Nikodemos, are you begging?" Cyrus chuckled. "I don't think I feel the sincerity in your tone."

"You can no longer barter with her. I won't play your games."

"What an extraordinary gift of language she has. Did you think you could keep her all to yourself?" Cyrus sipped his tea. "Shame on you. Here I was, thinking you joined that band of misfits for the betterment of mankind. But you joined to protect your investment, didn't you? An impregnable mansion, numerous hiding places, and a collection of despicable Breeds who would protect you. You should have stayed with me. We could have ruled this world together."

"The only things you rule are spineless worker bees."

"Careful. I still have a stinger just as sharp as your tongue."

Niko worried that Cyrus might use Gem to translate the ancient text. "She's never seen the book. She doesn't know those languages."

"And how would *you* know what *she* knows?"

Niko laughed and shook his head. "What is your intention? To hold on to a girl who will only become a nuisance? She's talkative and opinionated. I know how much you abhor that in a woman."

"True. Not to mention she's fair skinned. You can't trust them. But you know a little bit about that, don't you, my blue-eyed friend?"

Niko lifted his chin and abandoned his civil tone. "You gave me your word earlier that you didn't harm her. She told me otherwise."

"Arcadius had no choice but to drown the woman to keep her quiet."

Niko's energy spiked at the thought that someone had drowned Gem in her one place of sanctuary. He couldn't imagine the terror she must have felt, not even having the ability to scream for help. No chance to fight. Arcadius had a shielding ability that protected him from the elements as well as Mage gifts. Niko had long suspected that Arcadius was a Unique—one of a rare group of Mage immortals with extremely uncommon gifts. His sensei had told him stories about Uniques who were hunted by their own kind. Men who—according to legend—had received their first spark when the gods were at war and lightning crashed all around. Whatever the truth was, Cyrus was smart enough to keep strong men like Arcadius at his side, and Arcadius was too ignorant to realize that his power far surpassed that of the man he followed.

"You better tamp down that energy," Cyrus warned him.

Niko cursed in Old Japanese.

Just as soon as he heard Cyrus rise to his feet, an object whistled through the air and struck his back. Niko winced from the sharp sting of a whip.

"Lykos! Arcadius!" Cyrus bellowed.

Niko spied their energy entering the home through the front door. They flanked him and must have taken visual direction to seize his arms.

"I've waited a long time for this," Cyrus said, basking in his words. "A long time."

The whip struck Niko again, and he grimaced.

"Take off the shirt. I don't want to get blood on it. Those are your special clothes, brother. We must take good care of them."

Niko didn't have to comply—Lykos and Arcadius had already lifted the garment away. Niko seethed. He wanted to fight back, but his team's lives were more important than his discomfort and pride.

"What are you doing!" Gem shrieked.

Niko snapped his head up to the purple light streaking into the room. "Go in the other room, Gem."

"You can't let them do this!"

Cyrus's laugh was low and malicious. "Foolish girl. He has surrendered himself as my slave, and he is bound to me. A slave who steps out of line must be punished for his insolence. If he chooses to fight, it's at his own peril. Or yours. Or perhaps that young boy you think you're protecting. Or perhaps so many others connected to your team. Where should I start first?"

Gem's light was no longer deep amethyst and silver. The deep blue flutters indicated she was afraid, but she was also angry and confused. Niko could read every detail as her emotions fluctuated, including her strength and determination to win.

"Please don't do this," she begged.

The whip struck Niko again. Lykos and Arcadius released their hold, and Niko fell forward.

Gem choked back a sob. "I'll do whatever you want. *Please.*"

When Niko heard a slap, he shot to his feet and launched himself at Lykos. It was *his* energy that pulsed just moments before Gem fell. Niko struck Lykos with a closed fist and then put him in a choke hold. Niko squeezed the trachea, so much rage powering through him that he would have cut off this man's head if there had been a sword in his hand.

Gem shrieked, and by the scuffle and grunting, it sounded as if someone was holding her down. Niko lost focus. His eye exploded with pain when Lykos struck him. When Niko fell onto his back, someone grabbed his ankle and locked a metal object around it.

"Hold him still," Cyrus ordered, his patience wearing thin. "He has no power anymore."

Niko felt the absence of his core light for the first time in his immortal life. The link that had once been around Gem's ankle was now around his, and the place deep down that had once held his immortality now felt like an abandoned lighthouse. He had no sense of his energy, and though his powers were only suppressed, it was the first time in almost two thousand years that he felt mortal again.

Vulnerable.

Fragile.

And it was dark. So very dark. His gift to see energy was now gone, thrusting him back in the world where he once lived as a boy.

"Will you do anything?" Cyrus mused.

"I could kill you all," Gem declared in a small voice as if toying with the idea.

"Including your friend? Do so," Cyrus challenged her. "Show us your powers." He erupted with laughter.

Gem had little control over her energy balls and how destructive they could be if not properly formed and launched. Niko had seen the energy for himself, and it was immense. But he knew she'd never be so reckless as to wield her power within a small space. Not only could Cyrus and his men flash out of the way by the time she created an energy ball, but Gem could inadvertently kill everyone in the process, including herself.

"What a shame," Cyrus remarked. "I was curious what gifts you might be hiding in those tiny hands of yours."

"What do you want?" she asked.

"Do you see that feeble man before your feet? If you don't do as I ask, I'll whip him more. His wounds won't heal with that cuff on. I'll make him suffer."

Gem gasped.

"Return to your home and bring me the book."

Niko struggled against the two men holding his arms. "Gem, *don't.*"

"I can't give you the book," she argued, ignoring Niko. "I don't have it. I don't know where to look."

Niko winced when Cyrus kicked him in the back.

"This one will never tell," Cyrus said. "But you're a crafty woman. I have faith you'll find it now that you have the right motivation. If you succeed, I'll remove the cuff from his ankle. He still remains my servant, but he'll live."

"And if I fail?"

"Have you ever seen a man flayed? I can also rupture his eardrums and pour liquid fire in there so he'll never hear again."

"Don't do it, Gem," Niko insisted. "Don't listen to him. He doesn't keep promises."

"Oh?" Cyrus walked in front of Niko. "I promise that Kallisto is ready to end a life. I won't say whose life, but would you like to find out if I keep my promises?" He snapped his fingers. "Lykos, lock him up for now. Arcadius, please escort the Mage partway home. She'll have to walk the rest of the way barefoot."

Lykos gripped Niko by the hair and yanked him up, a sharp knife poking against his back. Niko tried to resist, but the blade threatened to pierce his spine.

"I don't even know what I'm looking for," Gem whimpered.

"A book," Cyrus said matter-of-factly. "An old book with red leather binding. The pages are old, but they shouldn't be damaged. And the first page has a symbol of the ouroboros. Do you know what that is?"

"I don't care. Niko, please tell me where it is," she pleaded.

Niko paused near the hall, and Lykos let him. They wanted him to answer.

But he couldn't. Even at the risk of Keystone, that book could never fall into Cyrus's hands. Especially now that Cyrus knew about Gem's ability to decipher language. She didn't realize it, but she was about to become his instrument. Gem would probably jump at the opportunity to learn something new, but she had no idea of the repercussions.

Knowledge is power, and the knowledge inside that book had the power to destroy.

Gem flashed home after Arcadius dropped her off a mile from the mansion. They had blindfolded her and put her in the trunk so she couldn't identify her location. She had a number to call when she was ready, and they would provide her with a destination point to meet. Cyrus knew their home was protected, so he took no chances.

Gem couldn't get out of that car fast enough. She had spent the entire drive wondering if she should wield an energy ball and destroy Arcadius as soon as he opened the trunk, but he had the power to shield himself. Aside from that, Niko was still in danger, and no telling who else Cyrus planned to target.

Once Gem found the book, she'd figure out the rest. After punching in the code to the gate, she slipped between the iron bars as it opened and flashed up the road.

A wolf exploded into view, gathering speed and bounding toward her. Gem shrieked. When she reached the locked door, she spun on her heel and sharpened her light to blast the animal before it tore her apart.

The wolf slowed his pace, his coat as black as midnight. Before he reached her, his sharp canines disappeared and his tail started wagging. Gem held off her attack, uncertain if he was friend or foe. When the black wolf sniffed her, he lifted his head and howled. Other wolves in the vicinity howled back, and a chill ran up her spine.

Gem pounded her fist on the door. A few seconds later, the door swung open and Wyatt gaped down at her.

"Son of a ghost! Where did you come from?"

She briefly took notice of his *Déjà* Boo shirt of a ghost. He looked so normal considering their world was crumbling around them. "Why are there wolves?"

Switch appeared behind him, his long hair framing his stern face. "Are you alone?"

She pushed her way inside.

Wyatt gripped her arm. "Where have you been? Why are you still in a nightgown? If this was some kind of prank—"

She wrested her arm free. "I don't have time to talk to you." Without answering his questions, Gem hurried up the stairs.

"Hold your ponies," Wyatt called from behind her. "You can't just ditch us in the middle of the night and come strolling in like nothing happened. I've fallen out of contact with Keystone, Niko vanished looking for you, and all hell's broken loose."

She flashed to get ahead of them and made it to the second floor. Niko had a room on the same floor as her but nowhere near her room. Gem had a nice view of the courtyard, but when she opened the door to Niko's room, he had no view at all. She had been in his room twice but never took notice of anything other than the wardrobe. His space was so dark that she had to retrieve a lantern from the hall to see in front of her nose.

Once inside, she closed the door behind her and slid the lock into place. The first thing she noticed was the wood floor against her bare feet. Why hadn't she thought to put wood in her room? It was so warm and inviting. She remembered him once saying how he liked the feel of wood, how it had a life to it. It was once trees, and now those living things were artifacts of a former life. A mink blanket covered his bed on the left side of the room. At least, she thought it was mink. Today's artificial furs made it impossible to tell. It felt luxurious beneath her fingertips as she made her way to the bedside table on the left. Usually people put lamps on them, but his had no personal or decorative items.

She set the lantern down and searched the drawers. The top drawer had a burlap pouch with something crushed up inside. It smelled like flowers, but she wasn't good at identifying scents. The bottom cabinet held a neat stack of knitted hats on the right and gloves on the left. Everything was so organized and simplistic.

Gem got up and went to the wardrobe on the opposite side of the room. He had replaced the pulls with ones that were knobby glass, and it occurred to her that everything in his room was about space and texture. When she opened the doors and looked at his black shirts, a terrible pang clenched her heart. The pink shirt she'd slipped in there was staring her right in the face. Gem ripped it off the hanger and flung it onto the floor, furious that she'd been so insensitive. It was only a reaction to his all-black attire, but what right did she have mocking someone's disability?

Niko was offering himself to Cyrus as a slave in order to save Gem, and what generous thing had she ever done for him?

"Well, that's going to change," she muttered.

Different styles of black pants were neatly folded at the bottom. Gem lifted each one to search for a hidden book. She even pulled the heavy wardrobe away from the wall to look behind it. Alas, there were only a few cobwebs. Niko kept his shoes lined up against the wall to the right of the wardrobe, all below a long bench. Every other shoe had a pair of socks rolled up in it.

Wyatt and Switch were banging their fists on the door, but Gem took her time, tapping and pushing on every single wood plank in the flooring. She'd seen enough movies to know about trick floors and secret hiding spots. After that, she tugged and pushed on the stones in the walls, but none of them came loose or activated a secret hiding spot.

The bathroom had absolutely nothing of interest but a standing shower, toilet, and sink. But she checked inside the toilet tank, just to be thorough.

"Will you open the door?" Wyatt shouted, his fist still banging. "I've got a chain saw, and I'm not afraid to use it."

Gem sat on the edge of the bed and thought about the countless rooms in the mansion. This could take eons! She considered Niko's warning. He didn't want Cyrus to have this object, even at the risk of people's lives. Gem had always respected Niko as her elder, but was he making the right choice for Keystone? Older immortals were often emotionally detached and therefore impervious to death. They knew everyone died eventually, and so they were less likely to make emotional decisions.

Gem was about as emotional as they came. His unwillingness to compromise could bring death and destruction to those she cared about, and she couldn't let that happen.

She wrung her hands and remembered Cyrus's description of the book. Red leather binding and old paper. That described so many books that she'd seen in her lifetime. But the symbol... something about an ouroboros rang a bell.

The door shook when someone kicked it. After another second, it swung open and struck the wall.

Switch lowered his foot and looked at the broken frame. "I'll fix that later."

Wyatt hustled in and knelt in front of her. "What's going on, kiddo? You can't shut me out of this. Are you in trouble?"

"We're all in trouble. Niko especially."

"I don't get it."

"I have to find something."

"You mean clothes?" He glanced at her scant attire. "Are you hurt? Never mind. You're a Mage, so probably not. But you know what I mean."

She slowly shook her head.

Switch remained in the hall, which put her at ease. He wasn't supposed to get involved in their affairs, and she didn't know him well enough to trust him. Hunter poked his head in. Switch quickly took his hand and led him away.

"Oh, Wyatt. I'm so awful at making decisions. I don't know if I've made the right one."

"I felt that way in 1973 when I bought a Gremlin. It had a red stripe down the side."

She pulled his slouchy beanie over his face. "When's the last time you shaved?"

"Probably the last time I slept." He yanked the hat off his head, his hair sticking out in all directions. "What are you looking for in Niko's room?"

Gem pondered for a moment whether she should keep Niko's secret, but this house was enormous, and she didn't have much time. "A book."

Wyatt snorted. "Then you're in the wrong room, sister. Who's looking for a book?"

"Some guy who's after Niko."

"Is that who took you?" Wyatt scratched his neck. "What happened to you?"

Her heart pounded against her chest when she thought of drowning again. She'd never experienced anything so terrifying. "It doesn't matter anymore."

Wyatt leaned back and tilted his head to the side. "Is he Asian?"

She furrowed her brow. "How did you know?"

"I've seen one of his dead buddies hanging around lately."

"The rest of his friends are alive." Tears welled in her eyes when she remembered the whip cracking against Niko's back. "I have to find that book. I just have to!"

"Fine. What's the title?"

She gave an exasperated sigh. "I don't know! He just said it was old with a red cover."

Gem froze when a light bulb went off. *Could it be?* She remembered the old book in her secret study that she'd never been able to decipher. Occasionally she would pull it out to compare the archaic language to the new books she purchased. Lately she'd been too busy with work to fool with it. When Viktor had given her that room, it already had a few books in there, but that wasn't one of them. It turned up later, but she couldn't place the exact time. Could Niko have found her secret room and put it in there? But why?

Because he knew she'd keep it safe. He knew she'd never dispose of a book, especially one she hadn't translated. Everyone

knew how much Gem loved a challenge, and Niko was probably
confident that she would never decipher the symbols in that book.
She thought back to the day she first found it on the bottom shelf,
intentionally out of view.

Gem sprang to her feet, knocking Wyatt onto his butt. "By
George, I think I've got it!"

With lightning speed, she flashed out the door just as nimble
as a fairy. When she reached the first floor, she sped toward the hall
on the east side. Gem finally stopped at the recessed alcove where
the secret door was located. She lifted the lantern off the wall and
went inside the room.

Her latest discoveries littered the large work table. She placed
the lantern on a hook near her reading chair before locating the
large red book and placing it on the table. The spine crackled as she
opened it up and turned to the first page. Right there in front of
her this whole time was a symbol of a snake eating its tail.

"Eureka!"

She hadn't made the connection when Cyrus mentioned an
ouroboros. Gem had opened this book dozens of times but always
skipped to different sections. Just like a cream-filled chocolate, it
was the middle that mattered. Gem scooped the book in her arms
and sat down in the leather chair in the corner. Cyrus wouldn't
expect her to find it this quickly, so maybe she had time to figure
out what she was dealing with.

Gem sat there for a long while, flipping the pages and analyzing
the symbols. Just when she was about to close the book and call
Cyrus, she came across a glyph that looked familiar.

"I've seen this before," she whispered, the Relic knowledge in
her mind flipping like the pages in a book.

Not everything a Relic read was put to memory. They had
selective memory, and any new material they wanted to string
to their DNA, they memorized at will. So whatever that symbol
represented wasn't something in her Relic knowledge, but she'd
seen it. And recently.

Recently.

Gem stood up and set the book on the table. The only books

that she'd been looking at lately were the ones acquired at Pawn of the Dead. She grabbed a shawl from the back of her chair and draped it over her shoulders before searching her shelves.

Gem found the fragile book and gingerly opened it. It was handwritten in an extinct Semitic language of ancient Mesopotamia. On some of the pages, above the passages, were symbols written with a different ink—a more modern one, because it was blue. Gem held her breath when a symbol caught her eye. She looked back at the red book and saw that they were an identical match.

Identical!

"Behold, I have found the key!" she sang. Gem jumped up and retrieved her pen and paper. This was when the magic happened.

The newer writing must have been direct translations of select passages. It could have been notes, but she decided to go through and analyze each one. Some languages using symbols weren't structured the same. The shapes might represent a phrase or have separate scripts, or it could be a combination of sounds to form words. Gem could easily translate the original language in the small book, and once she connected the patterns between those words to the symbols written above some of the passages, she could tackle Niko's book.

Gem didn't want to touch the pages of the red book more than she had to. The paper looked so old, and yet as she ran her finger along the edge, something felt different about it. As if the harder she scraped her nail against it, the stronger it felt to the touch.

Gem spent the next two hours jotting down possible translations. She compared every single symbol to search for repeats but had difficulty finding any. Translating a completely new language was a daunting task that took time, but it was exciting. If she managed to crack the code, she could store that knowledge in her DNA. It almost made her regretful she wouldn't have any offspring to pass it on to, but at least her own knowledge base would increase.

After it grew too dim to read, she replaced the candle in the lantern. Her feet were ice-cold even though she'd kept them on the footrest of the desk chair. She yawned loudly and stared at several sheets of paper she'd compiled in search of a pattern—anything that might connect to a word or idea. One symbol appeared in both books, and Gem double-checked in her dictionary to see if there were other definitions for that word. Then she pored over each line using that symbol to consider the context of its use in the sentence.

Her gaze drifted over to the open pages of the red book, and she pulled it to her. She pondered over the word, wondering if it was the correct translation. All signs pointed to yes, but she needed to translate a passage of complete sentences to know for sure.

She traced her finger over the symbol. "Sun."

Her fingers warmed, and she turned around when the flame in the lantern grew brighter. Had it? There was no sudden burst of oxygen in the room.

"I must be sleep-deprived."

As she stood up to leave, something compelled her to stay.

Maybe she wouldn't be able to decipher this language in one night, and maybe it didn't even matter. But if she could learn just enough of it, she might understand its value. Perhaps that alone would give her an advantage. Had she not found this latest book at the pawnshop, she would have never made any progress. What were the odds that something like that would have landed in her hands at this very time when she needed it most?

The fates must have been looking out for her.

Chapter 23

I SAT NEAR THE FIRE TO dry my hair while Shepherd passed out beef jerky to the kids. They were ravenous—a perpetual state that all teenagers seem to exist in—so Shepherd had given up his own resources to keep them content.

The temperature hovered in the forties, but the fire kept us warm enough. Viktor tried calling Wyatt twice on the satellite phone to get a status on Gem, but something must have been going on, because nobody answered. Probably for the best. We had enough to worry about, and we needed to keep focused on what was outside our cave and not hundreds of miles away.

With my hair now dry, I stood up and squinted at the trees.

"No sign of them," Christian said. "They're probably regrouping."

"It's what I *can't* guess they're up to that makes me nervous," I admitted.

He put his arm around my shoulder and tucked me against his chest. We stood at the mouth of the cave, the fire burning brightly behind us. There was plenty of wood to last us a day or two, but staying in one spot was the worst idea. Especially without backup.

"Why won't Viktor call our destination spot and see if they'll send reinforcements? They're probably close enough to help."

Christian guided my hand beneath his shirt to warm my icy palm against his stomach. "They won't help. It's not part of the protocol. It would make them vulnerable, and they might think this is a trap."

"So I guess it's just us."

"Aye." He gave me a quick squeeze before letting go. "I need to step outside and listen for a while."

"Stay close."

He flashed a crooked smile and looked down at me. Christian didn't say anything in response, but that was okay. Sometimes we bantered with just our eyes. After a playful bow, he slipped into the shadows.

Carol moved past me like a ghost, and I jumped before I realized it was her.

I caught her arm and tugged her back. "You stay here. I think you've caused enough trouble."

Carol turned, her crazy curls framing her pale face. Claude's tan coat was comically large on her, but she didn't seem to mind. "I just wanted to see what was going on." She kicked a few pebbles around. "If y'all hadn't made Joshua stay behind, he could have protected us."

"Really? A sixteen-year-old boy could have saved the day?"

"He's a cougar!"

I pointed to the woods. "And those are lions. Like the kind you see in Africa. You should thank Viktor for making him stay behind."

She folded her arms and lifted her stubborn chin. "He's out there somewhere."

"If he's smart, he went home."

"Joshua loves me. He'd never leave me."

I tucked my hands in the pockets of my black sweatpants. "Why can't you two just wait a few years? You're only fourteen."

"Almost fifteen," she chimed in.

"You don't even know what real love is yet. All that changes when you get older."

"Haven't you ever felt that way about someone? Like you just can't be without them? How would you feel if you were separated for four years? I'm not waiting that long. Four years is a lifetime."

"If he loves you, he'll wait."

She twisted her lips and glanced up at me. "Remember when I said that true love was when you'd die for someone? We have that. And it's not because he's a Shifter. I wouldn't care if he was a human. But Joshua can't be like me, so I wanna be like him. And you can't stop us. You can lock me up in a camp for another four years, but what's the point? I already know what I want. That's four years you're denying me to be with the person I love. What if he dies before then?"

I shrugged. "That's life. You can't predict what's going to happen. Haven't you ever wondered what a sixteen-year-old is doing with a fourteen-year-old girl?"

She huffed and looked at the woods. "We're not that far apart in age. Anyhow, it's not like that with us. We've barely kissed. He respects me, and he's the one who doesn't want to do anything more than kiss. He says Shifters don't mate with girls who haven't gone through their first change, and usually that happens in their older teens or twenties. Joshua looks out for me. Just because we're young doesn't mean we don't know what love is. Romeo and Juliet were only thirteen."

I turned to face her. "Romeo and Juliet were not only fictional, but they died. That story wasn't a romance—it was a tragedy."

She straightened her arms and looked up at me defiantly. "The *real* tragedy is keeping us apart. I never had a family before, and he makes me feel loved and wanted. I want to meet his parents and brothers. I want to be a part of that while I'm still young. He said that they'll take me in and look after me until I'm old enough."

I sighed and put my arm around her, leading her back in. "Don't be in such a rush to grow up, kid. Love isn't what you see in the movies." I thought about my rough road with Christian. "If love puts one of you in danger, the other has to love you enough to let you go. Even if it's just for a little while. Joshua loves you, or he wouldn't be following you across the country. But look at the danger he's in now. Don't let love destroy you. It's like that fire behind us. It can either warm you or kill you, so maybe you should be careful about getting too close." When we reached the crevice where the kids were sleeping, I faced her. "Look, I was a kid once. I know how strong those feelings are. If they're real, they won't change in four years. But you need protection. If he respects you enough not to mate with you this young, then he's a good guy. But he can't protect you. You're still a human, and if anyone finds out what you are—"

"They won't! I never show anyone my mark. I always cover it up."

There was no convincing this girl. I patted the cold wall. "Get some rest. If there's another attack, you can't run if you're sleep-deprived."

Carol looked like she wanted to retaliate with a better argument, but she capitulated and crawled into the space.

Claude used a long stick to stoke the fire. The wood crackled, and tiny embers skated upward in a cloud of smoke. Viktor was fast asleep, and Shepherd had taken a seat on a rock so he could rummage through his gear.

I stepped past the two men and sat down next to Matteo against the wall. "Thanks for all your help. Look, you can take off now. It's too dangerous." I lowered my voice. "I don't think my team trusts you."

"What reason would they have?"

"It's our nature to be suspicious of strangers putting their lives on the line for someone they don't know."

"I gave you my word."

"Yes, but they don't see it that way."

He snapped a small twig in two. "I promised to take you as far as I could. I can take you all the way."

"What do you mean?"

"I know where they keep the children."

Shepherd's dark eyes flicked up.

Matteo held out his hand to placate him. "Rest assured, I have no interest in what goes on in that place. They're protecting children, so that's all I need to know. These woods belong to the people who live in them. You can't expect a man to be blind to those who traverse across our land. I've seen other children pass through. They were never afraid, and those who guarded them left behind an emotional scent I can trust. Nothing ever alerted me that something indecent was afoot." He shook his head. "Not my business."

Shepherd digested his answer with care. His bloodshot eyes made him look like a crazed serial killer, and the scruff on his face wasn't helping. He always had a stone-cold look, but now even more so.

"You should get some rest," I said to Shepherd. "We'll keep an eye on things."

"I'm fine," he fired back, still staring at Matteo.

"You'll be real fine when one of those kids needs stitches and you can't see straight."

Claude set his stick against the wall. "I'll take the first shift. Get some shut-eye, you stubborn fool. I'll tap your shoulder when I need rest."

Shepherd grumbled beneath his breath as he stripped off his shirt and put on a dark green one with long sleeves. After collecting his things, he chose a spot by the far wall and folded up his leather coat as a pillow.

The gun stayed strapped to his hip.

It made me realize how silly I felt with a belt around my sweatpants, but it was the only way to carry my daggers. "Thanks for the boots," I said in earnest. "They're warm."

Matteo stared at them for a beat. "It's good to see them getting some use."

I thought about the tiny pair of shoes I'd seen him pull out, and while curious, I didn't want to pry into a piece of his life that might be upsetting. I could speculate all I wanted, but as long as he was here to help, dredging up the past might only upset him. A pair of woman's boots in the home of a single man was never a happy story.

"What troubles the girl?" Matteo asked.

"Teen angst."

"I can smell her sorrow."

"She tried to escape earlier in the trip to be with her boyfriend. I think we should tie her up, but Viktor would never go for that."

"Can the male not wait? She's hardly of age to entertain the idea of love."

"Tell that to a fourteen-year-old. They know everything at that age."

"What's her Breed?"

I leaned forward. "Human."

He drew in a breath, and I hated the way Chitahs could smell truth and lies without hearing a word.

"Not my business," he said at the tail end of a sigh.

I turned to look at him. "If you want to help, guide us to our destination. Shepherd might also know the way, but we could use your protection. Those lions will hurt these kids. If they don't keep them, they'll sell them as sex slaves."

Matteo's lip curled in a snarl.

When Christian reappeared, his hands were caked in mud. He flicked a peevish glance at me while heading to the other room. "Don't ask."

I smiled as he went to wash his hands. It was a juicy story I'd probably never hear, and somehow that made it even funnier.

"You didn't tell me you were mated," Matteo remarked.

"What makes you say that?"

His golden eyes locked on mine, and it was as if he could see every secret.

Or smell it.

"What would a Vampire want with a Mage?"

I chuckled and dusted off my hands. "What would a Mage want with a Vampire? Some things you can't explain."

"In my time, they would cast out anyone for interbreeding. It's unnatural."

"Unnatural? Look at us. We have fangs and run at light speed. Breed has no place to call anything unnatural when it's the core of who we are. We go against the natural order of things. We stop aging, we heal, we can pass knowledge down to kids through our DNA. We're the monsters that humans make up stories about, so you're not exactly in a position to decide which monsters should and shouldn't hook up."

His eyes hooded, and he smiled lazily. "You must be a Learner.

The newly made ones always have different ideas. That will change in time. You'll see."

"Maybe you're the one who'll change."

"Humans die with age. Old ideals die with them. Immortals live for centuries or even longer. People respect their elders and listen to them. No matter their initial beliefs, Breed will separate naturally and find comfort with their own kind."

"Someday you might feel differently about that."

"Intruder!" Claude growled. Not loud enough to scare the kids or wake Viktor, but it had Matteo and me on our feet. Shepherd, on the other hand, had nodded off in less than two minutes and was snoring.

I passed the fire and stood at the entrance. "What do you see?"

He lifted his long arm and pointed. "It's not what I see, it's what I smell."

Matteo stepped close and drew in a breath. He walked out a few more paces until the smoke didn't interfere with his senses.

"It's not a lion," he announced.

"How can you tell?" Claude shook his head. "Animal scents mingle."

Matteo turned on his heel. "Because I know every scent in these woods, city boy."

Claude dipped his chin, and a growl rumbled low in his throat.

I patted Claude's arm. "He's right. You can single out two criminals in a club filled with dancers, but this is Matteo's territory. He can probably tell a squirrel's ass from a raccoon's."

Nobody laughed.

Matteo looked like a primitive man in his animal pelts. Especially with his unkempt hair and long beard. It wasn't a bushy beard that hid his face; it grew thinner than most, and he had a band tying it together like my father often did. For a man in his prime, he didn't seem to care about his looks.

"It's a Shifter," Matteo explained. "But it's not one of the lions."

I scanned the woods but saw nothing. "How can you tell it's a Shifter?"

"Too many emotions lingering with animal scent. Animals

don't have complex emotions that constantly shift. There aren't any packs in this area. I know of two rogues, but it's not their scent."

I glanced back at the cave and then at the men. "I'll go."

"You'll go where?" Christian asked as he wedged himself between the men and me.

"I think it's Joshua. If he's in animal form, he won't come close."

"You can't go out there alone."

Viktor had ordered Christian to stay near the cave. He was the only one strong enough to fight off an attack if the lions got in. Viktor said he could walk the perimeter as needed but go no farther.

"I can't leave him out there," I said. "The lions might use him against us."

Christian gripped my shoulders and gave me a pensive stare.

I searched his eyes. "He's just a kid. Maybe he's not part of this group, but we can't leave a sixteen-year-old to the lions."

Despite Christian's dark past of countless murders, he still had a conscience. Especially when it came to children. If not, I wouldn't be alive.

I gripped his wrists extra hard to remind him I still had a little residual strength from his blood.

"Don't get yourself killed," he finally said.

I darted ahead and went in the direction Claude had pointed. Hopefully Joshua's animal would recognize my scent.

"Joshua," I whispered.

I weaved around the trees and stepped over a fallen limb. Every so often, I'd stop to listen. If General's men were this close, they wouldn't have allowed Joshua to get through. Not without a fight, and we would have heard it. It was just a matter of finding him.

I walked a familiar path that sloped down. The clouds had passed, and the moon lit up the world like a torch. At some point during the walk, I gave up on Joshua. I didn't have the skills to track a wild animal, but Blue was out there somewhere, and I'd made Viktor a promise. When the ground leveled, I flashed as far as I could to shorten the journey back to the first campsite.

Charred smoke lingered in the air. With my heightened senses,

I made sure I was alone before investigating. Once I crossed a tree line, I circled the perimeter around the dying embers of a fire.

"Blue," I whispered, swinging my gaze upward. She retained consciousness while in animal form, so maybe her falcon had just separated from the group. "Blue!"

My heart ricocheted in my chest when I spotted the shape of a man standing not too far away. I blinked a few times to make sure I wasn't just mistaking a tree for a person. My vision sharpened as he drew near, his broad shoulders and swagger familiar. As he moved into view, the moonlight caught the waves of his long blond hair. The scruff around his mouth only added to the animalistic look in his predatory eyes. General was a beast in human and animal form, and I remembered all too well his cruel heart.

I lightly gasped when I noticed the falcon perched on his arm. Despite the hood over her head, I recognized the beautiful coloring of Blue's breast.

"We meet again," he said with a growing smile.

One I wanted to wipe right off his face with the bottom of my shoe.

I searched the area for his brothers.

"Funny how you're always meddling," he went on.

"What are you doing out here? This doesn't look like loan shark business."

He lifted his arm, causing the bird to hop. "She won't fly with the hood on. She also won't shift."

"Don't be so sure."

He blinked slowly. "I'm a Shifter. We know how to move when we shift to slip out of our clothes and jewelry. Most of us don't wear necklaces or rings because it hinders the process and might cause injury. Just imagine what a hood might do." He tugged on the tassels hanging from it.

"What do you want?"

"Compensation. You slaughtered two of my brothers. Not my favorite brothers, but you owe me."

"Owe you? I paid you the money, and you tried to kill me anyway. I was defending my life. I was defending my father's life."

"I can no longer conduct business with the higher authority breathing down my neck. We could have settled this privately, but you had to take matters to the law." He flashed his teeth at me. "A mutual acquaintance told me about this opportunity, and I couldn't resist. I'm intrigued that you have such a prestigious job. I wonder what would happen if you failed at this mission."

I pulled out a push dagger and gripped the T-shaped handle. "You don't know what you're up against."

He clucked his tongue at me and stared at the bird. "We stopped your caravan to see *exactly* what we were up against. How many of you there are, what Breed, and I especially wanted to see the children."

My eyes narrowed. "What the hell do you want with those kids?"

Something flashed in his eyes. "Those *kids* are Potentials, aren't they?"

I feigned confusion. "They're orphans. There's nothing special about them except that they don't have parents."

General chuckled. "And I'm supposed to believe that the higher authority would take such interest in orphaned humans?"

I tried to come up with a quick lie to throw him off his game. "They're the human children of Chitahs, you idiot."

Doubt flickered in his eyes. "Liar."

"We were ordered to move these kids out of a Breed orphanage where they were wrongfully placed. Someone lied to you."

Doubt clouded his expression, and I scanned the trees again.

"I call your bluff," he said, his voice a low register. "If I'm wrong, I'll still ruin your mission and sully your reputation. Either way, you lose. If those children are Potentials, I can make enough money off them to live comfortably for two lifetimes. But maybe… maybe I want to get a closer look first. Finding a female companion isn't as easy as you might think. Especially one who knows her place. Humans are such timid little creatures, and that appeals to me so much." General licked his chops as if thinking about a tasty morsel of obscenity.

"If you put one paw on those kids, I'll make confetti out of your intestines."

Christian would have been proud of that line. He loved a creative threat.

"Is it money you want?" I asked, trying to stall him. Could I stab him faster than he could hurt Blue?

"Do you think I'd come all this way just for a few dollars?" His lips peeled back. "I want your precious cargo."

"Blue, jump!" I flashed at General and punched him in the stomach, my blade piercing his gut.

Blue's falcon hopped to the ground and collapsed, her wings flapping chaotically as the hood remained on her head.

General swung his arm and struck the side of my head. An explosion of pain radiated throughout my temple. With my fingertips dripping in light, I reached out and blasted him.

He stumbled backward and bellowed in pain. Despite my dizziness, I lunged and sliced my blade across his chest. It tore his thin jacket, but had it penetrated his skin? I flashed behind him and kicked him behind the knees. General dropped like a stone, and I was certain that bones snapped. Nothing like *that* had ever happened before, but I was also juiced up on Vampire blood.

General twisted around and, in a fluid motion, shifted to a lion. A giant mane crowned his massive head, and my little knife wasn't going to cut through that skin. He swatted his paw at me, and I hopped away from his razor-sharp claws.

Blue's falcon cried out, the sharp sound piercing the night. When he turned toward her, I panicked.

"No!"

I stabbed him repeatedly in the haunches, and he roared before pivoting around. I flashed to the side, trying to draw him away from the bird, who could easily become a meal in one bite.

"Come on!" I shouted. "You're not a real Shifter. You're a chickenshit! That's right. And so were your dead brothers."

He charged after me, and I weaved around the trees. General was nimble and swiped at my leg. He got my boot, but his claws didn't go deep enough.

I scurried up a hill, adrenaline firing me up like fuel in a race car. Once I reached the top, I was horrified to see his lion ambling back down in the other direction.

Toward Blue.

I scurried down the hill, branches tangling around me as I snapped them away. "I'm over here!"

Once he reached her, he swiped his paw. The falcon went airborne before landing in a pile of leaves.

All sense of reality vanished along with any rational thought. As I tumbled toward them, something caught my eye on the right.

A force of power, a blur of movement—Matteo sailing through the air. His long hair streamed behind him, and his eyes were as black as coal. The grimace on his face revealed his four canines, and he clutched a dagger in each hand. When Matteo collided with the animal, they rolled across the ground and fought like two ancient enemies.

As much as I wanted to taste blood, I reached Blue and slid to my knees. Her feathers were red, and I shuddered to think that her chest might have been ripped wide open. I pulled off the hood and stared into her glassy little eyes.

I cradled her small head in my hand. "It's Raven. It's me. You need to shift. I know it hurts, but you have to. Can you hear me in there? Hurry! Please… don't be dead."

I had no knowledge of bird anatomy or where to check for a heartbeat. Despair came over me, and images of a funeral flashed through my mind. One of her wings was bent in an awkward position, and I couldn't imagine how much pain she was in if she was even still alive.

"Please be in there. You can't do this to us—you can't do this to Viktor."

It was as if her skin blurred and became liquid. As I watched her shift, it wasn't as fast or as effortless as I'd seen before. It was slow and grotesque as the feathers fell away and revealed the gashes across her body and wing. She morphed to a human shape, but the wounds barely healed. One went from her left shoulder over her right breast. Another had cut through between her breasts, and two across her belly. Blood ran down in rivulets from the wounds. Blue's brown hair carpeted the forest floor, her jaw slack and eyes shut.

I patted her cheek frantically. "Blue, one more time. Wake up!"

Matteo knelt at my side, his hands bathed in blood. "She doesn't have time. Can your friends heal her?"

"I don't know. Maybe."

I glanced over my shoulder at the knife handle protruding from the lion's skull. General would never bother us again.

"Guard my back," he said, scooping her into his arms. Matteo gingerly lifted her while looking down at the gashes on her belly. He grimaced when one of them opened. "My flashlight's in my pocket."

I patted him down until I found the slender tool and switched it on.

With the wind at his heels, Matteo turned and ran back to camp. He moved through those woods as if he could run them blindfolded, and I struggled to keep up while simultaneously guiding his way with the light.

My lungs burned as we picked up speed. Blue was losing too much blood, and some of it was probably spattering on the ground.

What's that noise? I halted in my tracks and heard a wildcat. Not a lion's roar, but the one that sounded right after it was.

Joshua.

Torn between helping the teen or Matteo, I caught up with the Chitah and shined the flashlight to guide his way. Blue didn't have time.

"Christian!" I shouted. "We need help."

I wasn't sure how far he could hear, but the third time I yelled for him, he appeared.

"*Jaysus wept.* What happened to the lass?"

"Lion," Matteo said. "Your friend will die if she doesn't shift."

"Have her drink my blood."

Not only did Matteo swing away from Christian, but Blue's arm flew up to cover her mouth.

"For feck's sake. You'd rather die?"

We continued our jog.

"Christian, Joshua's out there," I said, out of breath. "General's dead, but his brothers aren't. He's just a kid. He's—"

"Let Viktor know where I went."

Without another word, Christian shadow walked out of sight. When we reached the mouth of the cave, Claude sprinted toward us, his eyes wide with fright.

"Viktor!" he bellowed.

We moved inside the cave, and Claude led us to a pile of his clothes that he'd spread out on the floor. "Set her down gently. Gently!"

Matteo placed Blue on the floor, her naked body bathed in blood. She moaned in agony before passing out.

Shepherd appeared out of nowhere with his bag. "Get out of the way."

We all backed up as Viktor knelt by her side and cupped her face in his hands. "Wake up, Blue. Wake up. Shift." In the chaos of the moment, he started speaking to her in Russian.

"Christian tried to give her his blood," I explained. "She refused."

"Of course she wouldn't," Matteo said. "Vampire blood taints the purity."

I shook my head. Not long ago, I'd felt the same way. But knowing the healing power, I didn't understand why she would rather die than have a little Vamp juice in her.

Shepherd took out a syringe and a small vial. Before he did anything, he set her broken arm. The sight made everyone cringe.

"Shouldn't you stanch the bleeding?" Matteo snarled.

Shepherd ripped a package open with his teeth. "I can't put hemostatic granules on her stomach. Pressure doesn't work on the torso—not where she's got it."

"She's bleeding out."

"Let me do my fucking job, Chitah." Shepherd quickly prepped the needle.

Viktor stroked her cheek. "Stay with us. It is not your time to leave this earth."

"What's happening?" Eve peered down at us from their sleeping spot.

None of us had time to worry about the kids.

Watching blood weep from Blue's open wounds was agonizing, and Viktor had his fingers on her pulse the entire time. "Hurry."

Shepherd slid the needle into her arm and pushed the plunger.

Blue gasped for air and opened her eyes.

Viktor's tone was harsh. "Change," he commanded.

Her gaze flicked down, but Viktor held her firmly so she couldn't see the wounds. Tears trickled from the corners of her eyes, and she shifted. Her falcon flapped one wing and looked intoxicated, blood still staining its feathers. The kids were aghast and crying, and I held my breath.

Blue shifted back to human form. She swayed in a sitting position, her eyes hooded and hands holding the wounds on her chest and stomach. Though they had sealed, the scars were horrific.

"Once more," Viktor urged, but Blue passed out in his arms.

"She's gonna be fine." Shepherd pulled out bottles from his bag. "That was enough to seal up organ damage and broken bones."

"The scars," Claude said, his voice rough and filled with dread. "She can't stay like that."

Shepherd shot him a baleful look. "A man can live with scars. At least she's alive."

Shepherd would know. He was covered in them.

He cleared his throat. "Look, if she doesn't shift, I've got some ointment that'll speed up healing. It won't fix it all the way. There's too much damage."

Matteo removed his long, sleeveless coat, which was a patchwork of different furs. He draped it across Blue as a blanket. "You should move her closer to the fire."

I turned and looked up. "Kids, go to sleep."

They all looked horrified. Adam might have just gotten his first glimpse of a naked woman. He was probably traumatized for life and, at the very least, would never choose to become a Shifter, if he chose to become anything at all.

Claude spread out his clothes near the fire, and we all worked together to move her.

Viktor stayed by her side. "Someone get her water. She's lost blood, and she'll need fluids."

Shepherd reached in his bag. "I've got a bottle of electrolytes. A few capfuls in her mouth every hour will help, but she really needs to wake up and drink. Claude, why don't you—"

"Give to me," Viktor said in broken English as he reached for the bottle.

Claude paced. "Who did this? I want them dead."

I sat on a large rock. "General's dead, but his brothers are still out there. I don't know if they'll give up or come at us hard."

"How many?"

I shrugged. "Three?"

"Two," Christian said from beyond the fire. When he appeared, Joshua was in his arms, naked and unconscious.

"This is a clusterfuck." Shepherd rose to his feet. "What the hell happened to him?"

Christian gave him a sharp look. "He fell naked into my arms after declaring his undying love. What the feck do you think? He's hurt. Get your arse over here."

Christian set the boy down alongside the wall.

"I don't see any wounds," Shepherd muttered, looking him over. "Head injury?"

"I found him that way. Next to a dead lion." Christian folded his arms and sauntered up to me.

"That must have been some fight," I said.

He sat next to me on the rock. "Had I arrived a moment earlier, I would have had front-row seats."

Shepherd smacked the boy on the cheek. "Kid, wake up. You hear me? Wake your ass up."

"Maybe you should give him an injection," I suggested.

Shepherd scratched his bristly jaw. "That's for life-and-death emergencies. His pulse and breathing are normal. I think he just passed out."

"How is she?" Christian asked quietly.

I followed his gaze to Blue. "Shepherd got her to shift again, but she's still cut up bad. Do you think she'll scar?"

"Aye, if they're deep enough. Shifters heal, but it depends on the wound."

"I met a guy in a bar once who was showing his off like it was a medal of honor. Why do they use liquid fire to keep the scars if all they have to do is not shift?"

"If they accidentally shift too soon, they'll lose the scars. They're just dumb eejits who want to look like a scratching post."

I rubbed my face and stared at Joshua, who was lying on the opposite side of the room. "We have to find those lions."

"Joshua!" Carol flew out from her sleeping spot and hit the ground with a loud smack before scrambling over to the sleeping boy. She reached him just as Claude dropped a hat over the boy's privates.

"That was *my* hat," Shepherd grumbled while he dug around in his bag.

"Joshua, wake up," Carol pleaded, tears staining her flushed cheeks. She quickly took off Claude's coat and draped it over his body. "He'll freeze to death. Doesn't anyone care?"

Claude looked dismayed at his good jacket lying on top of a naked man, and Shepherd chuckled when he noticed. Neither appeared concerned about Joshua's well-being.

I leaned over and whispered, "Do you think he's faking it?"

Christian answered with an arch of an eyebrow. It was possible. Then again, the kid might have shifted so many times to heal that he passed out.

Carol curled up against him and looked like a mother protecting her young.

Claude patted Shepherd on the shoulder. "Get some sleep. I'm still on shift duty."

Sensing Viktor's anguish over our plan unraveling and Blue almost dying, I stood up and squatted next to him. "I've never met a stronger woman. I used to think I was pretty badass, but Blue takes the cake. She'll be okay."

We both watched her sleep, knowing the consequence if she

didn't wake up soon. Viktor had a tough decision ahead of him. Either we left her alone to fend for herself, or he would have to cut another person from the mission to look after her, diminishing our numbers and putting the kids at risk.

Unless we could eliminate the threat.

I stood up. "I'm going back out. General's dead, Joshua killed one, and we got two others. Whoever's left might find General and leave, but they're weak without him." I snapped my fingers to get Shepherd's attention. "Do you have an extra dagger? Full-length?"

"Yep."

"I'll go with her," Christian said, inviting no argument. He pushed up the sleeves of his dark brown shirt, the kind of move a man makes when he's preparing to get down and dirty.

I wanted to promise Viktor that we'd take care of all his troubles, but all I could do was accept the knife that Shepherd handed me. "We'll be back by dawn. They won't have the balls to come in here, but Matteo and Claude will keep an eye out for trouble. You don't have a thing to worry about."

I waited for his permission, but Viktor continued stroking Blue's forehead with his thumb. His silence was answer enough, so I palmed the dagger.

I didn't need a sheath.

"Try not to stab them in the back like you did with the last one," Matteo said.

I gave him a bemused look. "Why?"

"I need a new rug."

"That's illegal, you know."

"Not according to the old laws. Not in battle."

I stalked past the flames. "If we're not back by dawn, leave without us."

But I already knew they would.

Chapter 24

"I F YOUR TUMMY KEEPS RUMBLING like that, you'll draw the lions to us," Christian remarked.

"Maybe that's my master plan."

"How long have we been walking?"

"Three hours." I tugged his sleeve until he stopped. "Give me your blood."

He did a slow turn, and his lips disappeared behind his beard. "I'm beginning to feel like an ATM."

"Quit your brooding, Vamp. I want you." I dropped my dagger and wrapped my cold fingers around his neck, which made him smile. The great thing about Christian Poe was how he could regulate his internal body temperature.

He encased me in his arms and gently kissed my lips. "It's better you not have too much."

"The power you gave me earlier is mostly gone, and if we run into the lions—"

"Then *you'll* shock them and *I'll* destroy. Just as we planned."

"Things don't always go as planned." I nibbled on his bottom lip, and his fangs punched out. "I need you inside me."

Christian pinned me against a wide tree and pressed his hard body against mine. There was a dance involved when taking Vampire blood, especially Christian's. He wanted it, but he didn't want it.

He just needed a little convincing, and I knew exactly which buttons to push.

"I need it," I whispered, nipping on his earlobe and trailing kisses down his whiskery neck.

When I licked his artery, he sucked in a sharp breath. Pieces of bark fell from the tree where he gripped it. While most Vampires were easy to seduce, Christian was particular in how he liked his blood foreplay. I had to make him hungry for me in more ways than one. My fangs lengthened, and I teased him with tiny pricks while pulling his hips to mine.

Christian was hard like granite, ready to fill me up with more than just his blood. He cradled my neck in his hands. "I want to feast on your body, but not here. Not in the woods like animals."

I wanted to invite him in, to feel his hands on my body and his tongue in my mouth. But he was right. This wasn't the time or place. Was it too much to ask to have sex on a bed for a change? Or at least somewhere less public? Our love life had taken a left turn out of the gate, and as delicious as the sex was, maybe I needed to pull back on the reins a little.

I sank my teeth into his neck. When my fangs retracted, warm blood flowed past my lips and down my throat. Instead of fisting my hair and grinding against me like a savage beast, Christian tenderly stroked the back of my head with his fingertips and held me to him.

His blood awakened my Vampire soul, and the power culminated within me. After a final swallow, I sealed the puncture wounds with a single lick.

When our eyes locked, a connection formed between us like an open channel. We had a bond based on love and respect, but blood linked us in some indefinable way.

Christian leaned in and kissed my bloodstained lips. The intensity of his gaze made my stomach flutter.

"What do you taste?" he asked.

While I could taste his desire, I hadn't yet learned all the complexities of blood reading. Perhaps my gift was weaker than most.

"Lust." I smiled imperceptibly. "Love."

"Is that all?"

I furrowed my brow. "I'm not sure."

He tapped my nose. "You spend too much time with Niko learning to be a better Mage. But one day you're going to have to learn how to read the language of Vampires. In my time, we drank more freely, so we learned faster. Now they frown upon recreational drinking. No wonder the younglings are numpties."

I nudged him away with a strong hand. "Watch who you're calling a numpty."

He inclined his head. "Present company excluded."

I wiped my mouth on my sleeve and drank in the night. It was clearer than just moments before, the moon bathing the new leaves overhead in a silver glow. "I can only imagine what you see."

He admired the view. "I can see every insect in the trees. Your night is my day."

"And what's our day?"

"My hell."

I snorted. "Thank God for sunglasses, huh?"

We continued our walk.

"How's your hearing with my blood?" he asked.

"Improved, but not by a lot. It's like someone turned the volume up a notch or two."

"Ah. So you can't hear your stomach rumbling. Shall I fetch you a rabbit?"

"I'm not hungry. My throat was dry, so I was swallowing a lot. I must have swallowed little air bubbles."

"Better you belch them out."

"Afraid they'll come out the other end?"

He glided ahead of me. "The mortal body is a repulsive thing."

"Is that so? I guess that means you don't want to feast on mine."

He spun on his heel and clutched me in his arms so fast that I gasped lightly. "You're the exception. You bewitch me, Raven Black. Through and through. My soul is dark, but I feel the light when you're near."

I threaded my fingertips through his soft brown hair. It was longish, just enough to cover the tops of his ears. "You're a pretty man, Mr. Poe. Anyone ever tell you that?"

When he leaned in to kiss me, I leaned away.

"We have lions to kill."

His eyes stirred with excitement. "I love hunting with you. I don't think I've ever met a woman with similar desires."

"One who murders with glee?"

His gaze darted back and forth between each of my eyes.

"What are you looking at?"

"Your soul."

I slipped out of his arms. "What do you mean?"

He shook his head. "It must be the moon talking. Let's keep moving." Christian took my hand. "Are you certain we won't get lost?"

I lifted my dagger from the ground as we passed by it. "I've got a built-in compass. I don't know the exact location of the cave, but I can guestimate my way back, and you'll be able to hear everyone once we're close enough."

We penetrated a thin layer of fog. My foot struck something solid, but it didn't sound like the usual underbrush. I bent over and gripped a smooth wooden handle. "It's Blue's axe."

Christian lifted a handful of garments. "I found the rest."

I swung the axe against a tree and left it lodged in the trunk. "What do you think the compound is like where the kids are going?"

Christian dropped the clothes by the axe. "If they're all the way out here, they're not going to be making regular runs to the grocery store. I wager they have gardens and hunt. Perhaps they own livestock so they don't have to leave the facility."

"I don't see why they can't take an extra kid."

Christian rested his hand against a tree and leaned on it. "If you're thinking about Joshua, you can bet your sweet arse they won't let him within twenty feet of the front gate. An underage Shifter, free to walk about Potentials? That's a security risk if I ever saw one."

"You act like he's going to sleep with all the girls."

Christian strode toward me. "All he has to do is bed one. Teenagers make foolish decisions and aren't always responsible with free will. They're emotional creatures who are easily influenced."

I sighed. "That's what I'm afraid of. Joshua won't stop until he finds her."

"Assuming he stays behind. If Viktor brings him along, we'll have no choice but to scrub his memories."

"What if he remembers? What if he finds the compound after we leave and they shoot him?"

Christian lowered his arm and stretched. "That's not our problem. Our job is to deliver three children to a holding camp, not to worry about the fate of two lovestruck teenagers."

I took his hand and touched the ring I'd given him. "Have you ever been lovestruck?"

He looked at me with those arresting black eyes, his dark eyebrows sloping down. "We have lions to kill, and all you can think about is drinking my blood and romanticizing about love."

I blinked innocently. "I was just asking a simple question."

He caressed my cheek, moonlight glinting off his onyx ring. "Only once, Miss Black."

"Tell me about her."

"Her eyes were like day and night, her legs as long as her history of killing men, and her hair as black as a sinner's heart."

"How could you love such an evil woman?"

He drew closer. "Because she wore my heart around her neck." Christian's eyes twinkled in the moonlight. "And she never tried to bury me in a pine box."

I slowly slinked by him. "Just be sure you keep bringing her coffee in the morning."

"Is that a threat?" he asked from behind, amusement in his voice.

I smothered my laugh.

"What was that you just said?"

I smiled. "Nothing. I just had a tickle in my throat."

"You hear that?" His tone sharpened, and I spun on my heel. Christian stood like a marionette frozen in place. He did that when isolating a sound.

I held my breath so he could hear better.

Then I heard it too. A rustling of something large moving through the forest. "Could be a deer."

"Could be a bear."

"Perish the thought." I gripped the dagger with my right hand and turned in a slow circle.

Christian suddenly covered his ears and grimaced.

My eyes flicked back and forth between shadows and light as Christian dropped to his knees, blood dripping between his fingers from one of his ears.

A lion rushed at me with alarming speed, and I had only seconds to formulate a plan. Instead of fleeing for my life, I ran toward him and reduced the distance between us. We both kicked off the ground simultaneously and crashed into each other. I drove the dagger into his neck, and his massive teeth punched through my shoulder.

When we hit the ground, I shoved him off me with ease. He flew back and struck a cluster of trees behind me. The wound on my left shoulder began to heal thanks to Christian's blood, and I rotated it in a circle to get the feeling back.

So *this* was what it felt like to be a Vampire. Having that small taste of power during a time when I needed it made me feel like a different woman.

I spotted Christian stalking off. Then I heard the sound of hard plastic being crushed, followed by a few creative swear words. It must have been another sonic weapon.

The lion swiped at my feet, knocking me onto my stomach. The air whooshed from my lungs. When he pounced on my back, I twisted around and blasted him in the shoulder before wriggling free from his massive paws.

The lion roared before chasing me as I bolted in the other direction. I veered toward a large tree and kicked my feet off it, cartwheeling over the creature and landing behind him. Niko had taught me that move in the training room, and it was one I practiced repeatedly.

From my crouched position, I grabbed his haunches and gave

him a shock to remember. He convulsed, and as I raised my fist to break his spine, a second lion blindsided me.

I struck a tree with enough force to break bones. My arm was in his jaws until Christian's hands appeared in a hurried attempt to pry the animal's mouth open before it severed my limb. I wrenched free just as the first lion savagely attacked Christian from behind.

When the lion above me fled into the woods, I sat up and stumbled to my feet to reach Christian in time. The lion had him pinned on his stomach and was about to take his head.

I flashed at him with impossible speed and grabbed one of the lion's fangs. With a hard yank, I broke his tooth at the root. The unexpected attack gave Christian enough time to turn and punch the animal in the face.

The lion crumpled to the ground and shook his head. His long tongue lapped at the blood dripping from his mouth, and his face wrinkled in anger.

Spying the dagger on the ground by a tree, I jogged around the animal. My foot skidded down an uneven patch of earth, and I fell on my side.

Dammit, I missed the city. I missed concrete and level floors. I missed electricity and makeshift weapons found in alleyways. I missed fire escapes.

"Come here, you blundering little shitebag." Christian stalked toward the lion in the moonlight, but the feline kept his distance. "*Jaysus wept.* Can we move this to the shadows?"

I crawled over to the dagger and gripped the muddy handle. Blood stained the blade, matching the crimson on the back of the lion's neck. A switch had flipped inside me that took me from Raven Black to the Shadow, back to the days when I used to trap criminals and kill them for sport. That part of my life was so ingrained in me that I didn't think I'd ever be able to erase it from my DNA.

In that moment, I didn't care about dying or even living. I only cared about winning.

When the lion catapulted toward me, I flipped through the air and landed beside him. Our movements were a blur of blood and moonlight. I continually dodged his attacks without using my flashing ability, as if the Mage inside me was gone and all that remained was a Vampire. Attuned to the sound of his body pivoting, I countered the attack each and every time, wearing him out as he struggled to catch me. I hadn't even realized my fangs were out until I jumped onto his back and drove them into his neck.

My thighs clenched tight against his thrashing body, and my fingers gripped his mane. With the dagger still in my hand, I reached below his neck and sliced his throat. Warm liquid spilled onto my hand. The lion crumpled beneath me as he surrendered to death. The compulsive need to drink gripped me in the same way the need to breathe does when deprived of oxygen. I didn't dare crawl beneath him while he was still conscious, so I ripped a large gash in his thick coat to get to his blood. Only then did I sample a taste of pure Shifter in animal form.

Blood used to always repulse me. The more evil the man, the more vile the taste. Only Christian's had ever coated my palate like ambrosia, and that probably had to do with his being a Vampire. After recently feeding from Christian, it must have changed how I experienced things. Or maybe it was the fact that I'd never tasted blood from a Shifter in animal form.

In any case, that blood was so sinfully delicious that I crushed him in my arms.

More. I need more.

"Raven!"

My instinct to hold on to my prey kicked in when Christian attempted to pry us apart.

"Raven, not when he's dead." Christian hauled me off the lion and held me in his iron grip with my back against his chest. "*Never* drink from the dead."

"Why?" I rasped.

"You'll get sick. Some go mad. Dead blood is unpredictable."

I went limp in his arms. "Where's the other lion?"

"Long gone."

"We should go after him," I said drunkenly, the back of my head resting against his shoulder.

"You were magnificent," he said, putting a shiver up my spine. "*That's* your Vampire nature, Raven. When you fight like a Mage, you think too much. When you fight like a Vampire, you don't have to think at all. You just… feel."

When my feet touched the ground, I turned and looked up at him.

Christian cast his dark eyes on mine. "What do you feel now?"

"His power. His anger."

Christian ran his finger across my lower lip. "Consider this your first day of school."

"University of the damned?"

"Focus, Raven. Not all Vampires are good at this. Someone should measure your skills. Tell me everything you can read in his blood."

I ran my tongue around my mouth and licked up every drop. "It's different than anything I've had before. It was like… like I could live in his skin. I wasn't thinking like a human anymore. I could taste his life like a curse on my tongue, but I've had darker. And…"

"What?"

I swallowed hard and felt a lick of shame. "I was so lost in his blood that I wanted to drink away his life. I don't feel sick like I usually do."

"Maybe you're cured of that. Or maybe you can't taste the sin from an animal because an animal is without sin."

I pondered on his theory. Shifter animals listened to the command of the human that shared their body, but they didn't plot or scheme. They obeyed, protected, and hunted. There was nothing inherently evil about their nature, so maybe this was what it was like for other Vampires.

My hands were still soaked in blood. Jesus. I probably looked like some deranged monster on the back of that lion.

I lifted my gaze to Christian, and my breath caught. "How can you still look at me like you love me?"

Christian took my hand and led me to a small clearing. The moonlight played on his features, enhancing his sharp cheekbones and deep-set eyes. Christian had a naturally rigid posture, but something about the way he stood in front of me was easy and casual.

I looked between our hands and saw all the blood. It was smeared across my face, but when I reached up with my other arm to wipe it off, he grabbed my hand.

Christian bowed and then slowly pulled me toward him. Clasping my right hand, he slipped his other arm around my waist and shifted from one foot to the other. The crickets harmonized as the forest created a symphony of music.

I looked up at him in disbelief. "Are you dancing with me?"

He twirled me around, and the next thing I knew, we were dancing in the moonlight.

"The kids are waiting," I argued.

He spun me around until I landed against his chest. "Can I have just one irrational moment with my lover?"

I peered up at him. "We look like demons."

When he grinned, the light glinted off his sharp fangs. "Aye, Precious. That's what we are. Now dance with me, you gorgeous Vampire."

I laughed blithely and fell into step. "You're not lovestruck. You're moonstruck."

We danced as if we were two ordinary people. In a morbidly beautiful scene that would have sent others fleeing in terror, we relished our victory. We also celebrated my Vampire half, who had single-handedly taken out a lion without hesitation or magic. But mostly we just stole a moment in time and forgot about everything else.

In the midst of madness, Christian made me feel normal. That my life—no matter how dark or twisted—had meaning. There were sides of me that no mortal could ever understand.

I finally had a man who loved every bright and dark thing about me.

Chapter 25

I EXAMINED BLUE'S AXE AS WE neared the cave. "I wonder why she carries this thing all the time. A knife is lighter."

"An axe is scarier." Christian lifted a branch out of my way.

"I beg to differ. I can do just as much damage, if not more, with a dagger."

"An axe is a primitive weapon. If a man is faced with either that or a knife, he'll choose the knife every time. The knife goes in clean and quick. The axe? Well, nobody wants to be a tree."

The predawn sky was shifting from a deep indigo to azure, announcing that we had no time remaining to hunt down the last lion. Prior to leaving, Christian and I had swung by the first campsite and collected the stray bags left behind.

"They're here!" Eve cried.

Christian and I shared a puzzled look.

"What's she doing up at this hour?" I asked.

"I don't know, but they're all in a tizzy. I can't make out what they're saying."

I noticed the dried blood on his neck that trailed from his ear. "How are your ears?"

"Grand." He shuddered. "If the last lion left is the one who put that fecking device on a bullhorn, I want him all to myself."

"You can have him."

Christian rubbed at his neck and then looked at his fingers. "My eardrums healed an hour ago, but I can't get that infernal squelching out of my head."

"Hope you don't have tinnitus."

"Thank the heavenly angels that isn't possible. Perhaps a tiny drop of your blood might speed along the healing," he said with a wink. "Maybe a thimbleful?"

Christian was teasing, but the request lingered in the air. What *wasn't* I willing to do for him? Sharing blood in large quantities wasn't a good idea, but neither of us seemed influenced by the other's power.

I put my finger in my mouth and pricked the skin with my fang. A pearl of blood formed on the tip and glistened.

Christian did a double take and then stopped. "Jaysus, I was just having a little fun with you."

I held out my finger. "Just take it."

He clenched his jaw and averted his eyes from the bright drop of blood. "I'm not feeble."

"How will you be able to hear the lion if your ears are ringing? I'm just helping you get your revenge."

"Or are you just trying to tantalize me?"

"Come find out."

He sucked my finger into his warm mouth, his eyes never leaving mine. When his tongue swiped across the cut, his eyes rolled back before he closed them. Christian moaned as if he were a starved man devouring meat for the first time in fifty years.

When I yanked my finger out, it left a streak of blood on his bottom lip.

"You'll be the ruin of me, Miss Black." He licked his lips and smiled. "And I taste your satisfaction, so don't think you pulled the wool over my eyes."

I shrugged and kept moving. "How are your ears?"

He caught up in two strides. Instead of answering, he took my hand and squeezed it. There was no telling what that man could taste in my blood. Christian had lifetimes of experience, and his powers far exceeded my own.

But I didn't mind the hand-holding.

At the mouth of the cave, grey smoke clouded the air from a dying fire. Claude passed through a veil of darkness and into the open. He had changed into a long-sleeved brown shirt with a high collar. Despite lack of sleep and everything we'd been through, his curly golden hair seemed perfectly styled. But his eyes were narrower than usual, and his nostrils flared.

"What happened?" I asked, letting go of Christian's hand.

When he spoke, all four of his fangs were showing. "He kidnapped her."

"Who kidnapped her? And who is her?"

"Carol."

My heart sank. General's brother must have run ahead of us. "Is anyone hurt? We got one, but we didn't think the other one would come back here right away."

Claude shook his head slowly. "That vile Shifter she calls her beau took her."

Christian chortled and hefted his bags. "They're probably off diddling in the woods somewhere."

Claude gave Christian a reproachful look as the Vampire strutted into the cave without a care in the world.

"Did you try to find her?" I asked.

"Viktor won't allow anyone to leave, not with the two left behind. Matteo went out, but he doesn't own her scent."

"How did it happen?"

"I think Carol was secretly carrying firewood to the second cavern. She created a dam, and water quickly flooded the room. It caused a panic because we had to get Blue off the floor. They must have slipped out and made a run for it. That young child couldn't have devised that plan all by herself. He coerced her."

"Nobody noticed they were gone?"

He shook his head and turned toward the cave. "The kids poured out of their spot so we could move Blue up there, but it was no easy feat. Then we had to stop the flooding since it was putting out the fire."

"Maybe Matteo will find them. How's Blue?"

"She's awake."

A weight came off my shoulders. "Good. I have a present for her."

He noticed the axe in my hand, but clearly other things were on his mind. The feeling of helplessness was almost tangible. "You say you killed one lion?"

"With my bare hands."

"Sounds delightful."

"I think there's only one left. He took off, so I don't know if he'll be back."

Once inside the cave, I tossed the bags down in a dry spot on top of some rocks. Adam and Eve spotted their stuff and went to rifle through it. After removing some of their extra clothing, they began organizing what little property they had.

I approached the corner where Viktor and Christian were talking. Viktor aimed his flashlight at the ceiling while Christian detailed our encounter with the lions.

"We cannot stay here," Viktor said. "We have to keep moving."

"It's a risk," Christian cautioned him. "If the last lion wants revenge, he'll be merciless."

"If we stay, the danger is greater," Viktor said firmly. "What if he has access to a satellite phone and calls for backup? We must keep moving."

Christian inclined his head. "What'll you have me do?"

"Break more firewood. Blue must stay behind."

Christian left the cave as if he had fire beneath his feet.

In the crevice behind Viktor, long hair spilled from the flat rock where Blue was sleeping. Viktor followed my gaze.

"She has plenty of water," I said, hoping to ease his worry. "We can leave her some of our rations. I don't need to eat, and neither does Christian. I've got a few packages of peanuts and cookies I took from the train. Claude said she's awake?"

"Da. She is too weak to shift again and refuses."

"Why?"

"The more we shift, the weaker we become. It helps us to heal, but shifting is akin to running a marathon. She will sleep for a day or two, but she cannot afford to sleep any longer than that. Shifting again will make her vulnerable to predators."

We both knew what that meant—Blue would carry those scars forever.

I climbed onto a rock and rose up to the height of her chamber. It curved around her like a cozy pita pocket, and it would be a safe place for her to recover. Claude had dressed her in his clothes, Christian's trench coat covered her feet, and Matteo's furs blanketed the cold stone beneath her. She lay at an angle with her feet tucked in the back and her head near the edge.

"Are you awake?"

She mumbled sleepily and looked at me. Her sapphire eyes sparkled in the light of breaking dawn.

"We found your clothes and bag at the old campsite. I didn't go through it, but you probably have supplies in there. I also brought you this."

When I held the axe in front of her, she smiled weakly. I set it down next to her along with her belt, which had the sheath that covered the blade.

"Thank you," she said, clearing her throat and looking more alert.

"Are you hurting? Shepherd probably has pain medicine."

She propped up her head. "No, just tired."

"I killed a lion with my bare hands."

"Is that so?" She chuckled quietly. "I always knew you were a badass since the day I took all your weapons."

Shepherd rested his arm on the ledge of her crawl space. "Here, drink this."

She looked warily at the pea-green liquid inside the bottle he offered her. There were chunks floating around, and it didn't look anything like a protein shake or energy drink.

"It'll help you heal up faster. You really need to shift one more time."

Blue leaned on her elbow and sniffed the drink. "Do I want to know what's in this?"

"Probably not. Just pretend it's beer and chug it down."

"Easy for you to say." Blue grimaced after a few gulps of her drink. "I'll shift later on when my falcon has enough strength to fly. If I do it now and she's still weak, I won't have any energy left to shift back."

I saw the bigger picture. It wasn't just about Blue being vulnerable but also her animal. If her falcon couldn't fly, any wild animal could come along, trap her, and gobble her up. What a gruesome thought.

"I'm sorry I slowed everyone down." Guilt bled from her expression. "I should have been paying attention."

Viktor joined Shepherd's side and patted her head. "You are alive. That is all that matters."

She leaned into his palm. "I made a stupid mistake. I shouldn't have wandered that far from camp. But it was too risky to keep trash in the open or store it close to where we're sleeping. I found a spot and started digging a hole with my axe. I didn't even hear him coming from behind. A knife cut through my shoulder, and I shifted on instinct. Then he grabbed my feet and covered my head."

I stepped down from the rock. "If it's any consolation, we stabbed him back. Karma's a bitch, and so am I."

She lowered her arm to lie back down on her side. "I wish I could have stabbed him myself, but I couldn't do anything with that damn hood on my head."

Viktor set down the satellite phone beside her. "I will leave this with you. I do not know if the compound will have outside communication. If they do, you'll be the first I call. If we do not return in three days, contact Wyatt and get yourself out of here."

She pushed it away. "You might need it."

He stroked his silver beard. "This is not up for debate. We are many; you are one."

"Thank you," she rasped.

"You have been a great service on this mission, and your duty is not over. I want you to have Wyatt arrange for transportation. We will need a way back home, and that will be one less worry."

Her eyes gently closed. "I will."

I patted Viktor's arm. "Do we have enough in the budget for a helicopter?"

Viktor gave me a "hell no" look.

"Just thought I'd ask. I'm homesick. When I get back, I'm making a special trip to Ruby's for hot apple pie and ice cream."

Blue smiled, her eyes still closed. "And hamburgers."

Shepherd walked away and ran his hand over his short hair. "I just wanna see my kid."

"And I want to see my partner," Claude added while he put more dry wood on the fire.

Matteo appeared like a ghost as he stalked into the cave. He clenched his fists and snarled. "I lost their scent."

Claude cursed and kicked the wall. The twins flinched as he paced around the growing fire.

Matteo stood between Viktor and me. "The young male shifted and marked his scent all over the place. With the wind blowing, I couldn't track him." He put his hands on his hips and lowered his head.

Viktor tapped his watch. "We cannot exhaust our time and resources searching for runaways. Perhaps after we deliver the two siblings, we can search the woods. It is unfortunate that she could not see the necessity of protection."

Blue scooted closer to the edge and lifted her head. "I'll look for them as soon as I can. They're probably long gone by now, but they won't get far on foot. Not many people trust hitchhikers."

Matteo was giving me a funny look.

"What?" I asked.

"I smell lust on you," he said matter-of-factly.

My cheeks heated, and I dodged his stare. Chitahs were unnecessarily invasive when it came to emotional scents, and the residual smell on my clothes must have detailed a lot about my evening.

More than I wanted anyone else to know.

"You tricked me," he said.

"How so?"

"You promised me a kiss with no intention to honor your word. Not if you're mated to that Vampire."

"Technically, I didn't promise to kiss you. I just promised you would get your kiss. I know lots of women who would leap at the chance with a stud like you."

His eyes narrowed.

Viktor branched away and attended to the twins.

I faced Matteo. "Wouldn't you rather have money? After everything you've done, you deserve a nice fat paycheck. I'll give you half my salary for this job. That's a lot of supplies you can buy for your home."

Matteo's masculine features and distinct bone structure hardened to stone beneath all that long hair and his beard. He didn't accept my offer, but the doleful look in his eyes reminded me of how important the kiss was to him.

Why would this be his last kiss? Was he swearing off women, or did he want to end his life? Maybe it was none of my business.

I'd promised him a kiss. A simple, harmless kiss. Yet in my heart, delivering that promise felt like a betrayal to Christian. It would mean nothing to me, but it might mean something to him. At some point our job might require us to get close to someone else for information or setting a trap, but this was different. I hadn't tried hard enough to negotiate a deal from the start, and now I'd painted myself into a corner.

"I'll do it," Blue volunteered.

I blinked up in surprise.

Still on her side, Blue tucked her hair behind her ear and lifted her head to win the Chitah's attention.

Matteo looked between us with disappointment. "That wasn't the deal we made."

"Am I not suitable?" she inquired. "My scars don't reach my lips. Close your eyes and pretend I'm a whole woman."

He gripped the ledge and leaned in close. "*You*, female, are exquisite. I am not worthy of your lips."

I snorted. "But mine will do?"

He gave me a look so icy that it could have given me frostbite. "You're my mortal enemy. It means less. This female is closer to my Breed. We have similar traits and family values. I just wanted the memory of a kiss, not the hope of a life I'll never have."

Blue shifted her sapphire gaze up to Matteo. "Let me kill any hope you might have, Chitah. I'm not sentimental about kissing, so I won't be keeping the bed warm for you at night. I don't want a mate. But if Raven promised you a kiss, I'll gladly pay her debt. I owe you."

His head jerked back. "Owe me?"

"For carrying me here. For lending me your coat."

Matteo reacted as though someone had told him the earth was flat. "I did what any decent male would do for a wounded female. You are not beholden to me."

"Is that so?" She rested her head against her arm as if struggling to stay awake. "Kiss me, Chitah. Claim your reward, unless you don't think I'm worthy enough."

Oh, Blue was good. Real good. She knew exactly how to push the right buttons. Watching her work Matteo over was like watching a baker kneading dough.

Matteo inclined his head. "You would honor me."

I mouthed "Thank you" to Blue. She gave me an imperceptible nod before Matteo stepped onto the rock, despite his height, to lean over her.

Maybe it was wrong to pawn off my favor on a wounded friend, but Blue was an unpredictable woman, and this was her choice. Most of us had needs and filled those sexual impulses on the side. But Blue shunned all attention from men. Maybe she didn't want to get close to them in any way that might jeopardize her position with Keystone.

Matteo didn't rush his reward. He tenderly brushed her straight hair away from her golden skin and gazed into her eyes.

Viktor gave them a cursory glance when the kids started giggling. "Go to the bathroom," he said tersely. "We leave soon."

Eve rolled her eyes and dawdled toward the second room, her bag in hand.

When Matteo leaned in for his kiss, I pivoted on my heel and watched the sunrise. The twinge of guilt in my conscience forced me to turn around more than the intimacy. Blue didn't like Christian. Hell, she didn't like Vampires. So I didn't understand why she'd bent over backwards to protect our relationship.

But when Christian came in with an armload of wood and gave me a smoldering look that burned hotter than the fire, I knew

I'd done the right thing. Christian always liked to say: "Your lips belong to me."

And they did.

Chapter 26

GEM HADN'T SLEPT A WINK all night. She'd combed through every page of her recent book acquisition to analyze the scribbling written above the text. She had mapped and memorized enough passages to locate matches in the red book. It would take far too much time to come up with definitive translations. The book she'd purchased at the pawnshop only had partial translations, and that would require extensive research to fill in all the gaps. Gem couldn't contact the owner because Cosmo had said that all those books and other items in the back had come from the deceased.

In a daze, she carried the red book up to her room. Her nightgown hung flat like a red nightmare, and she couldn't get it off fast enough. The thought of returning to Cyrus filled her with dread, but Niko needed her. She'd spent all night ruminating over their situation and concluded that she had no choice but to return.

Gem's wardrobe was whimsical and comfortable. She didn't really own anything that said "I mean business." After putting on camo leggings, she pulled out her chunky black boots—the ones she used to wear when Viktor would invite her on dangerous assignments—and laced them up. Cyrus wasn't very tall, so maybe matching his height would give him a complex. Poor Niko. She couldn't imagine how helpless he'd felt as a boy, and to wind up stuck with a repugnant brute like Cyrus?

She yanked on her black sweater. "Servant? More like a slave," she grumbled, thinking about how Cyrus was treating him.

Tattered rags? Whippings? Serving tea on his knees? The thought infuriated her.

After twisting her purple hair into two small buns, she grabbed her crystal pendant and slipped it around her neck. Gem needed all the positive energy she could get.

"Disgusting mouth breathers."

A throat cleared.

Gem squeaked and spun around.

Wyatt lingered in the doorway, wearing nothing but socks, jeans, and a loose grey hat. "Who are you talking to?"

Gem blew out a breath. "Myself. No one." She gathered the red book into her arms and clutched it to her chest. "I have to go."

He planted his hands on either side of the door. "I don't think so."

Gem strode across the gold rugs, which overlapped and weren't lined up in any particular direction. She liked it that way, and it gave her bedroom a real bohemian feel.

When she saw that Wyatt wasn't budging, she poked her cold finger into his belly button and gave him a tiny shock, which made him hop back. "I have no choice," she informed him before squeezing her way past him.

"Hold up, buttercup." Wyatt jogged ahead of her and walked backward. He looked so boyish in that hat that Gem sometimes wondered why a man as old as him would wear it. "What the immortal hell is so special about that book, and why can't you mail it to them?"

Gem slowed her pace. "I don't know what's in this book. I can't read all of it. But if I don't bring it to him, he'll kill Niko."

"Kill? As in…" Wyatt made a slicing motion across his neck.

"Yes. *After* they torture him."

"And you think they'll just let him go if you give him the book?"

Flustered, she stopped and swung her eyes up to the high arched ceiling. "I don't know."

Wyatt folded his arms. "So you're telling me you don't have a plan. You're just going to walk into the fire?"

"Do you have any better ideas? Because I don't. And there's

no way I'm going to stay here and hold on to this book if it means Niko dies."

"Can't he fight them? He's tough, Gem. We've all seen him fight."

Gem couldn't explain what Niko had done, and she wasn't sure Niko would want Keystone to know he'd signed away his freedom. "They put a metal cuff on him, and I don't know how it works, but he's mortal."

Wyatt anchored his hands on his hips and slid his lower jaw from side to side. "That changes things, doesn't it? I've seen those pop up once or twice on the black market, but they're hard to acquire. They say the metal's infused with some kind of magic that suppresses immortal gifts."

"I know. He put one on me."

Wyatt's eyes widened as she walked past him. He bounced in front of her again and gripped her shoulders. "What did it feel like? What did it do?"

"I couldn't feel my light anymore. I felt like a human."

He pinched the whiskers on his chin. "I wonder if it would work on a Gravewalker. Imagine, walking into a graveyard or public place and no spooks. Nothing but fleshwalkers."

"Flesh what?"

"Us. The living."

"I don't know. It didn't seem to affect my Relic knowledge."

"Yeah, but that's wired into your brain cells."

Gem closed her eyes for a moment and took a micronap while Wyatt rambled on about the possibilities of blocking a Gravewalker's power.

"Hey, you should sleep." Wyatt startled her awake when he shook her shoulders.

The book almost slid from her arms, and she clutched it tighter. "I wish Viktor were here. He'd know what to do."

Wyatt tucked his hands in his pockets. "Haven't heard from him since yesterday, but that's not unusual. It's the last leg of their journey. They're on their own."

"And so are we."

He scratched the back of his neck. "Look, we've got a bunch of wolves guarding the property. You're safe here."

She stalked off. "But Niko isn't safe."

He tugged the back of her sweater, forcing her to stop. "If I can't talk you into staying, at least let me tag you with a chip."

Her brow furrowed. "Huh?"

He robbed her view of the stairs when he jumped in front of her again. "A tracking device. I got a new batch in, and they're the size of a coin. I can slip one into the heel of your shoe. Or maybe cut open the leather on that book and—"

She swung away. "You're not touching it."

"What's the big deal? It's just an old book."

"Wyatt Blessing, if you put a knife anywhere near this book— or any of my books, for that matter—I'll invite every ghost in Cognito to the mansion for a big party, and you're the guest of honor."

His eyes widened, and he looked at her sideways. "You wouldn't dare."

"Wouldn't I?" She rocked on her heels. "Books are precious, and we must protect them."

"If you say so, Mother Teresa. At least give me your shoe." He gestured to her feet. "I'll put it inside, near your toes. Don't worry, I won't cut them up if you don't want me to. Just don't take off those slippers, or you'll never find your way back to Kansas."

She smiled at the *Wizard of Oz* reference.

Wyatt folded his arms. "I can't come get you myself, but at least I'll know where to find you if he doesn't let you go."

"Or find my body," she murmured.

He put his hand on her back and led her toward the stairs. "If you ever die, go where you're supposed to go. Don't linger in the afterlife. You might see a light or a person or hear a voice, but whatever you do, don't hang around."

She smiled up at him. "I'll hang around and haunt you."

"You know what's worse than dying? Becoming a lost soul. They inhabit the earth and forget their life. Even if you stayed here, you would lose pieces of yourself."

"Are you scared of death?"

He slowed to a stop, eyes downcast. "Pain scares me. Dying? Not so much. The best advice I can give you is not to get attached to anyone."

"Why?"

"Besides revenge, it's the number one reason souls stay behind. Fleshwalkers never see what happens to a soul that chooses to stay. I had nine sisters who died, but they all went to the next life. Gravewalkers don't linger, because we know exactly what a mad soul looks like."

"But Gravewalkers can see the dead. Doesn't that change things when it comes to family members? If you know the spirit, you can remind them about their life, can't you?"

He shook his head. "A soul without a body is like water without a container. It has nothing to channel and move it. Imagine tossing water into space. The droplets would spread out and lose form."

"Doesn't water vaporize in space?"

"Smarty-pants."

Gravewalkers had such a peculiar way of looking at death. "Have you ever lost anyone who stayed behind in the afterlife?"

Wyatt blanched and rubbed his hand down his stomach, eyes fixed on a faint trail of hair. "Just promise you won't linger."

"I don't plan on dying."

When his green eyes lifted, he gave her a grim look. "No one ever does."

After Wyatt put a tracking device in her boot, Gem called the number Arcadius had given her to let them know she was ready. Wyatt wanted the number, and Gem didn't see the harm since it was probably untraceable. It would keep Wyatt occupied. Just in case she didn't return, Gem left a note in her room for Viktor. It explained her actions, removing any blame he might place on Wyatt for not intervening. Wyatt was just doing his job, and a Gravewalker was no match for these men.

Gem placed the book in a brown bag, slung it over her shoulder, and let Raven's father drive her into the city. Crush didn't pry into her business, but he also had no idea she was going back into the lion's den. Her silence during the drive must have bothered him, because he kept giving her long looks at every red light. Gem wasn't a naturally quiet person, and the first time they met, she'd talked his ear off.

"If you need help, give me a call." Crush handed her his business card, which had the number and address for his auto shop. "My cell phone number's on the back."

What a loyal man he was. To do all this without asking any questions, all because he was Raven's father? Gem would forever envy those who knew that type of love and devotion.

She thanked him and got out. As tempting as it was to accept his offer, Gem wouldn't dream of involving Raven's father in her deadly affairs. It was brave of him and his Shifter buddies to guard Keystone, but Gem drew the line when it came to endangering a mortal.

As soon as Crush sped away, Gem let the business card slip from her fingers into the storm drain. She couldn't chance Cyrus finding that card.

After a short walk, she passed a tobacco shop and waited in an abandoned alley. Three minutes later, Arcadius backed up into the narrow space, and when the trunk popped open, she got in. He bound her hands in front and blindfolded her. She could have easily removed the blindfold, but to what avail? During the drive, she cried a little into the blindfold. No choice was the right choice. Every decision yielded a number of different outcomes.

She hugged the satchel and listened to the tires humming across the pavement. Arcadius hadn't searched the bag or attempted to take it from her. It gave Gem the impression that these men who followed Cyrus didn't think independently; all they did was follow orders. They were less like a team and more like soldiers. And Cyrus was less of a general than he was a dictator.

The car finally stopped, and Arcadius hauled her out of the trunk. As he led her into the building, he kept a tight grip on her arm. She thought about Niko's experiences as a blind man and wondered how much information she could gain from her other senses.

Concrete beneath my feet. A curb. Smells like cigarettes. A smoker must be standing close by. Definitely in the city. Seven steps to a door. The inside smells musty. Linoleum floor. This isn't someone's mansion. Fifteen, sixteen, seventeen steps. Another door, but it's locked. He's got a key.

Gem coughed and heard the sound of her voice bouncing off walls. It wasn't a large room or even a hallway. More like a foyer. Arcadius punched something into a digital keypad, and a lock clicked.

This place was probably in the Bricks, but it was likely an apartment building with a basement. Maybe there were multiple doors to multiple dwellings, but she was certain Cyrus didn't share a hall with anyone, because when they reached the bottom of the stairs, they were still in a narrow corridor as Arcadius opened the door to his home.

The door wasn't steel—that much she knew. From the inside, it reminded Gem of a hotel or apartment door. It made her wonder why they bothered with all the digital locks if someone could probably kick the door down or break in with a battering ram.

These men were ruthless and strategic, but they weren't very bright.

He shoved her inside, and Gem stumbled over her chunky boots before falling to her knees. The bag hit the floor, and she quickly removed the blindfold.

Moisture dripped from Cyrus's dark hair, but it wasn't sweat. He looked relaxed, his skin flushed and smelling of soap. She stared at his bare feet and sausage-like toes. None of them wore shoes in the house. Maybe it was their custom or maybe it was to protect the wood floor, but she hoped that he didn't make her take off her shoes. The tracking device needed to stay with her at all times.

Cyrus knelt in front of her, a paring knife in one hand, half an apple in the other. He bit down on the apple to hold it in his mouth and then gripped her wrists with his meaty fingers. Cyrus shoved the slim blade between her hands and cut the zip tie. The hard plastic fell to the floor, and Gem quickly scooped up the satchel.

He chewed a bite of his apple and stood up. "Don't disappoint me, girl. Is that what I think it is?"

"Where's Niko?"

He jerked his head to the side. "In the back. Alive."

"You promised to let him go."

His narrow eyes darkened. "If you don't let me see what's in the bag, I'll never let you go. How would you like that?"

Gem swallowed hard and slowly unbuckled the flap. While she did that, Cyrus handed his apple and knife over to Lykos before wiping his fingers on his black pants.

She pulled out the heavy book, and Cyrus's eyes glimmered at the sight of it.

"You promised," she reminded him.

He knelt down and pulled the book in front of him. His expression altered as he looked upon the cover with reverence. His fingers skimmed across the red leather binding. "There she is." After flipping open the first page, he let out a breath. Then he looked at Gem as if she were an afterthought. "I will remove his cuff."

She sprang to her feet and darted down the hall. Gem pushed open every door in search of Niko, but she found him kneeling in the middle of her bedroom, his head down and long hair obscuring his face.

Gem sat in front of him. Could he ever forgive her for taking matters into her own hands? "Why did you hide it in plain sight? In *my* study, of all places?"

"Because the only place a book would be safe is with you."

When Niko lifted his gaze, Gem clutched her pendant. A deep cut severed his bottom lip, and his left eye was swollen shut.

"When I first joined Keystone, I searched for a place to hide it," he explained, his voice tired and hollowed out. "A man never hides something truly valuable in his immediate space. It lived in one of Viktor's libraries for a while until he mentioned donating books to auctions and charities. I had no choice but to move it to your secret room."

"But nobody knows where my study is. Well, no one except for Viktor and Raven. I've never taken anyone in there. Not that it's a big secret, but I need peace and quiet when I'm working, and if people know about it, they'll pop in any old time they want. How did you find it?"

A phantom smile briefly touched his lips. "You leave behind an energy trail. The ribbons of light always led me to the wall. One day when you were out with Claude, I went inside." Niko heaved a sigh. "I should have buried it."

Gem sat on one leg and bent her other knee. "Weren't you afraid I'd find and translate it?"

"Before the owner died, he mocked us. He said that not even the high scholars could read that language."

"But someone wrote it. Someone obviously knew." Gem glanced at the closed door and lowered her voice. "I found a book, Niko. One that had direct translations of an old language written above select passages. The translations are symbols, and they're the same as the ones in your book. Someone figured it out. Maybe he was a Relic like me, or maybe he found the book and had no idea what any of it meant, but he kept it anyway."

Niko's face went ashen. "Tell me you did not bring that book."

"No," she said quietly. "But someone knew the language. If there's one, there could be more. You can't hide from this, Niko. People from that era might still be alive. You can't protect language. Does Cyrus know it?"

Niko shook his head but looked uncertain.

"He's had a thousand years to learn it."

Niko clenched his fists and leaned forward. "Then *why* did you bring it?"

"For the same reason you came here in the first place. Viktor would have never allowed you to negotiate on Cyrus's turf. You came here knowing that you'd never leave. Keeping the book away from him hasn't solved your problems, so let's see what happens."

She laced her fingers over her knee. "It's a spellcasting book, isn't it? I said a word, and it worked."

He frowned. "What worked?"

"Has anyone ever explained how to cast spells from the book? You don't just read the words, Niko. You have to touch them, and it activates the energy. I'm willing to bet that only a Mage can unlock the power. It's a process of give-and-take when you read the words, like it needs your core energy." Gem reached out and seized Niko's wrist. "Don't you understand? Even if Cyrus learns how to read it, does he know how to use it? I bet he doesn't, and that means it'll always be useless to him."

"Then what do you propose?"

Gem straightened her posture. "If I can convince him to let me stay and translate the book, I might find something in there I can use against him. Something that will get us out of this mess."

"You don't understand the power in the book."

"If I can wield energy balls, I can wield words."

Niko appeared statuesque before her. So much taller than she was. His stony expression gave nothing away as he sat quietly and stared into the void. Though Gem was a Mage of fifty, she felt like a child at his feet. Ancients lived more lifetimes than she could imagine. They had witnessed the evolution of science and religion. Some immortals went mad after a few thousand years, and others took their own lives. The vast majority simply died in battles or after attacks. Gem had rarely met anyone Niko's age, and she'd most certainly never met anyone who was over five thousand, but she knew they were out there. Immortals that old terrified her. No one lived that long because of luck.

Even now as she sat before Niko, a man she considered a friend, she felt intimidated by his power and knowledge. She always had.

"Do you hate me?" Gem's voice quavered as she reached out and held his wrist.

Niko immediately loosened her grip and held her hand between his. "No, braveheart. You did what you thought was right, and for that, there is no fault. My sensei taught me an important lesson: choices are not about results; they're about intentions. Perhaps my choices worked for a long time, but now I can no longer avoid making different ones. My intention has always been to protect the book, but if it comes at the cost of your life or someone else's, I have failed."

She stood up and tugged on his arm. "Well, the first thing we're going to do is get that bracelet of doom off your ankle. Cyrus is making good on that promise."

Niko rose to his feet. He was naturally more than a half a foot taller than her, but Gem's shoes gave her extra height.

"What's your plan?" he inquired.

Gem liked that Niko trusted her even if she didn't have all the answers. "My plan is to convince Cyrus that he needs me. The more time I can spend with that book, the better."

"Gem, you should go. If there's an opportunity for you to leave—"

"Then I would be a fool to take it. I'm not leaving you here, not with that insidious monster." She waved her hand in front of his face. "Niko, can you see my light?"

He shook his head. "My world is dark again. Even in an empty room, I've always been able to see my own energy. Stones and fire give off light. The stars and moon shine. But now I'm alone in the dark."

Tears welled in her eyes. If Cyrus didn't make good on his promise to remove the ankle cuff, Gem would make his life a living hell. "How many are still out there, Niko? Who's the threat?"

"Kallisto."

Only one. As long as the others remained here, she would only have to worry about the one. "Raven's father and all his Shifter friends are guarding the mansion. I don't see how one man could get past all those wolves, and even if he did, there are so many rooms in the mansion to hide in. Switch is keeping a close watch on Hunter. This Kallisto person wouldn't act without permission, would he?"

"Cyrus speaks with him every three hours. Knowing Cyrus, if Kallisto doesn't hear from him, he'll execute whatever order he was given."

Gem seethed at the idea. "Even if Cyrus is dead? He'll be free to do what he wants. Why would he have any desire to remain loyal?"

"They were once Tengrists but did away with religion when Cyrus became their god. That's what an evil genius does. He doesn't just become a leader; he becomes a deity over his followers until they no longer question him or allow anything external to influence them. They doubt everyone's word but that of their leader. That's why Plato follows him even in death. They weren't always like this, but I recognized the turning point. And when Cyrus discovered the power in this book, I knew my only choice was to steal it. You've given him more than a book, Gem. You've given him true power."

"Power that I promise he'll never understand how to use," she said firmly. "We just have to figure out a way to find Kallisto. That's the only wild card."

"And if we cannot?"

Gem shifted her stance and gripped the cuffs of her black sweater. "Then I guess we have to figure out a way to outsmart him."

Niko drew closer. "You're a young Mage full of optimism, but before you make this choice, I want you to consider what's at stake. You could die. Your immortal life will end along with your knowledge, and he will cast you into the fire without a second thought. This isn't your battle to fight. You can walk away, and Keystone will go on without me. I might find a way out of this, or I might not, but this is my burden to bear. Gem, you could die," he said, his voice cracking.

Gem's heart clenched when she felt the raw emotion in Niko's tone. She had never known the feeling of someone caring about her. Even her own Creator had taught her that death was inevitable for most, so it was better to avoid emotional attachment. Gem had broken that rule with Hooper, and to some degree, she had allowed herself to care for Keystone. Enough that she was willing to die for them.

Gem sprang into his arms and hugged him tight even though he barely touched her back. "Oh, Niko. Don't you see? Keystone is the only family I'll ever have, and I'll never leave you behind. *Never.* If that means we die together, then at least we won't be alone."

"Are you sure about this? There's no going back."

She rested her head on his chest. "I've never been more sure about anything in my life. I don't want to die, but I also don't want to live if it means someone else dying in my place."

He cradled her head in his hands. "As you wish, little flower. As you wish."

Chapter 27

SHEPHERD WALKED AHEAD OF ME and bent a branch, which thwacked me in the face when it snapped back.

"Thanks for that," I grumbled.

It had been a long hike, and my boots were getting toasty. The temperature was easily in the sixties, so the kids had taken off their jackets and tied them around their waists. My jacket was weighing down my pack, and I started pondering the worth of a well-packed bag. Viktor was a smart man, and this test had taught me a valuable lesson. Next time we had to pack for a mystery trip, I'd leave behind the heavy leather and invest in a good pair of thermals and a windbreaker.

"How much longer?" Eve whined.

"Who wants gum?" Shepherd reached in his pocket and flourished a pack of mint gum.

"Ooh, me! Me!" Eve turned around and cupped her hands while Shepherd gave her a piece.

I chuckled and nudged Christian. "He's good at diversion. My dad used to do stuff like that."

Christian propped his foot on a rock, his sunglasses shading his sensitive eyes. "I figured your da gave you everything you ever asked for."

"Dads who love you don't do that."

"And why is that?"

"Because kids don't always know what's best for them."

"Aye, but parents do?"

I gripped the shoulder straps of my backpack. "Did your father give you everything you ever asked for?"

Christian ran a hand through his scruffy hair, which hadn't seen a comb in days. "The only thing my da ever gave me was a pickaxe, a plow, and callused hands."

Eve tossed her wrapper on the ground, and I caught Christian staring at the shiny foil. The bright sun was clearly agitating Christian, because his temper was as short as my list of past boyfriends. I once had my eyes dilated for a vision test, but that wasn't anywhere near as uncomfortable as it must have been for a Vampire in daylight.

"Good thing you never married," I remarked, still staring at the gum wrapper.

"And why is that?"

"I'm imagining what you would do if everyone started throwing rice or confetti."

"It doesn't bother me."

A gust of wind blew the wrapper.

I smiled. "Is that so?"

Christian glanced down at the buttons on his Henley and did them all up as if he weren't bothered by the sound of that paper tumbling through the woods. "I'm only annoyed by the inconsideration for others."

"Good thing nobody's out here to notice."

It had been an uneventful morning with no sign of the last remaining lion. We had walked a good seven hours without incident, but the journey was arduous and the hills steep.

I wiped my brow and searched the woods. "I feel bad for leaving Blue."

Christian looked over his shoulder. "I fear that Blue's in more danger than we are. His brothers are dead, so if he wants revenge, he'll go for the weakest in our group. With his family gone, he doesn't have use for the children. General was their leader."

"Do me a favor, and never be the one who gives our team a pep talk. You suck at it."

"I'm only calling it like I see it."

I glanced up the hill, relieved that it leveled out. "We better catch up."

As we headed toward the incline, Christian fell back a step. "I need to water the flowers."

I chortled. "Nice try, Vamp, but I don't think I've seen you drink any water since we left the city."

"Nature calls!" he said, hurrying into the woods.

"I hope you never find it!" I yelled back, tickled to death that he couldn't let that tiny wrapper go.

Christian would walk by trash in the street and didn't go around cleaning everything up. But it was a different story when he actually saw someone tossing litter on the ground. That was a button pusher for him.

I guess everyone has their thing.

Eve shrieked, and I hauled ass up the steep hill until I reached the top.

With my dagger in hand, I closed in on the group and scoured the area for the lion.

Claude stood by a large tree with Eve sandwiched between him and the trunk. Her eyes darted around, but Claude had her head in a protective grasp.

Viktor stood behind a mossy tree, his gun drawn and aimed at the woods on the left. When I spotted Shepherd dragging Adam's unconscious body behind a thicket of bushes, I flashed to Viktor's tree.

"What happened?" I peered back at Shepherd, wondering why the kid wasn't bleeding.

Viktor fired his gun twice and shifted before the handgun even hit the ground. When his wolf took off, I picked up the gun and bolted toward the bushes to find Shepherd. There was a wall of earth on one side, and he had the kid tucked safely against it.

"What the hell's going on?"

Shepherd's hands were amazingly steady as he pulled a small bottle of liquid from his bag. "He has a motherfucking blowgun."

I crawled over Adam and put my finger on his pulse. "He's still alive."

"Not for long. Not unless I can figure out what he used for poison." Shepherd dropped a slim bamboo stick into the bottle and swirled it. The cotton-wrapped tip still had Adam's blood on it, and it mixed with the liquid. Shepherd set down the bottle and unfolded a leather flap with numerous small instruments inside. He opened two separate pockets, each containing a test strip.

"What is that?"

"I need to find out if the poison is plant or animal based."

"Why?"

"Because I only have two antidotes, and if I give him the wrong one, he'll die." He handed me two vials, one with a red label and the other a green. "Here, hold these."

Shepherd pulled out the bamboo dart and dabbed the end onto each test strip. Then he glanced at his watch and wiped beads of sweat off his brow.

"Why don't I suck out the poison?" I suggested.

"Be my guest, but I don't have enough antidotes for everyone." He stared at those test strips as if they were going to turn into unicorns. "Humans don't have anything like this. When I worked in the hospital, they would run elaborate blood work to find toxins."

"Where did you learn this?"

"Maggie. She knew everything about human genetics and biology. Breed Relics have unique antidotes similar to these, but they only work on Breed. Maggie developed something that would work on humans, but she didn't have the capability to create a universal antidote. It's based on animal and plant protein or something like that. You don't have to add saline. All I need is a vein."

"Don't you need to tie off his arm?"

"I've got a tool."

While both strips were tinged red, one was beginning to change color.

Shepherd had the syringe in one hand, and when he saw the strip turning, he reached for the red vial in my hand and extracted the medicine. With haste, he gripped Adam's arm and held a small plastic device over it. A laser illuminated his skin.

"You got good veins, kid." Shepherd slid the needle in and pressed the plunger.

"How long till he wakes up?" I asked.

Shepherd sat back and dropped his equipment near his bag. "I don't know. I've never done this before."

"What do you mean, you've never done this before? Are you fucking kidding me?"

He stared at the kid and pulled up one of his eyelids. "Maggie had all this knowledge but couldn't put it out there. Humans have regulations and approved test studies. She had all the science in her head, but she couldn't test it on anyone. She tried getting a job at a pharmaceutical company but never got that far. After her murder, her family put her things in storage. They let me collect my stuff, but I also took these. Maggie said they would save lives and change the world."

"Let's hope for your sake she was right."

Adam's face took on a pinkish hue, and his eyes fluttered. He still looked poorly with bluish lips and a cold sweat all over, but seeing him respond gave me hope.

Shepherd touched his hand but wasn't feeling for a pulse. His tactile ability allowed him to sense Adam's emotions, his pain, and what he was experiencing in that moment. It made me consider how Sensors could be exceptional doctors.

A tear rolled down his cheek and disappeared into his whiskery jaw. "It worked, Maggie."

Adam groaned and rolled to his side, just in time to retch.

Shepherd took off his backpack and found a bottle of water. "Drink this, kid. Even if you want to puke, hold it down and drink. You need to stay hydrated for the medicine to work through you."

Adam reluctantly took the water and gulped it. "Eve," he rasped.

"She's fine," I said, even though I had no idea what was happening behind us.

I looked at Shepherd in disbelief. "Do you know how to make more of that stuff?"

He shook his head. "These are the only two in existence. Doesn't matter anyhow."

"Why not?"

He wrapped up his instruments and put them in the bag. "This is Hunter's legacy. He knows all this shit, and when the time comes, what he does with that knowledge will be up to him. At least I can tell him it works."

"It would save a lot of lives."

"Yeah, tell that to the pharmaceutical companies. You think they want people getting their hands on cures?" He drew his gun and looked to the right. "The sicker you are, the more money they make."

"You should give it to a doctor or something."

He shook his head. "That's your human side talking. Toss out everything you know about the world you lived in. There's a lot of red tape. You can't just walk up with a cure in your hand, and we have to be careful about how much attention we draw to ourselves. All shit like this does is put a target on your back."

I could see that. There were a lot of factions who wouldn't like the idea of us giving cures to humans.

Shepherd touched the boy again. "Hopefully he doesn't have any nerve damage. I don't feel anything."

I jumped when Claude crashed onto the scene with Eve. They hurtled over the bush and dropped to the ground.

Eve crawled over to her brother. "Adam! Are you okay? What happened?"

"Get back before I puke on you," he said, still working on the water and struggling not to throw it all up.

Claude was on the verge of flipping his switch, but if Matteo was right, his first instinct was to protect the children and not hunt down the person responsible.

Speaking of...

"Where's Matteo?" I scanned the woods behind Claude.

"Searching," Claude growled. "Female, *sit down.*"

Eve obediently sank to the ground after trying to peer over the bushes.

As much as I wanted to run into the fray, Viktor and Matteo were out there, along with Christian. There was no way in hell I could abandon these kids.

"Put your jacket on," I said to Eve. "I don't think poison darts can penetrate jean jackets. It'll give you an extra layer of protection. Adam was an easy target in a short-sleeved shirt."

Eve did as she was told and helped her brother into his jacket.

Shepherd touched Adam's hand again. "If you start to feel funny or have trouble breathing, let me know right away."

That put a fright on the kid's face.

Shepherd zipped up his bag and met eyes with me. "They waited until it got warmer so we'd start stripping out of our clothes from all the hiking. Whoever's out there is fucking smart."

"Or stupid," I countered. "We've got Chitahs, a Vampire, and a Shifter. They won't get away."

Shepherd wiped his sweaty brow. "Maybe they don't care. And a man who doesn't care is more dangerous than a patient man."

Claude lifted the bottom of his black T-shirt and wiped his face. The adrenaline was making us all sweat as we kept our eyes on the woods. "Where's Christian?" he asked. "Wasn't he with you?"

I touched the necklace beneath my shirt. "Hopefully killing a lion."

After Christian compulsively branched away from Raven to grab the gum wrapper, he heard two things. The first was Adam cursing before hitting the ground, followed by Eve's scream. The second was the quickened footfalls of someone on the run.

Knowing the team would be protecting the children, Christian pursued the runner.

Isolating the sound took seconds. He snapped branches that stood in his way and went sailing over fallen limbs. Christian felt strong when he ran, even at human speed. Vampires didn't tire easily.

When he lost the sound, he skidded to a stop and sharpened

his hearing. His heart was still beating at a regular pace, and he held his breath to isolate as much of the sound as possible without internal interference.

Wood snapped in the distance. Christian took off, water splashing beneath his feet when he ran through a small stream. He weaved around fat trees and closed in on the sound. A heartbeat filled his ears, and it was strong.

Not human.

Animal.

Christian's fangs punched out. The Vampire in him behaved like a separate entity, and surrendering to that raw power was the greatest way to honor the ancient blood coursing in his veins. Seeing Raven fully give herself over to her Vampire nature when she killed the lion had roused a deep admiration within Christian. His blood might have been the push she needed to fully awaken. And she'd looked like a fecking goddess.

Steering his focus back on the lion, he crested a hill and caught sight of the beast. Its tongue hung out as it panted and paced. When it caught sight of Christian, it drew in a deep breath and roared. Predators couldn't identify a Vampire from afar. It was only when they got close and didn't pick up a scent that they would flee. From this distance the animal didn't know who the hell he was dealing with, and right now Christian was wrath.

The two predators stared each other down. In a split second, they collided in a savage attack, and Christian wrapped his arms around its head in a crushing grip. Large teeth sank into his shoulder and back, piercing a nerve and causing him to lose his hold when they hit the ground.

Christian sank his fangs into the lion's throat and tore open a hole. He could taste a mixture of self-preservation and the desire to kill, but fear was the underlying emotion, and that wasn't common in a beast like this. Not unless he'd figured out what Christian was.

When he tried to get ahold of the animal's jaw to rip it off, the lion took off.

"You little shite!"

He sprinted after the animal. Birds evacuated a bush when he tore through it like a tornado. Christian jumped for a branch and swung over a large fallen tree before dropping to the ground. The lion might be able to run faster, but Christian could run for a lot longer. It was only a matter of time.

Then he heard Raven and Claude talking. A wolf snarled, but all Christian could see was a never-ending pathway of trees, vines, and weeds.

"Run!" he shouted, hoping the group would hear him. "Raven, run!"

Christian slowed his approach. The lion's tail swished as he faced Viktor's grey wolf, who acted as a barrier between the lion and the team. Viktor was half his size and nowhere near the same weight, but he circled the animal and bit him wherever he could. The lion swiped his massive paw and knocked Viktor down.

Christian shouted once more, hoping that Raven wouldn't take that as her cue to come after him. The scent of fear must have been in the air, because the lion kept turning toward the group and taking deep breaths.

Viktor's wolf tore at the lion's legs, haunches, and even his tail. Blood stained the mossy ground below the animal's feet from the open wounds.

"Come and get me, you little fleabag, so I can give you a good throttling."

As soon as the animal pivoted, Viktor's wolf went for his belly and showed no mercy.

When the lion turned, Christian jumped in and struck his back with a closed fist. The creature moved at the last minute, so the blow didn't break his spine, but it was enough to do some damage. The pain on the lion's face was visceral, and he scuttled backward to get away.

There was no such thing as an easy kill. Every Breed had unique abilities and, in some cases, rare gifts. Shifters were complicated. A fast animal could escape, and a strong animal could pin him long enough to bite off his head.

And Christian was rather attached to his head, so he chose his moves carefully.

Blood stained the wolf's face, but his steely eyes locked on that lion like a target.

Christian inched closer, taking a step each time the lion turned away to fight off the wolf.

Fifteen feet.

Ten feet.

Six feet.

Hungry for the kill, he could wait no more. Christian lunged and wrapped his arms around him. The lion thrashed and roared, and while Christian could have crushed his neck, he refrained. No, that would be far too quick. He wanted this Shifter to suffer. He wanted to hurt him just enough to make him shift to human form.

Then maybe they could have some real fun.

Viktor's wolf rushed headlong toward the lion and went for his neck. It was like a jungle rodeo, with Christian straddling the lion and trying to hold on. Viktor moved in for the kill, and Christian's arms were in the line of fire. Blood sprayed from his attack, but Viktor suddenly whipped around and darted into the woods toward the rest of their group. Better that he stay with them. Christian had some business to attend to.

This stubborn bastard wouldn't shift. Christian squeezed tighter, breaking a few bones in the process. The animal bellowed in pain before collapsing in a heap. Christian felt the change before he saw it shape-shifting. When the process completed, his adversary was nothing but a weak, naked man with a bad haircut.

"King of the jungle, my arse."

Christian straddled the man on all fours, eagerly waiting for him to turn over and get a gander at a pissed-off Vampire. When he did, Christian patted the poor bastard's cheek. "Welcome to the party. So... you're the one who blew out my ears with that infernal device, aren't you?" Christian leaned in and smiled warmly, his fangs fully extended. "Why the glum face? You and I are going to have some fun."

Chapter 28

"**W**E HAVE TO STAY TOGETHER," I reminded Claude. He crouched with his knuckles pressed to the earth. When the lion roared in the distance again, Claude's golden eyes pulsed black.

"If you flip your switch, I'll knock you over the head with a stick," I warned him.

"I can't help it. You wouldn't understand what it's like."

I kind of did. Claude was like the Incredible Hulk in some ways. If he got angry, the beast inside him took control. The only problem being that this wasn't the right time for the Chitah cavalry.

"Fight the urge. If you take off, that just leaves Shep and me to protect these kids."

Eve huddled closer to her brother against the wall of dirt.

Shepherd touched Adam's hand again and chewed on his lip. "He needs medical attention."

"That's you," I pointed out.

Shepherd gave me an icy stare. "He can't keep the water down. He needs a fucking IV drip, and if I do that out here, he'll get sepsis."

"What's sepsis?" Eve's brown eyes were wide and fearful.

Shepherd crawled next to me and created a private huddle. "I still don't know what the hell they used for poison. He looks okay, but he might still have system failure. Heart attack, breathing problems… I don't know. But I sure as hell don't have the supplies he'll need in my bag. Look, I'm not a doctor. I know basic shit that I picked up by watching doctors in the ER. What if he needs a blood transfusion or antibiotics?" Shepherd glanced over his shoulder. "He's still not moving his legs very well. He won't make it if he goes into shock. We need to get this kid medical care and fast."

This was disastrous. I didn't know a damn thing about medicine, but Shepherd's concern gave me enough reason to worry. Paralysis was bad enough, but what if he died?

"Run!" we heard someone shout.

It was distant and spread all around us. Viktor was in wolf form, so that left only one person: Christian.

I didn't wait for a second warning. Neither did Shepherd.

He hooked his arm around Adam and launched him to his feet. "Let's roll."

Claude squatted in front of Eve. She climbed onto his back, and he stood up, her legs wrapped around his waist as she clutched his neck.

Shepherd was struggling between his gear and the boy. "Help me."

I got on the other side of Adam and put my arm around him. We took off as fast as we could, Adam's feet dragging behind. He tried to run, but he mostly held on and let us do all the work.

"Run!" Christian yelled again. This time it was closer.

I looked back and saw the lion coming for us. Viktor's wolf got between us, and all I heard were snarls and roars as I ran my ass off. For a brief moment, I entertained the idea of going back and helping, but then Adam whimpered in pain.

That was all I needed to hear.

"We got you," I said as we powered up a hill.

Claude was ahead of us by maybe twenty feet, the girl riding on his back. If this were flat pavement, he would have been long gone already.

Shepherd stumbled and almost dropped Adam in the process. When he got his footing again, we ran so fast that I thought my heart would explode in my chest. Once we crested the hill, the terrain leveled off.

My light pulsed against my palms, and I fought to control it before I accidentally blasted Adam.

On the flat terrain, Claude and Eve suddenly swooped upward in a blur. Leaves showered all around, and Eve screamed. Something clicked below our feet, and the next thing I knew, we launched into the air. As I felt myself twisting at an odd angle, a loud thud made me shudder.

Upside down, I stared at the forest floor beneath me through gaps in the thick rope netting. Our bodies were like one giant pretzel, my left arm and leg hanging from the open gaps, making it impossible for me to change position. This was like one of those traps I'd seen in the movies, only on a larger scale.

Now I knew what a fish felt like in a fisherman's net.

"What the fuck!" Shepherd growled.

I noticed a mechanism painted brown against a tree, and a steel cord going up to the top of our netting. A large log sat at the foot of the tree and must have been part of this contraption.

"Someone's sitting on my fingers," Adam complained, but all I could see was his leg.

With my free arm, I struggled to reach my push dagger. Sweat beaded on my brow, and once I removed my knife from the sheath, I made a sawing motion against the strong rope. The blade was too damn short. When I tried to put it back, fearing it might cut Adam by accident, it slipped through the net and landed on Shepherd's bag.

Something approached. I tucked my free arm and leg against the net so my limbs wouldn't become a snack for a hungry lion.

"Where's your gun?" I asked Shepherd.

"I can't reach it."

Is this how it all ends? Slowly eaten by a lion while dangling over his head? Bleeding to death as he laps at my bloody stumps? This wasn't in the brochure.

When I turned my head and looked through the gap, I was greeted by a man with a sparkling smile and big brown eyes.

He walked all the way up to the trap, just an inch from my face. "You made it. We've been waiting for you."

The man who'd captured us in his net went by the name Reuben. After cutting us down, he led us to the gates of their compound. Nestled in the middle of steep mountains was an open pasture. They'd fenced off the entire area to protect acres of farmland, and they grew herbs and vegetables inside a long greenhouse. Built against the greenhouse was a covered patio with long tables, providing an incredible view. There were a few barns, but the entire facility was underground. A hatch inside the greenhouse led below, which was where they rushed Adam.

Visitors were prohibited from going below, so Keystone remained topside. We finally got a minute to sit down and catch our breath. Mostly we marveled at the compound. We enjoyed miles of blue sky and listened to cows mooing in the distance where they grazed near a pond. This place had everything. Crops, sheep, pigs, horses. Hell, it even had turkeys. Someone brought us buckets of water, and when the sun began to set, Viktor arranged for us to sleep in the greenhouse overnight. He had returned to escort us into the camp, leaving Christian behind to take care of the lion.

I finished the last of my minestrone soup. "Eve, you need to eat."

She stared at her half-eaten bowl from across the wooden table. "Is Adam okay? I want to see him."

Viktor scooted beside her and patted her hand. "They are looking after him. But what help can you be if you are weak from hunger? Willpower alone does not make us strong. Even if you are not hungry, eat what you can."

Eve reluctantly lifted her spoon.

A man in a straw hat emerged from the oversized barn and closed the door. A woman in overalls helped him before they headed toward the greenhouse, their gait weary but smiles wide.

Reuben set a basket of fresh bread in front of us before sitting next to me. It wasn't quite dim enough for lights, but he lit a candle anyhow and set it in the middle.

Reuben gestured to my arms. "A little sunshine will remedy that. Nothing like fresh air and hard work."

I held out my pale arm. "You don't like my moon tan?"

He chuckled and shook his head. Reuben was an affable guy, and it made me feel easier about leaving the kids here.

Steam rose from the breadbasket, and Reuben pushed it toward Eve. "This came fresh out of the oven. Everything on the table came from our land. We're self-sustaining. Did you know that, Eve? We grow our own food, and you'll help with that."

"Oh boy. Chores," she muttered.

"Sometimes," he said, pushing away his smile and giving her a serious answer. "But first we need to find out what you're good at. That way we can give you a job doing what you love. Doesn't that sound nice?"

She shrugged. "I guess. Where's Adam?"

"He's fine. Just fine. I checked on him myself. You can't see him just yet, but I think by tomorrow evening they should be ready to release him."

"Release him from where?"

"Medical."

"You have a hospital?"

"We built a whole world down there," he said, tapping his finger on the table. "Up here, it looks like farmland. We grow crops and livestock. But down below? We have artificial light that looks like the sun. We have to keep the chickens underground though. They get their own room."

"Why?"

"Something was gobbling them up at night. They outgrew their chicken coop, so we're building more. Not enough hands on deck, especially with all the work we had to do over the winter. Are you good with building?"

"I don't know. What about the turkeys?"

"The turkeys can stay up here and take their chances. They're too loud." He rocked with laughter and winked at me.

Viktor helped himself to a slice of warm bread. "It is a good thing that you do here. I am very impressed. The conditions they came from…" Viktor shook his head in disgust.

Reuben nodded, his eyes trained on Eve. "You know, when

they first assigned me this job, I didn't want to come. Who wants to live in the middle of nowhere? Seems boring, right? But I fell in love with it. Did you know we have a movie room with a big screen? Leather seats, surround sound…"

Eve grabbed the heel of the bread and ate it without butter. "Candy?"

"We make homemade candy, but everyone likes the popcorn best. There's lots of stuff to do. Rock climbing, game rooms, swimming, a library. Over the years, kids like you made suggestions on how to make this place more like a home. Some of them never left. They turned eighteen and applied to work as a farmer or teacher. We have a lot of shepherds to keep you kids safe."

She jerked her head back. "Don't you mean guards?"

He pinched his chin and gave her a long look. "I don't know what it was like where you came from, but this isn't a prison. It's a home. We don't have guards; we have shepherds. We give you the best life we can until you're old enough to choose your own path. You'll receive an education in both human and Breed history. We don't shelter Potentials from Breed knowledge. Even if you don't choose to be a part of this world, you'll always be a trusted human. You and your brother will have a whole week to settle in and get to know everyone before school starts."

"How many kids are there?"

Reuben gave us a cursory glance. "I can't say exactly. Not in front of guests. But we have a diverse group of boys and girls. Some are black like me, some are brown like you, and some are as white as the ghost sitting next to me."

I chortled.

Reuben winked at me and crossed his arms. "A few children were sent here from other countries. We have a boy from Nigeria who's teaching his language, and we encourage everyone to celebrate and learn about their heritage. This isn't a place of conformity. No one is transferred out and separated from their friends. You get a chance to say goodbye to those who turn eighteen, and because it's not easy to bring them back for visits, we have it set up so you can video chat with them. You'll like it. Just you wait and see."

Reuben had successfully abated any fears the girl had about their situation. She tried to straighten her appearance. Her hair was tangled, her cheek smudged with dirt, and her hand marred by a small cut. "Do you have any clothes? I ripped my only jacket."

Reuben beamed and sat up straight. "Clothes? We have a large inventory we bought years ago, but we also make our clothes. There's a sewing and knitting class. Nothing here goes to waste. The rabbits we eat give us fur, the chickens give us feathers, and the sheep give us wool."

I frowned. "What about the cows?"

"Milk. Though we have fish and some livestock, we encourage a plant-based diet. Feeding our large group hamburgers every day would require more cows, and we have a lot of work on our plate right now. Venison is in abundance. We also trade with a few locals, but they don't know who we are." He glanced at Viktor. "We never bring anyone here to do trading. We're careful. Real careful. The less we have to trade, the better."

Viktor nodded. "I am impressed. This is nothing like what we have in the city. They do what they can, but I have not heard good things about those places." Viktor admired the pasture. Because his clothes were still in the woods, Reuben had lent him a pair of blue trousers with suspenders and a long-sleeved white shirt.

Reuben reached across the table. "I know shaking hands isn't customary, but someone told me that you're a big contributor to our charity, and I want to personally thank you for all your support. Not everyone gets to see where their money goes, but your generosity makes a difference."

Viktor looked at our host's hand for a moment before shaking it. "You were a Potential, weren't you?"

Reuben gave an impassive smile. "Once. Long ago. I wasn't lucky enough to find a place like this as a boy."

The handshake broke, and the two men sat back. Claude and Shepherd were chatting away at the end of the table, something about their respective dream homes.

I yawned while Viktor broke off a hunk of bread and tempted Eve with another piece.

"Don't worry," Reuben said, noticing my concerned expression as I glanced toward the front gate for the millionth time. "We'll find your friends. If they're in one of our traps, it might take a while to get them out."

"What's this place called?" Eve asked. "Does it have a name?"

Reuben rose from the table and stacked our empty bowls. "Wonderland. We had a vote years ago."

She snickered. "What were some of the other choices?"

"Oz, Metropolis, and one girl wanted to call it Fern Valley. That name almost won." He circled around the table and touched her shoulder. "Are you ready to pick out your room?"

Her eyes brightened. "I get a room of my own?"

"Of course! You can paint it, draw on the walls, decorate it any way you want. All you have to do is keep your bed made up and your room tidy. If you and your brother want adjoining rooms, we can arrange that, but everyone has their own space. No sharing."

"We slept in an open room in the other place. Adam can sleep somewhere else. I want total privacy." Eve stood up and addressed Viktor. "Thanks for bringing us here." She gave him a quick hug and then bypassed Shepherd as she circled the table and stood before Claude. "Thanks for saving my life."

Claude's cheeks flushed. He took her hand and bowed his head. "It was my privilege, little one. Pay it forward someday." He let go and smiled up at her. "Cherish your brother. You're lucky to have each other. You have a big decision to make someday, but I know you'll make the right choice. You've already seen the dangers, and maybe now you'll see all the good. Have a long, happy life."

"Um, you too. Thanks." Eve averted her eyes and fidgeted. "I heard everything you told Carol. I'm sorry about your sister."

What the hell had I missed? I'd never heard Claude talk about his family.

Claude tidied her hair with a sweep of his hand. "I was always her protector."

"I kinda know what you mean. I fight with Adam sometimes,

but he takes care of me. I don't know what I'd do without him."
Tears shone in her eyes as she turned and looked at Shepherd.
"Thanks for everything you did for my brother."

Shepherd nodded but kept his eyes trained on his hot coffee as
he took a slurp.

"You're not as scary as you look."

Shepherd spit out his coffee as Eve returned to her chair to
gather her belongings.

Reuben gestured to Claude. "You mentioned you're a
hairstylist?"

Claude straightened his shoulders as if there was no doubt.

"We have a few girls who, uh, they don't like what we've done."

Claude narrowed his eyes. "And what have you done?"

Reuben shrugged. "A hairstylist isn't in the budget. Last week
the new guy gave them all the exact same cut. They're not happy."

Claude rose from his chair. "If you bring them up here, I'll fix
your mistakes. But only on the condition that someone with an
ounce of talent pays attention and takes notes."

"I don't think you can fix what's been done, but you can show
us a few tricks."

Claude folded his arms. "You don't think I can fix bad hair?
Challenge accepted. Bring me all your supplies, and let's get this
done before their bedtime. And for future reference, cutting hair
isn't the only way to give someone a fresh new look. I'm also going
to show you how to create buns and properly braid."

"Lord have mercy," Reuben said on a laugh. "You're gonna
make some kids happy." He looked at Shepherd and me. "Anyone
else have talents we can borrow?"

I shrugged. "I can suffocate a man with my thighs."

Reuben's smile waned when he lifted his gaze to the field
behind me. "It looks like we found your friends."

I twisted around in my chair and rested my arms on the

railing. Christian swaggered across the field with a roguish smile on his handsome face. No glasses, his Henley shirt shredded and bloodstained, and Viktor's bag in hand. A man accompanying him branched away toward the entrance to the greenhouse.

Christian reached the side porch and crooked his finger, calling Eve over.

She cautiously approached the wood railing and was eye level with the Vampire. Her plump cheeks bloomed red when she looked down at the palm of his hand.

Christian returned her wadded-up gum wrapper. "The next time you decide to toss your trash and there isn't a trash receptacle, use your pocket instead. Don't be a litterbug, you hear? Have some respect for the world around you."

Eve took the wrapper and fled.

"Says the man covered in blood," I muttered.

He leaned in and gave me a chaste kiss.

"I take it by the glint in your eye that you killed the lion?"

"Aye."

"Took you long enough." I wiped his bloodstained beard with my sleeve. "Did you play with your food?"

"That's why I'm late." He dropped the bag. "I've certainly worked up an appetite."

"There's soup and bread."

"That's not what I'm hungry for, lass." His eyes lowered. "What's wrong with your hands?"

A strange golden light drew my attention, and I lifted my palms. *What the hell?* I shook them as if I could somehow remove the glow with a flick of my wrist.

"That's never happened before," I said, rubbing them against my jacket.

Christian gripped my wrists and looked me firmly in the eye. "You're not doing that yourself?"

I shook my head. "It doesn't feel like anything. Energy always tingles. Sometimes it heats up my hands, and other times it causes pain. This is just... weird."

I held up my hands and looked at them as if they were giant lightning bugs from a prehistoric era. A few seconds later, the light extinguished.

Chapter 29

T HE EVENING AIR WAS COOL but not unpleasant. Claude
had a line of customers in the greenhouse who were getting
their first professional haircut, and Shepherd reluctantly
acted as his assistant.

The rest of us sat on the long porch, lanterns on the walls
brightly lit.

"If you have power downstairs, why don't you set up some
lights out here?" I asked.

Reuben crossed his feet, which were propped on the railing.
"Artificial light attracts outsiders. It also attracts bugs."

Viktor enjoyed a sip of beer, something they'd brought up
from their private stash. Reuben said they didn't like alcohol on
the premises, but some of the shepherds kept a few bottles locked
up for special occasions.

This qualified.

I passed on the offer, much to Christian's surprise.

Viktor stood up from the table, his gaze fixed on the dark field
behind us. "What is that he has?"

Christian and I turned. Matteo emerged from the darkness,
flanked by two men. He looked like a man who had traveled out of
time with his fur-lined boots and layers of tattered clothes. He was
dragging something large behind him, and as they came into view,
I realized it was an unconscious man. His legs left two flat trails in
the grass. Matteo had rope looped over his shoulders like a harness,
and the other end of each rope was tied to the man's hands.

Viktor descended the steps to meet up with him, and I followed.

When Matteo reached us, he let go of the rope and panted, out of breath. "Anyone know this Mage?"

Viktor turned a sharp eye toward Christian. "Did you not kill the last one?"

"I don't think this is one of General's brothers," I said, taking note of the man's Asian features. "Who's this guy?"

"This is the one who shot the boy with poison arrows." Matteo nudged the man with his foot. "I spotted him in a sycamore tree with a clear shot of your group. I started to climb the tree, but he escaped."

Christian strolled up. "Escaped a Chitah? Aren't you supposed to be excellent climbers?"

Matteo glowered. "He's a Jumper. Have you ever seen one of them move? He took me on a long chase, and I had to wait until he used up his energy."

The man's long braid jostled my memory. This was the archer I fought on a snowy rooftop a few months back when a bunch of goons were attacking Niko.

Matteo heaved a sigh. "I threw a stunner at him, but—"

"It didn't work," I said, finishing his sentence. "He's immune to stunners."

"How do you know that?" Viktor shifted his stance.

"Because I fought him once. His group is after Niko." I knelt down and checked the man's pulse, and it was still ticking away. Maybe he was paralyzed. I looked closely at Matteo's mouth and chin but didn't see any blood. "Did you bite him?"

He shook his head. "Never had the chance to. After his last jump, he hit the ground running and then… collapsed."

"Collapsed?" Christian looked at him with a start. "Are you fecking with me? That's a Mage. They don't just pass out like one of those fainting goats."

"I couldn't see well from the ground, but it looked as if he had switched on flashlights. I thought he might have more poison on him, so I waited behind a tree."

Viktor knelt down. "Raven, hand me your blade. Perhaps he is pretending. Let us cut off his manhood and find out."

With a smile, I handed Viktor my push dagger. This might be fun.

When Viktor pressed it forcefully between the Mage's legs, every man watching winced and shifted his stance.

The only one who didn't move was the Mage. His eyes didn't flutter, and when I checked his pulse, it was steady and slow.

"Maybe he pricked himself with his own poison," I suggested.

Matteo folded his arms. "Wouldn't he have come out of it by now?"

I lowered my voice to Viktor. "What the hell was he doing out here? And a poison dart? I think you need to call home as soon as you can and find out what's going on."

Viktor stood up and rubbed the back of his neck. "If he's immune to stunners, we'll have to tie him up."

One of the men behind Matteo said, "We have chains in case of intruders. I'll get them." The man jogged toward the barn.

Reuben descended the steps of the porch and approached the scene. "You'll have to take him with you when you leave in the morning. You're responsible for him, and I trust you'll do the right thing and turn him over to the higher authority. If he knows where this place is, he's a liability."

I stood up and dusted off my sweatpants. "Reuben, if you have extra guards, you might want to put them around the property tonight. This guy has friends, and we don't know why he was gunning for the children. It wasn't an attempted abduction; he wanted them dead."

Reuben snapped his finger at one of the men, who then hurried off.

Matteo glanced at the greenhouse and looked around. "This is quite a piece of land you have."

Reuben stared at the rogue Chitah for a long time. "You're the one who lives in the cabin south of here, aren't you? Our scouts reported you."

Matteo stroked his beard. "No need to scrub my memories. I've seen children traversing through my territory. You can't keep that a secret. What you do with them, however, *is* a secret. One I don't understand. But I've never scented any fear on their part, so I left it alone."

"You've seen other kids?"

"You travel the same path each time. That's a fool's errand. When you create a recognizable scent trail, you catch the attention of local rogues." Matteo lightly kicked at the ground. "Consider taking a different path every time."

Reuben looked up at the stars blinking in the night sky. "The transporters would only get lost."

"No kidding," I chimed in. "*We* almost got lost. This mountain is nothing but a maze of trees and no clear landmarks."

"Is that bread I smell?" Matteo lifted his nose when a breeze picked up.

Reuben gestured toward the greenhouse. "You're welcome to it."

After a curt nod, Matteo strode past him and climbed the steps.

I eased up next to Reuben. "I get why you hire people like us to bring the kids. But we're city people, and it doesn't take much to get lost. Maybe what you need is a guide who knows these woods inside out."

Reuben arched an eyebrow. "Mm-hmm. And you know of such a man?"

"Would you be willing? You hire outsiders to work here, but maybe you need a local to keep an eye on things and help the teams move through without incident."

"That is not a bad idea," Viktor agreed. "When we moved off the trail, it became difficult to navigate. Matteo was very resourceful. It would be a shame if you treated him as an enemy."

Reuben tightened our circle. "Our hands are tied with local landowners. We don't have the power to kick them out, but we have to keep a close eye on them and make sure they don't get too nosy. We appreciate that he's kept to himself. Not everyone has."

"He's a skilled trapper," I added. "You should see the trap he built that I fell in."

Reuben stole a glance at Matteo, who was feasting at the table by candlelight. "Is that right?"

When Viktor signaled that he wanted to speak to Reuben alone, I wandered back to the porch and ascended the steps.

"How's the bread?"

Matteo had claimed the entire basket and didn't bother buttering it. "Fresh. Not as good as my recipe."

I sat down across from him. "Maybe you could teach them."

He chewed off another bite, flecks of bread crumbs clinging to his beard and scattering on the table. "I doubt they need any help."

"Don't be so sure about that."

"That Mage climbed high to conceal his scent," Matteo said. "If these people want to protect their land, they should build tree stands outside the perimeter. Someone high enough to see or smell trouble."

Matteo had solid ideas, but he was emotionally disconnected from the idea of pursuing anything meaningful in life. His last kiss with Blue hadn't escaped my mind, and while he might have been shunning everyone because of an emotional trauma, maybe he was a lost soul who just needed a purpose in life.

Hell, don't we all?

"You should think about offering your services here. They could use someone with your expertise. You know these woods better than anyone. You could protect the groups who come and go."

He swallowed a mouthful of bread. "And why would I do that?"

I folded my arms across the table. "Because despite your surly attitude, I think you care about what happens to children."

"No one is offering me any job, and I'm not here to beg for one."

"You could escort them yourself, or maybe you could just give them better ideas on how to secure this place."

He set down the heel of bread. "In exchange for what? Money means nothing to me."

"Take it from me, finding a purpose in life can pull you out of hell. Isn't that better than money? I spent a long time in hell, so I know what it's like. You think you don't need anyone, and maybe you don't. But that's not what it's about. It's who needs you. Think of all the kids you could help. I don't know you very well, but you stuck your neck out for us. I'm sorry about the whole kiss thing, but maybe I can give you advice."

"And what advice is that, Mage?"

I felt my father's wisdom filling me up. "Don't sit around waiting for life to get better. Breathing isn't enough. I don't know anything about your past and your woman, but what do you think she'd say if she knew you were living alone in the woods? What do you think she'd want you to do if given the chance to help innocent children? I can't tell you what path to take. I don't even know half the time if I'm on the right path. But you need to choose something instead of sitting on your ass, growing tomatoes."

I stood up and turned my back.

"Raven?"

I caught the railing and looked back.

"You're a fierce woman with a fiery heart. Don't ever let that Vampire change you."

I half smiled. "He's the one who brings it out in me."

Chapter 30

Earlier that day.

"WE GO," SWITCH SAID DECIDEDLY.

Wyatt stood up from the dining table and huffed. Since when did these guys think they called the shots? "Hold your ponies. You have an obligation to guard the property. The only place you go is two steps behind Hunter."

"He's got a point." Crush twisted a small rubber band around his grey goatee. "You need to protect that boy. Kids come first. Always."

Switch folded his arms on the table. "You put a tracking device in her shoe. How can you just sit here when you know exactly where she is?"

Wyatt knew Switch had good intentions, but tough shit if he didn't like the plan. "Look, we appreciate all your help. But when it comes to making countermoves, you don't get to make those decisions. *I* don't make those decisions," he said, pointing to his chest. "Maybe you're *top dog* around the packs, but that doesn't mean you call the shots when it comes to Keystone."

Switch leaned back in his chair. "Boy, if you make air quotes one more time, I'm going to snip off those fingers."

"Boy?" Wyatt bristled at the remark. "My name's Wyatt Blessing, and I was born in 1803. If anyone here's a boy, it's you."

"Boys hide in their castle while men fight battles."

Wyatt kicked over a chair. "It's not my choice! You think I like having my hands tied? But what happens if you take off and they bust in here and slaughter everyone, including the kid. Huh? You gonna feel like a hero? What the immortal hell do you expect me to do?"

Crush casually sipped his coffee. "Calm your ass down—the both of you—and we'll figure something out. You're both right. He can't call the shots any more than you could in a pack, Switch. Wyatt, you've got exact coordinates on your friend. Switch has a point. How much time before they find that little device on her? Let's put our heads together."

Wyatt returned to his seat across from Crush. He didn't like having this decision on his shoulders.

Crush laced his fingers together and addressed Switch. "Son, if you want this job, you better curb that impulsive behavior of yours. Remember where it got you last time."

Switch's long hair fell in front of his face when he lowered his head. "I'm not trying to stir up trouble. I just want to help. I know this isn't my family, but I guess pack instinct kicks in. Can't help it."

Wyatt rubbed his tattooed fingers. They were in a real pickle. The game changer was finding out that Gem wasn't on the dangerous side of the Bricks. That made a rescue more feasible. Wyatt had pinpointed her location at a hotel built in the thirties. The tracker could only signal the general area, so Wyatt had no clue where in the building she was. If he botched the rescue, he'd be the cause of her death. And knowing that girl, she'd haunt him from the afterlife.

Switch tapped his fingernail against his coffee cup. "So why don't you go get her, and we'll stay here?"

Wyatt snorted. "You think I can just shirk my duties? I'm central intelligence. I don't get to leave unless it's a direct order from my boss. What happens if he has an emergency and I'm not here? I also have to make travel arrangements to get them the hell out of there. If something happened to their vehicle, I'll have to figure out the safest way to get them to the nearest airport."

These guys didn't know what it was like to bear this kind of responsibility. Wyatt had to coordinate travel plans on the fly, and that was no easy task. He mapped their routes and made himself available around the clock in case something went awry. He also had the daunting responsibility of search and recovery should the team not make it out alive.

Wyatt was getting an ulcer, and Gravewalkers didn't get ulcers.

Crush sipped his coffee, his blue eyes trained on Wyatt. Despite him being a gruff guy, Wyatt didn't sense any derision in his tone. He was the kind of fella who wanted to get it done, and Wyatt respected that. It made perfect sense where Raven got her personality.

"We stay here," Crush stated. "Every man on the property accounted for. But I got more friends than this—friends who owe me favors I've never called on."

Wyatt frowned. "You'd use up all your favors to help someone you barely know?"

Crush tugged on the collar of his tight white T-shirt, which had a bottle of orange soda printed on the front. "That's the only way to do it in my book."

"Maybe that's not such a hot idea, old man. It's dangerous."

Crush sat back. "Good versus evil, my friend. Sometimes that's all a man needs to make a choice."

"I don't want any of your buddies haunting me from the afterlife."

Crush gave him a stony look, but there was something else in that look that Wyatt was all too familiar with: prejudice. "Just don't do any of your voodoo shit to make them zombies."

Wyatt groaned. "You don't know anything about Gravewalkers, do you?"

"I don't like the idea of ghosts."

"Me either. Why do you think my job is working with computers? Anyhow, I don't have magical powers to bind someone to the living world. That's their choice. I just don't want them following my ass home."

"So I'll make my boys promise not to die on me. How's that?"

Wyatt took off his hat and stretched it between his hands. "So what's the plan, Stan? Set up a surveillance van? Drive them out with tear gas?"

Still staring at Wyatt, Crush turned a skull ring on his finger. "Guns blazing. That's the only way to catch them off guard."

Wyatt got a quick visual of what that might look like. "I think you need to make an appointment somewhere else, because I'm all booked up on crazy. Your wolves will tear my friends apart. And if they don't, they'll die trying."

Crush's ring clicked against his cup when he wrapped his hands around it. "We'll take a piece of dirty laundry from their rooms. Once their animal gets a whiff, they won't attack anyone with that scent."

Wyatt wrinkled his nose. "You want me to fish out their dirty underwear?"

"Don't be a peckerhead. Just grab a shirt. That'll do." He lifted his cup. "And wolves can kill a Mage. Tear him to pieces. They start with the hands first, that way the Mage can't blast them with energy. After that—"

Wyatt turned green and held up his hand. "I don't need details."

Crush let out a deep belly laugh. "No, son. You don't. Every Breed has weaknesses. A Mage has power, but they don't have absolute power. Don't let 'em fool you; they're afraid of Shifters. That's why they used to enslave them."

"I know all about it," Wyatt said matter-of-factly. "I'm older than you, remember? I lived in the days of slavery, and just about every single Mage where I came from had a Shifter servant. Sometimes they'd hook the horse Shifters up to carriages and parade them around town. They hated that the most. Worse than being a maid or tilling the fields. Shifters didn't like having their animal demeaned in public."

Crush narrowed his eyes. "You ever own a Shifter?"

"Do I look stupid?" Wyatt put the hat back on his head. "Don't answer that. No, I never owned a Shifter. I only saw them with Vampires or lightwalkers. A lightwalker is—"

"A Mage. I know."

Wyatt shook his head. "Old-fashioned word. Never even

made sense. It's not like they walk on light." He held up his finger. "Gravewalkers, on the other hand, do walk on graves."

"Time's a-wasting," Switch reminded them as he laced his fingers together, much calmer than before. "I've never been the type to sit around and do nothing when there was a chance to make it right. But there's a Polish expression: not my circus, not my monkeys. That's the biggest lesson I've got to learn. So that means concentrating on my job and not sticking my nose in your business. Hunter's my responsibility when his dad's not around. I'll stay. I'm sorry if I'm coming across as bossy, but you're the one who invited us in on your problems. We can't tell you how to run your show, but we can help. Take it. People who do nothing change nothing."

"People who do something they're not supposed to also get fired. Maybe to you it's just a job, but this is the only thing I've got."

"What if your friend dies?"

"I'm a Gravewalker. Dangling death as an incentive doesn't work. The only reason people are afraid of death is because they don't know what happens next. They think it's over, like a curtain at the end of a play. But I know what happens. Death isn't a big deal. Just the dying part."

Switch covered his circle beard with both hands as if he were trying to keep himself from saying something he'd regret. Wyatt wasn't going to apologize for his views on death; he couldn't afford to get attached to people. Nobody understood Gravewalkers. Wyatt had lived his entire life watching specters come and go. Some people were better off dead.

Still. Gem was a sweet girl. He didn't like the idea that someone could be hurting her. Not only that, but she'd willingly walked into the face of danger. She could have abandoned Niko and stayed here, but she'd gone back. Blast! Wyatt wanted to be a hero, but Raven would kick his ass if any of her father's friends died because he decided to send them on a mission.

Or would she kick his ass for *not* doing it? Did she love Keystone more or her family?

Wyatt chewed on his fingernail, conflicted about the choice before him. "Fine. But you stay here."

"Someone needs to control them," Crush countered.

"I thought you said they wouldn't attack my guys?"

Crush arched his brow. "You know how wolves are when they get blood in their mouth. I don't think they'll touch them, but it'll go better if I'm along for the ride."

"I don't want you going."

Crush stood up and turned his pockets inside out. "I'm all out of fucks to give. Don't worry. I know what you're thinking. Raven will kill you if I get myself killed. I'll hang back and play it safe, but this isn't up for debate. If Viktor has a problem with it, he can deal with me. If everything goes well, you take all the credit for approving the plan. I just need to make some calls."

Wyatt got out of his seat and stretched. "Maybe you should wait until after dark. If you go prancing into the Breed district in broad daylight, you'll end up in an eternity box."

"Doesn't matter," Crush said. "Vamps are out all night, and if someone's gonna notice us, they'll notice us. Day or night."

Switch rose to his feet. "What do you want me to do?"

"Work on that dickish personality of yours?" Wyatt clapped Switch's shoulder as he passed by him. "I liked you better when you were losing at pool."

Switch gave him a short grin. "And I liked you better when you were losing at darts."

Hunter dashed into the room, a black mask covering his eyes.

"Well, hey there, Zorro." Crush put his hands on his knees and looked Hunter in the eye. "Bad guys are trying to storm the castle. Think you can stay here and protect everyone?"

Hunter nodded exuberantly.

Crush rumpled his hair. "Good man. We're counting on you. All these doors need to stay locked, and if anything bad happens, you and Kira need to hide like little mice." He glanced up at Wyatt. "Is that her name?"

Wyatt looked into the gathering room. "I should go find her.

She ain't supposed to wander off. I want everyone together in case something happens and we need to fly the coop."

Switch chuckled. "I'd never guess in a million years you were from the South."

Wyatt frowned. "How did you know?"

"Lucky guess," Switch said. "Lucky guess."

Chapter 31

G EM SHIFTED THE PILLOW BENEATH her, cramps settling in her legs from having sat at the tea table all day, trying to translate Niko's book. Her Mage power indicated the time of day was now reaching sunset. Had Viktor and the team completed their mission? She wondered about them a lot.

Much to her surprise, Cyrus actually knew one short phrase in the book. He bragged about remembering it word for word after all these centuries, but little good did it do him when he had no understanding of how to unlock the book's true power. He had memorized the symbols and found someone who could translate them. Unfortunately for Cyrus, that Relic died a short time after from the plague. Cyrus hadn't bothered asking the man to teach him the language. It was far too complex for a pea brain like him.

Gem rubbed her temple and stared at her papers. She had smartly left the translation book behind. There was no way she would chance Cyrus getting his hands on that, not if it meant relinquishing what little power she had. After a tedious night of learning, memorizing, and coding data into her DNA, she'd spent all day translating pages of the red book… in her head. The words she scribbled on paper were gibberish, incorrect translations for the symbols. If Cyrus discovered her deception, he would kill them both, so every word and phrase had to be matched whenever repeated and also required some semblance of logic when reading it.

Her brain hurt. This was by far the most taxing thing she'd ever done under pressure.

"Why does this take so long?" Cyrus said angrily, shoving her head toward the book.

So long? Was he insane? She was lucky she'd gotten as far as she had.

Gem gave him a cross look as he circled to the other side of the table, his arms folded like some kind of toddler on the verge of a tantrum. "Because it's thousands of years old. Because Rome wasn't built in a day."

Cyrus looked at Arcadius. "I don't like her tongue."

Arcadius steered his gaze down to her. "Want me to cut it out?"

"She's tired." Niko interrupted, taking on a conciliatory tone. "Tea will help. Gem is extremely adept at deciphering complex languages. You will find no one else who can match her skills."

Gem refrained from smiling, but his compliment warmed her. That feeling was extinguished when she noticed his tunic. Gem wasn't used to seeing him in clothes that weren't black, and she found herself hating it. Hating the bloodstains. Hating the untied drawstrings that hung from the neck. And, most of all, hating the meaning behind them.

Servitude.

Gem rubbed her ink-stained fingers across her camo leggings, guilty that she had warm boots and Niko walked around barefoot. At least Cyrus had kept his word and removed the cuff.

After Niko finished pouring her tea at the long table against the wall, he carefully turned and knelt beside her.

She scooted the papers out of the way. "You can set it down."

He bowed his head. "I did not want to disturb your work. Cyrus is a generous man to offer my freedom in exchange for your services."

With Cyrus still looming over them, Gem wanted to roll her eyes. Cyrus would never let him go. But she marveled at how easily Niko could manipulate his Mage brother.

Niko had put on quite a show to secure an agreement with Cyrus. He remarked how Gem could hasten his rise to power, but then he quickly revoked the offer and demanded that Gem leave immediately. That was enough to pique Cyrus's curiosity on what exactly Gem could do. Instead of threatening her, Cyrus offered Niko's freedom in exchange for her services.

It was all she needed to buy time. This book was unlike anything she'd ever read before. A maze of incantations specific to different Breeds. Before leaving Keystone, she noticed it was broken up into parts, but without a table of contents, the only way to determine the theme for each part was to translate the first page.

Gem sipped her green tea while Cyrus crossed the room and sat on the wooden sofa. Lykos joined him while Arcadius remained by the door.

"You shouldn't overwork yourself," Niko said quietly. "There's no rush."

They hadn't concocted a plan to get out of this. The only thing they'd managed to accomplish was staying alive. But Gem held a secret plan that kept her reading, kept her searching for just the right thing. She wasn't sure if it would work, but they didn't have many other options, and time wasn't on her side. Eventually Cyrus would realize that she'd created a false translation and take out his anger like a wounded dragon.

"What was your Creator's name?" she asked.

"Artemon."

"Cyrus says he forced immortality on him. Was that how it was for you?"

Still kneeling, Niko sighed and cupped his hands in his lap. "Yes."

She set down the teacup. "I've heard stories about people forced into immortality, and I can't imagine. I'm sorry." Those last words seemed woefully inadequate.

"The past is where it belongs."

"Is it?" She pushed up the sleeves on her black sweater. "How did you find out the book had power?"

"Remember the Relic I told you about whom we stole the book from? When he didn't cooperate or respond to blackmail, Cyrus tortured him for information. The only thing he learned was that the book had the power to rule all."

"If that's all he told you, how did you know a Mage infused power into the pages?"

Niko raised his head and observed the men in the room before answering. "My sensei told me about such books and how they were created. He said they were the alpha and the omega."

What Niko hadn't known all those years was that the spells weren't activated by reading them alone but by touch. After a long night, Gem noticed strange occurrences whenever she ran her fingers over the symbols and read them aloud. It didn't even matter which language she used so long as they matched up with the symbol. It was as if it drew from her power in order to work. If she had to guess, only a Mage could activate the spells. Otherwise, the Relic who owned the book would have figured it out and been a powerful man.

"Did you show it to your sensei?" she asked.

"I have never shown the book to anyone."

"Too much talking." Cyrus snapped his fingers three times. "Nikodemos, bring me food. You still remember how to cook, don't you?"

Niko's lips thinned. "Don't say anything to anger him. I'll just be in the next room."

"It's okay. I'll be fine. Just toiling away on a dead language and writing nonsense on paper."

He gave her a worried smile and left the room. Niko was in on her fictitious translating of the passages—it was the one thing they both agreed on. If something went wrong, at least Cyrus wouldn't be able to read the book himself, which would be bad even if he didn't know how to unlock the power.

From their brief conversation, Gem had acquired a valuable piece of information needed for one of the spells. It was the name of Niko's Creator, who was also the Creator of these other men.

Artemon.

Cyrus had given her a quill and inkpot instead of a regular ballpoint, and the ink stained her fingers. By the looks of his home, he didn't embrace the modern world. Ancients were like that, and she wondered if she might one day be clinging to relics of her past.

What might those be? Microwaves? Toilets? Hair dye? Battery-operated lights? What did the future hold in store?

She sipped her tea and gathered her thoughts.

Can I do this? What if I'm wrong? What if it doesn't work? What if he catches me?

Gem had been waiting for an opportune time, but fear gripped her spine. Cyrus was Niko's Mage brother, but were the others as well? She couldn't remember. These past two days she'd been without sleep, and she couldn't remember the details of every conversation. Kallisto was still unaccounted for, and that presented a threat, especially if he didn't share the same Creator.

She patiently waited for Niko to finish cooking. The smell of grilled meat wafted from the kitchen, a delicious blend of pork, vegetables, and rice. Once he fed these ogres and returned to his position, she would ask him more questions.

"Did I say you could rest?" Cyrus asked, his tone as sharp as a razor blade. "Each time I see you lift a finger away from that pen, I'm going to cut one of them off. Starting with the pinky."

Arcadius drew his sword. He pressed the tip of the blade against the floor and rested his hands on the pommel.

Gem loathed Cyrus for killing her ex, but it was Arcadius who made her tremble with fear. Every time she closed her eyes, she saw him smiling at her as she gulped water into her lungs. With a shaky hand, Gem lifted the pen from the stand and continued her work.

Thirty minutes elapsed before Niko returned with a tray of food. He carefully made his way toward Cyrus, and when he reached the couch, he knelt and offered the tray.

Gem wanted to stab Cyrus in the eyeball with her pen.

The only way to placate Cyrus was to continue working, so Gem had to tamp down her anger and focus. After all, they still had Kallisto to worry about. Niko revealed that when she had returned to Keystone, Cyrus received a call every three hours or so. But Gem noticed the phone hadn't rung all afternoon. Not since she made the agreement with Cyrus to translate the book. He must have called off Kallisto. Perhaps he'd been outside in the hallway this whole time.

Then again, what if he had infiltrated the mansion and slaughtered everyone? If only that phone would buzz. The silence wrecked her, but it also galvanized her into taking action sooner rather than later.

Gem continued reading a specific passage, one she had successfully translated and quadruple-checked. It was the only spell she'd managed to find that might actually help them, so she had devoted most of the afternoon to deciphering it.

What if it didn't work? While she'd dabbled with the power within the book, she had only gone so far as to feel the energy lift from the page, but it hadn't actually done anything outside of brighten a few candles.

"Not bad," Cyrus said while tasting his food. "Your seasoning technique has improved, but the rice is underdone. When I'm finished, you can prepare a plate for everyone else. Well, everyone except the girl. She doesn't get to eat until she's done with that book."

Gem nearly knocked over the inkpot when Cyrus abruptly kicked Niko, knocking him onto his back.

"What have I told you about giving me that look?" he said absently while gathering his chopsticks.

Niko's body had twisted so he faced her, his palms on the floor and his head slowly rising. Fire burned in his ice-blue eyes, and threads of blue light leaked from his fingertips.

Cyrus looked more interested in the plate of food on the armrest. He pushed around pieces of meat with his chopsticks until he found one that pleased him.

"You're nothing but a pig!" she spat, the words leaving her mouth before she had a chance to stop them.

Chopsticks tumbled to the floor when Cyrus rose to his feet.

Niko's eyes widened, and he slowly shook his head at her.

But Gem was on her feet. She couldn't stand another minute of it.

Cyrus strode toward her with the intensity of a gathering storm. "Arcadius, cut out her tongue."

The moment Arcadius lifted his sword, Niko moved so heart-stoppingly fast that he blurred before her very eyes. The sword was knocked out of Arcadius's hand, and the men crashed against the wall.

"Get him!" Cyrus ordered.

Lykos, who was leaner than the other two, launched from his seat and into the fray. Niko had his hands around Arcadius's throat, his grip so tight that the man's eyes bulged. Lykos punched and assailed Niko from behind, and in a matter of seconds, Niko was fighting both men. They kicked and pivoted, each one skilled in martial arts. Gem had never seen anything like it. The way they moved was a ballet, the artistry behind each attack sublime.

When she had a moment to catch her breath, she saw beyond the fast moves and flawless execution. Niko's cheek split. Blood spattered on the wall and streamed onto the floor from Arcadius's head. They fought in the center of the room with Cyrus on one side and Gem on the other.

Cyrus circled behind the couch and reached for a sword mounted high on the wall. He moved languidly, his face stoic.

Gem's heart quickened. She clenched her fists, tempted to wield an energy ball but going against all instinct. It would destroy them all in this confined space. Cyrus gripped his sword with both hands and moved toward the men.

She rushed back to the table and dropped to her knees, her hands shaking uncontrollably as she flipped through the pages. There wasn't time to look, to see what was happening over her shoulder. He wouldn't kill Niko. He'd promised! But would that stop Cyrus from maiming him?

When Gem placed her fingertips on the page, the world had never felt so fragile. She began the chant in a quiet voice. "Children of light, I call on you."

Her jaw went slack when she took her fingers off the page, and golden light encompassed her hands. She glanced at the men, and theirs were glowing too. Cyrus held his sword, waiting for an opportune moment. Even *his* hands were illuminated.

Gem swallowed hard, and when she put her fingers back on the page, the light in her hands extinguished. "Dim the light of all except the children of Artemon." Once again, she let go of the page, and the golden glow quickly faded from her hands. But that was not the case for all the men in the room.

Cyrus snapped his attention to her and back to his hands.

She needed to hurry, but she was afraid for Niko. Based on the spell's behavior, she was certain that whoever was touching the book was immune to any spellcasting, and by that logic, surely that would apply to anyone touching her. "Niko!"

He knocked Lykos unconscious and shoved Arcadius against Cyrus's sword. It impaled him through the stomach but didn't kill him.

"Come here!" she called out. "Hurry!"

Niko rushed to her side. "Are you hurt?"

"Touch me, Niko. Please sit as close to me as you can."

"What are you doing?"

"Hurry!"

He knelt beside her and placed his hands on her shoulders.

"Bind their light. Bind their minds." She grimaced as the symbols sent sharp currents of energy into her fingers. "Make them sleep for all time. No sun will heal, no light will wake."

"Stop!" Cyrus bellowed. "Stop what you're doing!"

He flashed across the room and lifted his bloodstained sword. Niko rushed him before the blade swung and severed her neck.

Gem shut her eyes. "Sleep, children of Artemon. The dreamworld awaits."

She flew back, raw power exploding from the book and showering golden light across the table like a fountain. Her fingers burned hot with energy, the heat radiating up her arms and into her shoulders.

"It worked. It worked!" she exclaimed. Gem watched the embers of light glittering as they floated to the floor and disappeared.

When the light show ceased, Gem felt the silence more than

heard it. She sat up and spied Niko on his stomach. Filled with dread, she scurried across the floor to his side.

"Niko! Wake up. Please, wake up!" After shaking him, she turned him onto his back.

He looked like a fallen angel, his black hair carpeting the floor and his eyes closed.

"Wake up!"

Niko didn't move. Nothing moved except for the easy rise and fall of his chest.

Horrified, Gem sat back, tears streaming down her face. "*No, no, no.* What have I done?"

Part of her was still in jubilation that it worked. It *actually* worked. Even though she'd read it in English, the magic somehow translated the idea and intent of the passage, drawing energy from her to charge itself up. But she quickly came off that high with the grim scene before her.

When Gem noticed the bloody sword in Cyrus's hand, she dragged Niko toward the door and away from the blade. It seemed irrational, but how long would the spell hold? A minute? Forever?

She cupped Niko's face and leaned in close, her lips trembling as she struggled to speak. "Niko, I'm so sorry. I thought if you were touching me that it wouldn't affect you. Why did you have to let go and stop Cyrus? I could have protected you."

She bowed her head, tears splashing onto his tattered garments. Niko had saved her. Again. If the blade had come down, Gem would have had just enough time to recite the final words. She could have saved him even if it meant her own death.

Gem recoiled at what sounded like vicious dogs attacking the door. A loud blast deafened her and punched a hole through the door. When a hand reached in to open the locks, Gem shielded Niko with her body.

Crush swung open the door. "Get 'em, boys."

She clung protectively to Niko, but the wolves sailed over them and pounced on top of the fallen Mage brothers.

Artemon's progeny.

Gem watched in horror as the wolves savagely tore them apart, limb from limb. No mercy. She wondered if those unconscious men were aware of their impending death. Could they feel the pain? Were they afraid?

She hoped so. With all the fire in her heart, she wished they felt every moment of their skin peeling back and bones breaking. They deserved it for all the misery that they'd left on this earth. One of the wolves shifted to human form and stood in the middle. He pried the sword from Cyrus's hand, which was no longer attached to his arm.

A wave of nausea moved over her like an ocean tide when Cyrus's head rolled across the floor.

Crush seized her arms and forced her to sit up and look at him. "You okay, honey?"

Dumbstruck, she simply shook her head.

Crush's gaze lowered to Niko's body. A Mage simply didn't die unless it was by gruesome means. Beheading, fire, Chitah bites—but none of those applied.

He lifted Niko's eyelids and felt for his ticking pulse. "What the hell happened to him?"

Gem had cast a sleeping spell with not a clue how it worked. She had vastly underestimated the power of words. Crestfallen, she replied, "I played God, and I failed."

He put a hand on her shoulder even though he didn't understand. "What's done is done. Help me get him out of here, and maybe I can fix him."

Gem wiped blood off Niko's chin with her sleeve. "Only I can fix this, and I'll spend the rest of my life trying. Until the day I die."

Chapter 32

AFTER I CLIMBED TO THE top of the watchtower, I circled the overlook and admired the view. The moon had risen with a sliver taken from her crown. Being a lover of heights, I'd asked Reuben's permission to come up. He agreed on the condition that I would act as the night watchman. No problem. As tired as my body was, my mind was wide awake and needed something to do.

Down below, many yards away, candlelight from inside the greenhouse twinkled. The windowed ceilings allowed me to see movement inside. Viktor was savoring a bottle of wine at a table they'd brought in from the patio, and Claude was sweeping up the hair trimmings from the numerous haircuts he'd given to the children. Shepherd was probably asleep in one of the sleeping bags Reuben had given us, but I couldn't see him among the long rows of plants. From my vantage point, I spotted a second greenhouse beyond an inlet of trees.

I climbed onto the ledge and sat down with my legs hanging over and my palms on the wide handrail. Man, what a view. The sky was infinitely dark and the stars blinding. A meteor flashed across the sky, and I searched for more.

"Careful, lass. You might fall and break your neck." Christian draped my leather jacket across my shoulders.

"What would you do if I died? Carry me all the way back home?"

"I'd bury you in the potatoes and sing you a song."

"The potatoes?"

"Think of all the lives you'd save with your rotting corpse nourishing the crops."

"You always say the things that make my heart go pit-a-pat." While I put my arms in the sleeves of my coat, Christian gripped the back of my sweatpants with one hand as if I might fly over the edge.

"Then perhaps I can make you swoon by pointing out that you still reek of urine."

"I'd bathe in the pond, but I might get a parasite."

"*Oh, Danny boy, the pipes, the pipes are calling,*" he sang.

"You're a terrible singer."

"I have to practice. Ashes to ashes, dust to dust."

"Potatoes to potatoes."

"Nothing beats a warm bowl of Irish coddle."

I scanned the property. "At least I haven't seen any mosquitoes. Say, what happens when a mosquito bites a Vampire?"

"They meet the palm of my hand."

"Seriously. Do they get super strength? Immortality?"

He brushed his hand over his beard, which had grown wild down his neck. "Hard to say. Those little feckers have been around for over two hundred million years."

"How old are Vampires?"

Christian bit back his smile and studied me for a moment. "You're inquisitive tonight. Perhaps I'll dig up a Breed history book so you can read all about how nobody knows how it all began. Some believe that Breed are the originals and humans were the defects born of Chitahs, Relics, and Shifters. Some think it's the other way around. It might explain why our DNA is relatively close. Nobody knows, Raven. If you ever meet an immortal old enough to tell the tale, you'll probably meet the most insane man who ever walked the face of the earth."

I shuddered at the thought of living that long. "Where's Matteo? I haven't seen him in hours."

"Down below."

I studied Christian closely, but he wasn't joking. "They're not going to hurt him, are they? Scrub his memories?"

"Why don't you come down from the ledge and we'll talk? I feel like a wee lad looking up at you."

I turned toward him but straddled the railing instead. "You shoved me off a bridge and out of an airplane. I'm not sure why my sitting on the ledge of a watchtower makes you so damn nervous." My eyes skated down to the long rips in his brown shirt, his wounds long since healed but the fabric still stained with blood.

"If you fall to your demise, I'd rather it not be accidental," he said with a crooked grin.

"Fine." My boots stomped on the wood floor when I scooted off the railing. "So what are they doing with Matteo?"

"I overheard Viktor showering him with praise, and the leader down below was impressed with his silence."

"Silence?"

"The Chitah noticed the caravans, the children, and the compound and yet never interfered. Never said a word to outsiders. Apparently they've run into trouble with a few nosy locals."

My heart lightened at the thought that Matteo might be rewarded for his selflessness. He could have released me and chosen to walk away. Even though he had only asked for a kiss, maybe all he really wanted was to feel like a human being again.

I fidgeted with the zipper on my coat. "I hope it's a long time before we ever have a job like this again. I miss home."

Christian winked. "I always thought traveling was a perk of the job."

"Maybe for you, but I like Cognito. I like the graffiti on the walls, the rude taxi drivers, the street performers, the food trucks, the mystery, the diversity—it's less stressful. It's familiar."

"The world is unpredictable, and if you don't immerse yourself in the unfamiliarity of it, you'll never survive. Do you think you'll always live in Cognito? Someday, Raven, you'll move on. You'll experience wanderlust, or maybe you'll be seeking asylum. The world can change in the blink of an eye. War. Famine. Civil unrest." He swung his gaze upward again. "Humans might find out about us someday and force us to leave. What if they close their borders and banish us to godforsaken places like the desert? That would be a sure way to kill us all."

"Then I put you in charge of building our sand igloo." I rested my forearms on the flat rail. "God, I'd kill for a hamburger and milkshake. It's too quiet out here. I miss the sound of traffic. I even miss the smell of cigarettes in bars and trash in the gutter."

Christian chortled. "Should I ask Reuben to bring you up a bin?" He pinched my chin. "How can you be sentimental over a crime-infested city when you have miles of gorgeous mountains?"

"Cognito is my home and always will be. I can't imagine living anywhere else. It's nice out here. Lots of sky, fresh air, and freedom. But it's not home."

He leaned on the ledge beside me. "So it's chaos you like."

I briefly thought about Houdini. It was hard not to think of him whenever the word "chaos" was uttered. Maybe moving somewhere would put the distance I needed between us. But why would I go through the trouble at the cost of my happiness? "What made you leave Ireland so young and travel across the world to a foreign country? Was your home that bad?"

"We were poor. I told you this story." He gazed up at the sky. "People search for a better life when they have none. When they're hungry or fearing for their life. 'Twasn't a pleasant experience having to suffer poverty and rejection in a new land, one I thought would be filled with opportunities and hope, but it taught me a valuable lesson."

"And what's that?"

"Persevere. It's better to take chances than to do nothing at all. Had I stayed behind, I'd be nothing but bones on a hill. We wouldn't be having this conversation. I wouldn't be looking at stars or saving your arse from lions."

I nudged his shoulder with mine. "I killed one of those lions, or have you forgotten?"

"And I killed two."

"If we're keeping score, then I get bonus points for catching Joshua and Carol on the run."

He chuckled softly. "And a lot of good that did. You went to jail and didn't collect your two hundred."

I stared into the dark woods, wondering if they had made it home.

"Perhaps I should go after them," Christian said. "They can't be far, and they'll be on foot unless he managed to hitch a ride naked."

I straightened up. "Nah. I think they'll be okay."

He looked over his shoulder and gave me a complicated look. "Why the change of heart?"

I shrugged. "If he really loves her, he'll do what's best for her no matter what. Joshua thinks he can give her a better life. Who are we to say he can't? Maybe Carol would have been safer in that utopia they've got underground, but nothing beats family. She's never had that before. This might be the worst decision she ever makes, but what's the point of dragging her back if she'll just find a way to escape? Reuben said this place isn't a jail, but to her it will be. Besides, now that Viktor knows how to find Joshua's family, I suspect he'll be checking up on her."

"To be sure." Christian looked down at me with a hint of concern. "Maybe you should see a Relic."

"For what?"

"That light show earlier with your hands. You might have a leaky battery."

I rubbed my palms. "Real funny."

Christian straightened up and faced me, causing me to do the same. "Do you see me laughing? I've not seen that color before—not from a Mage."

Usually the light was blue or sometimes white, but sparkling gold?

"I'm just tired," I said, blowing it off. "It's been a long trip."

"I've seen you knackered before, and never has that happened." He tilted my chin up with the crook of his finger. "You're mine now. You hear? That means I look after you."

I folded into his embrace and relished the heat of his chest against my cold hands, which had slipped inside the rips of his shirt.

"Mmm, keep touching me like that, Precious."

I felt his cock growing as it pressed against my lower belly. "Control yourself, Poe. I've got a job to do." My lips touched his delicious skin. "I'm the night watchman."

Christian's hands cupped my ass and pulled me against his hard erection. He let out an anguished groan. "Then turn around and do your job, lass. I'll be right behind you."

"Not a good idea. Someone might see us."

Christian released a shaky breath. *Of course* he liked that idea. And I had to admit, the thought of holding on to the rail while he pulled down my sweats and buried himself inside me gave me a thrill. I didn't have to wonder if it would happen.

I knew it would.

"I stink," I whispered.

He tenderly kissed my ear. "I'll stuff my shirt up my nostrils."

"I have blood in my hair."

"That's gravy on a steak."

When his tongue found a sensitive spot on my neck, I quivered. His beard brushed against my jaw as he made his way to my lips.

"Do all Irishmen kiss as good as you?"

"Only the well-hung ones."

We fell into a fervent kiss, and his hot tongue entered my mouth. When I sucked on it, Christian's hands slid into my sweats and beneath my panties. After a demanding squeeze, they ventured up my back with unhurried attention.

He leaned away. "Jaysus wept. Can't a man have privacy?"

I gave him a quizzical stare. "What?"

"Claude," he ground out. "Said he can smell sex in the air and told me to put an end to our party or he'll tell Viktor."

"I thought Chitahs couldn't smell us this high?"

Christian frowned. "You have a point. I think he's having a go at me. Should we call his bluff?"

I smiled wickedly, enjoying this game. "Let's wait until he's asleep. We should be able to hear his snoring from here."

"He better hurry it along, or I'll spike his tea with some of that valerian growing down there."

I walked around one of the four posts that secured the roof

overhead. A mountain lion moved stealthily by, the shepherds protecting their flock. "Have you been back to Ireland since leaving?"

He held his position. "Aye."

"Your home?"

"The place I grew up? There's probably nothing left of it now. What's to see?"

I neared him, my fingers skittering across the railing. "Memories."

He folded his arms. "Memories live in your mind, Raven."

"I know, but you're not curious if the house is still there? Don't you want to walk through a familiar field?"

"You mean the same field where I twisted my foot and did backbreaking labor? I'll pass."

When I reached him, I couldn't help but feel flummoxed by his answer. No matter how many years passed, I'd always want to return to my father's piece of land and walk through familiar streets to recapture those memories. How could he be so apathetic about his beginnings? About his family?

I leaned against the railing with my back to the woods. "Your brothers are all dead?"

"Aye." He strode toward me and cupped my neck.

"Did they have children? Do you have great-nieces and nephews?"

Christian's black eyes swallowed me up. "That wouldn't matter, now would it? I had to leave behind my human life, and I have no wish to return. I became a monster. It would be a sin for me to walk near their graves. Would you have me knock on some poor human's door and invite myself in? 'Hello, I'm your great uncle removed more times than I can count. You might have read about my crimes in the newspaper. Invite me in for a cup of tea?' For feck's sake, Raven."

"I just want to know more about you, what makes you tick."

He gave me a devilish smile. "My heart makes me tick. And sometimes my cock."

Would I be like these immortals someday, lecturing the youth on how our former life didn't matter? Christian was haunted by the sins of his Vampire life, so why wasn't he drawn to the one place in his past that held good memories of his family? Everyone had an anchor that held them somewhere, and I wanted to find his.

"Christian, you've traveled the world and lived in many different times and places. Everyone has a home. A familiar place you always want to return to, a place that fills you up when you feel empty. If it's not your first home, then where is it? I refuse to believe you're content with being a nomad. Everyone has that one place where they belong. Mine is Cognito." I stepped as close as I could get. "Where is your home?"

Christian placed a hand over my heart, his gaze reeling me in. "Don't you know? You're my home, Precious. Always will be."